FAR GONE

ALSO BY LAURA GRIFFIN

Exposed

Scorched

Twisted

Snapped

Unforgivable

Unspeakable

Untraceable

Whisper of Warning

Thread of Fear

One Wrong Step

One Last Breath

AND

"Unstoppable" in *Deadly Promises*

FAR GONE

LAURA GONE

LAURA GRIFFIN

G

GALLERY BOOKS

New York   London   Toronto   Sydney   New Delhi

G

Gallery Books
A Division of Simon & Schuster, Inc.
1230 Avenue of the Americas
New York, NY 10020

First Gallery Books hardcover edition April 2014

GALLERY BOOKS and colophon are registered trademarks of Simon & Schuster, Inc.

For information about special discounts for bulk purchases, please contact Simon & Schuster Special Sales at 1-866-506-1949 or business@simonandschuster.com.

The Simon & Schuster Speakers Bureau can bring authors to your live event. For more information or to book an event, contact the Simon & Schuster Speakers Bureau at 1-866-248-3049 or visit our website at www.simonspeakers.com.

Manufactured in the United States of America

10 9 8 7 6 5 4 3 2 1

Library of Congress Cataloging-in-Publication Data

Griffin, Laura.
  Far gone / Laura Griffin.—First Gallery Books hardcover edition.
    pages cm
1. Women detectives—Fiction. 2. Brothers and sisters—Fiction.
3. United States. Federal Bureau of Investigation—Fiction. 4. Murder—Investigation—Fiction. 5. Serial murders—Fiction. 6. Terrorism—Prevention—Fiction. I. Title.
  PS3607.R54838F38 2014
  813'.6—dc23
                                                    2013033910

ISBN 978-1-4516-8934-1
ISBN 978-1-4516-8937-2 (ebook)

For Doug

FAR GONE

Three messages.

The first to create shock and awe.

The second to deliver a terrifying blow—but only to the few who understood it.

The third was his favorite. It would be understood by everyone and bolder than they ever imagined.

chapter one

THE MESSENGER PULLED UP to the stoplight and scanned his surroundings. People streamed up and down the sidewalk, headed to jobs and meetings and classes under the colorless Philadelphia sky. The older ones wore dark overcoats and moved briskly down Market Street, with cell phones pressed to their ears. The younger ones were casual, dressed in jeans and bright-colored scarves and hats. They had backpacks slung over their shoulders and read texts from their friends as they walked.

He glanced at his watch. Eight minutes. He rolled his shoulders to ease the tension as he waited for the light. Three hours ago, he had woken up in a motel parking lot. He'd had a solid night's sleep in the front of the van—which was probably odd, considering his cargo. But years ago, he'd learned how to sleep anywhere.

The car ahead of him rolled forward. A silver Accord, late-model, female driver. She hooked a right, and the man followed, keeping his moves cautious.

A utility crew occupied the left lane, squeezing traffic down to a single line as they tore up the asphalt. The construction was good and bad, he'd decided. Bad because it might throw off his timeline. Good because it added to the chaos and created another reason for him to go unnoticed.

The man surveyed the sidewalks, skimming his gaze over the now-familiar takeout restaurants and shops hawking Liberty Bell replicas to tourists. Another glance at his watch.

Six minutes.

He reached into his jacket to check his weapon, a sleek FN Five-seveN with a twenty-round magazine. The pistol was loaded with nineteen SS195 jacketed hollow-point bullets, one already in the chamber. He was good to go.

Five minutes.

The messenger circled the block again. His stomach growled as he passed a doughnut store for the third time. He scanned the faces along the street, forcing hunger and fear and all distractions out of his mind as he made what he hoped would be his final lap through campus.

The phone beeped from the cup holder. He glanced at the text.

Red coat. Coming from the trolley stop.

He spotted her. No hat today, and her blond hair hung loose around her shoulders. Tall black boots. Tight jeans. Short red jacket with a belt at the waist.

He checked his watch. Once again, she was right on time.

Easing the minivan to the curb beside a fire hydrant, he watched her. She hurried toward her destination, gripping the strap of her backpack with a gloved hand. The other hand held a cigarette, and she lifted it to her lips for one last drag as she neared the building.

The cigarette disappointed him. She'd probably taste like an ashtray, nothing at all like his fantasies. He looked her over for another moment before sliding from the vehicle.

The sound of jackhammers hit him, along with the familiar smell of busted-up concrete. He glanced up and down the block and noted the cop on foot patrol talking to one of the utility workers. Both guys were fat and complacent. Too many doughnuts. The cop would hoof it over here in a few minutes, but by then, it would be too late.

The messenger hit the sidewalk, keeping the brim of his cap low as he watched the woman.

Eye contact. Just an instant, but it sent a sweet jolt of adrenaline through him.

One minute.

He looked straight ahead as they passed each other. This was it. He reached into his jacket pocket and pulled out two bits of orange foam, which he pressed into his ears. He hung a right and saw the Ford parked in the designated place.

Ten seconds.

He pulled out his second phone. Took a deep breath as he flipped it open.

Message One: You reap what you sow. He hit send and braced for the concussion. For a moment, nothing.

And then the earth moved.

◆

Andrea Finch had never been dumped at a barbecue joint, but there was a first time for everything.

Her date looked out of place at the scarred wooden booth in his charcoal-gray suit. He'd come straight from work, as she had. He'd ditched the tie but still seemed overly formal in a restaurant that had paper-towel rolls on every table and classic country drifting from the jukebox.

"So." Nick Mays took a swig of beer. "How was your day?"

Andrea smiled. He sounded like a tired husband, and they'd only been dating a month.

"Fine," she said. "Yours?"

"Fine."

For the dozenth time since she'd sat down, his gaze darted over her shoulder. When his blue eyes met hers again, she felt a twinge of regret. He really *was* a nice-looking man. Good eyes, thick hair. A bit of a beer gut, but she didn't mind, really. His main problem was his oversize ego. Andrea was used to men with big egos. She'd been surrounded by them since she'd entered the police academy, and they'd only multiplied once she earned her detective's badge.

"Listen, Andrea." He glanced over her shoulder again, and she braced for the speech. "These last few weeks, they've really been great."

He was a terrible liar, which was too bad. As an assistant district attorney, he was going to need the skill if he planned to run for his boss's job someday.

He opened his mouth to continue just as a waitress stepped up and beamed a smile at him.

"Y'all ready to order?"

Nick looked pained. But to his credit, he nodded in Andrea's direction. "Andie?"

"I'm good, thanks."

He glanced at the waitress. "Me, too."

"So . . . y'all *won't* be having dinner with us?" Her overly made-up eyes shifted to Andrea. She tucked a lock of blond hair behind her ear and looked impatient.

"Just the drinks for now." Nick gave her one of his smiles,

which seemed to lessen her annoyance as she hustled off. The smile faded as he turned back to Andrea. "So I was saying. These past few weeks. It's been a good time, Andie. You're an interesting girl."

She gritted her teeth. If he insisted on using frat-boy speak, she was going to make this *way* harder for him. She folded her arms over her chest and cast her gaze around the restaurant, letting his comment dangle awkwardly.

The cowbell on the door rattled as a family of four filed outside. Tonight's crowd was thin, even for a Monday. Maybe the weather was keeping people away. Austin was set to get sleet tonight, and her lieutenant had called in extra officers, expecting the roads to be a mess.

"Andrea?"

She looked at him.

"I said, wouldn't you agree with that?"

The cowbell rattled again as a skinny young man stepped through the entrance. He wore a black trench coat and clunky boots. His too-big ears reminded Andrea of her brother.

She looked at Nick. "Agree with what?"

His mouth tightened. "I said it seems like neither of us is looking for something serious right now. So maybe we should cool things down a little."

She glanced across the room as the kid walked toward the double doors leading to the kitchen. She studied the line of his coat, frowning.

"*Andrea.*"

"*What?*" Her attention snapped to Nick.

"Christ, you're not even listening. Have you heard a word I said?"

She glanced at the kitchen, where the clatter of pots and pans had suddenly gone silent. The back of her neck tingled. She slid from the booth.

"Andie?"

"Just a sec."

She strode across the restaurant, her stare fixed on the double doors. Her heart thudded inexplicably while her mind cataloged info: six-one, one-fifty, blond, blue. She pictured his flushed cheeks and his lanky body in that big coat.

A waiter whisked past her and pushed through the doors to the kitchen. Andrea followed, stumbling into him when he halted in his tracks.

Three people stood motionless against a counter. Their eyes were round with shock, and their mouths hung open.

The kid in the overcoat stood a few yards away, pointing a pistol at them.

His gaze jumped to Andrea and the waiter. "You! Over there!" He jerked his head at the petrified trio.

The waiter made a strangled sound and scuttled out the door they'd just come through.

Andrea didn't move. Her chest tightened as she took in the scene: two waitresses and a cook, all cowering against a counter. Possibly more people in back. The kid was brandishing a Glock 17. It was pointed straight at the woman in the center, Andrea's waitress. She couldn't have been more than eighteen, and the gunman looked almost as young. Andrea noted his skinny neck, his *freckles*. His cheeks were pink—not from cold, as she'd first thought, but emotion.

The look he sent the waitress was like a plea.

"You did this, Haley!"

The woman's eyes widened. Her lips moved, but no words came out.

"This is *your* fault."

Andrea eased her hand beneath her blazer. The kid's arm swung toward her. "You! Get with them!"

She went still.

"Dillon, what are you—"

"Shut up!" The gun swung back toward the waitress. Haley. The trio was just a few short yards away from the gun. Even with no skill whatsoever, anything he fired at that distance would likely be lethal. And who knew how many bullets he had in that thing?

Andrea's heart drummed inside her chest. The smoky smell of barbecue filled the air. The kitchen was warm and steamy, and the walls seemed to be closing in on her as she focused on the gunman.

His back was to a wall lined with coat hooks. She counted four jackets and two ball caps, probably all belonging to the staff. Was anyone else hiding in the back? Had someone called for help?

"*You* did this!" the gunman shouted, and Haley flinched.

Andrea licked her lips. For only the second time in her career, she eased her gun from its holster and prepared to aim it at a person. The weight in her hand felt familiar, almost comforting. But her mouth went dry as her finger slid around the trigger.

Defuse.

She thought of everything she'd ever learned about hostage negotiations. She thought of the waiter who'd fled. She thought of Nick. Help had to be on the way by now. But the closest SWAT team was twenty minutes out, and she *knew*, with sickening certainty, that whatever happened here was going to be over in a matter of moments.

"I trusted you, Haley." His voice broke on the last word, and Haley cringed back. "I trusted you, but you're a lying *bitch!*"

"Dillon, please—"

"*Shut up!* Just shut up, okay?"

Ambivalence. She heard it in his voice. She could get control of this.

Andrea raised her weapon. "Dillon, look at me."

To her relief, his gaze veered in her direction. He was crying now, tears streaming down his freckled cheeks, and again he reminded her of her brother. Andrea's stomach clenched as she lined up her sights on his center body mass.

Establish a command presence.

"Put the gun down, Dillon. Let's talk this through."

He swung his arm ninety degrees, and Andrea was staring down the barrel of the Glock. All sound disappeared. Her entire world seemed to be sucked by gravity toward that little black hole.

She lifted her gaze to the gunman's face. Dillon. His name was Dillon. And he was eighteen, tops.

Her heart beat crazily. Her mouth felt dry. Hundreds of times she'd trained to confront an armed assailant. It should have been a no-brainer, pure muscle memory. But she felt paralyzed. Every instinct was screaming for her to find another way.

Dillon's attention slid to Haley, who seemed to be melting into the Formica counter. The others had inched away from her—a survival instinct that was going to be of little help if this kid let loose with a hail of bullets.

Loud, repetitive commands.

"Dillon, look at me." She tried to make her voice firm, but even she could hear the desperation in it. "Put the gun down, Dillon. We'll talk through this."

His eyes met hers again. He rubbed his nose on the shoulder of his coat. Tears and snot glistened on his face.

"I'll kill you, too," he said softly. "Don't think I won't."

"I believe you. But wouldn't it be easier just to talk?" She paused. "Put the gun down, Dillon."

She could see his arm shaking, and—to her dismay—hers began to shake, too. As if she didn't know how to hold her own weapon. As if she didn't work out three times a week to maintain upper-body strength.

As if she didn't have it in her to shoot a frightened kid.

He was disintegrating before her eyes. She could see it. His Adam's apple moved up and down as he swallowed hard.

"You can't stop me." His voice was a thread now, almost a whisper. He shifted his stance back toward Haley, and the stark look on her face told Andrea she'd read his body language.

"I'll do it."

Andrea's pulse roared in her ears. The edges of her vision blurred. All she saw was that white hand clutching that big black gun. The muscles in his hand shifted as his index finger curled.

"I'll do it. You can't stop me."

Andrea squinted her eye.

Lord, forgive me.

She pulled the trigger.

chapter two

ANDREA WOKE WITH A KNOT in her chest. She rolled onto the cool edge of the pillow and tried to hold on to the soft, dreamy feeling that she could slide out of bed and step into her routine. But even her sleep-drugged brain knew it was a lie.

She opened her eyes. The hum of traffic outside was inescapable. Beams of sunlight seeped through the gaps in the blinds, hinting at a bright, agonizingly blue morning that was already well under way.

As she sat up in bed, her gaze landed on the running shoes that had been taunting her for days now. She went into the bathroom and avoided her reflection in the mirror as she brushed her teeth. Then she padded into the kitchen and reached for the coffeepot.

Day three on leave. Just the prospect made her stomach fill with acid. She couldn't stand another stint in her apartment, but the thought of going outside was worse. As the coffee hissed and gurgled, she glanced around her tiny living room and made a list of all the chores she needed to do—laundry, cleaning, grocery store, bills. It was the same list as yesterday, only longer, and she felt a surge of disgust with herself.

She stalked into the bedroom and wrestled into her sports bra, then jammed her feet into sneakers. Back in the kitchen, she poured a mug of coffee, not bothering with cream, which she probably didn't have anyway. A few quick gulps. Pulling her tangle of dark hair into a ponytail, she grabbed a baseball cap and was almost out the door when her cell phone chimed.

Andrea eyed her purse. She dug the phone out and wasn't surprised at the number on the screen.

"Hi."

"Hi yourself," Nathan Devereaux said. "Where have you been?"

"Oh, you know. Lounging by the pool. Working on my tan."

Silence. He didn't like the sarcasm. Then he said, "Have you seen the news today?"

"No. Why?" Against her better judgment, she grabbed the remote from the coffee table and switched on the television.

"Forget it. Anyway, where are you? I thought you'd be in by now."

Andrea flipped channels until she landed on a news broadcast. But they were done with local stories, and a photo of the senator's daughter who had died in that university bombing filled the screen. Andrea studied the picture, which had been plastered all over the news for days now. Julia Kirby. She was beautiful.

And just eighteen years old.

The camera cut to a view of the smoldering building. First responders raced about, ferrying the wounded to ambulances and triage tents. Dust-covered civilians staggered down the sidewalk with wide, shocked eyes, some with shrapnel wounds and ears bleeding from the blast.

"Andrea? Are you coming in?"

"Why?"

"You've got an appointment with the shrink, I thought."

"I rescheduled."

More silence.

"Something came up." She switched off the TV and grabbed her sunglasses from the counter. Lot of good they would do her if some reporter was camped out in her parking lot.

"Andie—"

"I'll be in tomorrow. Eight o'clock sharp. Listen, I've got to go, okay? Call you later."

She stuffed the phone back into her purse and knew it wouldn't ring again. Nathan wasn't like that. He wouldn't call incessantly, but he *would* track her down some other way. He'd probably come pounding on her door late tonight when he knew she'd be home. And he'd probably refuse to leave until she let him in and at least went through the pretense of answering his questions. He was her assigned "sponsor"—whatever that meant—and it was his job to ask.

Nathan had been her mentor when she first joined Austin PD's homicide unit. They'd been through ups and downs together and many hellacious cases but nothing that came close to this. This was out of her realm of experience, and she didn't know how to talk to him about it.

Which was what shrinks were for.

Another chime emanated from her purse. She jerked the phone out but didn't recognize the area code.

"Hello?"

"Hey, it's me."

She felt a flutter of panic at her brother's voice. She'd considered the possibility of her grandparents calling. Dee and Bob read the paper every morning and might stumble across the story out of Austin. She'd planned what she'd say to them, but she hadn't given her brother a thought.

"Are you there?"

"I'm here." She cleared her throat. "What's up, Gavin?"

Now it was his turn for quiet. Andrea waited. Would he bring it up right away or dance around it?

"I need a favor."

The statement startled her.

"I need some money. Not a lot," he rushed to add. "And I'll pay you back, I promise."

He didn't know, then. This wasn't about her at all—he was hard up for cash. If he was like most college kids, she'd assume he needed it for beer or gas. But Gavin wasn't like most college kids. He wasn't like anyone. "You been taking your meds?" she asked.

"Come on, Andie."

"Have you?"

"Yes, all right? Gimme a break. Can you lend me the money?"

"How much?"

"Two thousand."

"Two *thousand*? You said not a lot!"

"It isn't a lot."

"Are you out of your freaking mind? I've got rent due next week. Jesus. What's it for?"

"I'll pay you back."

She snorted. "How? Last I checked, part-time busboys weren't making the big bucks."

"I quit that job."

Andrea thought about the number on the caller ID. Her stomach clenched with anxiety, and for the first time in days, it wasn't because she'd taken another human life.

"Gavin . . . whose phone are you on?"

"A friend's. Listen, can you lend me the money or not? I've got wiring instructions here. You can send it straight to my bank, and I'll pay you back, I swear."

"Where are you? Are you even in Lubbock?"

Silence.

"If you dropped out, I swear to God—"

"I didn't call you to get the third degree."

"You did, didn't you? You dropped out. Gavin! You're what? Fifteen credits shy of graduation?"

"Twelve," he said tersely. "And I didn't drop out. I took a leave of absence. For something important. I can go back whenever I want."

"Go back *now*. What the hell are you doing? And what's this money for?"

"Damn it, Andie. Why do you have to be such a bitch all the time?"

"Does Dee know? Don't you dare tell me you hit her up for money."

His silence confirmed her suspicions.

"They're on a fixed income! What the hell's wrong with you?"

She waited, half expecting an answer.

"Gavin?"

The call went dead.

◆

Jon North should have been fighting insomnia on a lumpy, too-short mattress, but instead he was speeding toward a crowded honky-tonk on the outskirts of Maverick, Texas, the capital of Middle of Fucking Nowhere.

All because he trusted Jimmy Torres.

Jon surveyed the array of cars and pickups as he pulled into the gravel parking lot. Located on a two-lane highway just south of Interstate 10, the Broken Spoke attracted its fair share of ranchers, roughnecks, and long-haul truck drivers looking for a break in the monotony between El Paso and San Antonio.

Jon swung into a space beside an ancient Chevy and checked his rearview before getting out. The chilly air smelled of dust and diesel fuel. The sky was clear, and a half-moon shone down on the desert landscape. Jon approached the dilapidated bar. Neon beer signs cluttered the windows, and the thin walls seemed to vibrate with every guitar riff.

Inside was stuffy and loud, just as he remembered. He stepped away from the door and skimmed the crowd. It was the Spoke's usual array of men, most well on their way to being drunk. The women were of the heavily made-up, bottle-blond variety, with plenty of cleavage on display. They were here to have fun or make a buck, maybe a little of both. Some faces were familiar, some not. He cataloged all of them, swiftly discarding the ones that didn't line up with his objective tonight.

Jon turned to the pool room, where a brunette with a cue leaned low over the green felt—a move choreographed to get the attention of the beer-swilling man behind her. Jon peered at her face.

Right hair color, wrong type.

He scanned the room again and his gaze landed on a woman seated on a corner bar stool. Slender build, leather jacket, straight dark hair that didn't quite reach her shoulders. She glanced toward the door, noticed him, and gave him a brief look of appraisal before shifting her attention back to the bartender.

Torres was right. She didn't fit. Before joining the Bureau,

Torres had put in five years on a Houston vice squad, and he was good at reading people. Jon was glad now that he'd hauled himself out of bed.

The woman lifted a drink to her lips as he edged around the crowd. He couldn't take his eyes off her. There was something about her alert expression, her posture. She noticed him again in the mirror behind the liquor bottles, and her gaze narrowed as he walked over and claimed a stool.

"Hi," he said.

No answer. She was about as approachable as a coral snake.

The female bartender lingered a moment, seeming amused, then slipped away to tend to other customers.

"Buy you a drink?"

She looked him over with cool blue eyes. "Thanks, I'm good."

"No, really, I insist." He nodded at her almost-empty glass. "What is that, whiskey?"

She seemed annoyed by his persistence but not surprised. "Jack and Coke," she said.

He caught the bartender's attention and held up two fingers.

The brunette shifted to face him, and he noticed the thin gray T-shirt beneath the leather. Faded jeans, snug. Scarred black biker boots. A slight bulge under her jacket told him she was packing. He pulled his gaze back to her face. She wore black eyeliner, and a trio of silver earrings dotted both ears.

The drinks arrived.

"I'm Jon, by the way."

She watched him over the rim of her glass as she took a sip.

"You're new in town," he said.

"So are you."

"Is it that obvious?"

"The accent. Michigan, is it?"

"Illinois." He tipped back the drink and tried not to cringe at the sweetness of it.

She was watching him while keeping a close eye on the mirror behind the bar. Clearly, she was looking for someone tonight, and it wasn't him. She rested an elbow on the counter and pretended to give him her undivided attention.

"Illinois is a long way," she said. "What do you do?"

"Search for people, mostly. And things."

At her questioning look, he expanded.

"I'm with ICE. Immigration and Customs Enforcement."

The corner of her mouth lifted, and he felt a warm pull he hadn't felt in a long time.

"Think I've heard of it," she said.

"They move us around a lot. I started out near Canada. Now I'm down here. So what about you? What're you doing in town?"

"Passing through."

"Where you headed?"

"Wherever."

He watched her eyes. Calm. Clear. Not lying, really, but giving nothing away. He was used to evasiveness. Most people out here valued their privacy and didn't let down their guard with outsiders.

Which was one reason so many leads in this case had turned to dust.

She was still watching him. She sipped the whiskey again, and he saw her gaze return to the mirror. A stocky cowboy type steered a woman through the crowd toward the door. Jon recognized him as one of the ranch hands at Lost Creek.

"I should get going." In a quick, fluid motion she slid off the stool and scooped up her purse.

"What's the hurry? You haven't finished your drink."

"That's okay." Her mouth curved into a coy smile. "It's past my bedtime. I need to get home."

He stared down at her, and the smile irked him more than the lie. She dug a crisp twenty from her purse and placed it beneath her glass.

"Nice talking to you." Another smile before she turned on her heel.

He watched her walk away. When she was gone, he slid the twenty into his pocket and replaced it with one from his wallet.

The bartender filled a few beers and made her way over. She had leathery skin and lines around her mouth that signaled years of hard living under the West Texas sun. Jon had talked to her before but never bothered to introduce himself, and now he regretted it as she cleared away the half-finished Jack and Coke.

He smiled. "I didn't catch her name, did you?"

"Don't think she threw it."

"You seen her in here before?"

"Nope." Her tone was clipped, and she darted a glance at the clock. He figured she was jonesing for a cigarette. After a moment, she looked up at him and seemed to give in.

"She asked about Lost Creek Ranch, same as you did."

Jon glanced at the door. He got up from his stool, even though he knew it was pointless to tail her. She'd be looking for it. He didn't know much about her, but he knew that.

He left another twenty on the counter and maneuvered through the crowd. He stepped into the parking lot and saw a pair of red taillights fading down the highway.

He called Torres.

"You were right, she's a badge."

Curses filled Jon's ear as he crossed the lot to his pickup. "I knew it!" Torres said. "The DEA's fucking us again. Did you run the plate on her Cherokee?"

"I thought you had it."

"Yeah, but something's screwy. Must've got it down wrong. I can swing by the motel later, see if it's there."

Jon looked out at the horizon, at the vast, empty desert. No traffic, no houses. Just a twinkle of lights on some distant oil derricks.

"Don't bother. She was heading for the interstate."

For a moment, Torres said nothing. Then he said, "Well, that's good, right? Maybe she's going back where she came from."

"Maybe," Jon said, but he didn't believe it.

Jon ended the call and pointed his truck toward Maverick. He checked the dash clock. Ten past midnight. Another day gone and nothing to show for it.

He trained his gaze on the endless yellow lines. Thirteen days. Less than two weeks left.

The clock in Jon's head continued to tick.

chapter three

ANDREA SWUNG HER ARMS over her head and gazed up at the clouds. She bent down to touch her toes, did a couple of deep lunges, and set off toward the lake.

She'd left her music behind so she could relish the sounds of traffic and construction and a city bustling with people. She'd actually missed the noise. She pounded down the sidewalk, passing commuters with umbrellas. She passed bus stops and coffee bars and bike shops with faded pictures of Lance Armstrong still on display. She passed aluminum trailers where the spicy scent of breakfast tacos wafted from the windows. Then she cut east at the lake, and as her feet hit gravel, she finally found her stride.

The running helped. Always had. Her breathing was a soundtrack, better and more vital than any music as she focused on the tree-lined path and picked up the pace. The trail was clear today—nearly empty, in fact. She glanced left toward the water, but the usual fleet of stand-up paddle-boarders wasn't out.

The sprinkling became a drizzle as she ate up the trail. Her heart thrummed in her chest. She passed the statue of Stevie Ray

Vaughan holding his guitar. She passed the dog park. She neared the Congress Avenue Bridge, home to the largest urban bat colony on the planet. The pungent odor of guano hit her, and she had a memory of her freckle-faced brother, age five, standing under the bridge in the black cape left over from Halloween. Gavin had idolized Batman, and their grandparents had taken them on a pilgrimage to Austin to witness the bats take flight over the city at sunset. Andrea had been twelve and thoroughly bored by it all as she'd sat on the hillside watching her brother zoom around pretending to be a superhero.

She pictured Gavin's ruddy cheeks and the unruly red hair that had earned him nicknames throughout his life. Once again, she was worried about him. Her brother was a genius but could be amazingly dumb when it came to people.

Andrea quickened the pace. As the trail curved, she glanced up to see the concrete headquarters of the newspaper that had been running stories about her all week.

Her chest pinched. Her breathing grew shallow. She looked at the building and fought against the panic.

Don't do it.

She focused on the path and tried to get her rhythm back. She had to get a grip. She was meeting the department shrink in less than two hours, and she needed to have her shit together.

And how are you sleeping, Andrea?

Fine.

Any nightmares? Insomnia?

No, nothing like that.

And have you experienced any flashbacks associated with the incident?

No.

What about sudden feelings of anger or hostility?

She'd had feelings like that most of her life, but she knew the answers. *No, no, no.* She might throw in an occasional *yes* to make it seem like she was being honest, but no way was she letting some shrink climb inside her head.

It was tougher to lie to Nathan.

He'd had that look on his face when he'd come over the other night. Nathan knew. He'd been through an officer-involved shooting, and he *knew*, which was why they'd assigned him to her. He was supposed to help her. But she didn't want his help. She didn't want anything from anyone, even though for days, she'd felt this constant low-grade anxiety, as if she was holding on to something by her fingernails, but she didn't know what.

Andrea veered right, away from the newspaper building, prompting a honk from a driver. She cut across a parking lot and turned southbound on a busy street.

For a while, she ran without thinking. Rain soaked her T-shirt. It seeped into her shoes, making her socks squish with every stride. She wove through residential streets, twisting and winding as she racked up mile after mile at a too-fast pace for the weather conditions. When her thighs burned and her lungs were about to explode, she looked up and spotted her apartment building. She set her sights on it and poured on the speed.

She stopped at the bank of mailboxes and gulped down air. Arching back, she let the rain pelt her face. Six miles, maybe seven. She bent over to flatten her palms on the cold pavement, letting the drizzle soak her back as thoughts flooded in to fill the vacuum. She thought of Gavin and Dillon and her grandparents. She thought of her mother. She thought of the dozens of things she'd failed to do in her life and the handful of things she'd done right.

A pair of shiny black wingtips stepped into her field of view, and she jerked upright.

"Detective Finch."

He wore a suit and tie. Jon something . . . who clearly wasn't an ICE agent. Her gaze dropped to the badge clipped to his belt.

FBI.

Water glistened on his dark hair. His broad shoulders were damp but not all of him, which meant he hadn't been standing out here long. His eyes were shielded by silver aviators, so she couldn't see his expression, just her own look of wariness reflected back at her.

"You have a minute, Detective?"

It was more of an order than a question. She glanced around the lot again but didn't see any sign of the reporters who'd been hounding her for days.

She turned and faced him. "I knew you weren't ICE."

The side of his mouth curved slightly, but he didn't smile.

"Is your name really Jon?"

"Special Agent Jon North. How about we find a place to talk?"

Andrea glanced at her apartment window. She didn't like the idea of taking him up there—not because he was six-two and armed and a virtual stranger but because she assumed he was nosy.

But if she took him to a coffee shop, they might get approached by a reporter.

"Third floor, no elevator," she said.

He gestured toward the stairs with a politeness that fit the suit. "After you."

She trekked up the steps, untying the key from the drawstring of her sweatpants as she went. She opened her door and made a direct line to the breakfast table covered in paperwork.

"Coffee's still on if you want some."

She scooped the papers into her arms and headed to the

bedroom, where she dumped everything on the dresser. Then she ducked into her closet and changed into a dry T-shirt before closing her bedroom door and rejoining him in the kitchen. He stood beside the breakfast bar, where she'd left her laptop out. Fortunately, it was off.

She leaned back against the opposite counter and folded her arms over her chest. "So what can I do for you, Mr. North?"

The sunglasses had disappeared, and he was watching her now with those hazel eyes she remembered from the bar. His hands were tucked casually into his pants pockets, putting his badge and gun on display. She wondered if he thought she'd be intimidated. His dark hair was thick, no gray. She put him at thirty-five, give or take, but what he lacked in years he made up for with a relaxed confidence.

"You been back long?" he asked.

"Two nights."

He nodded absently, and she could tell this wasn't news. She watched him taking in details as he glanced around her apartment: her cell phone charging on the counter, the droopy yellow plant in the corner, the unopened mail.

Nosy, just as she'd expected.

"Mind if I . . . ?" He tipped his head toward the coffeepot.

She crossed the kitchen and took a mug down from the cabinet. It was green, with a yellow John Deere logo on it, and she filled it to the brim. He didn't strike her as the cream-and-sugar type.

He accepted the coffee, took a sip, and put it down beside last night's dishes.

"You didn't mention you're a cop," he said.

"You didn't ask."

"You didn't mention your name, either."

"I don't usually give out my name in bars."

He smiled. "I don't blame you."

Her heart did a little flutter—something about his smile. Or maybe her system was responding to having an attractive man in her kitchen.

"How'd you find me?" she asked.

"Ran your license plate."

"Try again," she said. She'd borrowed that tag from the '86 Chevy Celebrity her grandfather kept under a tarp in his garage.

He watched her silently until she started to get irritated. "I need to know about your interest in Shay Hardin," he said.

"What interest?"

His eyes didn't change—they stayed locked on hers. "You interviewed no fewer than twelve people about him over the course of three days," he said.

"Interviewed?"

"Asked questions about him."

"So what? I can ask questions about whatever I want. It's none of your business."

He rested his hands on the countertop. "Actually, it is. My team's been conducting an undercover investigation of Hardin for the past four months."

She didn't say anything. She was aware of Hardin's background—he'd been arrested a few times on minor charges, mostly fighting in bars, but he'd never been convicted of anything. She was aware that he lived with some friends, including her brother, at Lost Creek Ranch outside Maverick. She was *not* aware until this moment that he was the subject of an FBI investigation.

She watched the agent's face and wondered if he knew that her brother had recently joined Hardin's little commune. Gavin's previous stint there had lasted an entire summer and would have been longer if Andrea hadn't found him and persuaded him to go back to school.

She adjusted her strategy now. If she stonewalled, he'd probably get more interested, not less.

"So what's your question, exactly?"

"I want to know why an Austin homicide detective is poking around my suspect," he said. "I don't need him getting spooked."

Andrea reached for the cabinet beside him and took down a glass. She filled it with water from the tap and took a long sip as North watched her.

She'd known right away that he didn't fit the profile of an ICE agent. Those guys tended to be bulkier and rougher around the edges. The ones in West Texas spent a lot of time hotshotting around the desert in their 4x4s.

North had the height. And he'd clearly spent time outdoors recently. But he looked different from the typical border cowboy. He seemed smoother, smarter. And he looked comfortable in a suit.

He was still watching her steadily, waiting for an answer.

"It's not police-related," she told him. "My interest is personal."

His brow furrowed. "You two have a history?"

"Something like that."

He seemed surprised. And maybe a little disappointed.

But it wasn't a bad concept. If he thought she had a relationship with Shay Hardin, that kept her brother out of it.

"So what did he say? I assume you tried to contact him while you were out there?"

"He wasn't really communicative," she said vaguely. "We're not on good terms."

"Any chance you could change that?"

"Doubtful." And that was the truth. "I tried to reach out to him, and I got nowhere."

"Did you visit the ranch?"

"Didn't get past the gate."

"Did you try calling him?"

"No luck." She shrugged. "Anyway, I hear he keeps to himself now. That's what everyone in town says."

North's look was intent, and the ball of dread that had been sitting in her stomach for the last five days grew heavier. Andrea had never liked Hardin. What was he mixed up in? And what was Gavin mixed up in by association?

"What's this about, anyway?" she asked. "Why's he under investigation?"

"I'm not at liberty to say."

She glared at him across the kitchen. Typical fed. Swoop in wanting a quid pro quo with none of the quid.

He stepped forward and gazed down at her. She noticed his eyes again and remembered how they'd looked back at the bar. She'd seen something else in his expression then, but right now he was all business. "A little friendly advice."

She glared harder.

"Leave Shay Hardin alone. I can't think of an easier way to ruin a promising career."

What the hell did *that* mean? She got the distinct impression he was taking a jab at her.

He set his mug in the sink. Then he crossed to the door and glanced back as he opened it.

"Trust me on this, Detective. He's a problem you don't need."

Jon slid his truck between some mesquite bushes and tossed a camo net over it. The night air was cold and brisk as he made the trek out to the meeting point. Nothing out here was a short distance away. At first, he'd been put off by the vastness of it, but it had grown on him. He'd come to appreciate the honesty of the desert, the hardworking people with their callused hands and skin as parched and cracked as the land. He crossed the field to a slight rise beside the dried-up riverbed—the Lost Creek for which the nearby ranch was named. Torres was right where he'd said he'd be, about half a mile south of the house.

"Hey, thanks for stopping by," he said.

Jon ignored the sarcasm as he settled in beside him. He stretched out prone and lifted the night-vision binoculars to his face.

"What do we got?"

"A coyote moved across the highway 'bout an hour ago," Torres said.

"You call it in?"

"CBP took it."

Jon glanced at him. "You in your truck?"

"Nah, Whitfield dropped me off."

Jon settled himself against the cold, hard dirt. He peered through the binocs and did a slow 180-degree scan east to west. It was flat country, only a low ridge running north-south to break up the landscape. The ridge would have been a better vantage point, but it was too obvious. Hardin had trained at Fort Benning. He would have spotted it in a minute.

Overnight surveillance of the ranch had been a priority ever since the eavesdropping crew had picked up a snippet from an outdoor conversation: *meeting us . . . oh-two-hundred hours.* They'd had a team stationed out here for the past three nights, but no one had entered or left the property, and Jon was convinced they'd missed something.

Still, he scoured the landscape for anyone coming or going. He listened for the crunch of footsteps or the low hum of an approaching engine. He listened for coyotes—either the furry or the human variety. He listened for rattlesnakes. This land was inhabited by things that would bite, sting, and stab—not to mention shoot—when threatened. Hardin had a sign hooked to the game fence that surrounded his land: NO TRESPASSING. WE DON'T CALL 911.

Torres rolled onto his back. He untwisted the lid from his thermos, and the aroma of hot cocoa wafted over. Most agents on surveillance downed coffee by the gallon. Torres was a Swiss Miss addict.

"Thought you were coming back yesterday."

Jon lowered the binocs. "Got tied up."

"How was the office?"

"Same. Jane says hi."

A flash of white teeth in the darkness. "No kidding?"

This assignment had been a dry spell in more ways than one, and Jon knew Torres was ready to be done with it. Jon wasn't so eager. In the four months since he'd come out here, his work had slowly turned into an obsession. Eight years with the Bureau, and Jon had never had a case grab hold of him like this one. After months of undercover work, after countless hours of painstaking digging, he was long on theories and short on evidence. Coincidence after coincidence had piled up, but he couldn't find a way to fit everything into a coherent picture.

He checked his watch again. Twenty more minutes.

"How'd it go in Austin?" Torres asked.

"Fine."

"So what's her story?"

Jon thought of Andrea Finch outside her apartment, her face slick with rain and sweat, her T-shirt plastered to her body.

"She said it was personal, not business."

Torres grunted. "Yeah, right."

"Said she has a history with Hardin."

"I don't buy it. She took what, three days off work? To come out here? I bet money she's on some kind of task force. DEA's fucking with us again, I'm telling you."

"She didn't take off," Jon said. "She's on the beach."

"She's what?"

"Suspended. Administrative leave, pending an investigation. She was in an officer-involved shooting. An eighteen-year-old died."

"No shit, she killed a kid?"

Jon pictured her face again. He wondered whether the shooting was the reason for that edgy look in her eyes. Or maybe she always looked that way.

"What's the verdict with Maxwell?" Torres asked. "He in or out?"

Jon peered through the binocs again and thought about their boss in San Antonio, who'd never really been on board with this operation. "We've got one more week. If we don't have a warrant in hand by that point, he wants to pull the plug."

Torres muttered a curse.

"Said we're needed on the Saledo case."

"We've already got ten agents staffed to that thing."

Jon shifted his gaze to the ridge, and his attention caught on a faint green glow behind some scrub trees. He adjusted the lenses. "What time'd you get here?" he asked Torres.

"'Bout ninety minutes ago."

"And where's Whitfield?"

"Off the highway near the gate, like we planned. Why?" Torres lifted his binoculars and tried to zero in on what Jon was seeing.

"Heat signature."

"Faint, but it's there," Jon agreed.

"It's not moving."

"I'm thinking it's a vehicle. Engine hasn't totally cooled down yet."

"Can't believe I missed it."

A flash of movement caught Jon's eye. He aimed the binocs west, where a much brighter green glow was now moving through the bushes.

Torres tensed beside him. He saw it, too, and it was right on time. Jon checked his watch to make sure. After so many nights of nothing, he'd all but written off this meeting.

The shape moved stealthily through the low scrub brush. The figure was small and hunched over but not sure-footed like many of the drug and human traffickers who slipped through the region. It progressed slowly up the incline and neared the clump of mesquite trees. Jon confirmed his first take that the fainter heat signature belonged to a vehicle.

The rumble of an engine disrupted the quiet. But it wasn't from the vehicle on the ridge. This noise came from the direction of the house.

"Someone's moving out." Torres rested his binoculars on the ground and dug for his radio. He used a secure channel to make contact with the third member of their team, who was in an ICE van not far from the highway.

"Yo, we got a pickup heading toward the gate," Torres told Whitfield. "Looks like Hardin's. And we've got a second vehicle parked up on the ridge."

The plan was for Whitfield to tail anyone leaving the property. The agent was almost as green as Torres, and Jon hoped he wouldn't get burned.

"Roger that." Whitfield's voice sounded staticky. "Just got a visual on the truck . . . exiting the southwest gate."

Jon looked at the ridge again. He adjusted his lenses. The stationary vehicle seemed to be waiting to leave until the pickup was gone.

Torres climbed to his feet and silently collected his gear. Jon stayed prone, trying to get a view of the second subject.

"You coming?"

The pickup's grumble continued to fade. Soon Whitfield would be on the tail, with Jon and Torres close behind, hoping to get into position in time to see something wherever this meeting went down.

Torres was on the radio with Whitfield. "Repeat that. You said they're turning *west*?"

"Affirmative."

"Why would they go west?"

"No idea," Whitfield said. "There's nothing out there—at least, not on the map I'm looking at."

"Okay, we're on our way."

Jon watched the ridge as the mystery vehicle eased out from behind the brush and moved slowly down the gentle slope. No headlights. It stopped near the dirt road leading to the highway, and Jon got his first unobstructed view of the car and the driver.

He lowered his binoculars. Un-fucking-believable.

Andrea Finch.

Part of him wasn't surprised at all.

✦

They were leaving, Shay Hardin behind the wheel and a man Andrea didn't recognize riding shotgun.

She waited at the base of the ridge as Hardin's taillights grew smaller. Why on earth were they going west? There was nothing in that direction. He'd have to drive a good twenty minutes just to pick up a highway.

Not her problem. She had the information she'd come for, and it was time to get gone.

Andrea kept the lights off as she moved cautiously down the road. Using only the moon for guidance was unnerving, but she couldn't risk headlights yet, so her visibility was limited to about ten feet beyond her front bumper. She eased over the uneven terrain, careful to avoid trees and cacti and boulders as she neared the dirt road that bisected Lost Creek Ranch.

The ride smoothed as her tires found hard-packed earth. She eased into the middle of the road and headed due east, toward the gate that linked the property with an adjacent ranch. She kept a careful eye on the odometer. In the light of the moon, she spotted the high line of the game fence and the eight-foot posts on either side of the gate.

It was closed.

She rolled to a stop and checked her surroundings. She'd propped that gate open with a rock, but it was shut now. How had it come to be that way? They'd had some gusts in the last hour, so maybe the wind had moved it.

Or maybe the landowner had.

She looked around, hyperalert for any sign of someone lurking nearby. In the dimness, she spotted the loop of baling wire that had been used to secure the gate. It lay in the dirt near the fence post, exactly where she'd left it.

Andrea climbed out. She paused beside her SUV and listened

for a full minute before trudging over to the post. She hauled the gate open, then slid behind the wheel and rattled over the cattle guard that separated Lost Creek from its neighbor. Again, she returned to the gate. She reattached the baling wire and let out a sigh. Home free.

A force slammed into her, plowing her face-first into the dirt. Her breath disappeared with an *oomph!* She bucked and tried to scream, but the weight crushed her lungs. Fire lanced up her back as the barrel of her own pistol dug into her spine.

Something clamped around her wrists. Her arms were wrenched back at an impossible angle. She sucked in a breath but got a mouthful of dirt, and panic set in as she struggled for air.

Then the weight disappeared. She rolled. She scrambled for her knees, and a bolt of pain seared through her abdomen. She convulsed into a tight ball. Another kick landed like a sledgehammer. The third time, she reacted, grabbing the boot and yanking with all her might, but it tore from her hands. Muffled curses as her attacker tripped backward.

She rolled away into something prickly. Cactus! Choking and gasping for air, she groped for her gun and got it out of her holster just as an engine roared to life nearby. She pushed to her knees and finally caught a breath—and a nose full of exhaust fumes—as the truck sped away.

✦

"Where the hell's he going?" Torres adjusted the screen on their navigation system. "There's nothing out here."

Jon picked up his radio. "Give us an update."

"Subject is still moving due west," Whitfield reported.

"Copy that. What's your speed?"

"We're doing about thirty. He seems to know the area pretty good."

Torres worked the GPS, trying to determine their destination. "Nothing on the map."

Jon tried to rein in his frustration as he steered over the bumpy ground. What did Andrea Finch think she was doing creeping around Hardin's property in the middle of the night?

"Think I remember a dirt road back here, when we did that first flyover." Torres looked out the window, but the rugged countryside was devoid of lights. "You remember anything else?"

"No."

"Okay, now he's changing course," Whitfield said over the radio. "He's heading northwest."

"Keep on him," Jon ordered. "He know you're back there?"

"Negative. I'm driving blind, using the NVGs."

Jon made headway through the desert brush, plowing over the low stuff but veering around any sizable rocks. Whitfield was doing the same but using night-vision goggles instead of headlights. The tactic would help him close the distance without being seen, but noise could still be a problem. Sound traveled pretty well out here.

They hit a rut, and Torres braced his hand on the dash as he reached for his radio again.

"Whitfield, any sign of a second vehicle?"

No answer.

"Whitfield?"

"Got an un-ID'd"—static—"west."

"Repeat?"

"I got an un-ID'd vehicle moving in from the west, maybe a mile out."

"Roger that."

Jon rolled to a stop and killed his lights. The terrain was flatter here, and he needed to avoid being seen by both parties.

"We're in the middle of nowhere," Torres said, looking around.

"Maybe that's the point." Jon got on the radio. "What do you see?"

"Looks like a white Tahoe," Whitfield responded. "They're parking near a low canyon that runs east-west. I'm pulling over. I've got the listening equipment. Lemme set up and see what I can get."

"We need tags on that Tahoe," Jon said. "You got your scope?"

"I'm working on it."

Torres looked at him. "He needs help. Want to try and get there on foot?"

Jon went still. He buzzed down the windows. "Hear that?"

Silence in the truck as they both strained to listen. And then Jon heard it again, a faint hum.

"We got company," he informed Whitefield, turning to look out the back window. He spotted a pair of headlights coming up fast. "A pickup, it looks like, coming out of the south, possibly from Hardin's ranch."

"Shit." Torres looked around. There was no time to move, so it was a matter of pure luck whether they were spotted or not.

"Whitfield, you copy?"

"Affirmative."

This was where their ICE vehicles came in handy. It wasn't that unusual to see border agents trucking through the desert in the middle of the night. The real problem was that if anyone spotted them, they'd abort the meeting, and Jon's team would miss a much-needed chance to gather intel.

The engine drew closer. Jon watched in the rearview mirror as the twin beams bumped over the landscape. The truck came within fifty yards of their location and zipped past without slowing.

"Whitfield, he's coming your way," Torres said. "It's a pickup."

Jon shoved the truck into gear and followed the taillights, keeping his own lights off and maintaining a safe distance. He skimmed the horizon, looking for the low canyon Whitfield had mentioned, but it was too dark to make anything out.

"Whitfield, there's a pickup moving toward you," Torres repeated. "You copy?"

"Shit."

"What is it, Whitfield?"

"I'm lit up like a Christmas tree. They definitely spotted me. Everyone's bugging out."

Jon hit the brake. There was a sudden flash of light as one of the trucks veered in their direction, then abruptly changed course.

"We're burned, too," Torres said into the radio. He looked at Jon. "What do you want to do?"

Jon spotted the white Tahoe and punched the gas. Torres picked up the radio.

"Tell him to follow the Tahoe," Jon ordered. "We need that tag."

Torres relayed the message as Jon checked the mirrors and saw two pairs of red taillights disappearing into the night, along with whatever intel they might have gleaned from this meeting.

Unless they could ID the Tahoe.

Jon switched on his strobes.

Torres looked at him. "You're gonna pull him over?"

"That's the plan."

The Tahoe sped up. Jon floored it.

"Looks like he doesn't want to talk to us."

They jerked and bounced over the terrain. Jon tried to close the distance.

"Where's the road?" Torres fiddled with the GPS as the engine whined and Jon edged closer.

The Tahoe veered south suddenly. Jon did the same, following the bobbing red taillights over the prairie. He barreled over low bushes and cacti, still keeping an eye out for boulders.

Jon glanced down at the navigation system. "He's going for the highway. Tell Whitfield to get ahead of us and head him off."

Torres relayed the message as they lurched over the uneven ground. Jon pushed his speed, trying to get close enough to read the tag, but they were too far away and the ride was bumpy. Torres took out the binocs.

"Anything?" Jon demanded.

"No."

Jon checked his speed. He was doing forty-five, but it felt faster with all the dips and rises. Once they reached the highway, he could open up the V8 and overtake them, but out here they were limited.

Jon tracked them doggedly through the scrubland. The brush grew thicker, funneling everyone into a tighter and tighter gap as they neared the road. Jon glanced at the GPS and tried to gauge how much farther.

They hit a rise and caught air, all four tires off the ground. Jon gripped the wheel, bracing himself as they crashed down and immediately hit a bump.

The wheel jerked right. Jon fought for control as they skidded across the dirt.

"Watch out!"

He swerved, missing a boulder. He pulled the wheel, but the truck was listing left.

"I hit something." Jon slowed and felt the rhythmic limp of a flat tire. He glanced up at the red taillights receding into the darkness. He pressed the gas and heard a metallic screech.

"Dude, you're on the rim."

Jon rolled to a halt and pounded the steering wheel. He grabbed the radio.

"Whitfield, we have a blowout. You copy?"

Nothing.

Torres muttered a curse.

"Whitfield, you copy? You need to stay in pursuit. We need that license plate."

Static. Jon looked at Torres as a scratchy voice came over the radio.

"I think they"—static—"them."

"You're breaking up. Repeat?"

"I said I'm on the highway."

"Where's the Tahoe?"

"Nowhere. I lost them."

chapter four

ANDREA WATCHED THE DOOR and waited, annoyed. She'd never been one for surveillance work—she was too impatient. She glanced around the parking lot to make sure she hadn't attracted notice, but the car wash was busy. No one seemed to be paying attention to the woman leaning casually against the building, watching the truck stop across the street.

She looked at the door as it whisked open and Hardin finally stepped out. She lifted her camera and framed the shot. He had a case of beer in one hand and he was looking the wrong direction, but when he veered toward his truck—

Snap.

Money shot.

Snap, snap, snap.

Three more, just to be sure. She lowered the camera and simply looked. He turned suddenly, as if sensing her gaze.

She held her breath, didn't move. He couldn't see her—she was in shadows. And she had a ball cap pulled low over her face.

His gaze darted away as he climbed into his truck and fired up the engine.

He peeled out, and she waited a full three minutes before crossing the lot to her Jeep, where she scrolled through the shots. His face was clearly visible and she even got the tattoo on his neck. Mission accomplished.

She motored across town and swung into the grocery to pick up a few things before returning to the Lazy Dayz Inn, which somehow managed to look worse in the light of morning.

Pulling in, she surveyed the low adobe building. By any standard, the place was a dump. But it was within her budget, so she'd been willing to put up with gritty carpet and ice cubes that tasted like rust. She parked and shoved open the door. Reaching for her groceries, she felt a hot zing of pain.

Son of a *bitch*.

She took a moment to blink it away. Her rib was broken. Either that or severely bruised. Gingerly, she reached across the console and collected the bags.

"Looks like you plan to stay awhile."

She turned to see Jon North standing there, backlit by the sun. The sight of him made her heart do a little jump.

She told herself it was the thigh holster.

"You always sneak up on people?" She yanked her keys from the ignition and slid out of the Jeep.

He didn't answer, just stood there blocking her way. He wore desert-brown A.T.A.C. boots, tactical pants, and a navy ICE shirt that stretched taut over his pecs. Except for the aviator shades, he looked nothing like the polished FBI agent who'd shown up at her apartment two days ago.

"We need to talk," he said.

"About what?"

"Not here."

She glanced at her motel room door.

"Not there, either. Come on."

He crossed the lot to a dusty white pickup that had the Immigration and Customs Enforcement logo emblazoned on the door.

Andrea sighed. She glanced down at her groceries. She hadn't bought perishables because her room didn't have a fridge. So she left everything on the seat, grabbed her coffee, and joined him at his truck, where he was already waiting with the engine running. He started backing out before she even closed the door.

The truck was full of gadgets—radio, GPS, notebook computer on an arm attached to the console. Exactly like their police units in Austin, except the inside didn't smell like vomit, and the equipment was from this millennium.

"Must be nice working for Homeland Security." She wedged her coffee into the drink holder.

He glanced in her direction, but she couldn't read his eyes because of the sunglasses. "I thought I told you to stay away from Shay Hardin."

She adjusted the vent in front of her. "I think you have me confused with someone who works for you."

He turned onto the highway heading east out of town.

Andrea fiddled with the switches on the dash until a puff of warm air shot from the vents. She leaned back against the seat and made a futile attempt to get comfortable.

"I could have you arrested. You realize that? You're interfering with a federal investigation."

She stared out the window as the arid landscape whisked by. Everything looked yellow and thirsty. So many barbed-wire fences, so few cattle. The Black Angus she *had* seen were rangy and underfed.

For three years running, this county had been ravaged by drought, and her heart went out to the ranchers. Not everyone was lucky enough to have liquid gold lurking under their property.

"Well?"

She turned to look at him and noticed the tightness of his jaw, the tense set of his shoulders. "You want me to say something? How about this, North? You're full of crap. You can't have me arrested for anything. I haven't broken any laws." She glanced out the window as he eased onto the shoulder. "Where are we going?"

Instead of answering, he swung onto a narrow dirt road that bisected a wide, open field dotted with creosote bushes and cacti. A couple of black pump jacks bobbed in the distance.

"Shay Hardin is under investigation for murder." He cut a glance at her. "Are you aware of that?"

She stared ahead as they bumped over the ruts. She'd been snooping around for days trying to figure out what the feds wanted with Hardin—and if her brother had anything to do with it. She'd considered a range of possibilities but *murder* hadn't made the list.

"Sounds like the sheriff's bag," she said. "Why's the FBI involved?"

"The victim was a federal judge."

"Who?"

"Arthur Kimball. Of the Western District Court."

Andrea frowned. "I don't remember hearing about it."

"This happened July fourth, six years ago."

Six summers ago, Andrea had been at the police academy. The training had lasted thirty-two hellacious weeks, and it had kicked her ass. She remembered the bruises and blisters and aching muscles. She'd hardly had the energy to crawl into bed that summer, much less watch the news.

"Think I missed the headline." She paused and looked at him. "You really think Hardin killed him?"

He pulled up to an oil derrick and shoved the gearshift into park. "Yes." He climbed out.

Andrea followed. She glanced up at the enormous steel structure looming over her. It looked like a cell-phone tower, only bulkier. She'd always imagined oil wells as loud and dirty, but this one was silent, clearly out of operation for some reason.

North trekked over to a wooden trailer. He mounted a few steps and yanked open the door.

Andrea glanced around. Another dusty ICE vehicle was parked off to the side, in the shade of the building. She reached under her leather jacket and touched the pancake holster at the small of her back. Her department had confiscated her service pistol as part of the investigation, so she was down to her backup weapon, a Kimber Ultra Carry II, which was compact enough not to be noticed by the untrained eye.

She had no doubt North had noticed it.

She followed his path up the steps and opened the door. The inside of the trailer was cold and dim, and it took a moment for her eyes to adjust.

A man stood on the opposite side of the room, leaning against the cheap wood paneling. Latino, medium height, medium build. Like North, he wore a T-shirt with the ICE logo on the front. He had his arms folded over his chest and was watching her with a look of guarded curiosity.

North was watching her, too. He'd taken off his shades now, and she could see the impatience in his eyes.

She took her time looking around. What had once probably

been the headquarters of a drilling operation was now some sort of comm center. In the middle of the room was a makeshift table made of sawhorses and a sheet of plywood. Several laptops were open on it, their screens facing away from her. A computer and a printer occupied a desk against the far wall. A faint noise drew her attention to the corner, where a police scanner sat atop a file cabinet.

"Have a seat." North nodded at a metal folding chair.

Andrea propped her shoulder against the wall beside the door. "I'm good."

He gave the other guy a look Andrea had seen before from countless male colleagues. *See? Didn't I tell you she was a pain in the ass?*

North dropped into a chair by the table. He leaned back and scrubbed his hands over his face. It was the gesture of someone who was supremely tired. Maybe she wasn't the only one who hadn't slept much last night.

He sighed. "Andrea Finch, meet Special Agent James Torres."

The man nodded in her direction.

"You're undercover, too, I assume?"

Another nod.

"Hey, what happened to your lip?" North leaned forward.

Andrea touched her mouth, where it was still raw and swollen. "I bit it."

His gaze narrowed, and she could tell he didn't believe her. She didn't care. She shifted her attention back to Torres.

With just two brief nods, he'd conveyed some important facts. One, they trusted her, which was interesting because they didn't have a reason to, as far as she could see. Undercover operations were some of the most dangerous activities in law enforcement. Andrea had been involved in more than her share as a newbie detective on the Austin vice team, where her slight build and young face had convinced plenty of johns and drug addicts that she was the real deal. It was dangerous work, and it could quickly become deadly if your contacts discovered you weren't who you said you were.

The second thing it told her was that they wanted something. Otherwise, why share even the slightest bit of information?

She glanced at North. The tired look was gone now, and he was watching her with a hawklike gaze.

"You were right," he said. "I can't really arrest you."

She waited.

"I would like to request, though, as a fellow law-enforcement officer, that you get the hell out of our way."

Andrea sighed. "Look, North—"

"It's Jon," he said. "That's my real first name. And I'd prefer you use it, because I gave you my real last name in Austin, and I don't need that leaking out. Far as anyone here knows, it's Jon Nolan and Jimmy Garcia. We'd like to keep it that way."

"Understood."

"Good," Jon said. "We'd also like it if you'd go back to your motel, pack your stuff, and head back to Austin."

"Not happening."

He and Torres exchanged looks.

"I want some answers first." She balled her fists in the pockets of her jacket and watched them carefully. "I want to know about the judge."

"What about him?"

"Tell me about your murder case."

He watched her, clearly debating how much to say. Maybe he thought if he answered a few questions, she'd back off. She hoped that was what he thought, but it couldn't have been farther from the truth. Something was seriously off about this setup, and she wasn't going anywhere until she knew what it was. And even when she did figure it out, she wasn't going anywhere until she was totally convinced that her brother was not involved.

Jon leaned back in his chair. "Judge Kimball supposedly died in a hunting accident six years ago."

"Supposedly?"

"That's what the family maintains. The ME ruled it a suicide."

"And you're not convinced?"

"We think he was murdered," Torres said.

"We *know* he was," Jon corrected. "We just have to prove it."

Andrea watched Jon carefully. He sounded sure of himself. She wanted to know what his evidence was, but instinct told her not to ask. At least, not yet. Right now, he was in sharing mode, but that could shut down at any moment.

"Why would Hardin want to kill this judge?"

"Vendetta," Jon said.

"About what?"

"Shortly before his death, Kimball ruled on a case of eminent domain. A chunk of land owned by Hardin's parents was designated to be used for a highway project. They were forced to sell for a fraction of the land's real value. Then they fell on hard times."

"Hardin's dad died of a heart attack a year later," Torres said. "And now his mom's in a nursing home with Alzheimer's."

She looked at Jon. "He blamed the judge for her Alzheimer's?"

"Hardin sees the court case as the cause of his parents' plight," Jon said. "Ever since then, he's had a deep-rooted hatred for the federal government. He's made threats, fired off letters to newspapers. In the months before the judge's death, Hardin had been following him around. He'd been calling his house, harassing his wife."

"Doesn't mean he killed him."

Jon didn't bite. He wasn't going to share whatever evidence he had, and Andrea didn't blame him. Most investigators she knew played it close to the vest until they had enough for a warrant. Obviously, they didn't have that, or they wouldn't be here.

She glanced around the room and noted the map tacked to the wall. It looked to have been created from a satellite image. She studied the red outline someone had drawn with a marker and recognized the shape of Pecos County. Several red pushpins were clustered near the site of Lost Creek Ranch. She recognized the juncture of two dirt roads—the precise location where she'd been jumped by a booted assailant last night.

Going out there in person to gather info had been a little risky. Armed trespassers weren't looked on kindly around here, even by law enforcement. She was lucky she'd gotten off with some scrapes and bruises and not an ass full of buckshot.

The whole incident wasn't something she wanted to mention, though, and not just because it made her look incompetent. If Jon knew about it, he'd use it as one more reason to try to shoo her out of town.

She glanced back at him. "How many agents you have working this thing?"

"Three undercover, including Torres and myself. And four guys on electronic surveillance, rotating shifts of two."

She gaped at him. "*Seven* agents? In this nothing little town? And you've been here four months?"

"Surveillance guys are based out of Fort Stockton," Torres said.

Andrea looked at him. She didn't buy this. Seven full-time people staffed to a six-year-old cold case? It would have been unheard of for her cash-strapped police department.

She studied the map again. Also pinned to the wall were some aerial photographs of Lost Creek Ranch. The pictures showed the house, the barn, and the outbuildings, along with the various vehicles scattered about the property.

Jon was leaning back in his chair now, watching her. If he was any kind of detective—which she assumed he was—he'd figured out that one of those five vehicles belonged to her brother. So much for keeping Gavin's name out of it. She looked at Jon and could tell he'd seen her notice the car. Okay, no more games. They both knew why she was here.

"Your turn," Jon said. "What's your beef with Hardin? I gather you're not a big fan."

"I don't like him," she said.

"Why?"

"He's a skinhead, for starters. I'm worried my brother's been hanging around him."

"Maybe your brother's a skinhead."

"He's not," she said firmly, but her stomach tensed. She hadn't seen Gavin since Christmas. He'd seemed perfectly normal then, but normal for Gavin was already outside the mainstream.

"How'd they meet?" Jon asked.

"In Lubbock last spring. Gavin was a junior up at Texas Tech when he met him at a gun show. Hardin later called him up and asked him to be a straw buyer for one of his friends."

"Your brother's into guns?"

She shrugged. "We grew up on a farm."

"In the Valley?" Torres asked.

"Near Victoria. My grandparents are rice farmers. They raised us after our mom died."

"Pearl Springs, Texas."

She glanced at Jon. "How'd you know?"

"The plates on your Cherokee are registered to a Robert Miller there."

"That's my grandfather. He collects guns, too, by the way—like about half the population. It's no big deal."

"So you have no problem with your brother being a straw buyer for some skinhead who's probably part of a militia group?"

"Of course I had a problem with it. He asked me if what Hardin wanted him to do was illegal, and I told him hell, yeah, and he told me he didn't do it. But next thing I know, he's quitting his job and moving to Maverick—"

"I thought you said he was in school," Jon cut in.

"This was in the summer. He had an internship at a software company. It was a good job, and all of a sudden, he quit so he could come here to shovel cow patties and mend fences. I spent all of last summer convincing him he should go back to school in the fall and get his degree. Then I found out he'd left school again, so I assumed he was out here, and I was right. Only this time, he's dropped out. So no, I'm not a fan of Hardin."

Jon glanced across the room. He had this silent-communication thing with Torres that was starting to get on her nerves.

Torres looked at her. "Your brother's twenty-two."

"Yeah?"

"Don't you think he's old enough to decide for himself where to live?"

Andrea bit back a retort. He was right. But she'd always been protective when it came to Gavin. She still thought of him as a kid, with his fiery red hair and skinny build. She remembered the stolen lunch money and the playground pranks. She remembered all the days he'd come home angry and sullen because he'd been tormented at school.

Andrea hated bullies. It was one reason she'd become a cop.

And although Gavin talked about Hardin as his friend, she thought the guy was just one more bully out to take advantage of him.

Jon was eyeing her lip with disapproval, and she wondered if he knew where she'd been last night. She looked at Torres.

"Yes, he's old enough," she said.

"Then why are you here?"

"I want to make sure he's not being brainwashed. Or talked into throwing his future away. Hell, I don't even know if he's being held there against his will."

"You think he is?" Jon leaned forward and rested his elbows on his knees.

"I don't know. I haven't talked to him."

"Then how do you know he's there?" Torres asked.

"He's there. People in town have seen him. He stands out."

And even if they hadn't, she'd been out there last night to confirm it for herself. Gavin's blue Ford Focus had been parked beside the rickety old barn.

"You're right," Jon said. "He's there."

She scowled. "Why are you asking me questions if you already know the answers?"

"We confirmed it this morning. He and four other people are living there with Hardin: Mark and Olivia Driscoll, along with Ross and Vicky Leeland." He paused. "Any of those names ring a bell?"

"No."

"Latest batch of images just came in, and you can see Gavin's license plate."

"What kind of images?"

"Homeland Security has drones patrolling the entire border area," Jon said. "One in particular is programmed to fly over

Hardin's place. It's ninety acres. They don't leave often. We think they're stockpiling food and supplies."

"And guns."

Andrea looked at Torres.

"They aren't using cell phones or landlines that we've been able to tell," Jon said. "And there's no Internet connection."

She scoffed.

"What?"

"If Gavin's living there, there's Internet. He's a computer junkie."

Jon glanced at Torres again and back at Andrea.

"And what's your plan?" Jon asked. "You can't stay here forever. Don't you have a job to get back to?"

She bristled. "My plan is to help Gavin. He needs to get back to Lubbock so he can graduate."

Jon stood up. He stepped closer, and she got the feeling she was about to hear the real point of this meeting.

"So you refuse to leave." He folded his arms over his chest.

"I'm not leaving until I talk some sense into my brother."

"Problem is, Andrea, you're a cop. Hardin is going to hear about you going around town asking questions about him, if he hasn't already. That puts him on guard and jeopardizes our investigation."

"Your investigation has nothing to do with me. *Or* my brother."

"Maybe, maybe not," Jon said.

"What's that supposed to mean?"

"We've been trying to build this case for months, and we could use someone on the inside," he said. "You could get your brother to help us."

"What, you mean get him to wear a wire?" She pushed away

from the wall and felt her temper rising along with her voice. "That's what you mean, right? Maybe I can persuade him to walk up to Shay Hardin and casually ask him where he was—oh, I don't know—July fourth, six summers ago? Great idea. Then my family can sit around for six long years waiting for you to solve the mystery after Gavin turns up in some ditch with a bullet in his brain."

Jon's expression hardened. "You should think about it, Andrea."

Both men stared at her. The only sound in the room was the faint crackling of the police scanner.

"I'd like a ride back to town now."

She jerked open the door and stepped out into the blinding sunlight. The wind whipped against her cheeks as Jon joined her on the steps.

"You get him to talk to us, you'd be doing him a favor," he said.

"Gavin was in *high school* when that judge died. He had absolutely nothing to do with it, so don't act like you have some leverage against him."

She stalked down the steps and across the dirt. She heard him follow, but she didn't look at him as she climbed into the truck.

"Think about it, Andrea. Hardin is bad news. You know it as well as I do. That's why you came all the way out here." He started the truck. His gaze was on her, but she refused to look. "He's using your brother for something—and whatever it is can't be good."

◆

Special Agent Elizabeth LeBlanc stared at the portly bank manager and waited for him to get to the point. She'd been listening for ten minutes, and still the man was totally in the weeds. Finally, she interrupted his description of the Italian sub he'd ordered for lunch.

"All right, and when you returned from the sandwich shop, which door did you use?"

"The back, like always," he said.

"Did you get a look at any of the customers in line?"

"Um, no. Not really."

Elizabeth jotted it in her notebook. So far, no one had noticed the robber except for the teller who'd received his typewritten note. No one besides the teller had even realized a crime was occurring until the perpetrator was out the door.

The bank manager shifted back and forth on his feet. His gaze flicked to her notepad, and he wiped his palms on the sides of his suit jacket.

She tried to put him at ease with a smile. "Well, it's too bad you didn't see him. But those are the breaks, right? I'm sure the lobby footage will be able to tell us more."

He looked at her blankly.

"The surveillance footage? Your assistant said—"

"Oh, yes, of course. Let me check on that."

He scurried into the back room, and Elizabeth sighed. This was going to be a long day. She'd been in Del Rio an hour already and had made virtually no progress. First, there had been a glitch with the security camera. Next, the traumatized teller had jumped up in the middle of the interview to rush into the bathroom and get sick. And then for an added challenge, the evidence response team had arrived late. They'd gone right to work, though. Both technicians were now crouched beside the bank's glass doors, dusting for fingerprints.

Elizabeth watched in surprise as a man ducked under the yellow tape and strode into the lobby.

Jon North.

She almost didn't recognize him in the border-agent gear. But there was no mistaking his face as he peeled off his shades and looked around. His gaze found her, and he moved in like a guided missile.

"How'd you get here?" she blurted.

"CBP guys gave me a ride to Laughlin."

She blinked at him. Laughlin Air Force Base was just a few miles away, which meant his "ride" had been a helicopter.

Of course. Because plenty of agents could just snap their fingers and conjure up a chopper on short notice.

"What do we have?" he asked.

"Well, it's a pretty straightforward robbery. A low take, too. Frankly, I'm surprised you heard about it."

He glanced at his watch, and she noticed his bare ring finger. It wasn't the first time. Jon North was single, smart, and impressively ripped. There wasn't a woman in the San Antonio field office who hadn't noticed him—Elizabeth probably more than most. She had an annoying weakness for alpha types.

She cleared her throat. "So . . . did someone call you or . . . ?"

"Jane called Jimmy Torres," he said, as if that explained what he was doing here. "I assume since they sent you out that it's connected to the one from November?"

She was getting the picture now. Maybe. The three similar bank robberies had occurred back in the fall, right before North and Torres were sent out to West Texas on some undercover assignment. The case was pretty hush-hush, but she'd heard through the grapevine that they were reopening the investigation of a judge who had died under suspicious circumstances.

Although what that had to do with this bank heist, she didn't have a clue.

But what did she know? She'd been on the job barely two years. She hadn't had time to achieve rising-superstar status like Jon North had.

He was staring at her now, waiting.

"Looks like a connection to the other ones, yeah," she said. "Maxwell wanted us to check it out. I'm waiting on the surveillance footage."

She motioned toward the back of the bank, where her colleague from San Antonio was trying to get access to the security video.

"Based on what we've got so far, it seems like the same MO," she said. "Man walks in during the early afternoon, totally nondescript, draws no attention to himself. He waits in line for a female teller, passes her a typed note, and then stands there quietly as she counts out a few thousand dollars and hands it over."

"Where's the note?"

"The evidence tech already packed it up, but I've got a copy." She reached for the file she had spread out on someone's desk.

North read the note, which instructed the teller not to alert anyone, not to sound any alarms, but simply to hand over the specified amount of money. In all the cases, the tellers had complied, because that was what they'd been trained to do. Banks were insured. No sense in employees risking their safety over money that wasn't even theirs.

"Six thousand dollars." North handed back the note. "Same as last time."

"I know."

"What about the video?"

She led him into the back room and was relieved to see that her partner had managed to get something up on the computer screen. He glanced up when they walked in.

"Security firm finally sent this over," he said.

She and North leaned in to get a view of the screen. The time stamp at the bottom showed 12:56. They watched the grainy black-and-white image as a man entered the bank. Baseball cap pulled low, zipped jacket. Nothing remarkable given the weather.

"Gloves," Elizabeth said. She wasn't surprised.

He waited patiently in line, keeping his head down, as if reading the slip of paper in his hand. When his turn came, he approached the teller.

"Hit pause." North leaned closer. "Damn it."

"Damn it, what?"

He glanced at her. "He's too short."

"Too short for what?"

"Shay Hardin."

Okay, *now* she understood. Shay Hardin was a person of interest in North's resurrected murder case. Several of the agents in her office had been helping out with the background checks.

"I'm going to need a copy of this tape," North told her.

"Sure."

He returned to the counter in the lobby and picked up the file she'd been compiling. "Vehicle?" he asked.

"We don't know yet. Last three robberies in San Antonio all involved different vehicles, and the plates were conveniently obscured by mud. Want me to send the outdoor footage, too?"

"Thanks," he said. "I'd wait for it, but I need to get back."

"Air taxi's leaving?"

He smiled slightly.

"How are things going out in Maverick?" she asked.

"So-so."

"You know, I'm not really up to speed on your case, but . . . I should probably give you a heads-up."

He lifted an eyebrow.

"Word is they're planning to yank you guys out soon."

He didn't look surprised.

"It's just something I heard," she said. "Think they need all hands on deck for the Saledo case."

North's jaw tightened, and he shook his head.

"Can you blame them? The cartels are out of control," she said. "They executed five people in Brownsville last weekend. And then there's Al Qaeda. Every office is stepping it up after the university bombing."

"I thought that was just a theory."

"Not anymore."

His gaze sharpened.

"You haven't heard? They traced the minivan used in the bombing through the number stamped on the axle," she said. "Vehicle comes back to a cleric at a mosque in Philly. He was pretty radical, from what I understand."

"Was?"

"It was a suicide attack."

North looked over her shoulder, his expression inscrutable as he stared out at the street. The afternoon sun slanted through the windows and made the stubble on his face stand out. She waited for him to say something. North wasn't a big talker. He was known for being a loner, as she was, and he had a reputation for going against the grain. But so far, that had worked for him, and he also had a reputation as a solid investigator.

He glanced at his watch.

"I'll send you that footage," she told him.

"Appreciate it."

"Say hi to Jimmy for me. And good luck with your case. Whatever you're looking for, I hope you find it soon."

◆

Andrea was on her eighth Hershey's Miniature when a knock sounded at the door. She padded across the room in her socks and peered through the peephole. Her heart lurched. She wasn't expecting visitors, and she definitely wasn't expecting Jon North in civilian clothes with an easygoing smile on his face.

She opened the door.

"Hi," he said.

She put her hand on her hip, instantly wary. They hadn't exactly parted on friendly terms.

"May I come in?"

She pulled the door back. He stepped inside and glanced at the bed, where her laptop was propped on a pillow.

"Working?" he asked.

"Yep."

"You had dinner?"

"Yep."

"How about a drink, then?"

She tipped her head to the side.

"There's a decent pub up the road," he said. "They've got a lot of beers on tap."

"Aren't you worried about your cover?"

"It's in Fort Stockton."

She looked him over. Gray flannel shirt tucked into jeans. Worn sneakers. Except for the Sig Sauer hiding under his brown leather jacket, he looked almost like a regular guy.

Yeah, right. If regular guys were built like action heroes.

But something about the running shoes got to her. They had some miles on them. They made him seem more human, less threatening. Although that was an illusion. Her brother was a key to his case, and she knew full well he'd come here because he wanted something.

Still, the drink offer was tempting. Better than staying holed up in her motel room with Mr. Goodbar, at least. She glanced down at her faded T-shirt and baggy sweatpants.

"Give me ten minutes."

He gave her that slow smile that made her heart beat faster. "Five."

chapter five

THIRTY MINUTES LATER, THEY pulled into a crowded parking lot on the outskirts of Fort Stockton. They were in Jon's personal vehicle, a gray F-150 with oversize tires. They walked to the bar entrance without comment, and he held the door open for her—more of those old-fashioned manners that seemed second nature.

Country music drifted from a jukebox. She'd expected to grab a seat at the bar, but he steered her toward a table in the back beside the pool room. Andrea poked her head in. Judging by the intense look of the men gathered around the table, there was some money riding on the game.

She stripped off her jacket and hung it on the back of her chair, and Jon's gaze lingered on her stretchy black top. The Kimber was in her ankle holster tonight.

"They have food here if you're hungry," he said as she sat down. "The wings aren't bad."

A waitress stopped by to take their drink orders. When she was gone, Andrea leaned forward on her elbows. "Look, I should tell you right off, so there's no misunderstanding. I'm not going to get my brother to wear a wire for you."

"You mentioned that already."

He seemed totally relaxed. She hadn't known him long, but she knew *relaxed* wasn't his natural state. He was trying to get her to let her guard down so he could pump her for information.

But two could play at that game, and she liked a challenge.

Their beers arrived, and he looked at her over his bottle as he took a sip. "You talk to your brother yet?"

"I'm seeing him tomorrow." She hoped.

"Let me know how it goes."

She kept her expression neutral as she glanced around the bar. Not a bad crowd for a Wednesday night. There were some golf shirts and khakis mixed in with the jeans and cowboy boots, probably tourists en route to Big Bend National Park.

"So." He leaned back in his chair, as if he was settling in for a story. "Tell me about Pearl Springs."

"What's to tell?"

"What was it like for you two growing up there?"

She held his gaze. "I've got a question first."

"Uh-oh. Sounds like a test."

"It is. How'd you find me in Austin?"

The side of his mouth curved in what might have been a smile. She waited. If he gave the bullshit story about running her plate again, she was officially done giving him information.

She should be done anyway, and yet here she was, having a drink with him. She was in a reckless mood.

"I ran your prints."

She blinked at him. Her mind scrolled back through their encounter at the Broken Spoke.

"You took the glass?" she asked.

"The twenty."

"You *stole* my twenty?"

"Don't worry, I replaced it. And then some."

She leaned back in her chair, annoyed. And maybe a little impressed.

"I knew you were a cop," he said. "I didn't know what kind. Once I ran it down, I called up your department, thinking maybe I'd chat up your supervisor, find out what you were doing out here."

"And?"

"And I didn't get a supervisor. They patched me through to some public-information officer, and I got a canned statement about your being on leave."

Which had probably piqued his curiosity. Which had probably led him to Google. Which had no doubt provided him with a slew of headlines about her killing a teenager.

She watched his eyes, trying to read them.

"Then I guess you know."

He nodded.

"Good." She picked up her beer and took a cold gulp. She didn't want to talk through it again. She'd been debriefed so many times she could recite it by rote now, and there was something terribly wrong with that.

"Are you all right?"

The way he said it caught her off guard. His look was so direct, as if he expected a straight answer.

"Flashbacks?"

She nodded.

He didn't say anything, but it seemed like he was waiting for something. His hazel eyes were calm and patient.

And it hit her, as it did sometimes. The stark finality of what she'd done. Because of her, a young man would never fully experience life. His family would never stop grieving. What she'd done had saved lives, but it had ruined lives, too. And she couldn't get away from it.

She glanced down at her beer bottle as she thought about what to say.

"You spend so much time training." She looked at him. "But when it really happens, it's different. I don't know. I'd thought about it, but I'd always envisioned some drug dealer drawing down on me in an alley or something. I never pictured a freckle-faced kid in a crowded restaurant."

He watched her intently. "They get you an attorney right away?"

He meant the officers union. She nodded.

"That's good."

She thrust her chin out. "I'm going to need it. I've already heard rumors about problems with my review."

"Why?"

"I'm not supposed to talk about it," she said, hating the way she sounded, like a lawyer or someone covering her ass.

"Are you going to leave?"

"No way."

He watched her.

"They can fire me, but I'm sure as hell not quitting."

"Good." He covered her hand and squeezed it, and she immediately tensed. She wanted to pull away, but his palm was heavy and warm, and she liked the way it felt.

"You were telling me about Pearl Springs," he said, changing the subject.

She tugged her hand into her lap. "Not much to tell. It's a pretty small town, like Maverick. I moved there in middle school."

"From?"

"Houston, where we lived with my mom. She died when I was eleven."

His brow furrowed.

"I came home from school one day. Cops were there. Social services. My mom had been in a drunk-driving accident. Single vehicle."

She could see the question on his face. *Yes, in the middle of the day.*

"She had a drinking problem. When she died, Gavin and I went to live with my grandparents."

"Your dad?"

"Not an option."

He turned his beer on the table, watching her.

"My parents divorced a long time ago," she explained. "Probably best for everyone. It wasn't a happy marriage."

"What about you?" he asked. "Ever been married?"

"Nope. You?"

"I was engaged once. She called it off."

Andrea looked at him expectantly, but he didn't elaborate. "Did you love her?" she asked.

"I wouldn't have proposed if I didn't."

"Do you miss her?"

The question seemed to make him uncomfortable, and for some reason, she felt glad. He looked down at his beer. "Honestly?"

"No, make something up."

"I haven't thought much about her in months." He met her gaze. "When she left, she told me I was an ego-driven workaholic and I was destined to end up alone."

"Ouch."

"Yeah, it wasn't exactly a smooth breakup." He glanced at his bottle, then at her again. "You ever come close?"

"God, no."

"Why not?"

"My job's hell on marriages. It's a proven fact."

"There are exceptions."

"There are." She shrugged. "But not for me. Relationships need nurturing. I can't even take care of a houseplant. What would I do with a husband?"

He laughed, and she felt the mood relax, even though it was a touchy subject for her. She'd been in dozens of relationships, and they were all the same: hot and brief. When she'd first recognized the pattern, it had made her sad and self-conscious, but now she'd accepted it. Mostly.

Every now and then, she wondered what it would be like to have something steady with someone. Something where she could count on him to be there. She thought of Dee and Bob and how they still went to movies together on Sunday afternoons and how he sometimes brought home a pint of her favorite ice cream just to surprise her. She thought about Dee nagging him to take his heart meds and get off his feet in the heat of the day.

Of course, they fought, too, and many of their conversations ended with the slam of a screen door. It wasn't a dream relationship by any stretch, but it was solid.

"So I've been reading about your brother," Jon said. "National Merit Scholar. Full ride to Tech."

She felt a swell of pride.

"Spent his sophomore year on academic probation."

"How'd you know that? That's part of his private record."

"So what's the deal there?" he asked, glossing over her question.

The deal with Gavin? Andrea wished she knew. "Gavin is very bright." She paused. "But it's a liability sometimes. He doesn't fit in well." She ran her thumb over the condensation on her bottle. "He's a sweet kid. Well, you know. He *can* be. He's twenty-two, so sometimes he's pretty selfish, and I want to strangle him."

She glanced up, and he was watching her, clearly waiting for her to say more.

"You have any siblings?" she asked.

"Two brothers and a sister. They're doctors in Chicago, like my dad."

"*All* of them?"

"Well, except my sister. She lives in St. Paul."

"But she's a doctor?"

"A cardiologist."

Wow. Andrea let that sink in, trying not to feel intimidated.

She picked up her beer. "So why didn't you follow the family tradition?"

"I went to law school instead."

She put a hand to her chest. "*That* must have been a shock."

He smiled, and she felt a warm rush. God, what was she doing here? She didn't want to like him. She didn't want to feel this *pull* of attraction. She definitely didn't want to help him. But something about him—or maybe everything about him—got to her. He was a man she'd have a hard time refusing, and that was dangerous.

"So if you went to law school, why aren't you practicing?" she asked.

"I did, for a while. Spent some time burning the midnight oil for a bunch of corporate clients. Then decided to apply to the FBI Academy."

"How come?"

He hesitated, and she prepared for a glib answer.

"Because I believe in accountability."

The simplicity of it surprised her. She watched him as she took a swig of beer, wondering if he was being honest here. She decided to push him. "Tell me about your murder case." She set her beer aside.

"I did."

"You really didn't. I want to hear about the evidence. Call it professional curiosity."

He seemed to consider that. Maybe he thought it wouldn't hurt to have a homicide cop's perspective, or maybe he just wanted to keep the conversation flowing. "It had been dormant for a long time," he said.

"Six years."

"Then Hardin's name came up in another investigation, and our SAC—that's the senior agent in charge—"

"I know."

"He asked me to take a look, see what our friend Shay's been up to the last few years."

"And?"

"And turns out he's been busy."

"Buying up ranches. Doing the gun-show circuit. Does he have a job to pay for all this?"

He stared at her.

"What?" she asked.

"What's he do for money? That's what I wanted to know, too."

"It's a logical question." The waitress passed by, and Andrea ordered another round.

"You're right." He paused, and she got the impression he was holding something back. "He didn't buy Lost Creek Ranch. Not like you're thinking. He bought the surface rights only. Height of the drought, too. Got it for a steal. The owner kept the mineral rights, which is where the real value is."

"So what's with the gun shows? Is he a licensed dealer?"

"Only thing he's licensed to do is drive a car," he said. "We see it a lot with these antigovernment types. They don't like their names in databases. Don't like the idea of background checks. It's probably why he asked your brother to be a straw buyer for his friend."

"What does he do at these shows?"

"Sells hunting gear—binoculars, ammo, camouflage jackets. Passes out leaflets railing against the government."

She raised an eyebrow.

"He's convinced the federal government is to blame for the failure of his parents' farm. Cutbacks in subsidies, that sort of thing."

"Not to mention they seized the land," she said.

"That, too."

"I can kind of see where he's coming from. I grew up in an ag town. A lot of people I know have been devastated, especially with the drought."

"Do they murder their public officials?"

"No, but plenty of them are mad. It's not easy watching your crops dry up because of water rationing when fifty miles away, they're watering golf courses."

Jon gave her a measured look. Maybe that sounded provincial to his ears, but it was how she felt.

"You were telling me about your evidence," she said. "The ME ruled it a suicide, but you think he got it wrong. Why?"

"Couple of things. One, Kimball had just bought a half-million-dollar life insurance policy three months before his death.

One of the clauses stipulated that in the event of suicide within the first six months, the policy would be void."

She tipped her head to the side. "Any chance Kimball missed the clause?"

"He had a law degree."

"Okay, so maybe he didn't care," she said. "Wanted to end it all anyway."

"Also, his favorite shotgun was a Winchester, custom-engraved. Belonged to his dad. He didn't use that weapon, though. He used a cheap twenty-gauge he'd picked up at Walmart a few years before."

"So?"

"So most suicides tend to be ritualistic. His wife insisted that if he'd intended to kill himself, he would have used his favorite gun."

"Guns are heirlooms to some people," Andrea said. "Maybe he wanted to leave it to his kids. Didn't want them having a negative association with it."

"They didn't have kids."

"This is weak, North, and you know it." She leaned forward on her elbows. "What's the real evidence?"

He looked at her for a long moment. Then he sipped his beer and plunked it on the table. "A fingerprint."

Her eyebrows tipped up.

"We have Shay Hardin's print on one of the shotgun shells."

chapter six

"HARDIN LOADED THE MURDER weapon without gloves?" Andrea couldn't keep the skepticism out of her voice.

"Not the shell used in the killing," Jon said. "We got the judge's prints on that. *A* shell. From the box in Kimball's car. He drove it out to a part of his ranch where he liked to dove hunt, parked, and walked out into a field with his shotgun. Never came back."

She watched him. "What's Hardin's story?"

"Has an alibi for the time of the crime."

"Of course he does."

"Four people put him at a bar in Killeen, two hundred miles away."

She cringed. "That hurts. What does he say about the shell? I assume someone interrogated him?"

"An agent *interviewed* him a week after it happened. Hardin claims the judge was at some of the same gun shows. Must have bought a box of ammo from him there." He paused. "Unfortunately, that story pans out. They were, in fact, at a couple of the same events. And Hardin sold ammo, so it's possible. But I'm not seeing it. The judge wouldn't stop at a booth to buy something from a man who'd publicly insulted him and sent scathing letters about him to the local paper."

"You're right, it's a stretch."

Jon leaned back in the chair. He rubbed the back of his neck, and she could see the stress of the case was weighing on him.

Still, she felt as if she was missing something. Such an old case with such fuzzy facts. "You know, I've been doing some investigating of my own these last few days," she said. "I made a few calls about you."

He waited.

"Nice job last year. I hear you helped nail those two guys who were plotting to blow up that bridge."

He didn't say anything. Did he catch what she was driving at? This seemed like an odd assignment on the heels of such a big win. Almost as though he and Torres had been put out to pasture.

She watched his eyes. He definitely got her meaning, but he wasn't going to talk about it.

She persisted anyway. She'd succeeded at interrogations because she didn't give up. Subject didn't want to talk? She kept hammering. She hit on a touchy subject? She didn't let go.

Other times, it was about finesse. During her patrol days, her stature hadn't been much help when she needed to get drunks into her car. But as a detective, she used it to her advantage. A lot of men blew her off, didn't take her seriously. They sat in the interview room shooting the breeze with her, waiting for the real detectives to show up. Meantime, she was getting the conversation flowing while listening to every word.

"This isn't just a cold case," Jon said now.

"No kidding."

"Hardin's been on our radar."

"Our?"

"Homeland Security."

Andrea had never liked the term. It sounded so ominous. It implied invaders, paratroopers, *Red Dawn*.

"You want to explain that?"

"His name keeps cropping up," he said. "He's a person of interest in the judge's death, he's in a white supremacist group."

"But he was in the military," she said. "I think he even earned a medal or something." She was being deliberately obtuse. He'd earned a Bronze Star in Operation Iraqi Freedom. He'd been a war hero. But then he'd dropped out. Why? She didn't know. And as a city homicide cop, she had no easy way of finding out. But Jon probably knew.

She sipped her beer and waited, hoping he'd answer the unasked question.

"Someone like him can be a problem," Jon said. "The military training, expert marksman. Great if he's on your side. But what if he decides to switch teams?"

"What are you saying, exactly?"

"I'm saying, here's a guy who goes from sending letters to the newspaper and intimidating a federal judge to quiet. Not earning any money—at least, not that he's reporting. Living in the middle of nowhere. Even by West Texas standards, the place is remote."

"You think it's a front? That he's keeping a low profile?"

It seemed like a reach to her, but he wasn't sharing everything he knew.

He watched her, and she felt her skin heat as she imagined being alone with him—far away from a crowded bar. The look in his eyes shifted, and she knew he'd read her mind.

"Come on." He plunked his beer on the table and stood up.

"Come where?"

"Let's play some pool."

"How do you know I play?"

"Because you do." His look pinned her. Resisting would only make her seem insecure.

"Fine." She shrugged, making it no big deal. She grabbed her jacket and her beer and followed him.

The previous players were filing out as Jon walked over to the rack of cues on the wall.

"This one looks about your size." He handed it to her.

"It's been a while for me." She tested the cue's weight in her hand as Jon flipped back the cuffs of his shirt.

"Same here."

She smiled. "Why don't I believe that?"

He racked the balls with the snap of his wrist. "Eight ball. Loser buys the other one dinner."

She lifted an eyebrow. She'd expected him to bet cash or maybe a round of drinks. No matter the outcome, he was locking in a date with her.

Was this part of his information-gathering mission, or did he really want to take her out? She still didn't trust his motives.

"Ladies first." He handed her the cue ball.

"That's your first mistake. Making assumptions." She lined up her break shot, conscious of his gaze on her body as she leaned over the table.

Despite being rusty, she managed to sink a couple of solids. He followed up with a few impressive bank shots. After a five-ball run, he missed a curve shot and turned it over to her.

Another mistake.

She got down to business, nailing a long-rail bank shot. She studied the layout and planned her next move.

"Who taught you to play?" he asked.

"My granddad." She leaned over the felt and sent him a sharp look. "He never let me win, though. I had to earn it."

Jon watched her from the corner. Something in his gaze reminded her of the night at the Broken Spoke. She shouldn't be getting so comfortable, not with the fed investigating her brother. But she had that flutter in the pit of her stomach, and she felt the alcohol kicking in.

She sank another solid before tapping one of his stripes.

"Oops."

Jon chalked his cue, watching her. She reached for her beer, used it to cool her throat as he mulled his strategy. The next shot was all power. It made a sharp *crack* that sent a jolt of heat from the top of her head to the soles of her feet.

He studied the table for his final shot. "Corner pocket," he said, leaning over.

He killed it. Then he looked up at her.

He didn't gloat. But the look on his face told her she would have been much, much better off if she'd stayed in her motel room pecking away at her computer.

He took her cue and replaced it on the rack. He replaced the chalk and watched her as he dusted his hands.

"I owe you dinner." She shrugged into her jacket, putting an end to the evening.

They drove back to Maverick without talking. Tension hummed in the truck cab between them, and she spent the drive gazing out at the inky desert. Clouds were out tonight, so there was little to see besides a few ranch houses here and there.

He pulled into the pitted parking lot and slid into the space beside her Cherokee. Without a word, he came around to her door.

She was out before he reached it, digging through her purse for the keycard.

"Thanks for the drinks," she said.

He looked down at her, and her skin tingled in response. She read his intentions right there on his face—he wasn't shy about it—and her heart started drumming as his palm slid under her jacket and came to rest at her hip. She took a step back, but his grip tightened. His other hand came up and cupped the side of her face, and she held her breath as his thumb grazed the corner of her lip.

His gaze met hers. "What really happened here?"

"I bit it."

He dipped his head down and his breath was warm against her temple. "You're lying."

Her heart skittered, and then his mouth was on hers, warm and stinging against her swollen lip. The heat of him surrounded her. He smelled faintly of the desert air and the beer they'd been drinking, and she felt the warm slide of his hands as they splayed over her back beneath the jacket to pull her against the firm wall of his body. So much power, right there for her to touch. She let herself melt into him, knowing it was a bad idea, knowing she should step away, but she didn't want to yet. She combed her fingers into his hair and kissed him with the same pent-up longing she felt coming from him, and the thrill of knowing he wanted her spread through her body like fire. The night air was cold against her cheeks, but his arms were warm and strong, and his hot mouth melted away all her resistance, all logical thought. He pulled her up on tiptoe, and she strained against him, tasting him, giving herself a last heady moment of intoxication before she loosened her arms and forced herself to step back.

He looked down at her, breathing hard, just as she was, and she could hear the pounding of her own heart as she retreated farther and his hands dropped away. He searched her face as she leaned against the door, feeling cold.

She didn't say anything. She was afraid if she opened her mouth, she'd invite him inside. He watched her steadily.

"Good night, Andrea."

She nodded, still not trusting herself. And then he turned and walked back to his truck.

She went into her room. As she locked the door and secured the latch, she listened for the smooth catch of his engine, the throaty moan as the truck backed out. She closed her eyes and pictured him on that long, empty road as he drove away.

Switching on a lamp, she glanced around. The digital clock said 12:02. Her computer was still on the bed, waiting for her amid a sea of candy wrappers. Still feeling off-balance from the kiss, she simply stood there a moment and let her heart rate come down. Then she walked into the bathroom and stripped off her clothes, piling them in the sink with the ankle holster on top.

She stared at her reflection under the harsh fluorescent light, imagining how he'd seen her tonight. She looked . . . terrible. The makeup she'd hurriedly applied didn't hide the dark circles under her eyes. She ignored the cut on her just-kissed lip and looked at her torso, where a pair of rainbow bruises decorated her right side.

When she was a police cadet, her instructors had talked about muscle memory, that automatic reflex born of hours and hours of training that kicked in during pressure situations. Muscle memory was your friend. It could save your life. But pain had a memory, too, and it was stronger. Andrea remembered getting the wind knocked out of her at the academy. She remembered the sting of her mother's palm. She remembered her first sex. She stepped closer to the mirror, and the tendons in her shoulders tightened as she surveyed her bruises and relived the two sharp jolts of pain.

She turned on the shower and climbed in while the water was still cold. Closing her eyes, she stood still until the spray grew tepid, then warm, then scalding, and then she turned her back on it and let it pelt her neck until her muscles relaxed.

Why had he kissed her? Was it just some bullshit manipulation, or had he simply wanted to, a man kissing a woman?

Whenever she'd dealt with federal agents, they'd been tough, territorial, arrogant. Jon North was all those things, and it should have bothered her, but instead, it pulled her in. She'd catch him looking at her the way he had that first night, and the intensity in his gaze made her swallow, hard.

She didn't need this right now. She needed to be thinking about her brother and how to help him. She was in a unique position to reach out to him and maybe save him from something—save him from himself. Gavin had a habit of making self-destructive choices, and becoming friends with Shay Hardin was clearly one of them.

When the water turned cool again, she climbed out and slipped into a tank top and sweatpants and placed her pistol on the nightstand before sliding into bed. She squirmed into the valley of the sagging mattress and lay on her back, staring at the ceiling. She listened to the sounds around her—the distant hum of a TV, cars whisking down the highway, the deep echo of a long-haul rig. But no F-150 pulling into the lot. No determined man retracing his steps to her door.

She closed her eyes and willed her muscles to relax. She let her mind drift and tried not to think about the hard wall of his body and the taste of his mouth.

Her eyes flew open. She sat up and glanced at the clock: 2:16. Why had she—

Her skin chilled as she registered a change in the air, a tangible shift in the darkness that alerted all her senses.

A draft tickled her skin.

Rolling out of bed, she grabbed her pistol and padded silently to the front door. It wasn't latched. She stood motionless as the meaning sank in.

She checked her weapon before easing open the door and peering outside. Nothing, not even a passing car. The highway was deserted.

Gripping her pistol, she stepped into the chilly air and looked around. She spied two minivans down the way—the families from Oklahoma who had been checking in earlier. The front-desk clerk's car was gone. She surveyed the parking lot, and her gaze landed on an unfamiliar pickup beside the Dumpster.

Andrea ventured out, skimming her gaze over every shadow. Dropping to a crouch, she checked for anyone hiding low between the cars. Nothing. She crept across the pavement and calmly surveyed the area as she placed her hand on the pickup's hood.

Stone cold.

Her gaze went across the vacant lot to the nearby strip center that abutted the highway and harbored countless hiding places. Scanning for threats, she walked back across the pavement, pausing to check her Jeep and grab a flashlight. He'd been inside when she came home.

Her heart pounded. Her gut tightened. Maybe she was being paranoid.

You latched that door, and you damn well know it.

She returned to her room and kept the lamp off as she shone

the flashlight around, searching the bathroom, the closet, under the bed. She went down a mental checklist. How many times had she done this in strangers' homes, responding to a call? She checked behind the curtains, even checked the vents in the ceiling. No sign of forced entry. Still, her heart thudded. Her mind raced.

He watched you shower.

She secured the door again and swept the light around the room, over the bed, the dresser, the chair, then over the closet and back again.

Something glinted on the dresser. She stepped closer, aiming the flashlight at the lone bullet with the black tip.

A thirty-aught-six. An armor-piercing round, left like an offering.

A cop killer.

chapter seven

JON GLANCED UP FROM the array of surveillance photos as Torres stepped into the trailer.

"Some light reading." Torres dropped a stack of files onto the table.

"What's that?"

"Fleshed out the employment histories with the help of our IRS contact. I got everyone at the ranch: Shay Hardin, Ross and Vicky Leeland, Mark and Olivia Driscoll, and Gavin Finch."

"Anything new?"

"Haven't had a chance to read through it all. Figured you could help."

Jon opened the top file, which contained a thin sheaf of papers held together with a binder clip. A handwritten sticky note on top said "Vicky Leeland." Info on the two wives had been hard to come by.

Torres sank into a chair, and Jon felt a stab of guilt. The man hadn't had a break in days. While Jon had been putting away beers with Andrea, Torres had been stuck here working.

So much of this case was about digging. Since coming out here, Jon had culled through thousands of details searching for the one that mattered.

"Didn't find much we didn't already know about Hardin," Torres said.

"Still gaps?"

"Yep. After leaving the Army, he framed houses for a year, then stopped, although it isn't clear if he got another job. His records are still patchy, so if he worked, it was off the books. Same goes for Ross Leeland. He was at a brake-repair shop for a few months, then a lumberyard. He worked construction a couple years ago, but I couldn't find anything recent."

Jon pulled out another file, this one for Gavin Finch. "Texas Instruments, SoftSolutions." He glanced up. "I'm guessing that's software?"

"Yeah, they're out of Lubbock. He had an internship his freshman year of college. Unpaid, so there's not much record of it. We wouldn't even know about it if he hadn't listed it on another job application."

"Any three-oh-twos?" Jon asked.

"Yeah, the interview form's clipped there. Someone talked to his supervisor."

Jon flipped to the form and frowned as he read it. "Guy says he's a 'maestro on anything with a motherboard.' So looks like he's the resident expert on computers."

"That was my take, too."

Jon reached the bottom file in the stack and glanced up, startled. "Andrea Finch?"

Torres looked at him. "Wanted to make sure she wasn't bent."

"And?"

"Nothing stands out."

Jon opened the folder and skimmed the first page, which was her employment history.

"Currently on the beach, like you said," Torres reported. "This is her second time to be reviewed for possible excessive force. Last time was during her rookie year when she responded to a domestic, ended up Tasing the guy three times. He wound up in the hospital, along with his kid."

"She Tased his kid?"

"No, the kid had a broken arm. Dad went after him with a baseball bat."

Jon flipped to the second page and then closed it, feeling guilty for reading about her behind her back.

Not a good sign. Lines were starting to blur. From the look on his face, Torres knew it, too.

Jon had taken Andrea out last night to soften her up, get to know her better, maybe learn more about her background and consequently more about her brother. But by the end of the night, his goals had shifted, and Gavin Finch was the farthest thing from his mind. Andrea Finch intrigued him. Not just her family—*her*. And since the night he'd met her, he hadn't been able to get her out of his head.

Torres stood up and grabbed his keys. "I'm out, man. I need to grab some food before we head to Stockton."

"Thanks for getting this," Jon said. "I'll comb through all of it, but what's your takeaway?"

"My takeaway?" He snorted. "Next time, *you're* on file duty, and *I* get to take a girl for beers."

◆

You could tell a lot about a person by who bailed him out of jail, which was why Andrea had called Nathan. Now she sat in her Jeep, shivering and hungry, as she waited to hear the details of Shay Hardin's most recent arrest. Specifically, she wanted any information he could run down on the lucky recipient of Hardin's one phone call.

"Ross Leeland," Nathan said over the phone. "He's a real winner. I assume you already knew he had a sheet?"

"Just a guess. What's on it?"

"A pair of domestic disturbances. A DUI. A public intox," Nathan reported. "Leeland was arrested for assault up in Dallas but got it knocked down to disorderly conduct."

"Charming." Andrea watched the door to the restaurant. She checked her mirrors, but so far, no sign of Gavin's car.

"You should see his mug shot. He's got a swastika on his forehead like he's Charles Manson. Oh, and get this—he used to be the webmaster of a site called TKB. Triple K Brotherhood."

"That's on his arrest record?"

"Alex turned that up," Nathan said. His wife worked in the Cyber Crimes Unit at the Delphi Center, a world-renowned forensic lab. "She had her laptop out when I called in the request, so she offered to take a crack at this guy."

"I've never heard of TKB," Andrea said. "You're talking about Texas?"

"They have ties to Killeen, which is up by Fort Hood. But doesn't sound like they're exactly Aryan Nation. Maybe a few dozen members, from what Alex could tell. Their site's not up anymore, but she found some references here and there. Logo's a couple of crossed pistols and a skull. Highly original."

"So they're what, a neo-Nazi org? A militia group?"

"Could be both."

If Hardin had ties to a group like that, it would further explain the FBI's interest in him. They'd been keeping close tabs on those organizations since Oklahoma City.

"Alex might have more by tomorrow, though. She said she was going to look into it at work."

"Tell her thanks." Andrea checked her watch. She craned her neck around, but still no sign of Gavin's car.

"So you have a new boyfriend I don't know about?"

"Funny."

"Why am I running this dirtbag?"

Andrea got out of the car and headed for the restaurant. He was fifteen minutes late now. Maybe she'd missed him going in.

"It's a long story," she said.

"Yeah, well, I want to hear it in person. I assume you'll be in at three tomorrow?"

"That's the plan." She stepped inside the Dairy Queen. It was blissfully warm and smelled like onion rings.

"Listen to me, Andrea. Don't even think about canceling another appointment. Taggart will hit the roof."

"I know, I know."

"I shit you not. You'll be out of a job."

"I thought I already was."

Silence. It was the very thing she feared most, and they both knew it. Her job was everything. It was the only thing she'd ever really been proud of, the only thing that had ever given her solid ground. Now that ground seemed to be shifting beneath her feet.

"The facts are in your favor here, Andie."

"Not if you read the papers."

"That's crap. You play your cards right, it'll work out. But you can't keep screwing around with the process."

The *process*. Just the word put a bitter lump in her throat. It wasn't the press's grilling that had surprised her. A young man was dead, and she would have been shocked if they *hadn't* put her actions under a microscope. What surprised her was her department, the institution to which she'd devoted her career. Their lukewarm endorsement of her and their fervent pledge to fully investigate the "circumstances of the incident" had left her feeling adrift when she needed them most. *You did the right thing.* Five simple words they'd withheld from her. Maybe it was just bureaucratic ass covering, but it still stung.

Andrea suppressed the urge to whine to Nathan. This was her problem, not his.

It wasn't Jon's problem, either, and she wasn't sure why she'd opened up to him last night. Her instincts told her she shouldn't trust him. But the way he looked at her . . . He'd listened when she'd talked, and his concern had seemed genuine.

"Andrea?"

"I'm not screwing with the process."

"You've canceled three appointments in a week."

"*Rescheduled*," she said, but she could tell he was pissed now. "I fully intend to go."

"Yeah? Then have your ass here tomorrow so you can wrap this thing up and get back to work where you belong."

"I hear you," she said.

But he'd already hung up.

Andrea glanced around the restaurant. The dinner rush was over, and most of the booths were empty. Through the glass, she spotted a blue Focus. She crossed the restaurant, pushed open the door, and stood on the sidewalk, looking around.

"*Sneaky little hobbitses!*" hissed a voice.

She spun around and saw Gavin grinning at her.

"Damn it!" She elbowed him in the ribs. He loved to creep her out with his Gollum imitation.

"Hey, why so jumpy?"

She looked him up and down, and her heart lodged in her throat. His hair was short, *not* shaved. And no Nazi tats in evidence. He looked the same as he had at Christmas, and her relief was intense.

"You're late," she said.

"Save the lecture. I'm starving." He went straight for the register and ordered his usual: two double cheeseburgers, French fries, and a chocolate milkshake. Andrea ordered a chicken basket, and five minutes later, she was staring at her brother over a greasy pile of fries.

It felt good to see him. She'd missed his blue eyes and his dry humor and his teasing grin.

"So, how's Dee?"

"Fine," she said, pleased he'd asked. "Her birthday's next week."

"I know." He pointed a French fry at her. "And before you lay into me, I already put a card in the mail. I never forget her birthday."

"You should call her, too. She'd love to hear from you."

He shrugged, and she knew he wouldn't. He wasn't a phone person. Not that Andrea blamed him, really. She wasn't, either— one of the many ways they were alike.

"So what's going on, Gavin?"

"What do you mean?" He chomped into his burger with a gusto that annoyed her.

"I mean what are you doing here?"

"I told you. Working on the ranch."

"Lost Creek Ranch, same as last summer?"

He took another huge bite and nodded.

"I don't get it." She shook her head. "This place is a dust bowl. I saw an actual *tumbleweed* this morning the size of a Volkswagen. Why on earth would you come out here?"

He slurped his shake. "Yeah, and Lubbock was a real paradise."

"At least you had a purpose there. You were getting a degree."

He sighed. "If you're gonna start this up again, Andie, I'm taking off."

She tried to tamp down her frustration. She glanced at her chicken, but her appetite had disappeared. "Okay, fine," she said. "Explain it to me, then. What are you doing here?"

He ate a few fries.

She waited.

"I needed a change." He shrugged. "A chance to think about stuff."

"Such as?"

"Stuff, all right? It's none of your business."

He started in on the second cheeseburger. She watched him, frustrated because she knew he was right. He was an adult. It *wasn't* really her business. But she and Gavin weren't like normal siblings. After their mom's death, they'd formed a strong bond. The age gap didn't matter. In the podunk town of Pearl Springs, they'd been misfits together. Allies. It was the two of them against country music and Sunday school, against lima beans and prune kolaches, against their grandfather's cranky tirades. Throughout their unconventional upbringing, they'd had each other's back.

She remembered driving down from the University of Houston one weekend so she could chauffeur Gavin to the eighth-grade dance. He'd had a huge crush on his date. Andrea couldn't even remember the girl's name now, just how relieved she'd felt to learn her brother wasn't gay. It would have been just one more reason for the farm boys to pick on him.

He'd had a tough time of it growing up. Andrea felt partly responsible, because he'd never found his footing. The normal adolescent ups and downs had quietly morphed into depression. She looked at the raised pink scar on the inside of his wrist, and the familiar lump of fear rose in the back of her throat.

He saw her looking and pulled his arm into his lap.

"Listen, I'm fine, okay?"

"You don't seem fine," she said. "I don't get what you're doing."

"Maybe I like it out here, all right?"

"Why?"

He waved a fry. "I like the people. The climate. I like the free, fresh air."

"'Free, fresh air'? What does that mean?"

He shook his head.

"Seriously, I'm asking."

"Wake up, Andie. Civil liberties are going away in this country. I can't turn on the TV without seeing some jackbooted thugs kicking down someone's door."

"You're talking about those SWAT shows?"

"Yes! Ever since 9/11, the government's been using the threat of terrorism as an excuse to infringe on people's rights. We're heading toward a police state, Andie. Don't even get me started on the disarmament campaign. The Brady Bill, the Fisk-Kirby Act."

"Disarmament?" She blinked at him. "Are you kidding me? This is Texas. You can buy a gun on any street corner."

"Ha."

"Ha *what*?"

"Easy for you to say. You're the one with the badge. No one's going to come disarm you. You're one of the power brokers."

She folded her arms over her chest. "I'm a power broker now? This sounds like Shay Hardin talking, not you."

"Shay's right. Turn on the news if you don't believe me. The government's got surveillance all over the place. You can't hardly drive down the street without some camera taking your picture. They're everywhere, recording our conversations, our e-mails, taking photos twenty-four seven. It won't be long before everyone in the country's required to give a DNA sample."

Andrea watched him shovel French fries into his mouth as warning bells clanged in her head. Disarmament. Government surveillance. DNA sampling. He sounded more than a little paranoid.

Actually, he sounded like a nutcase.

Or maybe Shay Hardin was the nutcase. Maybe *he* was the paranoid one, and he was planting these ideas in her brother's head.

On the other hand, the man actually did have drones flying over his house. He might be justified in being a little suspicious.

Gavin looked sullen, and she could tell she was losing him. She needed to drop the ideological discussion and get down to pragmatics.

"Okay, let me ask something," she said. "How come you don't answer your phone?"

"I got rid of it."

She knew this. What she didn't know was whether he'd replaced it with another one. "How's anyone supposed to get hold of you?"

"Who needs to get hold of me?"

"Me. Dee and Bob. Your friends."

He shrugged. "They can e-mail me. Doesn't cost me a dime."

"You never check your messages. I've been e-mailing you for a week now, and you just responded yesterday."

"I told you, I've been busy."

"Yeah, hiding out at that ranch. Gavin, it's bizarre. All those gates and game fences. Do they even let you leave?"

He scowled. "I do whatever I want."

She pushed her chicken basket away and leaned forward on her elbows. "Don't you miss your computer science classes? Doesn't it bother you to be stuck on some ranch that doesn't even have Wi-Fi or cable? I would think you'd be going nuts with boredom."

He gaze darkened. Maybe he'd recognized the not-so-subtle probing. "I'm doing okay," he said.

"Yeah? Then what was the money for?"

No reaction. Zip.

"You asked me for *two thousand* dollars, Gavin. The least you can do is tell me who it was for."

"For me."

She watched his eyes, the same blue eyes as their grandfather's. "I don't believe you. I think it was for Hardin."

He stuck his chin out stubbornly, and she could tell she'd offended him by calling him a liar. Never mind all the crap he'd said about her profession—somehow *she* was the one being offensive here.

"The guy's a manipulator," she said. "I can't believe you don't see it."

"Don't insult someone you don't even know. Shay's a war hero. He's won *medals*. He has principles and ideals and he's not afraid to stand up for his beliefs. Unlike the rest of the sheeple in the country."

"You're changing the subject, Gavin. What was the money for?"

He shook his head. "I don't want your money anymore,

Andrea. I'm sorry I asked." He slid from the booth and stood up. "And I also don't want you meddling in my business."

"Gavin—"

"I *mean* it!" he snapped. "You're not my mother. You never were. So just go back to Austin, and butt out of my life."

Her stomach hurt as she watched him leave. She tipped her head back and stared at the ceiling.

Andrea pitched her food into the trash and stepped out into the cold desert night. She glanced down the highway leading to Maverick. He was already gone, not even a trace of taillights.

She slid into her Jeep and glanced around. She noticed the security camera mounted on the corner of the building, aimed down at the door. Government surveillance. Disarmament. He sounded like a crackpot. Did it ever occur to him that most of those cameras were put there by business owners trying to protect their property?

She shoved the key into the ignition.

The Fisk-Kirby Act. *Senator* Kirby.

Andrea froze. She stared through the windshield. Her skin turned icy as understanding dawned.

chapter eight

BY THE TIME HE put an end to his sixteen-hour day, Jon had
an empty stomach and a hand full of cactus needles. Undercover
work was a pain in the ass, because at some point, you actually
had to do whatever it was you told people you did.

Because of their SWAT training, Jon and Torres had been
pulled in on a number of ICE raids. They'd spent tonight executing a warrant at a home where a convicted sex offender was ru-
mored to be holed up. The guy had been deported twice already
but somehow had failed to get the message.

Like a lot of ICE raids, the whole thing was based on a tip,
which was always a mixed bag. Tonight's had panned out, though,
and they had turned up not only the sex offender but the unex-
pected bonus of a kilo of coke.

During the mayhem that ensued, the coke's owner had fled
through a back window. Jon and Torres had taken off after him.
The foot pursuit ended on the outskirts of town when the man
tripped face-first into a prickly-pear cactus the size of a grizzly

bear. He'd gone ballistic, howling and kicking and throwing wild punches as Jon wrestled on the cuffs.

Jon drove along the gravel road to his house now, more than ready to call it a day—except for the yawning hole in the pit of his stomach. That would have to be dealt with even before he got a shower. And then there was the other hunger that had been gnawing at him for days. He thought of Andrea's lithe body and her sensual mouth and the way she'd tasted when he'd finally gotten her to stop arguing with him. Unfortunately, the chances of doing anything about that craving tonight were slim to none.

Jon passed through a trailer park, where clotheslines and electrical wires stretched between homes. He entered an area of modest houses on lots surrounded by chain-link fences. The low adobe homes were lit up like jack-o'-lanterns. His didn't match, dark except for a bare bulb dangling above the door. He pulled into the carport and ignored the Rottweiler barking and hurling himself against the fence as he trudged to his back door. The dog's name was Loco. He and Jon had yet to become friends.

He unzipped his ICE jacket as he flipped on the lights inside. Half of them were out, a fact he only remembered at this time of day. He stripped down to his Kevlar vest and pulled open the fridge.

Reality kicked in. He stared at the shelves, then filled a cup with tap water and gulped it down.

A car roared up the street, and Loco erupted as brakes screeched in front of the house. Jon tossed his cup into the sink as three raps sounded at the door—*Pop! Pop! Pop!*—like gunfire.

He glanced out the window at the SUV parked diagonally across the patch of dirt that made up his front yard.

Pop! Pop! Pop!

He pulled open the door.

"You son of a bitch!"

"Nice parking."

Andrea stalked past him. "How dumb do you think I am, North?"

"Would you like to come in?"

"Did you think I wouldn't find out?" Her blue eyes flashed up at him, and she looked ready to spit nails.

He closed the door and sighed. "Find out what?"

Her eyes widened. Her fists clenched. She glanced at his groin, and he took an instinctive step back. "You lied to me! About your case and my brother and everything!"

Her whole body was vibrating. She wasn't wearing a jacket, but he could tell it was from anger, not cold.

He felt the first stirrings of alarm. He couldn't remember the last time he'd made a woman so furious. Probably never.

"Andrea, calm down."

"Calm down? You lied about some cold case to get me to open up to you!"

"What are you talking about?"

"What do you *think*? Julia Kirby! *Senator* Kirby! The real reason you want to use my brother!"

He didn't say anything. Heat flared in her eyes.

"I knew it!"

Shit. He tipped his head back. "Andrea—"

"No! You're done! I get to ask the questions now."

He looked down at her and felt an odd mixture of dread and anticipation. She was irate, and with good reason.

He'd underestimated her.

Torres had warned him. He'd wanted to be straight up with her, see if she'd agree to help them. Jon had wanted to do things his way, and as the senior agent on the case, he'd won. Didn't feel like a win right now.

"First question." She turned away, as if just looking at him was unbearable. "True or false, and don't you *dare* lie to me." She turned around. She took a deep breath. "Do you believe Shay Hardin had something to do with that bombing in Philadelphia?"

He watched her. He didn't say anything. As the seconds ticked by, all the color drained from her face.

"Oh, my God." Her shoulders slumped. She sank onto the arm of his sofa and buried her head in her hands.

"Andrea, look at me."

She didn't move. Maybe she was thinking about her brother. Maybe she was thinking about the sixteen people who had died in that attack. The images on the news had been bad, but the raw police footage was far worse—severed limbs strewn across the sidewalk, victims shrieking, mutilated bodies. The carnage was shocking, even for seasoned investigators.

But Jon didn't know what she was thinking about. She was so utterly still he couldn't even tell if she was breathing.

"Look at me, Andrea."

Nothing.

"*Look* at me, damn it, and I'll answer your question."

She lifted her head, and the bleak expression on her face made his gut tighten.

"Yes, all right? I think Hardin had something to do with it." He paused. "But I'm on my own with that. Except for Torres, everyone else thinks I'm crazy."

"What makes you think he did it?"

He paused.

"Tell me."

"You don't want to know."

"Tell me, God damn it!"

Jon was suddenly beat. His legs hurt. His head hurt. He had about a thousand cactus needles in his palms, and his hands were on fire.

He went to the fridge and pulled out a half-finished jug of Gatorade. He guzzled it down and tossed the container into the trash.

He sank onto the sagging armchair beside his weight bench and started untying his boots.

Andrea was still watching him with a look of despair.

"You know this investigation all started with a bank heist?"

She didn't react.

"Six thousand dollars, back in September. This was in San Antonio." He tossed his boot into the corner. The second one joined it with a thud. "Then, a month later, seven thousand. Both nothing amounts. Robber wasn't armed. After Thanksgiving, another bank got hit for sixty-five hundred. It would never have gotten on our radar, except one of our eager-beaver new agents noticed some similarities, thought the cases might be part of a series."

He stood up and loosened his vest. "Turns out this agent was right. We went back and looked at the tapes. Guy's wearing shades and a baseball cap or a hoodie each time, but you can tell it's the same perp."

"Shay Hardin?"

He pulled off his vest and tossed it onto the sofa. Now he was down to a sweaty T-shirt and jeans. He unfastened his leg holster and put it on the table. "No," he said.

She looked confused.

"Several aspects of the crimes pointed to an inside job. Someone who knew standard ops at these banks. Each hit, they took just under the amount that would attract the FBI's attention."

"Don't all bank robberies attract attention?"

"We get hundreds a year in Texas alone. We prioritize cases, like everyone else." He sat down and looked at her. "Besides the amounts, we also noticed the timing. First robbery happened while the bank manager was at lunch—but it was two in the afternoon, which was kind of an odd lunchtime. Also, the perp didn't say anything, just presented the teller with a note. But the wording was interesting. He used jargon that made us think he had inside knowledge of the procedures at this bank."

"So what did you do?"

Jon leaned back in his chair. "Checked out the bank employees, starting with the first hit, which we thought would be most revealing. Ran everyone's close relatives and significant others to see if anyone had ever been arrested or in trouble with the law. Guess whose name came up?"

"Hardin's."

He nodded. "We found four bank employees with exes who had rap sheets, but Hardin was the only one of those who'd been investigated for killing a federal judge."

She looked frustrated. And intense. And she had a little worry line between her brows that he hadn't noticed before.

"So you're saying Hardin's suddenly robbing banks now? Why would he do that?"

"Because"—he smiled tiredly—"that's where the money is."

chapter nine

"YOU THINK THIS IS *funny?*" She looked as if she'd just found gum on the bottom of her shoe. "I'm being serious here!"

"So am I."

He got up and went to the sink. He ran a dish towel under the faucet and wiped down his face, which was covered in grime. He could have used a shower and a pizza, but he wasn't getting either until he got rid of Andrea. It was either get her out or get her in his bed, and she looked like she'd bust his jaw if he so much as touched her.

He leaned back against the sink. "I started poking around, looking into what Hardin's been up to for the last six years. I didn't like what I found. Two weeks later, I persuaded our SAC to let Torres and me come out here to do some more digging."

"You had to convince him?"

"San Antonio's a busy field office. Besides antiterrorism and everything else, we've got our hands full with drug cartels and human trafficking. Not a lot of people sitting around twiddling their thumbs."

"And what'd you find?"

"I can't tell you all of it. But none of it's good."

She thrust her chin forward in that stubborn look that got his blood going.

"That's the way it is, Andrea. I can't tell you everything about my case. I probably shouldn't even be telling you this much, but for some reason I trust you."

"That, and you want me to get my brother to help you."

Again, he figured his silence was confirmation enough.

She walked into the kitchen and leaned against the counter, facing him. Some of her color had returned, but her expression still looked grim.

"So you came out here to dig, and now you have reason to think Hardin's going around knocking off banks. Why don't you arrest him?"

"There's the little problem of evidence. We've got some, but it's all circumstantial. Ditto the judge's murder. We need something concrete on either case to get an arrest warrant or even a search warrant."

He thought about the rumor Elizabeth LeBlanc had told him that Maxwell was ready to pull the plug. It wasn't a rumor. Maxwell had told him point-blank that he was getting ready to shut down this op. Jon was running out of time, but he'd never felt so close to a break, and he needed Gavin Finch to get it.

Andrea was watching him with suspicion. She still looked confused, too, and he didn't blame her. It was a complicated case, which was one reason he'd had a hard time selling his theory to his superiors. Much easier to believe a simple explanation—especially one supported by the evidence.

"But what does this have to do with Senator Kirby? And my brother?"

"I'm not sure. Could be Hardin is using stolen money to fund other illegal activities. When I investigate, I always follow the money." He suspected she did, too. She'd been asking about how Hardin earned a living.

"But why the senator?" she asked. "I thought Hardin had a vendetta against the judge."

"He did. But the judge is dead, and now he's moved on to bigger targets. Kirby's conveniently nearby, and he's controversial. He's been in the news a lot."

"I don't even keep up with politics, and I've heard all about him," she said. "He's ticked off a lot of people by putting his name on that gun law."

"He's trying to prove he's tough on crime."

"Well, it backfired. Now there's no shortage of people who'd like to see him lose the next election."

Jon nodded. "And a fraction of those who'd like to see him dead. Or hurt his family. Believe me, we know. Until this morning, we had a team of agents in Philly working 'round the clock on whether the university bombing was directed at the senator. They put together a list of groups that might be responsible, and you know what's at the top of the list?" He stepped closer. "Militia groups, neo-Nazis, and antigovernment orgs. And you know what else? We have no surveillance footage of Hardin on his property at the time of the bombing. None. But Torres and I *did* find footage from the parking garage at the El Paso Airport three days before the attack. Looks like Hardin was catching a plane somewhere. Two days after the attack, he's back on the ranch again."

"You checked—"

"None of the airlines has him on a flight, so he must have been traveling under an alias, probably using a phony driver's license."

There was a huge black market for fake IDs around here—no surprise to anyone working law enforcement in a border state.

"You said you had agents working 'until this morning,'" she said. "What happened this morning?"

He stared down at her. Of course that detail had caught her attention. It was all over the news anyway, so he might as well tell her.

"Our forensic lab traced the vehicle used in the bombing to a cleric at a Philadelphia mosque. Now it's looking like an Al Qaeda cell. Everyone's efforts have been redirected."

Her face brightened a fraction. "There goes your Shay Hardin theory."

"Maybe."

"Maybe *what*? You've got the whole Bureau saying international terrorists. And you're hung up on some yahoo out in West Texas?"

Jon tossed the towel away and folded his arms over his chest. "Okay, forget the university bombing for a minute. I *know* Shay Hardin has a deep-rooted hatred for the federal government. I *know* he's capable of violence and that he killed a judge. I'm *almost* positive he's masterminding a string of bank heists that may be funding his violent activities. What are the chances your brother's living there and not involved?"

She fumed up at him. He could see the answer in her eyes. The chances were zero, but she refused to admit it. "You don't know my brother. He's never even had a traffic ticket. He would never get involved in any of this."

"How sure are you?" Jon edged closer and watched her body stiffen. "Don't tell me—just think about it. Because I'm offering Gavin a chance here."

"Right. A chance to get thrown in jail for something he didn't do. Or get his face on the evening news. Or get a target on his back. All because you can't do your job and put together a case against the guy you're really after."

She strode over and yanked open the door, leaving just as hot as she'd arrived. He clamped his hand over hers on the knob. "Hardin's going away, I promise you. Your brother's better off helping us."

She jerked her hand away and stepped outside. Loco was going crazy, barking and lunging at the fence, but Andrea didn't even seem to notice.

"I'm serious, Andrea."

She glared at him. "I'm serious, too. You think your case is so good? Go make it."

◆

Andrea was too mad to sleep. She flipped onto her stomach and punched at the pillow, but there was no way to get comfortable. No way to relax and let go of the arguments volleying through her brain.

She flipped onto her back and stared at the ceiling. Even in the faint glow of the bathroom light, she could still see the chipping paint.

She was sick of this motel. She was sick of this town. She was sick of this dry, dusty air that made her skin itch. She was sick of eating gas-station food and sitting on this bed, hunched over her laptop at night.

More than anything, she was sick of leaving Gavin message after message that he refused to return. He wanted her to butt out. He'd made that clear. And yet with every day that ticked by, she felt more and more pulled in.

What are the chances your brother's living there and not involved?

She knew good and well that the chances were nonexistent. It wasn't just her experience as a cop that told her so, but it was also her grasp of common sense, a trait she'd inherited from her grandfather. *You lie down with dogs, you wake up with fleas.* Gavin had been spending way too much time with Hardin not to be involved on some level.

She squeezed her eyes shut as images of those smoldering ruins flooded her brain. The charred building looked like some huge monster had just taken a bite out of it. Sixteen people killed, most of them students. Dozens more injured, some who'd lost limbs or been permanently scarred by flying shrapnel. Who could do such a thing? Who could murder and maim a bunch of innocent people on the very threshold of life?

Plenty of people could. Andrea knew it. She'd seen enough slain gangbangers and branded hookers and abused children to know there was really no limit to human cruelty.

Wind howled against the building, rattling the windowpanes. A scratching noise sounded on the pavement outside. Andrea glanced at the door. The noise drew closer. She kicked off the covers, grabbed her gun, and parted the curtains to peer outside.

Scritch-scratch. Scritch-scratch.

It sounded like something small. She unlatched the door and cautiously opened it to poke her head out.

A truck roared down the highway, and an armadillo scampered out from behind her Jeep. It darted to the corner of the lot and disappeared into the field surrounding the motel.

Andrea stepped outside and stared after it. Another gust of wind had goose bumps springing up on her bare arms. She glanced up at the clear night sky.

Thousands of stars. Millions. She tipped her head back to

look at them, and for the first time all day, the clutch of anxiety loosened. Maverick, Texas. During the day, it was dry and prickly. Same as its people. But tonight it seemed . . . peaceful. For a full minute, she simply gazed up at the glitter and let her thoughts drift away from the turmoil.

I like the free, fresh air.

She shuddered. And she thought of Jon North.

He was a solid investigator. And he believed he had a case against Hardin for robbery and murder and maybe even mass murder.

If he was right, then Gavin had to at least know *something*. The question was what. And what had happened to his moral compass? What had happened to the gentle little boy she'd grown up with?

Jon knew a lot, but he didn't know Gavin. This was a kid who'd steadfastly avoided rough sports. Who loved target practice but refused to hunt. Who caught lizards in the house and carried them outside where they'd be safe from his grandmother's broom.

Andrea looked glumly at the vacancy sign in the window of the motel office. She'd been here a total of seven days. A full week of her life, and what did she have to show for it? Many more questions than answers. A pair of nasty bruises. A brother who ignored her messages and had basically told her to get out of his life.

An inconvenient attraction to a man she knew was using her.

Why had she let him kiss her? Why had she shared so much about her past, her job, her *self*? Why had she let her guard down?

Because she felt a connection with him. Attraction, yes, but a connection, too. Even though she knew she shouldn't.

Everything about her being out here was so screwed up. She should be home, saving her career from ruin, not stuck out in this dust bowl, investigating a case that wasn't even hers.

She sighed and stared out at the highway. She remembered Nathan's advice when she'd first joined homicide.

You don't find something under one rock, turn over another.

Nathan knew what he was talking about. Andrea had never once solved a case by sitting around waiting for evidence to fall into her lap.

She went back inside and zipped her pistol into her purse. She threw on some jeans and shoved her feet into Nikes. She chucked her toiletries into her duffel, packed up her laptop, and glanced around the drafty little room.

She checked her watch: 11:50.

She hurried to the motel office, where someone was switching off lights and shutting down early. Through the window, she wasn't surprised to see the listless teenager who'd checked her in. What was his name? She remembered chapped lips, pierced eyebrows, and an abundance of greasy hair that hung past his shoulders.

Andrea yanked open the door and leaned in.

"Just letting you know, I'm checking out."

He looked at her with blank, dilated eyes.

"Room eleven. Jeep Cherokee."

Another empty look. Then his gaze dropped to her tank top and seemed to focus.

"Any messages for me tonight? Or anyone stop by while I was gone?"

He dragged his attention to her face. "Oh, hey. So the room rate—that's nonrefundable."

"Yeah, got it. Did anyone swing by here tonight? Maybe a blue Ford Focus?"

He shook his head.

Andrea noticed the glowing vending machine across the

room. She quickly pounded out two Cokes and a Snickers bar and gave the desk clerk a wave on the way out.

She piled into her SUV and stuffed the snacks into the cup holder. She popped open one of the Cokes and took a long gulp. Then she rolled down the windows and braced herself for a five-hour drive.

She felt better. Buoyed. Doing something felt infinitely better than *not* doing something. She was still pissed at Jon, but maybe she could harness all that anger and put it to use.

◆

The converted tack room smelled like leather and animal sweat, and Shay liked it. The smell put him in a mind to work.

Message Two was coming.

He finished with the metal file and sat back to admire his handiwork. Not bad. The device was simple yet elegant and reminded him of the Colt revolver his grandfather used to keep in the glove compartment of his truck. No automatic anything, nothing fancy. Just perfectly constructed parts that moved together for the desired effect.

Ross stepped up to the table and gazed down at the device. "Looks almost finished."

Shay pulled off the latex gloves he wore in case agents from ATF or the Federal Bureau of Incineration managed to collect any debris. "I still have to hook up the timing mechanism."

Ross folded his arms over his chest and pursed his lips. "I been thinking. Maybe we should skip this one. Kinda off-topic, if you think about it."

Shay looked Ross up and down, disappointed. He would have expected something like this from the others. But he and Ross had been at Benning together. They'd been to Fallujah. He knew the tough decisions required in war.

Still, there had been warning signs. Ross had once been lean and fast, capable of humping a sixty-pound pack over dozens of miles, but eight years had taken a toll, and now he was soft and bloated, with a beer gut and a wife dragging him down. Maybe he'd lost sight of his creed. Maybe now he was just doing this for money. No mission commitment.

Shay didn't need this shit now. He needed soldiers who weren't afraid to engage the enemy.

"I didn't define the rules of engagement," Shay reminded him. "They were defined by the aggressor. Our government's at war with its people."

"Yeah, I know, I just . . . I think there's gotta be a better way to make a point."

Ross looked at him, oblivious to how pathetic he'd become. Pathetic or not, though, he was still a necessary element of the plan.

"Are you in or out? I can get someone else. Olivia will do it."

Ross tipped his chin up, proving his ego was intact, at least. "I'm in."

"Fine."

Shay turned back to his work. The barn door creaked open, then whisked shut again. Shay was left with the cold silence of his task. He pulled his gloves back on. He'd finish now, while he felt inspired.

Message Two was coming, and it was brutally simple.

There are no innocents in war.

chapter ten

THE GUARD NOTED ANDREA's badge number on his clipboard before raising the electronic arm and waving her through. She wended her way up the driveway, not sure why she felt nervous. She'd been here many times before. This time it seemed different, though. She took a deep breath and tried to settle the butterflies in her stomach.

Through a line of oak trees, she glimpsed the tall white columns of the Delphi Center. The sight was imposing, but the gleaming building atop the hill was just the tip of the iceberg. Besides the upper floors, the Delphi Center included a multilevel basement that housed a firing range, the Bones Unit, and a complex warren of research labs.

Andrea hiked up the wide marble steps and produced her ID for the receptionist just as the person she'd come to see strode into the lobby.

"Hey, you're back." Alex Devereaux changed directions and came to meet her. In her hand was a paper bag from the on-site coffee shop.

"Got in this morning," Andrea said.

"Nathan's going to be surprised."

Andrea was surprised, too. She'd fully intended to cancel another shrink appointment, but at the last minute, she'd decided to suck it up and go since she was in town. It had been every bit as miserable as the last one.

Nathan's wife was watching her, her expression unreadable. Despite her petite stature and cute pixie cut, the brunette was known to be a ball buster. Before coming to the Delphi Center, she'd been a PI helping women in abusive relationships who wanted to disappear. Alex was highly skilled at both finding and losing people in cyberspace.

"Sorry to show up like this, but I have a request for you," Andrea said.

"I thought you were on leave still."

"It's personal."

As she said it, Andrea pinpointed the source of her nerves. All her other trips to Delphi had been work-related. She hated asking people for favors, especially personal ones.

Alex waited for her to collect a visitor's badge and then led her to the elevator. "How was your trip to Marfa?" she asked as they zipped to the top floor.

"Maverick. Not great, which is why I'm here."

The elevator doors slid open, and they were faced with a long wall of windows. Andrea stepped up to the glass and gazed out over the treetops. After days in the desert, everything looked so *green*. The view was beautiful except for the trio of turkey vultures circling above some low bushes. Besides being a world-renowned crime lab, the Delphi Center was also home to one of the nation's largest decomposition research centers.

Alex led her past the DNA laboratory and ushered her into a dim room filled with glowing computer monitors, most piloted by scruffy twentysomethings. Action figures and bobblehead dolls perched on some of the cubicle dividers.

Alex took her to a corner cube.

"Then I'm guessing this is about your brother. How is he?"

"I'm not sure." Andrea took a seat. "He recently dropped out of school to become a ranch hand."

"Okay."

"If you'd ever met my brother, you'd know how improbable that is." She pictured him back at the Dairy Queen, with his pasty skin and his delicate fingers. "He's working for some people I don't trust, and I think they hired him for his technical skills, maybe setting up some sort of communications for them. But law enforcement's got an eye on this group, and they say there's not even any phone service out there."

"Landlines or cell phones?"

"Neither. Cell coverage is spotty in the area anyway, but they haven't come up with much, and they've been paying attention."

"That kind of surveillance—you're not talking some hayseed sheriff."

"FBI."

Her eyes widened. "Damn, Andrea."

"I know."

Alex didn't say anything right away, and Andrea could tell she was now carefully choosing her questions. "What do you want me to do?"

"I need to know if they have it right. I can't swallow it. I think the FBI's missing something."

Alex gave her a pensive look. "So surveillance. I'm not as

current in that area as I used to be. I've been spending most of my time lately on SpiderNet—that's our new software program that traces pedophiles who troll the Web for kids."

"I see." Andrea tried to keep the disappointment out of her voice. It sounded like an excuse, and she didn't want to strong-arm Nathan's wife into helping her if she wasn't comfortable.

Alex stood up and craned her neck over the cubes. "Hey, Ben."

"Yo."

"Can you pull up that activity map?" She looked at Andrea. "This is more Ben's thing right now."

They moved to a spacious double cubicle with no fewer than four monitors going. The man in the chair appeared about Gavin's age, but he had a mature look in his eyes that said he'd seen a thing or two—maybe tracking down some of the trolls Alex mentioned.

He tipped back his chair and looked at Alex. "Wazzup?"

"Andrea, Ben." She didn't waste words. "Andrea's with Austin PD. She's looking at a subject who's also being investigated by the feds. They're coming up with two different profiles, and she thinks the FBI's missing something."

"You can count on it," Ben said.

"You mind taking a look? She's interested in Internet or phone activity at a certain location."

"They're saying there's nothing there, but I don't see how that can be true," Andrea said.

"Well, if they're just using Stingray, they're probably missing something," Ben said.

"Stingray?"

"It's a cell-site simulator."

At her blank look, he continued.

"A surveillance device. It secretly dupes phones within a certain area into jumping on a fake network. The feds don't like to talk about it because it's controversial for a lot of reasons, partly because it scoops up data about innocent people who aren't even being investigated."

"Do they need a warrant?" Andrea asked.

"That's up for grabs," Alex said. "The courts haven't really caught up with a lot of the new surveillance techniques."

"They're probably using everything they have," Ben said, "but there are plenty of ways around a system like this. What I'm working on is a program that picks up cell-phone *plus* Internet activity, without having to trick devices into using a fake network."

"How does it work?" Andrea asked.

He sighed. "I could explain it all, but . . . why don't I just show you what it does? Give me a zip code, and we'll take it for a spin." He closed out of what he'd been doing and clicked open a new program as Andrea rattled off the zip code of Lost Creek Ranch.

"Hmm . . . that's a new one. Whoa." His screen had turned white. He looked at her. "That's another planet. Where exactly is this?" He zoomed out on a map until the screen showed Interstate 10 cutting through the outskirts of Fort Stockton. The edge of the city was covered with yellow and orange dots.

"What are those?" Andrea leaned in.

"Hot spots," he said. "Internet or cell-phone activity. In the more populated areas"—he zoomed out until all of Fort Stockton appeared on the screen—"we break down the spectrum. Yellow, light activity. Purple, lots of usage. This town's yellow-orange. This zip code here"—he zoomed back to the original area—"no hot spots. Practically a glacier."

Andrea felt a ripple of relief. But she didn't trust it. Her instincts told her something was up. She felt apprehensive as she looked at the screen. Did she really want the answers to these questions? Would she have the guts to act on the information if she got it?

"Of course, this is all real-time." Ben checked his watch. "Peak Internet hours are early to mid-morning and nine P.M. to one A.M. I'd have to monitor it for a few cycles to really get a true read."

"Cycles?"

"Days," he translated. "The info you're after could take a while."

"What if I narrow it down?" Andrea took out her phone. "I brought GPS coordinates."

Ben looked at Alex and grinned. "She brought GPS coordinates. A woman after my own heart."

Andrea's phone chimed, and she read the number with surprise. She hadn't expected him to return her message. "Sorry, I have to take this." She ducked into an empty cubicle and answered the call.

"I'm looking for Detective Finch?"

"Speaking."

"This is Ryan Copeland in the governor's office. I had a message you called?"

✦

Government buildings had a sameness about them, but the FBI field office in San Antonio bore very little resemblance to the Murrah Federal Building in Oklahoma City. This was by design. In the immediate aftermath of the attack that killed 168 people, including nineteen children under the age of six, the U.S. government launched an effort to reexamine federal buildings across the country to determine which were most vulnerable to attack.

San Antonio ranked high on the list. Located in the city's densely populated downtown near the Alamo, the River Walk, and other tourist attractions, the FBI field office ticked off more than a few criteria for a soft target. It was decided it was time to relocate.

Jon passed through the security gate leading to the new building, a marvel of American engineering in the terrorist age. It was on the outskirts of San Antonio, with deep setbacks from other structures and roads. The facility had a state-of-the-art surveillance system and an external security checkpoint, complete with metal detectors and X-ray machines for visitors. The building's outer shell was made of bomb-resistant material and specialty glass that—unlike the glass in Oklahoma City—wouldn't shatter into deadly shards in the event of an explosion.

What was most notable to Jon, though, was what the building lacked: children. Because when Timothy McVeigh parked his yellow Ryder truck in the Murrah Building's drop-off area beneath the America's Kids day-care center, he introduced the public to a whole new type of horror.

Jon had been sixteen at the time of the attack, and he'd watched the coverage from a television in his American history class at New Trier High School north of Chicago. Earlier that morning, his life's ambitions had included college and med school. But by sundown on April 19, all that had changed.

Jon passed through another gate and pulled into the bunker-like parking garage. He'd always been uneasy with the knowledge that he worked in one of the most secure buildings in the nation. Most Americans weren't so lucky. Most Americans lived and worked in places that would be classified by engineers or terrorists or anyone else as soft targets. Just yesterday, Jon had read a news story about the hardening of America in which the reporter suggested that security needed to be beefed up at every school and church in the nation.

The article had depressed him. It had also driven him to squeeze in yet another trip to San Antonio so he could try to persuade his boss not to yank his team out of West Texas.

Jon headed for the door, catching some curious looks from colleagues who were shedding jackets and loosening ties as they hurried for their cars. The dusty ICE-agent attire, which was practically invisible in Maverick, made him stand out here. And maybe the leg holster was a little much, but Jon had gotten used to it.

Then again, maybe it wasn't his clothes that were causing the funny looks but the fact that he was going *into* the office at five on a Friday while everyone else was streaming out.

His phone vibrated. He pulled it out and was surprised by the number. He'd thought he was at the very top of Andrea's shit list.

"Where are you?" she demanded.

He considered lying, but then he thought of her laptop and the bedspread littered with candy wrappers. She was a workaholic, too.

"Heading into work. Why?"

"Maverick or San Antonio?"

"San Antonio." He stepped through the door and slipped out of the traffic flow. "Torres and I have a meeting with our SAC tomorrow."

"Can you get to Austin tonight? Come by my apartment at eight, and we'll go from there."

She wanted him to come over. On a Friday night. He pictured her in his house last night, with her fists clenched and her eyes blazing. He'd thought about her today through those long stretches of highway.

But something in her tone told him she wasn't inviting him over to finish what they'd started in the parking lot of her motel.

"Why?" he asked.

"I've got a new angle for you. Investigation-wise."

"I didn't know you were helping me."

Silence on the other end. He'd bet money this new angle had nothing to do with her brother.

"What's the catch?" he asked.

"No catch."

He didn't believe her.

"I'll explain when you come," she said. "Be here at eight."

◆

Jon's F-150 showed every sign of a recent road trip: dusty running boards, bugs on the windshield, empty cups in the console.

"It's eight fifteen," Andrea said as she slid inside.

"Had to go home and change."

She checked him out. "You look like an agent again."

He wore a dark suit with a blue silk tie, and his clothes looked fresh and unwrinkled.

"Where to?" he asked

"The Four Seasons on Cesar Chavez."

He swung into the Friday-night traffic headed for the bridge.

"What's at the hotel?"

"Ryan Copeland," she said. "He works in the governor's office. Jon looked at her.

"He used to work for Kirby's reelection campaign."

"Inside dirt. Not a bad idea."

"Believe it or not, I actually *am* a detective." She looked at him and noticed a few details she hadn't taken in at first glance. He hadn't just changed clothes; he'd showered, and he was wearing aftershave—something subtle and masculine that she was going to have to try hard to ignore. Had he done that for her? Would it matter if he had?

Andrea looked away. There was more going on here than two cops working a case together. She needed to remember that they were coming from totally different places and had conflicting agendas.

He wanted to solve his case, period. She had to keep in mind that as attractive as he was, as *helpful* as he was, his primary motive was to achieve his objective. He didn't give a damn about Gavin except as a means to an end.

A few minutes later, Jon held the door open as she stepped into a hotel that looked nothing like the Lazy Dayz Inn. Polished floors, huge fireplace, oversize leather club chairs. A ridiculously tall flower arrangement dominated the lobby, and piano music drifted from the bar.

Andrea spotted their contact. He stood beside a staircase, talking on his phone and checking his watch. His attention landed on Andrea, and he tucked the phone into the pocket of his pin-striped suit as she walked over to make introductions. The man's expression sharpened when she mentioned that Jon was with the FBI.

"I thought you all were with the police?" He looked at Andrea.

"I am. Austin PD. Listen, I know you don't have much time. Is there somewhere we can talk?"

Jon's badge seemed to be making the man antsy. He glanced over his shoulder to where people in cocktail attire were milling around outside a ballroom. Tonight's event was a high-dollar fund-raiser benefiting the governor's reelection campaign.

"Let's step outdoors," Copeland said, leading them onto a patio.

The weather was cool, and Andrea stuffed her hands in the pockets of her leather jacket. Copeland lit a cigarette and looked Jon up and down as he took a drag.

"I assume you work with McMurphy?" Copeland asked.

"Who's that?"

"Philadelphia office. I returned his call. Twice." He blew out a stream of smoke. "Guy never got back to me."

Jon looked at Andrea.

"When you were with Senator Kirby's election campaign," she said, "you filed a complaint with Dallas PD about someone harassing the senator and his staff."

"It was the staff, mostly." He flicked his ash onto the patio. "I'm not sure Kirby even knew he existed."

"You didn't inform him?"

"We can't tell him about every wing nut who shows up to complain." He looked at Jon. "Especially a guy like Kirby. The minute he put his name on that gun bill, he had people coming out of the woodwork. We were getting calls, letters, people showing up in person to rant."

"What sort of security does the senator have?" Andrea asked.

"In Washington, the Capitol Police," Copeland said. "But everywhere else, it's thin—just some private bodyguards. We're not talking Secret Service caliber or anything. They're a step up from rent-a-cops."

"So he was getting lots of threats," Andrea said. "What was different about this guy?"

Copeland leaned back against a wrought-iron banister separating the patio from some manicured flower beds. She watched him through the veil of smoke.

"*He* was different."

"How?"

"Persistent, for one. And smart." He tossed his cigarette butt onto the concrete and crossed his arms. "Frankly, he scared the shit out of me."

"You met him?" Jon asked.

"Just the once. At least, I *might* have met him. I don't even know his name, just that he liked to call and lurk around the campaign headquarters. I talked to him on the phone one time, too. At first, I thought he was a donor, but then he roped me into a debate about civil liberties and the theft of democracy."

"Was this before or after the confrontation?" Andrea asked.

Jon cut a glance at her, clearly annoyed to be playing catch-up. She had a copy of the police report, but there hadn't been time to show it to him.

"Before," Copeland said. "The confrontation came later, maybe a few weeks. I was leaving the office, and he was waiting in the alley between the building and the parking garage."

"So no name," she said. "How can you be sure it was the guy from the phone and the letters?"

"He talked to a lot of us. Kirby's staffers. He had certain phrases he used over and over."

Andrea glanced at Jon, who was intent on their interview subject now. She took out a notepad and reviewed what she'd written.

"In the report, you describe him as six-two, goatee, shaved head, jeans, and a bomber jacket?"

She looked up, but he didn't confirm.

"You also mention an eagle tattoo on the side of his neck."

Again, no comment.

"How did he threaten you, exactly?" she asked.

"He showed up, ranting about the usual antigovernment stuff. But the whole time, he's holding his jacket open, showing me his holster. 'Give Kirby a message. Tell him I'm watching him.'"

"What kind of gun was it?" Andrea asked.

"What's in the report?"

"A black handgun."

He nodded. "That sounds right."

Andrea glanced at Jon, whose steely look told her she was botching this interview. She took an envelope from her jacket pocket and pulled out a five-by-seven photo.

Copeland stiffened.

"Does this look like the man you saw?"

He flicked a glance at it. "I don't know."

"You didn't even look at it."

Copeland returned her gaze coolly.

"Mr. Copeland," she said, "why do I get the feeling you're not being entirely straight with us here?"

He looked at Jon, then back to her again.

She shook her head. "Lying to the police, Mr. Copeland. Never a good idea."

He sighed. "Fine, all right? It wasn't actually me in the alley."

God damn it, she knew she should have vetted this witness. But she hadn't had time.

"*Who* exactly—"

"Carmen Pena." He folded his arms over his chest, wrinkling his nice pinstripes. "She didn't want her name on the police report."

"Why?" Jon asked.

"The beat reporters read those things. She'd already been in the news that week. Someone started a rumor that she was having an affair with the senator."

"Was she?" Andrea asked.

"Of course not. Those rumors are a dime a dozen for any politician. But this one came at a sensitive time, and we needed it to die down. I told her I'd put my name on the report, but we should at least get it on record. You know, that this guy showed up with a gun and everything."

"Filing a false police report is a serious offense," Andrea said.

He lifted an eyebrow. "You going to arrest me?"

"What happened with the report?" Jon asked, picking up the slack now because Andrea was busy being ticked off.

She was mad at herself for not seeing through this. And she was embarrassed that she'd called Jon all the way up here to interview this man.

"I'm not sure. I would guess Dallas PD referred it to the local FBI, but we didn't have a name or anything, just a description. And we're not even sure it's the same guy who sent the letter and called—that's just a guess. So what can they really do with that?"

"Where's Carmen now?" Jon asked.

"She left right after I did. Last I heard, she was working for the mayor."

"Did she leave on her own or get fired?" Andrea asked.

"She was let go."

"Fired?"

"People come and go on campaigns. There's a lot of turnover."

"What about you?" Jon asked. "Why'd you leave?"

Copeland tapped his breast pocket. She could tell he was battling the urge for another cigarette, but the urge to wrap up this interview was stronger.

"Look, I need to get back in there. I'm on meet-and-greet tonight."

"Last question," Jon said. "Why'd you leave the campaign?"

He sighed. He tucked his hands in his pockets and met Jon's gaze. "I worked for Kirby five years. We didn't see eye to eye on a lot of things."

"Didn't like his ideology?"

He sniffed. "Nothing that noble. The governor's camp offered me more money."

✦

Andrea seemed oblivious to his anger as they returned to his truck. He squeezed back into traffic and cut her a glance.

"Where'd you get that photograph?"

She looked at him. "What, of Hardin?"

"Yes, of Shay Hardin, a suspected murderer."

"Truck stop in Maverick."

Jon shook his head.

"What?"

"He see you take it?"

"I was careful."

Jon didn't believe her. If she really wanted to be careful, she'd stay the hell away from Maverick. Despite going to the effort to hide her license plates, she'd still been attracting too much attention to herself and asking too many questions.

"We're not the only ones who turned up that report," she said now.

"We?"

"Okay, me. Whatever. Your friends in Philly had it, too."

"I know."

"Why didn't they follow up?"

Jon turned onto the bridge leading back to the south side of town. "Our team there's inundated. They're following up on thousands of tips and leads. And as of this week, they're pushing harder on the foreign-terrorist angle."

"But you still don't believe it."

"No."

She turned to face him. "See, that's what I don't get. You seem like a decent investigator."

He shot her a look.

"So explain it to me. If this Shay Hardin theory's so plausible, why are you and Torres the only ones buying it?"

Jon didn't want to explain.

But part of him did. It bothered him that she obviously thought he was way off-base.

He glanced at her across the truck. She was watching him with those clear blue eyes, waiting for an explanation.

"Look at everything the senator stands for," he said. "He's become hated by antigovernment orgs. Militia groups believe he betrayed them. They think he's a traitor, and they haven't been shy about making it known. Surf the Internet if you don't believe me. A lot of these websites are packed with thinly disguised threats against Kirby. Some even posted stuff celebrating the death of his only daughter."

"That's sick."

"That's free speech."

"Why'd he switch sides on the gun thing?" she asked.

"Who knows? Maybe he took a poll. Or conducted a focus group. Maybe he had a genuine change of heart."

Andrea sneered. She was a cynic like he was.

"Maybe he's fickle," Jon said.

"But I still don't get the tunnel vision. If that agent in Philly—what was his name, McMurphy?—if he knows about this possible suspect, why wouldn't he follow up? Even if they've got a good case coming along with the Al Qaeda angle, it's only logical to develop other solid leads."

Jon slowed as he neared her street. "Yeah, well, the Bureau doesn't always do what's logical." He glanced at her. "You want to get dinner?"

She looked startled. Then wary.

Jon glanced away and waited for an answer. Damned if he was going to beg her to have dinner with him. But he wasn't ready to take her home yet. Even when she pissed him off, he still liked her company.

"You a fan of Tex-Mex?" she asked.

"No."

"How about barbecue?"

"Fine. Where to?"

"Just pull in up here on the left."

He turned into a large parking lot that had been converted to a food court. About a dozen mobile trailers of different shapes and sizes were set up in rows facing the street. He found a parking space beside a bike rack, then stripped off his jacket and tie and tossed them into the backseat. He unbuttoned his cuffs and flipped his sleeves back as Andrea stood off to the side and pretended not to notice.

The air smelled like grilling meat and funnel cakes, and he realized he was starving. Andrea stepped up to a silver Airstream with an inflatable pink pig perched on top.

"Bubba's BBQ." He looked at her. "Nice."

"Everyone calls it the Pig. Don't worry, it's good. Think I'd take you to a dump?"

"Maybe."

She smiled slyly and they placed their orders. She insisted on paying, and he let her. Then they staked out a graffiti-covered picnic table and waited for their number to be called.

Jon glanced around. It was a typical Austin crowd of college kids, musician types, and aging hippies. Andrea looked right at home in her leather jacket and faded jeans, with all the extra metal in her ears.

He glanced over her shoulder at the redbrick apartment complex across the street. Interesting that she'd picked a busy dinner spot just footsteps from where she lived as the place to settle their bet. Not really what he'd wanted. She could walk home, no need for him to drive her.

This woman was an expert at keeping him at arm's length. He was going to have to change that. Soon. Her mouth had healed up, and he'd spent the last two days thinking about it.

"What?" She tipped back her beer. He'd been staring.

"I need a copy of that police report," he said. "Particularly if there's a letter with it."

"There is. I've got it at home."

Their number was called, and Jon got up to get their food. They'd both ordered pulled-pork sandwiches and beer-battered French fries, Andrea's with an extra side of mustard. Jon slid her basket in front of her, and she plunged right in.

"You read the letter?" he asked.

"Yeah."

"What did you think?"

"Well, it's not signed, so we don't really know who sent it." She dipped a fry in mustard. "I think it's a man, though."

"Why?"

"I don't know. The tone? Sounded masculine. Sort of military.

And he quotes the Constitution, the Bill of Rights, some Supreme Court justice."

Jon narrowed his gaze at her. "Brandeis?"

"Yeah."

"You remember the quote?"

She hesitated. "Something about 'if the government becomes a lawbreaker'—"

"—'it breeds contempt for the law; it invites every man to become a law unto himself; it invites anarchy.'"

She lifted an eyebrow. "Someone paid attention in law school."

He took a sip of his beer. That wasn't why he knew the quote, but he didn't want to discuss it. Instead, he changed the subject. "You always eat like this?" he asked.

"Sure. Why not?"

"You're pretty little for that appetite."

She shrugged. "I run a lot."

"You run in college?"

He already knew that she had. He'd done a preliminary background check after their first meeting. He'd intended to go deeper, but now their relationship had shifted, and it felt like cheating.

"High school, college." She popped another fry into her mouth. "Running's a poor kid's sport. You just need shoes."

He watched her eat and realized he couldn't remember the last time he'd shared a meal with a woman who actually seemed to enjoy food. It was refreshing, sort of like the way she wasn't falling all over herself flirting with him because he was an FBI agent.

Then again, he wouldn't have minded a little flirting. She seemed intent on keeping her distance. Every time he started to draw her out, she seemed to pull back again. She had trust issues—not surprising for someone who'd essentially been orphaned as a kid. But he wanted her to let him in. He wanted her to see him as more than an FBI agent investigating her brother.

"What?" she asked.

"Nothing."

"Back to the letter. It was long and well written. Whoever wrote it seems very articulate."

Jon took a sip of beer and rested his bottle on the table. "You think he's smart?"

"I think he has a point."

He didn't mask his surprise.

"Obviously, I don't agree with killing people to make it—if that's what he's doing—but I'm sure there are a lot of people out there who sympathize with his views. I mean, even if Shay Hardin didn't kill that judge or target the senator's daughter, someone else could have done it for all the same reasons."

Jon watched her silently as he ate. She was right, and that's what bothered him.

"You know, a lot of law-abiding people aren't crazy about the federal government," she said. "They remember Ruby Ridge and Waco, and now they look around and see the increasing surveillance, the militarization of police. Rubs a lot of people the wrong way."

"I'm aware of that. And for the record, I think we took the wrong road at Waco. We should have used less lethal tactics. We were after a cult leader, and we should have arrested him off-site and avoided the whole confrontation."

"I'm surprised to hear you say that."

"Why? It's the truth. We fucked up. Hopefully, we learned from it."

She watched him, looking thoughtful. "Copeland called this guy—who we think might be Hardin—just another wing nut."

"What about it?"

"So why *this* wing nut? Why do you think Hardin's the one responsible for this attack? Where would he get the funds? The materials? And I'm still not seeing him behind a Pennsylvania plot. He's a thousand miles away."

"I told you, we don't know his whereabouts at the time of the bombing. We have no evidence that he was at the ranch or even in Texas at that time."

She dipped a fry in mustard. "That doesn't mean he *wasn't*. And anyway, Lost Creek Ranch doesn't strike me as much of a place to launch a revolution. It's not exactly a hive of activity. They don't even have Internet."

"That's something that concerns me," he said.

"Why?"

"A lot of these organizations went underground after OK-BOMB."

"OKBOMB?"

"The Oklahoma City bombing. That's the case name." He had to remind himself that not everyone was as fixated on that case as he was. "That was when the FBI really started taking a hard look at homegrown terrorism. We stepped up surveillance, efforts to monitor communications. And then all that increased even more after 9/11."

"And the Patriot Act."

He nodded. "In a way, I think that made it harder for us. We drove a lot of groups underground. They started changing tactics. There's been more focus on decentralization. Instead of having cohesive groups, it's more of a leaderless resistance." He paused. "I think the most dangerous players are the ones we don't even know about. Silent cells. They don't communicate openly. They're not on our radar. Most people don't even know they exist."

He could have told her more, but she had a guarded expression in her eyes, and he could tell she didn't want to believe any of this. She was fiercely loyal to her brother. He knew that. He even admired it to an extent, but it could become a problem, too. For both of them.

He glanced at their baskets. They'd put a good dent in the food, despite all the talking. For a long moment, they just looked at each other, and he tried to read what she was thinking.

"It's late." She stood. "I was up all night driving. I should get home."

"I'll come with you."

She looked surprised.

"I need that report."

They crossed the street and walked toward her apartment. Traffic whirred, and the bars were filling up. As they neared her building, the last few bars of a John Coltrane song drifted from a courtyard. Jon stopped and let the music wash over him. A couple emerged from a purple door.

Andrea glanced over at him. "So what time's your meeting tomorrow?"

"Not so fast."

"What?"

He took her hand and pulled her toward the bar. Before she could come up with an excuse, he led her inside.

chapter eleven

THE INTERIOR WAS DARK and noisy. Jon read a chalkboard sign and handed a twenty to a fedora-wearing man as big as an oak tree.

The club was packed. Jon pulled her past a blue-lit stage, around the bar, and then outside to a brick patio, where he spied an empty table.

Andrea eyed him suspiciously as he pulled a chair out for her. "Very smooth."

"What?"

She glanced around and sat down. "The bet was dinner."

"This part's on me."

But that didn't seem to put her at ease. He flagged a waiter, and she asked for a Jack and Coke. He ordered straight whiskey.

She peeled off her jacket and draped it over the back of the chair. Tonight she wore a fitted black T-shirt, and he'd already noted the Kimber tucked into her ankle holster.

Jon liked looking for the Kimber. Whenever he saw her, it was the first thing he noticed, right after her eyes.

Which looked annoyed right now.

"Relax, Finch. It's just drinks."

"Ha. Coming from you."

"What?"

"Not to point out the obvious, but you're not the most re-laxed person in the world."

He leaned back in his chair, facing the propped-open door. Music drifted through and enveloped the courtyard in a bluesy haze.

He sat back and listened. And watched her.

She scanned the patio, observing, checking, looking for trou-blemakers. It was a cop's gaze, and finally, it came to rest on him.

"I wouldn't have picked you for jazz," she said.

"Why not?"

"I don't know. Too free-form?"

Their drinks arrived. She stirred the ice cubes with her straw, and he sipped his whiskey. It was good. Smooth.

"I'm surprised they have jazz here," he said.

"This is the live-music capital of the world. They have every-thing."

The song ended, and applause went up inside the bar.

Jon looked at her. "You like it?"

"It's okay. I've never really listened to it."

He leaned closer. "I got my first fake ID so I could go to a jazz club in Chicago."

"Hoodlum. How old were you?"

"Sixteen."

"They let a sixteen-year-old into a bar?"

"I was tall."

"I bet you were." She smiled, and for the first time all night, it seemed genuine.

He looked around at all the people talking and drinking and enjoying the music. He looked at Andrea, at the dark swing of her hair and the smooth line of her neck. Her lips were soft and lush, and he thought about taking her home.

She slid him a look. "What?"

"Nothing."

"You were thinking something."

"I'm trying to picture you growing up in Pearl Springs."

"God, don't."

"Why not?"

"It wasn't pretty." Her expression clouded, and he knew she was thinking of her brother. "That's one of the reasons I am the way I am. About Gavin."

"How do you mean?"

She poked at her ice cubes, and he waited, watching her. He'd been steering the conversation to Gavin for days, but now he felt a stab of guilt. He'd been manipulating her, and she knew it, and he wished they'd met under different circumstances.

"It wasn't always easy for him, being my brother." Her gaze lifted. "Especially when I hit high school."

"Why?"

"I don't know. I cut my hair short. Wore black lipstick. Didn't lust after the football team. They didn't know what to think of me, so they called me a dyke, which by some twisted logic made Gavin a fag, so . . . he was pretty much doomed from the get-go because of me."

Jon watched her, trying to visualize the misfit teen. He could picture the lipstick and the attitude but not the insecurity. She seemed so confident now.

She glanced around. "I should come here more."

"It's right next door. I don't know how you stay away."

"I never think about it. I mean, it's *here*. All I have to do is open a window."

He shook his head, and she smiled.

"Oh, like what? You'd be down here every night if you lived in the neighborhood?"

"Maybe."

"No, you wouldn't. You're a workaholic like I am." She grinned and sipped her drink.

An ego-driven workaholic who is destined to end up alone.

Jon tried not to think about it. He tipped back his glass, and for a while, they listened. Without drinking, without talking. Without even moving—just letting the music flow around them and fill the space. It was nice listening with someone who didn't feel compelled to talk.

When the waiter came by again, she shook her head tiredly.

"You look beat," Jon said.

"I feel like roadkill. Too much driving."

As much as he didn't want to, he stood up and peeled off some bills. He held her jacket as she slipped into it.

"You don't need to walk me home," she told him.

"I still need that report."

The night was cold and clear, and the sidewalks were crowded with Friday-night traffic. She took out her purse as they neared her building.

"The letter's just a copy. No prints or anything." She glanced at him over her shoulder. "What are you going to do with it?"

"Take a look. Run it through our anonymous-threat-letter file."

"I already thought of that." She trudged up the stairs. "I submitted it today, but you should follow up. I'm sure you'll get a quicker response."

She unlocked her apartment and stepped inside. He followed her but waited near the door. Her place smelled good, something distinctly feminine but not overwhelming like perfume. He remembered the scent from his first trip over here.

"It's all yours," she said, bringing the folder. She propped her shoulder against the doorframe.

He glanced up from the paperwork as she stifled a yawn. Her eyes looked glassy. "Go to bed, Finch."

"What about you?"

He stared down at her. No, that hadn't been innuendo. She was that exhausted. "Back to work," he said.

"Tonight? You're going back to the office?"

"I have to take care of some things."

"Oh. Well . . ." She cleared her throat. "Sorry about Copeland. I should have vetted him first and not wasted your time."

She hadn't wasted it. But he didn't tell her that. "It's okay." He stepped outside. "The jazz made up for it."

chapter twelve

SHAY LAY IN THE bed of Lost Creek and peered through the scope. He pressed his cheek against the stock and forced all of his muscles to relax. He closed his eyes, took a deep breath to fill his lungs, and slowly exhaled as he looked through the crosshairs. He felt relaxed. One with the rifle. It was an extension of his body, his mind, his thoughts.

He pulled the trigger and heard the distinctive sucking sound as the bullet traveled through the suppressor and found the target.

Dead on.

He'd developed a taste for killing in the desert. He liked the efficiency of it. Men in suits could argue all day long, negotiate all day long. But war required action. Blow a man's head apart like a melon, and the debate was over. End of discussion.

Gravel crunched, and he turned around to see Mark walking up the creek bed. The morning sun cast his long shadow over the rocks.

"Live fire, huh? Thought you were doing dry training."

"Shooting is a perishable skill." Shay shifted into sitting position, feet apart, digging his heels into the ground as he rested his arm on his knee. He positioned the rifle and got on target again.

Mark spit on the rocks. He shifted the chaw in his mouth and looked out at the canyon.

"What's on your mind, Mark?"

"I'm worried about the girl."

"Don't be." Shay glanced at the makeshift range flag—a bandanna duct-taped to a tree branch.

"Shouldn't we take care of her?"

He peered through the scope. "We'll play with her awhile first. Plus, we don't want Gavin to lose focus if his pain-in-the-ass sister suddenly goes missing."

A wind kicked up. He glanced at the flag again and made adjustments mentally as he gazed through the crosshairs. He relaxed, took a breath, and blocked out all distractions. Conditions were never perfect.

He sent another round downrange. Again, it hit the target pinned to the berm a hundred yards away.

"You know she's a cop, right?"

Shay glanced at him. The comment didn't merit a response. He'd known she was a cop when she came out here last summer. He made it his business to know. But he wasn't worried. Gavin's sister didn't have a federal badge. She presented an obstacle, but one that was easily dealt with at the right time.

This op was all about timing.

Shay checked his watch and loaded another round. He lined up the shot. Glanced at the range flag. Took another breath.

He squeezed the trigger.

Mark whistled. "Damn."

Shay stood up. "We need to go."

Mark glanced at the sky. He fell in beside him as they trekked back toward the house. He didn't say anything, and the only sound was the crunch of gravel under their boots.

Shay looked at him. "Everything in place for later?"

"Just about."

"We leave at oh-nine-hundred."

They neared the barn, and a faint noise droned overhead. Mark glanced up. "Uncle Sammy, right on time." He looked at Shay. "How did you know?"

"I make it my business to know. You should, too." He stepped into the barn's cool shade. "'Those who understand the enemy never suffer defeat.'"

✦

There were numerous ways to ID someone who'd fled a crime scene: eyewitness accounts, fingerprints, DNA, vehicle. Elizabeth's top choice was vehicle, every time.

She had a thing for cars, which made her unusual among female agents, particularly in the South. Elizabeth chalked up her interest to the summer she'd turned seventeen, when she'd worked at her uncle Gary's Toyota dealership. As a minimum-wage file clerk, she'd spent her days getting griped at or getting her ass pinched by Gary's more senior employees, which was pretty much everyone.

By her second week on the job, she'd picked up a few survival skills. She'd learned to file with lightning speed in order to minimize her time in the hallway beside the break room, a high-traffic area for ass pinchers. She'd learned to alphabetize backward. She'd also learned to classify the men at the dealership into three categories: Touchers, Talkers, and Gawkers.

Today had been packed with Talkers, but none of them

had provided any useful leads. Elizabeth turned into the lot of Moore's Pre-Owned Vehicles—GET MORE FOR YOUR MONEY AT MOORE'S!—feeling deflated. She was now down to the tenth dealership on her target list, and she'd made absolutely no progress in her quest to find the getaway car used in Wednesday's bank robbery.

The problem wasn't her strategy—at least, she didn't think so. She'd based her list on logical assumptions. One, that because all three San Antonio robberies had occurred within one hundred feet of Interstate 10, the perp was using I-10 as his route to and from the crime scenes. Two, that because each robbery had been committed by what appeared to be the same unidentified man using different vehicles, he was most likely getting rid of the vehicles shortly after committing the crimes. And three, that a robber hitting banks for relatively small amounts of cash would be more likely to sell or trade a vehicle than to ditch it outright. And car dealerships kept records.

So to find her perp, Elizabeth simply had to find one of his vehicles. And to find a vehicle, she simply had to check car dealerships along I-10 in and around San Antonio. Easy peasy. Except that it wasn't.

Elizabeth whipped into a front-row space near Moore's showroom. She freshened her lipstick and smoothed her long blond ponytail, well aware that her arrival had already been registered by the men loitering around the sales floor.

She got out of her little white Honda, and before her feet even touched the sidewalk, a burly man in a dress shirt and tie swooped in to nab her.

"Afternoon." He smiled and thrust out a hand, textbook Talker.

"Good afternoon."

He gave her a quick once-over, only lingering a moment on her breasts before turning his attention to her Honda. "Looking for a car today? Maybe something a little roomier?"

"Actually, I am. But not for myself." She flashed her creds. "Mind if I speak with a manager?"

The smile faltered briefly, but he managed to hold it. "That'd be me. I'm Jack Moore."

Elizabeth glanced around at the sea of cars. "So this is your place?"

"It's a family shop."

She took that to mean it belonged to his father.

"I'm hoping you can help me. I'm looking for a car that might have come in last week, probably Wednesday or Thursday. A ninety-six Pontiac Grand Am, teal green."

His brow furrowed. "We don't acquire stolen vehicles. I can tell you that right now."

"I'm sure you don't." She smiled. "This isn't about a stolen car. The car doesn't even matter, really. We're looking for the person driving it."

"Well, either way," he said, "it doesn't ring a bell."

She glanced out at the expanse of automobiles. "Looks like you all do a lot of business. Would you mind checking your records?"

"Believe me, we got a Pontiac like that on the lot last week, I'd have noticed it. That color green's a tough sell."

She tugged a list from her purse. "I've got several others I'd like to check on. Maybe these would ring a bell?"

He stepped closer and scanned the list, which included makes, models, and approximate dates for the three other vehicles used in the robberies.

"Those are from the fall."

"That's right."

"I'd have to check the files." He looked behind him at the glass building. "We've got a girl that handles all that, but she won't be here till Monday."

"Would you mind if *I* check? I've been doing this for days, so I'm quite familiar with the filing system."

He frowned skeptically.

"It would just take a minute, and I could cross you guys off my list. I've got four more dealerships to visit this afternoon."

His attention strayed as a minivan pulled onto the lot. When he glanced at her again, she could tell she almost had him.

"Ten minutes." She smiled. "That's all I need."

Moore handed her off to a junior salesman, who showed her to a wall of file drawers in the corridor between the repair garage and the vending-machine alcove. It was déjà vu all over again. Elizabeth kept her butt tucked in, half expecting some sweaty mechanic to come along and make a grab.

The auto world did everything by Vehicle Identification Number, and the seventeen-digit VIN provided a wealth of information. With just a glance at the digits, someone who knew their stuff could tell a car's make, model, and year and where in the world it was manufactured. Elizabeth knew her stuff. And she'd memorized the prefixes of all four cars on her list. Her fingers combed nimbly through the file drawers as she checked out the sections for all the relevant VIN numbers.

She found nothing. No invoices that would reflect a trade-in, a sale, or a repair on one of the vehicles she was seeking.

She noticed that the most recent invoices in the files were from around February.

"Finding what you need?"

Junior was back. Another Talker, which was pretty standard for sales guys.

"Actually, I'm striking out. I need to check something from this week, and these files don't look updated."

"Ah, that's probably because Jill—the girl who does it—she's pretty backed up." He propped a shoulder against the wall. "Anything I can help with?"

"I'm looking for a green Pontiac Grand Am. A ninety-six." She pulled a black-and-white surveillance photo from her purse. She'd stopped using the pictures this morning after noticing everyone's guard went up when they realized they were looking at a surveillance picture. But she was at the end of her rope now, so she handed him the pic.

"That's definitely not one of ours," he said. "Busted taillight, dented quarter-panel. Looks like it was just in a wreck. We wouldn't touch it."

"You're saying your customers never bring in cars that need body work?"

"Oh, sure. Happens all the time." He handed back the photo. "I'm saying we wouldn't keep it around. We get those in, we send 'em straight across the street." He nodded at the window.

Elizabeth followed his gaze. She hadn't even thought about body shops. How had she missed that? Three of her four vehicles had visible dings or dents.

She tried to imagine how many body shops were in the San Antonio area. Maybe she should have followed her supervisor's advice and simply put this case on the back burner until the labs came back on the robbery note.

But then she thought of Jon North. He'd had that determined gleam in his eye when she'd last seen him. He'd been so certain these bank robberies were connected to something important.

Elizabeth left Moore's and motored over to Hill Country Automotive across the street. She passed the repair bays and pulled right up to the front. It was already four o'clock, so she'd keep it quick. As she strode toward the door, her gaze landed on a shiny green Pontiac.

She halted. A Grand Am. She pulled the photo from her purse and stepped over for a closer look.

Identical.

Except for a few key details. This car lacked a broken taillight, a dented quarter-panel, and a license plate obscured by mud.

She crouched down beside the bumper, which had a scuff mark. She studied it. She studied the photo in her hand.

Her pulse sped up.

"Help you with something?"

She turned around. A man was watching her from one of the repair bays. Short, beefy, tattooed arms, buzz cut. She walked over and glanced at the name embroidered on his gray coveralls. *Randy.*

"Is your manager here?"

"You're looking at him."

She smiled, but it didn't work this time. He'd made her for a cop the second she pulled out that photograph.

She went ahead and introduced herself, flashing her badge. His blue eyes turned a few degrees cooler.

"I'm interested in that Pontiac," she said. "Would you happen to know who the owner is?"

"That'd be me, temporarily. It's on its way to auction."

Elizabeth looked him over. He seemed guarded but not un-cooperative.

"I take it you bought it from someone?

"Couple days ago. Quoted him a price on the body work, and he decided not to bother. We get that sometimes. If it's worth it, we do the body work here, then bundle a few vehicles together and take them out to auction."

Her heart was pounding now. She tried to keep her tone neutral. "Do you remember the day, exactly?"

He squinted. "Wednesday, I think. I'd have to look to be sure."

"Would you mind?"

Without a word, he led her into a building as a trio of Gawkers watched from the nearest service bay. Inside, the air was warm and smelled of motor oil. A UT basketball game was playing on a TV mounted in the corner. He scooted behind a counter and tapped at a computer.

Elizabeth held her breath as she watched his hands. The creases of his knuckles were black with grease.

"Wednesday. Paid fifteen hundred for it." He gave her a dark look. "I can show you the title, too. We're not running a chop shop here."

Elizabeth pulled out her notebook. "Could I get the name of the person who sold it to you?"

"David Woods."

He rattled off a San Marcos address as she jotted it down.

"And do you remember what he looked like?" She glanced up, and the manager was watching her. "White, black? Tall, short? Old, young?"

"He was white." He had the expression of someone who wasn't crazy about helping the police but didn't see a way around it. "Medium build. Maybe late twenties."

Elizabeth scribbled it down and felt a surge of excitement. She looked up from her notepad and smiled.

He didn't smile back.

"Thank you," she told him. "You've been very helpful."

◆

Andrea was downtown when her phone buzzed, and she recognized the number of a cop she knew from her patrol days.

"Hey, Andie. I got that info you wanted," she said. "She's at an address over on Cherry Knoll."

"In Pemberton Heights?"

"That's right."

Andrea veered into the turn lane. "Wants or warrants?"

"Negative. Clean as a whistle. You need me to text this over?"

"Thanks, that's a big help. I owe you."

"Forget it. Hope to see you back soon."

Andrea pulled an illegal U-turn and headed north. As she turned onto Cherry Knoll she surveyed the charming old bungalows and towering new McMansions. The neighborhood was expensive. Not her usual stomping grounds, either on or off the job. Almost every driveway seemed to have a BMW or a Saab, with the occasional Volkswagen thrown in. Just keeping it real.

Andrea scanned the street numbers and spotted the house she wanted—a white clapboard one-story with black window shutters and a red front door. There was a Kia parked out front—with a crumpled bumper, no less. Andrea noted the other cars up and down the block as she rolled to a stop.

Instead of approaching the door, she walked up to the gray sedan on the opposite side of the street. She pulled open the passenger door and slid inside.

"Hi."

Jon checked his side mirror. "What are you doing here?" he asked flatly.

"Same thing you are. I take it she's not home?"

"Woman who answered the door said she's due back any minute."

"Who was she?"

"Didn't ask. Sister, roommate, maid—she could be anybody."

Andrea pulled a notepad from her jacket and took down the Kia's license plate. It wouldn't hurt to check.

Jon watched without comment, and she figured he was a step ahead of her.

"So." She tucked the notepad away. "How's your day going?"

"Busy."

"Me, too. Went for a jog. Hit the gym. Ate a big lunch. I feel like a million bucks."

He looked at her.

"You, on the other hand, look pissy."

He glanced at the side mirror. He was in a suit and tie again, with his badge clipped to his belt alongside his gun. She remembered him at the bar last night, with his tie gone and his sleeves rolled up, watching her with that dark, steady gaze that made her heart thud.

"Tell me what's wrong," she said.

He checked the mirror again. "I met with Maxwell this morning. He gave us one more week."

"Okay." She paused. "That's good, isn't it?"

"I wanted three. And more resources. It's impossible to monitor six different subjects with the team we have now."

"I assume you asked for all that?"

He didn't respond.

Well, that explained his sour mood. She doubted he was used to losing an argument.

They sat in the tense silence. The street was empty of people. She glanced at Jon staring a hole in that red door.

She dug into the pocket of her jeans and pulled out a bullet.

"What's that?" He frowned at her open palm.

"A thirty-aught-six."

"I know what it is. Why's it in your pocket?"

"Someone left it in my room Thursday."

He stared at her. "You're serious."

"Yes."

His face hardened as he looked at the bullet. She placed it on the dash, where it gleamed in the sunlight—except for the black tip.

"You dust it for prints?"

"None. Big surprise. Anyway, I know who left it. It's like you said, he hates law enforcement. He's playing games."

"*Games?*" He leaned closer. "Do you realize how dangerous he is?"

"If he'd wanted to hurt me, he could have. Instead, he's taunting me because he knows I've been asking about him."

"That's just—" He shook his head. "Why didn't you tell me?"

"I'm telling you now."

A flash of movement pulled their attention to a sleek black Jaguar turning into the driveway. A woman got out: slender brunette, black pants, black heels, black sunglasses. A shimmery white blouse balanced out all the dark.

Andrea slipped the bullet back into her pocket as she looked the woman over.

"You know if she's married?" she asked.

"Divorced."

"Looks like the mayor's gig pays pretty well." She glanced at Jon. "You want to do this together?"

"No." He shoved open the door. "This time, I do the talking."

They approached the woman as she strode toward her front door, clearly in a hurry.

"Ms. Pena?"

She halted on the front step and turned to look at them.

"I'm Special Agent Jon North." He flashed his ID. "This is Detective Finch. Are you Carmen Pena?"

"I can't talk right now," she said briskly. "I'm late for an appointment."

"This won't take long."

She shoved a small Chanel handbag under her arm. "What is this about?"

"Would you mind if we come inside for a moment?"

"Yes."

Andrea cut a glance at Jon, but he looked unfazed.

"I understand you used to work for Senator Richard Kirby's campaign," he said.

"I have no comment about Senator Kirby."

"Did you work for his campaign?"

"I said I have no comment."

Andrea folded her arms over her chest. "Ms. Pena, we hear you had a confrontation with a man outside Kirby's campaign headquarters about eighteen months ago."

She peeled off the sunglasses, and Andrea got hit with a blast of hostility. "What part of 'no comment' do you not understand, Detective?"

"Ma'am, we'd just like to ask you a few simple questions," Jon said.

"And I'd just like *you* to listen to a simple answer: No comment." She headed for the door.

"*Ma'am.*" Andrea used her cop voice, and she turned around. The curtain in one of the windows shifted, suggesting that someone was watching them from inside the house. A dog walker had stopped in front of the neighbors' place, ostensibly to admire the landscaping. "We just need a moment of your time."

"Do you have a warrant of some sort?"

"No."

"Then I suggest you step off my property. If you'd like to talk to me, discuss it with my attorney. He's at Biskell and Klein downtown."

She strode into the house and slammed the door.

Andrea looked at Jon. "And I thought I was a bitch."

He walked back to the car.

"So what now?" she asked his back.

He pulled open the door and rested his elbow on the window as he looked at her. "I've got to go home. Change. I have a five-hour drive ahead of me."

"You're leaving now?"

"I've only got seven days left, Andrea. I don't intend to waste them."

chapter thirteen

TORRES STRODE ACROSS THE parking lot, feeling more energized than he had in weeks. It was good to be home—only for
a few nights, yeah, but that was better than nothing. He'd missed
San Antonio. He'd missed the green. He'd missed the lights. He'd
missed the restaurants and bars and even the traffic. Most of all,
he'd missed the women.

He held the door for a young agent juggling an armload of
files. Saturday-night case work. The life of a rookie. Torres flashed
her a smile, but she didn't return it as she squeezed through the
exit and hustled toward her car.

Undaunted, he made his way upstairs to the desk he hadn't
seen in weeks. The bullpen was deserted tonight, except for a
few wrung-out agents talking on the phone. Torres booted up his
computer to check e-mail before thumbing through the paperwork crowding his in-box.

Across the room someone slammed down a phone receiver.
Torres glanced over his cube and spotted a blonde hunched over

her desk, squeezing the bridge of her nose as if she was fighting off a headache.

Elizabeth LeBlanc. She hadn't been around that long—just long enough to raise a few eyebrows.

No one could figure LeBlanc out. She was hot, but she didn't date. Guys asked her out—nothing, not even a drink after work. Some people thought she had a secret boyfriend in the Bureau, maybe someone married. Some people thought she had a secret girlfriend. But Torres didn't get that vibe.

He'd observed her on more than one occasion. He'd noticed the way she listened in meetings and took copious notes. He'd noticed her habit of arriving early and leaving late. If she was having a love affair, it was with her job.

She leaned back in her chair and rubbed her neck tiredly.

So much for paperwork.

"Long day?" he asked, sauntering over. It was a lame opener, but he was out of practice.

"Long week. Long, crappy week, if you want to know the truth." She frowned. "I thought you were in Maverick."

He rested an arm on the wall of her cubicle. "Headed back tomorrow."

"Any chance you guys might make an arrest soon? Put me out of my misery?"

"You're working on *our* case?"

"Evidently."

"How'd that happen?"

She sighed and glanced down at a stack of files on her desk. "The Del Rio bank robbery. Someone thinks it's connected to what you're doing."

"It is."

"You want to tell me how?"

Torres hesitated. He probably shouldn't share too much. But on the other hand, if she was working it—

"That's what I thought." She had an edge in her voice. "Slaving away all weekend still doesn't put me in the inner circle."

"Slaving?" He smiled down at her.

"Sorry. I'm throwing myself a pity party. I spent my day interviewing used-car dealers, trying to track down your getaway vehicle."

"Any luck?"

"No. I thought I had a lead, but"—she lifted her arms to tighten her ponytail, and Torres's heart stuttered—"it's not panning out. At least, not tonight."

He gazed down at her. Wisps of hair curled around her neck, and her eyes were pale blue, almost gray. She really *was* pretty.

She glanced at her watch and started stacking files.

The blue eyes looked up at him. "You want to have dinner?"

Torres stared at her. Holy shit, was she . . . ?

"O-*kay*, forget I asked. Didn't mean to put you on the spot."

"No. I mean—you're not. I was just thinking, it's pretty late, right? I'm not sure what's open."

She stood up and glanced at her watch again. "Well, it's only eleven. Luv's is open."

"Luv's?"

"The truck stop. On I-35?"

He tried to picture her dining at a truck stop and drew a complete blank.

"I drop in there sometimes after working late." She stuffed some files into a computer bag and hitched it onto her shoulder. "It's not bad, actually." She hesitated a beat. "You want to join me?"

Fifteen minutes later, he slid into a parking space between

Elizabeth's Honda and a pickup with oversize tires. The separate cars had been her idea, which didn't really bode well for his chances of taking her home. Didn't rule it out, though. Torres was an optimist.

They took a corner booth with a view of the whole restaurant, and a waitress stopped by right away to take their orders.

"Hot chocolate?" Elizabeth smiled at him.

"Why not?"

She shrugged. "I don't know. I figured you for beer, but I guess that goes to show how little I know about you, right?" She folded her hands in front of her. "Such as what's this case you're working on out in the middle of nowhere?"

That was it, then. She'd invited him here for scoop, not because she wanted to jump his bones. It was a setback but nothing major.

He debated how much to tell her. He was pretty sure he trusted her, but he wasn't used to talking about this case. At least, not with anyone besides North and their team.

"You know much about OKBOMB?" he asked.

"Just what they presented at the Academy, really. Why?"

"You probably know, right, that some people think there might have been others involved? Not just individuals but groups."

"The mysterious John Doe Number Two," she said. "I thought all those accounts were conflicting. Different physical descriptions."

"Could be," he said. "Or could be there was more than one John Doe Number Two. You heard of the Aryan Republican Army?"

"Vaguely."

The waitress dropped off their drinks, and Torres stirred his cocoa.

"In the nineties, they pulled off a string of bank robberies," he said. "They saw the crimes as both symbolic and practical: rip off a government-backed institution, and use the money to fund an insurgency. Kind of a double 'eff you' to the feds. Some people think they funneled some of the money to Tim McVeigh to subsidize his plot."

Her eyes widened, and she leaned forward on her elbows. "Are you telling me . . . what I think you're telling me? You think these robberies might be connected to what just happened in Philadelphia?"

He didn't answer.

"You think Shay Hardin is the connection?"

"We're looking into it. He has a documented history of making threats against the government, and Senator Kirby in particular."

She leaned back against the seat, clearly shocked, which was good news and bad. Good news because Maxwell evidently had managed to keep a lid on what their team was up to out in Maverick. But bad news because it demonstrated just how little credibility their boss had given this theory.

The Philly case involved more than two hundred agents, and yet only a few were working the Shay Hardin angle. Obviously, no one at the top took him seriously as a suspect. Maxwell had emphasized that fact just this morning by giving them a one-week deadline before he pulled the plug.

Elizabeth shook her head. "That's . . . wow. That's quite a theory."

"You don't buy it."

She gave him a level look. "I think it sounds complicated."

"So?"

Elizabeth played with her straw and seemed to choose her words carefully.

"It's been my experience that when one explanation for something is complicated, and one explanation is straightforward, the straightforward one is more likely true."

Torres didn't say anything. He'd walked through the same logic a few hundred times during the course of this investigation. North was convinced they were on the right track with this thing, while Torres often thought they were in the weeds. Not just the weeds, the freaking wilderness.

North looked at Shay Hardin and saw parallels with OK-BOMB. He saw a homegrown terrorist who was about to strike again, big.

Torres looked at the man and saw a possible suspect for the judge's murder and maybe the bank robberies. But the rest of it? The rest seemed fuzzy. Vague.

Like his commitment to his job lately. Torres sometimes had a hard time scrounging up the motivation to really tackle this case.

North felt something for this case that Torres could see but didn't really understand. He felt a passion about it, a determination that they were going to get the guy and bring him to justice. Not just any guy, but *this* guy, Shay Hardin, someone who had—literally—gotten away with murder years ago and needed to be held to account.

Their food arrived. Elizabeth picked up her club sandwich and looked at him. "I heard the bomb in Philadelphia was made with fertilizer, right?"

"Ammonium nitrate and racing fuel, which is highly flammable," Torres said. "They make it for cars, motorcycles, powerboats."

"Any evidence Hardin bought those materials?"

"Nope." He chomped into his burger.

"Any evidence he was in Philadelphia at the time of the crime?"

"Nope."

She sighed. "You guys are way out on a limb here."

"I know."

For a while, they ate in silence. Torres knew what she was telling him, underneath the tact. If they blew it with this thing, it could affect their careers permanently. North had a law degree to fall back on, but Torres didn't.

"Why are you so convinced?" She watched him closely.

"I don't know."

"Sure you do."

He sighed. "North has a gut instinct about the guy. He believes he got away with something, and now he's trying to do it again, on a much larger scale."

"What about your gut instinct?"

Torres looked at her, surprised she'd asked. The answer that popped into his mind didn't come from North but from his own legwork.

He stirred his cocoa. "You know Hardin made it into Ranger school? Washed out after the first week."

"I didn't know that."

"He'd been in Iraq for a few years leading up to that, managed to get pretty out of shape. He'd trained at Fort Benning, and they really kick your ass while you're there, but once you're overseas, it can get pretty calm. There's a lot of sitting around, lot of people lose their edge. That's what happened to him.

"So all his life, he had this dream he wanted to be a Ranger, be part of this elite group. Then he finally gets his shot, and he botches it." He looked at her. "You ever met one of those guys who's obsessed with black ops—the toys, the lingo, the secrecy? Thinks he's Jason Bourne or someone?"

"Had a few in my Academy class," she said drily.

"Same here. Thing I noticed, they're arrogant. Think they're smarter than everyone. They give off the attitude with anyone they ever meet. Shay Hardin's like that. I've turned the guy's life inside out looking for stuff, and that's what keeps coming up."

"So you do believe in this."

"I do," he said, surprising himself. Maverick was a pain in the ass, yes, but he didn't actually believe he'd been wasting his time there. They had some solid leads; they just had to develop them. And they had to do it quickly, because if they *were* right about it all, then they were dealing with a ticking clock.

"Okay, sold." She gave a crisp nod.

"Sold?"

"You're closer to the case than anybody. If you think there's something there, that's good enough for me." She smiled. "I'll quit complaining about wasting my weekend."

Torres didn't know what to say. She glanced at her watch, and he braced himself for an excuse.

"It's late," she said on cue. "I should get home." She pulled some money from her purse, but he caught her hand.

"I'll get it."

"No, let me," she insisted. "I invited you."

He eyed her curiously as she scooted out of the booth, beating a retreat for some reason.

"Thanks for sharing." She stood and smiled down at him. "I'll let you know what I find."

◆

It was nearly midnight when Carmen pulled into her driveway. She collected her purse and a few files off the front seat and remembered to check her mirror before getting out of the car.

The street looked empty. No detectives or FBI agents camped out on the curb.

She mounted the steps to her front porch, averting her eyes from the empty flowerpots on either side of her door. Her mother would be horrified. It was April, and she hadn't planted a thing. She hadn't even set foot in her backyard in more than a week.

Carmen let herself in and dumped her purse and files on the table. She glanced at the living room, where Bella was sprawled on the couch watching *South Park*.

"How'd it go?" Carmen kicked off the heels that had been torturing her for hours.

"Good." Bella sat up and rubbed her eyes. "He went right down."

"How'd he eat?"

"Pretty well." She stood and picked up the hoodie draped across the sofa arm. "He had about six ounces at dinner. Another four at ten o'clock. Then he was out again. We did a walk earlier, so I think the fresh air wore him out."

Carmen felt her shoulders loosening. She smiled. "Thanks for coming on short notice."

Bella picked up her keys. "No problem. See you tomorrow."

She saw Bella out and then went into the kitchen. The remains of a frozen pizza sat on a metal baking sheet tucked beneath plastic wrap. Carmen poured a glass of wine. She'd already had two tonight, but that was over the course of six long hours. She never really drank or ate at fund-raising dinners—just enough to appear social.

She picked up the merlot and savored a long sip. She went into the living room, switched off the TV, and padded barefoot into the bathroom, where she set her wine on the counter. Then she tiptoed to the end of the hall to peek in on Lukas.

He was on his tummy, fast asleep, with his satin blankie bunched up against his face. Carmen resettled him on his back. She spread the blanket over him and touched her hand to his downy hair. She stroked his cheek. Velvet soft. She'd had no idea what soft was until she touched her baby's skin for the first time.

Carmen leaned over the crib. She stared down at her son and felt the familiar swell of emotion in her chest. From the first day, she'd been astonished by the utter *love*. She'd once been in love with her ex-husband, but that paled in comparison with this. This love was intense and fearsome, and she'd had no idea how much it would change her life.

His little lips moved—just slightly—like he was sucking a bottle. She wanted to scoop him up and squeeze him and smell his hair, but he was sleeping soundly, and he might be up later anyway. Instead, she wound up the Winnie the Pooh on the rocking chair and listened to the first bars of music as she eased shut the door.

Her cell phone was chiming from her purse across the house. She checked the caller ID. Ryan again. She plugged the phone into the charger on the kitchen counter. Then back into the bathroom for another sip of wine. She hung her robe on the hook beside the claw-footed tub and turned the water to scalding. A splash of bubble bath. Then time for the rounds.

She peered through the peephole and surveyed her quiet street as she flipped the bolt. Then she turned off the lamps, locked the back door, and switched on the floodlights that illuminated her driveway.

She returned to the bathroom, unbuttoning the tiny pearl buttons on her blouse as she went. Sinking into the fragrant water, she immediately felt her muscles relax. Sunday, midnight, and she was just now getting a chance to unwind from the week. In just six hours, she'd be up to do it all over again.

She hated nights like these. She hated smiling and chitchatting and making witty conversation with wealthy strangers when all she really wanted to do was go home and play with Lukas. When was the last time she'd had a full, uninterrupted weekend with him?

Carmen sipped her wine and sank deeper into the lavender-scented foam. She rested her arms on the sides of the tub and tipped her head back.

Something smelled strange. An odor. She opened her eyes. *Gas.*

She stood up and grabbed her robe. Bubbles streamed down her arms and legs as she stepped onto the bath mat and wrapped herself in terrycloth. Had Bella forgotten the oven? She hurried down the hall and into the darkened kitchen. The oven was off. She glanced at the stove. A faint hissing noise—

Creak.

She whirled around. A shadow loomed in the corner.

Lukas.

She lunged for the hall, but the man grabbed her arm and slammed her against the doorframe. Hands clamped around her neck and hurled her to the floor. Pain seared her scalp as he yanked her head back by the hair.

She bucked and kicked. She threw elbows and flailed under him, but he was heavy and strong, and he had her pinned against the wooden planks.

Lukas.

She reached back, clawing for the man's face, his eyes. Soft flesh. A grunt of pain, and his weight shifted. She bucked him off and scrambled to her feet, but he caught her ankle. She crashed to the floor, hitting her chin.

Stars swam before her eyes. The weight smashed down on her. Hands closed around her neck from behind.

Oh God, oh God. What does he want?

She could roll over. She could let him rape her and bite her tongue and not make a sound and pray Lukas would stay fast asleep.

Gas.

Panic set in as the odor filled her nose. She had to get down the hall to Lukas. She had to get him out. She bucked again, clawed at the floor.

The grip on her neck tightened. Her chin was pressed against the wood. The coppery taste of blood filled her mouth. She tried to scream, but she couldn't move her head, her mouth, and the only sound was a muffled wail.

The hand tightened again. One hand. Where was the other? His weight shifted, and her heart pounded wildly as she struggled to turn her head to see what he was doing.

A dark arm arced up. A flash of metal.

A raw sound tore from her throat, but it was too late.

chapter fourteen

ANDREA WOKE UP WIRED. She lay in bed, staring at the ceiling and trying to pinpoint the reason for her mood. She rolled onto her stomach, pulled the pillow over her head, and squeezed her eyes shut. Maybe she could sleep it off.

Yeah, right.

Nick Mays flashed into her mind for the first time in a week. She thought of that lopsided smile he'd used when he'd been trying to get her to sleep with him. It was a nice memory, but her brain quickly jumped to the more recent memory of Nick standing in the sleet outside the restaurant that night. She remembered his look of bewildered pity as he'd watched from across the parking lot while she gave the first of countless statements.

Remembering made her stomach hurt. Andrea despised pity, always had. And in spite of the concerned messages he'd left on her voice mail, she had no intention of ever calling him again, much less sleeping with him.

She flipped onto her back and gazed up at her ceiling. She

thought of Jon North. She thought of him in his dark suit and silk tie, with his badge clipped to his belt. She thought of him at his house in Maverick, all sweaty and grimy, with the two-day beard. She remembered him pitching his boots across the room and glaring at her. She liked that version of him. That Jon North could probably get her off. The suit-and-tie version tended to get on her nerves.

She closed her eyes and sighed. She needed to get a life.

There was always running. A good ten miles would probably do the trick, would leave her feeling energized and in control. Mostly. At the very least, it would put some of this humming energy to good use. She glanced at the clock on her nightstand. Unfortunately, she didn't have time for a run or anything else this morning.

She dragged herself out of bed and took a lukewarm shower. She pulled a brush through her hair and decided to leave it down instead of pulling it into a ponytail. She was, after all, on leave. Her gaze went to her badge sitting on the dresser. It was starting to collect dust.

Tears burned her eyes. She'd been a good cop. It had surprised her how quickly she'd taken to it. After the hell of the police academy ended, she'd sailed right into her job with so much energy and enthusiasm. It had felt like a perfect fit.

She'd liked the work. She'd liked the other cops. She'd even liked the ribbing. Criticism was the lifeblood of a squad, and she'd never taken it personally. It had given her a sense of belonging.

More than anything, she'd liked showing up on a call and taking charge of a situation. It was something she still liked, even as a detective. When she arrived at a scene, her presence gave people reassurance. Hope. They trusted her to help them, and she took that trust seriously. It made her who she was. It mattered. Her job *mattered*, and the pang of missing it was overshadowed only by the excruciating prospect of never getting it back again.

Andrea grabbed her leather jacket. She tucked the Kimber into the holster at her back and headed out the door.

It was a crisp blue day, and she left the windows down as she drove across the bridge to North Lamar Street. The restaurant parking lot was busy, and she had to circle the block twice to find a space.

City Diner was an Austin landmark. Open around the clock, it attracted the postparty crowd when the bars closed on Sixth Street. After sunrise, it was a magnet for foodies and health nuts. Sunday was definitely for the fitness patrons, many in biker shorts and yellow spandex shirts. There were runners, too, and even a few tennis players. Andrea preferred the runners, because most had the courtesy to change out of sodden T-shirts before crowding into the place for a meal.

She stepped into the restaurant and immediately spotted Alex at the bar. There was an empty stool beside her. Andrea squeezed through the throng of people and claimed the seat.

"Nathan's sorry he can't make it," Alex said. "He got a call-out."

She felt a twinge of jealousy, even though she typically dreaded getting called out of bed on a Sunday morning.

"You order yet?" Andrea asked.

"Just sat down."

Andrea scanned the menu. The restaurant's name was really a misnomer. Yes, it was a diner in that it served meat loaf, sandwiches, and mac-'n'-cheese. But given their location directly across from the Whole Foods headquarters, they put a gourmet spin on everything. The grilled cheese sandwich was stacked with Gruyère. The deviled eggs came with a side of organic, locally grown arugula. The waffles were made with Madagascar vanilla and served with Grade A Vermont syrup, which wasn't nearly as tasty as the Log Cabin that Dee always plunked on the breakfast table.

"You look stressed," Alex said.

She glanced up. "Just tired."

"Rough night?"

"Rough month."

The waitress stopped by, and although the mimosas sounded tempting, Andrea ordered coffee. Alex asked for a virgin Bloody Mary.

Andrea narrowed her gaze. "Are you pregnant?"

"What? No!"

She searched her face for any sign that she was lying. She didn't see anything but decided to ask Nathan. If he broke into a dopey grin, she'd know the truth.

"Nathan's really sorry he couldn't make it," Alex said, deftly changing the subject. "He wanted a chance to talk to you. You know, he's worried about you."

Andrea looked at the TV above the bar. "I'm fine."

"Really?"

She forced herself to make eye contact. "Really." She cleared her throat. "So any word yet? On that stuff Ben was checking for me?"

"Still working on it."

"Has he come up with anything?"

"You never know with Ben." She rolled her eyes. "He's very mysterious. Doesn't like to be pestered for updates while he's researching."

"I'll keep that in mind." She glanced at the TV again, where a local newscaster was standing in a street beside a red Suburban. It was the pushy blonde who had staked out Andrea's apartment for two days, hoping to get an interview about the shooting. Holly Something-or-Other.

"I'm concerned about you, too."

Her gaze snapped to Alex. "Don't be."

"You know, I was with Nathan when he went through this. I know it's tough."

Her attention drifted to the TV again, and she noticed the headline crawling along the bottom of the screen: GAS EXPLOSION 2200 BLOCK OF CHERRY KNOLL. CAUSE STILL UNDER INVESTIGATION.

Her stomach dropped.

"Andrea?"

"Nathan—you said he's on a call. Was it a gas explosion?"

Alex darted a confused glance at the television. "I think it was a house fire. Why?"

"So there were fatalities?"

"I don't know."

Andrea looked at the TV. The camera panned to the charred remains of a house. Beside the burned structure was a shiny black Jaguar.

She jumped up from her stool.

"Andrea, what is it?"

"Sorry." She snatched up her purse. "I have to go."

✦

The street had been blocked off with barricades. Andrea cut between them and skirted the black-and-white parked in the exact spot where Jon had been yesterday. She ignored the curious look from a patrol officer she vaguely recognized and found Nathan in the driveway with the fire chief. He frowned when he spotted her.

Andrea surveyed the property. A white crime-scene van was parked directly in front of the house—or what was left of it. The entire front of the structure was a blackened pile of debris. What remained of the back of the home was a smoldering mess.

Nathan got free from the fire chief and made a beeline toward her.

"Is Alex okay?"

Intense concern. Andrea would bet money that girl was pregnant.

"She's fine," she told him. "I need to talk to you."

He darted a look over her shoulder, and his frown deepened. Andrea turned to see a second news van pulling up to the barricade. The local media had obviously discovered there was more to this incident than they'd first reported.

"Here we go," Nathan muttered. He took Andrea's arm and steered her farther up the driveway, where the red Suburban would shield them from view.

Andrea caught a glimpse of the backyard. A blue plastic swing dangled from a tree limb.

Jesus God.

"Why are you here, Andrea?"

She looked at Nathan. She swallowed the bile in the back of her throat. "What happened here?"

He gave her a long, hard look. Maybe he figured she was missing the job, wanted to put her skills to use. "Gas explosion, just after midnight. Victim's thought to be Carmen Pena, but that hasn't been confirmed. Her child was there, too. The neighbor's a trauma surgeon. He rushed into the house and rescued the kid, got third-degree burns all over his arms and feet. Child's in ICU."

Andrea felt dizzy. She fought the urge to bend over and throw up.

"Why's homicide here?" she managed.

"The fire chief has questions," he said. "His guys were here all night, working the scene. He doesn't like this for an accident."

Andrea looked at the house. The bedroom wing had been less affected than the kitchen, and it was still possible to discern a bathroom with the sink standing upright amid the singed walls. "Where's the point of origin?" she asked.

"In the kitchen, near the gas stove." He glanced at the debris.

"So someone tampered with it?"

"Probably." He looked at her, and she knew she was missing something. "One of the fire investigators found shards of metal and pieces of a timing device. Looks like possibly a pipe bomb, but that's totally unconfirmed."

"Show me."

Nathan watched her, clearly debating with himself. He led her to a white crime-scene van with its back doors standing open.

"Hey, you got that pipe debris?" he asked one of the CSIs.

The guy glanced at Andrea, then reached into the van and pulled out a flat metal box with a see-through lid. It looked like an airtight container, the preferred method of transporting fire-scene evidence in order to keep accelerants from evaporating.

"Don't shuffle anything around," the guy told Nathan, then ducked between them and returned to what was left of the house.

The box was divided into numbered sections containing mangled pieces of what had once been a metal pipe. Other sections contained misshapen bolts and ball bearings, some coated with blood.

She glanced at Nathan. "Mind if I take a picture?"

He gave her a stony look. Then he unlatched the lid and turned the box to face her so she could snap a few shots with her phone camera. When she finished, he returned the box to its place, slammed the van doors shut, and stepped onto the water-saturated lawn.

"Where's the victim?" Andrea asked.

"Medical examiner's office. I called over there this morning. He said he's going to have to bring in a forensic anthropologist to get a positive ID."

Her gaze went to the swing again.

"Want to tell me why the sudden interest in my case?"

She looked at Nathan. And then she looked behind him, where a CSI in a white Tyvek suit was crouched beside the Jaguar, dusting the door for prints. All the windows were shattered, and shards of glass surrounded the car like ice chips.

"Andie?"

"I'll explain, but . . . I have to make a call first." She desperately needed to talk to Jon.

Another news van pulled up. A familiar reporter jumped out and immediately homed in on her.

"You shouldn't be here," Nathan said, eyeing the growing huddle of reporters.

Andrea squeezed his arm. "Don't worry, I'm gone."

chapter fifteen

DAVID WOODS WAS A BUST.

Elizabeth and another agent spent the better part of Sunday staked out in front of the man's apartment, simply trying to get a look at him. She'd enlarged the surveillance photos showing their un-ID'd bank robber in order to make a comparison. But they'd had nothing to compare.

After four hours without a hint of movement in the apartment, she'd tracked down the building manager, who'd let her know the tenant had disappeared two weeks ago in the middle of the night. One day the landlord was pounding on the door looking for rent money, next day the apartment was empty. Elizabeth insisted on seeing the place, in case he might have left behind a clue, but the only evidence of Woods was a fist-sized hole in the wall beside the bathroom door.

Elizabeth dragged herself into the office and tossed her keys onto her desk. This case was exasperating. So far, every lead she'd painstakingly uncovered had turned into a dead end.

She opened her e-mail and watched a torrent of messages fill the in-box. One was from a lab tech at Quantico. Subject line: "Letter Analysis."

According to the message, the letter from the bank robbery had yielded no fingerprints or DNA. Big shocker. The paper was twenty-pound multipurpose stock, common at any office-supply store. The ink was from an HP printer, nothing unusual. But the technician did want to discuss "one more observation."

Elizabeth stared at the message, irritated. Why hadn't he simply told her the observation right there in the e-mail? He'd provided his cell-phone number beneath his name.

Elizabeth recalled the technician. She'd met him briefly while touring the Questioned Documents section of the FBI Laboratory with her Academy class. The man had given their group a presentation on check forgery.

She glanced at her watch. Three o'clock on a Sunday. She pictured the guy at home with his feet up, watching a game and knocking back a few beers. You'd have to be pretty pathetic to willingly spend your entire weekend toiling away at work.

He picked up on the first ring.

"This is Elizabeth LeBlanc. I just read your message here about the letter I sent in?"

"A very *interesting* letter, I must say." His voice had a slight lisp, and she remembered wire-rimmed glasses and an underbite.

"Interesting how?" she asked.

"Interesting in that I wasn't able to glean very much from it at all."

"Is that unusual?"

"Usually, I find something. A watermark, a copy mark, a partial print. So I was very happy to find the indented writing. At least gives you a clue to work with, albeit a small one."

"Indented writing?"

"On the letter. You didn't notice it? Lower left corner. I attached a PDF for you with the e-mail."

She leaned forward and clicked open the file. He'd scanned in a copy of the letter that was all marked up. A red arrow pointed to the lower left corner, where some faint gray numbers were scrawled.

"How did I not notice that?" she asked, perplexed. She'd examined the thing with a magnifying glass before the CSI sealed it in an evidence bag.

"It's almost invisible to the naked eye," he said. "The writing's indented into the surface, as the term implies."

"You mean like when you write on top of something?"

"Exactly. I noticed the markings while examining it with oblique light and was able to visualize the numbers using an ESDA."

Elizabeth had no idea what that stood for—something she'd studied at the Academy, no doubt. She probably would have retained more information if she hadn't been dinged up and sleep-deprived throughout most of her training.

"It looks to me like a three-digit number: five-two-oh," she said. "Any idea what that is?"

"Could be a lot of things, depending on whether the last character is a letter O or a zero. Maybe part of a license plate, a serial number, a check number. If I had to guess? It's a phone number. You're probably aware the prefix five-two-oh is used in San Antonio."

"I was just thinking that," she said, doing some mental math. "So if it *is* a San Antonio number, that means it's seven digits and—"

"Ten to the fourth," he said cheerfully. "That's ten thousand possible combinations. In other words, ten thousand phone numbers for you to investigate."

"Great." Her head was already throbbing. "I can hardly wait."

◆

Someone pounded on the door, and Jon glanced up.

"Who the hell's that?" Torres asked.

Jon was pretty sure he knew. He crossed the trailer and opened the door.

"Where have you been?" Andrea stepped past him into the room. "I left three messages."

Jon stared down at her. Twenty-four hours ago, she'd looked rested and energized and ready to tackle the world. Now she looked . . . different.

Her gaze skimmed over the boxes blanketing the floor and came to rest on the coil of extension cord in his hand. "What are you doing?" She glanced up at him.

"Packing up."

"*What?*"

"We're shut down."

"Since when?" She shot a look to Torres, then back to Jon. "I thought you got more time. I thought—"

"Guess you haven't seen the news lately."

"What news?"

Jon looked at her for a long moment, trying to read the strange expression on her face.

He stepped over to the plywood table and tapped the keyboard of one of the laptop computers. The screen came to life. He navigated to CNN and clicked open the video clip he'd watched less than an hour ago. It showed footage of a bearded man in a turban flanked by FBI agents. The man wore a Kevlar vest over his gray robes, and his hands were cuffed in front of him.

"Who's that?" Andrea asked.

"Muhammad Samhat. This is his perp walk. They've been running it all morning."

A headline scrolled beneath the footage: SENIOR CLERIC, TWO OTHERS ARRESTED IN FBI RAID.

Andrea's gaze snapped to his. "So that's it? Case closed?"

Jon didn't say anything.

"We're due back in San Antonio tomorrow," Torres told her.

"But . . ." She looked at Jon. "But what about your theory? Your evidence? What about Shay Hardin?"

A week ago, she would have been elated to find out his theory had been discredited. Now she looked outraged.

"The DNA results came in," he told her. "The remains of Khalil Abbas, a leader at a Philadelphia mosque, were at the scene of the truck bombing. Philadelphia guys executed search warrants on three different homes this morning, all high-level members of the same mosque. Word is they found guns, computers, anti-U.S. propaganda. Looks like a terrorist cell."

"So you're saying you were wrong?"

"Looks that way." Jon tossed the extension cord into a box brimming with equipment.

"Carmen Pena is dead."

He looked at her. It took him a full three seconds to process the words. "She's—"

"She was killed in an explosion last night at her home," she said. "There was a gas leak involved, and investigators also found evidence of a pipe bomb."

"The house on Cherry Knoll," Jon stated.

"The one where we just were, yes." Andrea stepped closer. "And she wasn't the only victim. Her ten-month-old child is in intensive care."

Jon stared at her. There was a sudden absence of air, like when he'd fallen out of a tree as a kid and landed flat on his back.

She gripped his arm, and her eyes looked anguished. "Do you understand what I'm telling you?"

"*I* don't." This from Torres. "Who's Carmen Pena?"

"One of Kirby's staffers," Jon said numbly. "We went to visit her yesterday."

"Not just any staffer," Andrea added. "I think that rumor was true. I think she was having an affair with him."

"Whoa, whoa, whoa. Hold up." Torres stepped over a file box and stared down at Andrea, hands on hips. "You're saying Kirby's *mistress* is dead?"

"I'm saying the *mother of his child* is dead. They were over, but I think he was paying her hush money." She looked at Jon. "Think about it. The Jag, the house, the designer clothes. The detective on the case tells me she was making forty grand a year working for the mayor's office."

"I thought she was divorced."

"She was," Andrea said. "As of three *years* ago."

Jon felt as if a cold fist was gripping his stomach. Andrea met his gaze, and he now understood the look in her eyes.

"I think you were right," she said. "The senator *is* the target. And Shay Hardin is terrorizing him by going after his children. Even the ones no one knows about."

The room went silent, and the words seemed to hover. Torres muttered something in Spanish.

Jon stepped away. He raked a hand through his hair.

"Where *is* Hardin?" Andrea asked. "Anyone seen him the last twenty-four hours?"

"His truck is at the ranch," Jon said.

"That's according to the latest flyover," Torres added. "But he could have left the property in a different vehicle, maybe someone else driving."

"I thought you had the place under surveillance."

"It's ninety acres, with six people and five vehicles," Torres said defensively.

"When was the last time you talked to Gavin?" Jon asked Andrea.

She tensed, but he could tell she'd expected the question. "We exchanged e-mails last night."

"And?"

"And he said he's fine, same as last time I bugged him. He wants me to get off his case about going back to school."

"I saw the kid this morning," Torres told her.

"Where?"

"Tailed him from the ranch to the grocery store in town. He bought a few things, picked up some burgers, went right back. He was in his little blue car."

Jon stepped away from them. He turned to the map on the wall, tuning them out as different scenarios raced through his mind. "You have this relationship confirmed?" He turned to Andrea. "About Carmen Pena and the senator?"

"Not yet, but I will soon."

"How?"

"I've got two tickets to Phoenix," she said.

"What's in Phoenix?" Torres asked.

"Senator Kirby."

◆

Andrea could count on one hand the number of times she'd been in an airplane, but Jon was obviously a frequent flyer. A frequent *armed* flyer—he whisked them and their weapons through security in no time. They made a brief hop over New Mexico, and shortly after landing at Sky Harbor, he had them in a rental sedan, with their destination programmed into the navigation system.

"Black Hawk Resort and Spa, eleven miles," Andrea said. She glanced around, trying to gauge the traffic. "Think we'll make it in ten minutes?"

"Doubtful," he said, cutting into the left lane. "You made an appointment?"

"Six o'clock."

"I'm surprised he agreed to see us on such short notice."

She didn't say anything.

"He agreed to see us, right?"

"Pretty much."

He cut a glance at her. "What's that mean?"

"I might have been a little vague. He agreed to see *you*. And FYI, you're part of the task force investigating the university bombing."

"Perfect."

"What? You're on a task force, aren't you? And your investigation is possibly linked to the university attack."

"The real task force is working out of Philadelphia. And I'm sure whoever they've got covering the senator has never heard of me."

"So we'll wing it. I do it all the time."

Jon navigated the Red Mountain Freeway. Out her window, Andrea saw a steady flow of tile rooftops in varying shades of brown and gray. The sun was sinking low over the mountains to the west.

"I take it you've never met Senator Kirby?" Jon said as they neared their destination.

"No. Have you?"

"Yes."

She looked at him expectantly. The word had sounded weighted with meaning, but he didn't explain.

"You know he got a bounce from this," Jon said.

"From his daughter's death?"

"His approval numbers are way up. Sympathy effect."

Jon turned right at a rock waterfall, and the transmission shifted into lower gear as they made their way up a hill. The driveway wended past a rolling green golf course dotted with palo verdes. Palm trees and saguaros lined the road. Behind all the green loomed a craggy red canyon. Water, no water. She suspected the golf course's designers had been going for dramatic contrast, but to Andrea, it seemed jarring—just a glaring reminder that the entire place was man-made. An amusement park for the rich.

The sprawling adobe hotel was situated at the top of a bluff overlooking the golf course. More waterfalls, more saguaros. Jon bypassed the valet and pulled into an empty space beside a line of golf carts.

"She's meeting us in the lobby," Andrea said as they got out.

"She?"

"His scheduler. Her name's Kirsten."

Pointy green agaves lined the path. Hot-pink bougainvillea dripped over the adobe walls. Andrea and Jon entered an airy lobby with a giant adobe fireplace in the center. A flame flickered over fake logs.

Andrea skimmed the clusters of chairs and sofas. She saw plenty of sun-bronzed, silver-haired men lounging with drinks and cigars, fresh off the eighteenth hole. The women were equally sun-kissed. They perched on chairs and ottomans throughout the lobby, like spindly-legged tropical birds in their colorful visors and tennis skirts.

Andrea and Jon stood out. He was in a charcoal-gray suit with the same blue tie he'd worn yesterday. And she was in her go-to detective's uniform of black slacks and a blazer. Ignoring the curious glances, Andrea scanned the faces, looking for a twentysomething woman who might be named Kirsten.

No one even remotely fit the bill, so Andrea made a phone call.

Ten minutes later, a youngish man in an olive business suit stepped off the elevator and strode toward them. A gatekeeper. Andrea pegged him instantly by his brisk demeanor and the pseudo-concerned frown on his face.

"Sorry to keep you waiting. Agents North and Finch, is it?" He offered Andrea a limp handshake.

"Detective Finch," she corrected. "And this is Special Agent Jon North. We're here to see Senator Kirby."

A pained look. "I'm afraid that's quite impossible tonight. The senator is in a meeting."

"We have an appointment at six."

"I'm sorry." He clearly wasn't. "I wasn't informed of the appointment, and it isn't going to be possible to work you in tonight."

"I didn't catch your name."

He looked at Jon, who stood with his hands tucked casually in his pockets. "Ted Holloran." He cleared his throat. "I'm the senator's personal assistant. As such, I can tell you that his schedule is *completely* booked. I'm not sure who you talked to—"

"Kirsten," Andrea said.

"I see. Well, I'm afraid she wasn't informed of the senator's time frame this evening. Excuse me." He held up an index finger and pressed a cell phone to his ear. "Yes? No, it's at eight. Okay, call you back." He slipped the phone into his pocket and continued without missing a beat. "Despite what Kirsten may have communicated, it's simply not possible for me to squeeze you in—"

"Try."

Andrea glanced at Jon. His razor-sharp tone brokered no argument. She could feel the gatekeeper tensing up beside her.

"Well." He took out his phone again. "The best I can do is check tomorrow's schedule."

A blond woman glided up to them and squeezed the man's arm. "Twenty minutes, Teddy." Her voice was laced with anxiety, and he waved her off with a shooing motion as he scrolled through his calendar.

"I have a three forty-five." He looked up at Jon. "You can do fifteen minutes."

Andrea plucked the phone from his hand and dropped it into her pocket.

He went bug-eyed. "That's my *phone!*"

"Listen up, Teddy, because we seem to be having a failure to communicate," she said. "We are here to see the senator. Now. Not later. Not tomorrow. Now. And we're going to need more than fifteen minutes."

"But—"

"You may be aware that the senator's daughter was killed in an attack recently. Are you aware of that, Teddy?"

He continued to look apoplectic. His mouth opened, but no actual words came out.

"We are here to talk to the senator about the investigation into his daughter's death." She spoke slowly, enunciating each word. "I am not asking you this, I am telling you. Now, either you get the senator out of his meeting to talk to us, or we will locate him and get him ourselves. Do you understand?"

His gaze dropped to the bulge in her pocket, and his cheeks reddened. He looked at Jon, who lifted an eyebrow lazily. "Fine." He straightened his shoulders. "I'll see what I can do."

"Thank you." Andrea handed back the phone. "We sure appreciate it."

chapter sixteen

THE SENATOR WAS BOOKED in the Presidential Suite overlooking the golf course. Jon and Andrea waited for him in a spacious sitting room decorated with bronze cowboy statues and Navajo rugs. Teddy had handed them off to Kirsten and promptly disappeared—probably to go vent his indignation to his fellow staffers.

Jon leaned his shoulder against the wall and watched Andrea. She looked nervous, but he didn't think it was because she'd bullied her way in under false pretenses and was about to interview a sitting U.S. senator. This place reeked of privilege, and he could tell it made her uncomfortable.

She continued to surprise him, and he wasn't easily surprised by people. She was a mix of contradictions—brusque and sensitive, determined and hesitant, alluring and prickly—all at the same time.

He felt drawn to her, even though he knew he should keep his distance. He should have left her in Maverick, but he'd been strangely excited by the prospect of spending more time with her, so he'd given into impulse and let her come.

He'd probably regret it later, but for now, he was enjoying her company. Not to mention her unorthodox investigation methods.

"You notice the weapon on that guard?" She nodded at the doorway.

"An FN Five-seveN," he said. "Standard-issue sidearm for Secret Service agents."

"They're a step above rent-a-cops, I'd say. Guy told me he's with Wolfe Security. You heard of it?"

"Private firm from Texas, right?"

"I've run across them before," she said. "They've got a good reputation."

A commotion in the next room, followed by a frantic exchange in hushed tones, signaled the arrival of Someone Important. A moment later, Kirsten was back, clutching a leather folio to her chest.

"The senator will see you now."

Jon pushed away from the wall. Andrea clasped her hands behind her back. But the man who entered the suite didn't look senatorial. He had a shaved head, a thick neck, and a clear plastic radio receiver clipped to his ear. His gaze promptly zeroed in on Jon.

Jon knew the drill. He lifted his arms and allowed the guy to frisk him. Andrea did the same. He came up with nothing, because they'd surrendered their weapons to the man stationed at the door to the suite. Jon didn't like being separated from his gun, but since they hadn't gone through any formal screening process to get this meeting, he figured it was fair.

The guard gave them a brief assessing look before going to the door and giving a nod.

The blonde from the lobby was back, followed by Richard Kirby.

The junior senator from Texas carried himself like a cattleman—broad shoulders, straight posture, a hefty gut that spilled over his belt buckle. He wore suits most of the time but loved to be photographed at his ranch in jeans and his favorite Lucchese cowboy boots.

At the moment, he wore golf shoes, khakis, and a sky-blue polo. A white golf glove hung from his back pocket.

"North, is it?" He cast a look in Jon's direction as he walked straight to the bar.

"Special Agent Jon North, San Antonio field office." Jon didn't offer a hand, as the senator was tied up making a drink.

Kirby got out a highball glass, dropped in a few ice cubes, and filled it halfway with vodka. "And you are?" He nodded at Andrea.

"Detective Andrea Finch, sir. Austin PD."

He took a jar of onions from the fridge. "You like a drink, Detective?"

"No, thank you."

"Agent?"

"Not for me, thanks."

A splash of vermouth. Four pearl onions on a toothpick. He took a gulp and plunked the glass on the granite counter.

Then he eyed Jon with the stern look he was known for.

"The task force is out of Philadelphia."

"That's correct."

"You're not on it."

"That's correct."

"Mr. Spillman called to check." He nodded at the bodyguard, who now stood beside the doorway like a sentry. "That's why I'm paying the big bucks, right, Spillman? So someone can pick up the goddamn telephone."

Spillman gave an almost imperceptible nod, and Jon looked

him over. He had a relaxed but superalert look that Jon had seen before. The two other guys he'd seen with that expression were both former SEALs.

The senator stayed behind the bar, staring him down as if they were having a contest. "So you're out of San Antone. And you're not on the task force." He jerked a head in Andrea's direction. "She's not even a fed. Why are you here?"

"We have some news," Jon said. "Carmen Pena was killed early this morning in a gas explosion."

Kirby didn't blink. He just stared at Jon. Then his gaze shifted to Spillman. "Close the door."

Spillman closed the door—with himself inside the room—and took on the there-but-not-really-there look of a professional bodyguard.

"I heard about Carmen." The senator's voice had softened.

"Her son was badly injured, too. Lukas Pena." Jon paused. "He's in ICU."

Kirby looked him directly in the eye for a drawn-out moment. Jon saw a sheen of tears as he picked up his drink and took a swill.

"Sir, we need to ask you," Andrea said, stepping closer. "Are you aware of who Ms. Pena listed on her son's birth certificate as the baby's father?"

It was a bold move, Jon thought. But it was artful, too—asking the question without really asking it. If he knew anything at all about Lukas Pena's birth certificate, that told them what they wanted to know.

Kirby knew this, which was why he was eyeing Andrea sharply. He looked at Jon. "It's blank." Another swill of vodka.

No one spoke for several seconds.

"Sir, have you made the agents investigating your daughter's death aware of this situation?" Andrea asked.

"What situation is that?" His tone had an edge now as he emptied his glass.

Andrea darted a look at Jon.

"That baby's not mine. Far as anyone knows, he's got no daddy, just like it says on the birth certificate."

"You can't be—"

"Lukas Pena's parentage is critical to the investigation," Jon said, cutting her off. "The lead investigator needs to know about it."

"About what?" He came around the bar now, a slight swagger in his step, and Jon realized they'd played this wrong. He'd shifted from barely cooperative to defiant.

"Sir, the situation is obvious to anyone who looks," Andrea said bluntly. "There have been four deposits of fifty thousand dollars made to Ms. Pena's bank account over the last year. From some of your biggest campaign contributors."

"That's her business."

Jon looked at Andrea. This wasn't going anywhere. "Senator, we've been investigating a man in West Texas by the name of Shay Hardin."

He frowned at Jon. "Never heard of him."

"We think he's heard of you. We think he's particularly familiar with your stance on gun control."

Kirby muttered a curse. He refilled his drink, not bothering with vermouth this time, and crossed the room to sink into an armchair. "You're telling me some gun kook's responsible for Julia?"

"We're investigating that. We're also investigating the possibility that he may be responsible for the explosion that killed Carmen Pena." Jon paused to see if he was following, now that he'd knocked back about five shots of vodka.

Kirby gazed past Andrea, at the giant window facing out over the golf course and the desert beyond. His look turned wistful.

Andrea approached him, pulling his attention back to the conversation. She handed him a stack of photographs of Shay Hardin. They were good shots, all taken in Maverick over the past week. She'd shown them to Jon on the plane and didn't seem particularly concerned when he shared his opinion of her going around photographing a suspected murderer.

She didn't seem particularly concerned by his opinion on anything she did.

Jon watched the senator flip through Andrea's shots.

"Never seen him." He passed them back.

"Are you sure? Not at a stump speech? A campaign rally?"

"I've got a memory for faces." He gave a wry smile. "Comes in handy."

Jon was getting pissed off. "Shay Hardin has a history with antigovernment groups," he said pointedly. "A few of his friends are affiliated with the state's most outspoken militia and white-supremacy orgs."

"Is this supposed to scare me?"

"Senator, you need to be candid with investigators about your relationship to Carmen Pena."

"What relationship?" His gaze narrowed. "If one word about that baby leaks to the media, I will have your job, Agent. And yours, too."

Jon shot Andrea a look. Then he looked at the senator, whose cheeks were flushed now from both emotion and alcohol. They were on the brink of losing what little cooperation they'd had just a few minutes ago.

"Senator," Jon said levelly, "most of the investigation is focused on Islamic radicals on the East Coast. *If* it turns out that Shay Hardin is behind these crimes, then we have a potentially bigger problem. April nineteenth is only five days away."

Kirby scowled. "What's that got to do with anything?"

"It's the anniversary of Waco, the Oklahoma City bombing, and the opening battle of the American Revolution—the 'shot heard round the world.' April nineteenth is of critical importance to the antigovernment movement."

"So?"

"So it could be Hardin and whoever's working with him are planning something more in just a few days. Until we know for sure who is behind these attacks, you should cancel all your public appearances."

A chilling smile spread across his face. "You think I should just what? Go home? Pull the covers over my head?"

"Sir." Andrea crossed her arms. "With all due respect, you don't seem to be taking this seriously."

He jabbed a finger at her, and the ice cubes in his glass rattled. "I buried my daughter on Saturday, Detective. Don't tell me I don't take this seriously." The last word came out choked, and he bent forward. He tucked his head down, and his shoulders shook.

Jon glanced at Andrea. She seemed taken aback. He nodded at her, and she gave him a *Who, me?* look.

Jon nodded again. Yes, it was sexist, but she needed to do something. Comfort the man. Something.

Andrea stepped closer and lowered herself into a crouch beside the chair. "Listen, Senator Kirby." Her voice was softer.

"Julia was everything." His words sounded strangled. "*Everything.*"

"Sir, investigators need information that only *you* have to find out who is hurting your loved ones."

His head snapped up, and his eyes were pink and watery. "I know how this works. You think I don't know? Leak on top of leak on top of leak. It would ruin me."

Andrea glanced at Jon.

The senator bowed his head again.

"If you don't help the investigation," Jon said, "*you* could end up dead."

Kirby rubbed his forehead with his hand. He looked up again and smiled through the tears. "I lose the election, I'm dead anyway." He stood up and walked back to the bar as Andrea gaped at him.

She rose to her feet. "What about your wife?"

Jon heard the derision in her voice.

"What about her?" Kirby poured another drink.

"Do you mind if I ask where she is? What sort of security you have in place?"

"She's home in Dallas." He nodded at Spillman, who'd been standing like a statue for the entire conversation. "I've got another team of these guys with her."

"Around the clock?" Jon asked, and the senator nodded.

His shoulders were slumped now, and he didn't look senatorial anymore. He looked haggard.

"And exactly when did you hire this team?"

Kirby sighed heavily and looked away.

"Senator?" Jon persisted, knowing he was about to get his question answered and that their trip out here had not been a waste. Had he hired them before or after he found out about Carmen?

Kirby looked him in the eye. "This morning." He took another gulp and set the glass down with a *clink*. "I hired them this morning."

◆

Jon spent half an hour on his phone in the parking lot while Andrea waited in the front seat, getting angrier by the minute as she watched him in a heated conversation with someone. Finally, he slid behind the wheel.

"Okay, no more crap." He turned to face her.

"What the hell's that mean?"

"Call your brother. Now. Come up with a ruse—an emergency, a death in the family, whatever you want—but we need him interviewed ASAP."

"Don't you mean 'interrogated'?"

"Andrea"—his jaw tensed—"I'm done fooling around." He pushed his phone at her, but she waved it off.

"Even if I wanted to, I can't call him," she said. "He doesn't have a phone."

"Bullshit."

"Are you calling me a liar?"

"How can he not have a phone?"

"Because he doesn't have one. I checked. They shut off his account when he didn't pay his bill."

He muttered something and shook his head, then put the car into gear and shot backward out of the space. He gave her a hot look as he zipped past a row of golf carts and turned out of the parking lot. "You really want to get pulled into this as a material witness? Is that what you want?" He sped down the private drive leading back to the highway. "Philadelphia's sending a team down. They're going to want to talk to you. I can guarantee you that."

"That's good, right?" she asked, refusing to be intimidated. She didn't give a damn if they called her in. She hadn't witnessed anything, and she didn't believe Gavin had, either.

"How many are they sending?"

He didn't respond.

"Jon?"

"Two."

"*Two* agents? That's it?" It was a token effort, nothing more. Someone was covering his ass, not taking this case theory seriously.

"The perp walk didn't help," Jon said. "Not to mention the press conference this afternoon. The director has us boxed in—unless something new breaks." He shot her a look. "You want to help us with that?"

"*I'm* not the problem here. I've been helping you since the beginning."

He turned onto the highway and punched the gas, and Andrea's temper flared.

"Lose the attitude, North. You're the one who's been lying."

"When did I lie?" He looked offended.

"April nineteenth. What is *that* about? You ever think to mention we had a deadline here? You ever think that might be relevant?"

"I didn't lie to you."

"By omission—yes, you did."

"You're the one holding out," he countered. "Don't think I don't know that. If you really wanted to help—"

"I *am* helping!"

"—you'd have found a way to get your brother in a week ago."

"You're not being straight with me, and you want me to trust you with my brother's future? With his *life*?"

"*I'm* not responsible for your brother's life, Andrea! And neither are you. Get that through your head! He's an adult, and if he fucked up and robbed a bank and helped kill innocent people, he's going to be held accountable."

Andrea's heart clenched. "He didn't help kill anyone."

"How can you say that? Jesus Christ, open your eyes. He's *living* there. He's involved."

"He's *not* involved. He wouldn't do this." Andrea stared straight ahead. She couldn't look at him.

"You're a smart woman, Andrea. You're a goddamn detective, but you've got blinders on."

She slapped the door. "I know I've got blinders on, all right? He's my kid brother! And he can be selfish and stupid and infuriating sometimes, but he's my brother, and he's not a murderer! He wouldn't do it. You don't know him like I do." Her chest squeezed painfully. She turned away and had to grit her teeth to keep from screaming. Damn it, she was angry. She was angry at Jon for pushing her buttons. And at herself for letting him.

Most of all, she was angry at Gavin for making her doubt him, even for an instant. Hot tears burned her eyes, but she forced them back. She couldn't lose it in front of him. He'd see it as a confirmation of everything he'd said.

Jon didn't talk. He drove silently, navigating a river of taillights on the highway. She could feel the tension coming off him.

It was the phone call. Whoever it was he'd been talking to at the Bureau, it hadn't gone well. No matter how much circumstantial evidence he pulled together, they still weren't supporting his theory, and now they'd very publicly pointed the finger at Islamic terrorists through today's arrests. Typically, when investigators made a bold move like that, only concrete physical evidence could make them change course.

And such evidence would be hard to come by with everyone looking in a different direction.

Jon cut into the right-hand lane and swung into a parking lot. Andrea glanced around, alarmed, as he rolled to a stop beside a sign: PARADISE VALLEY INN.

"What are we doing?"

He thrust the car into park. "The last flight to El Paso left ten minutes ago. There are two in the morning."

"So we're spending the night?"

"I am."

She eyed the keys in the ignition, which seemed to tick him off more. Not that she cared.

"You want to spend your night driving, that's up to you."

"Fine," she snapped.

"Fine."

They stared at each other, gazes locked, and she felt the frustration of the day boiling up again. She turned and looked out the window as he got out and slammed the door.

chapter seventeen

TORRES CALLED ELIZABETH FROM his truck.

"Hey, I've got a question for you."

Pause. "Who is this?"

"Jimmy Torres. You said you were working our getaway vehicles."

"Yeah?"

He adjusted the binoculars, focusing on the door of the Broken Spoke as several men exited the bar. One pulled on a helmet and climbed onto the back of a motorcycle, while the others walked toward a pickup.

"So you have makes and models but no owner, right?"

"That's right," she said. "What's that noise?"

"A hog."

"What?"

"A Harley. I'm staking out a parking lot, and I need to know if any of your getaway vehicles happen to be a white Tahoe."

"A Chevy Tahoe? No. I'm searching for small cars—all four-door sedans—a Grand Am, a Ford Fiesta, a couple of Hondas."

"Damn."

"Why?"

Another man walked out, this one wearing a cowboy hat. Definitely not a biker. Torres watched him cross the lot. "Come on, come on, come on," he muttered as the man neared the Tahoe parked on the edge of the lot.

He pulled open the door.

"*Yes.*"

"What?"

"My guy just showed," he said. "I have to go. Keep me posted on those cars."

Torres dropped the phone into the cup holder and waited for a few moments to keep a low profile. It wasn't that late, so there was still some traffic to blend into as he entered the highway.

He followed the Tahoe, which he was almost certain was the same one he and North had been in hot pursuit of just a few days ago.

Almost certain but not quite. No one had managed to read the license plate that night. But the make and model fit, along with the approximate age. The Tahoe from the other night was a clunker, just like this one, and Torres had a feeling about it. Enough of a feeling to run the plate, which was from out of state. The registration had come back to a Brian Floyd of Las Cruces, New Mexico.

If that was Floyd behind the wheel now, the guy had a clean record. So who was he? And why was he in Maverick?

Torres kept an eighteen-wheeler between him and the Tahoe as he sped down the highway. He could be a tourist. Could be someone passing through. Could be someone looking for work in one of the oil fields that had attracted thousands of roughnecks to the area in recent years.

Could be a friend of Hardin's.

Torres didn't know who the hell he was and had no idea if he had a connection to his case or not. He just knew something had nagged at him when he first noticed the Tahoe pulling into the Broken Spoke.

Maybe he was just bored. Or restless. Or bitter that North was probably getting it on with a pretty woman tonight, while he was stuck in Maverick, suffering the mother of all dry spells.

But none of that mattered right now. What mattered was that he had a lead and a chance to follow it up.

◆

Andrea called Nathan from a dark and secluded spot on the hotel patio.

"How's it going?" she asked him.

"How's it going? Fantastic. I've got feds all over my crime scene, and now I hear some ATF hotshot's on his way down from Washington. You wouldn't know anything about that, would you?"

"It's a long story."

"Well, let's hear it, because these guys just pulled my case out from under me, and they're not telling me jack shit."

Andrea took a deep breath. She'd already told him that Carmen Pena was linked to a prominent politician and that her death might be a targeted hit. Now she explained about Senator Kirby and the possible connection to Philadelphia.

"And you're involved in this how? Wait, let me guess. Another 'long story'?"

She didn't answer. "How's Lukas Pena?" she asked instead.

He made a sigh that sounded extremely tired. "Same. He's still in ICU. Carmen's mother is there with him, and she refuses to leave. The woman's got a lot of family around her, so that's good."

Andrea's chest hurt thinking about it. She stared out at the swimming pool, where rectangles of light from the second-story windows shimmered on the water. "Any updates on the evidence?" she asked.

"I'm not getting much, but one of the CSIs said they found a partial fingerprint on one of the pipe fragments. So that's something."

"Hmm. You'd think he'd wear gloves making it."

"You'd think. They're running the print now. Or so I've been told. I'm not really in the loop."

The patio door opened, and a man stepped out. It was dark, but Andrea had no trouble recognizing Jon's tall silhouette and the athletic way he moved.

"You know, Andrea," Nathan said, "I'm all out of advice for you, and you don't listen anyway. But I will tell you this: if Taggart gets wind that you're out there investigating this when you're supposed to be on leave, or that you're involved at all, that's it. You're done."

"I understand."

"The man's allergic to bad publicity."

"I understand, Nathan."

"Do you really? Because you're not acting like it."

"Listen, I have to go. I'll call you tomorrow, okay? Keep me updated on that fingerprint."

She hung up. Jon stepped through the wrought-iron gate and crossed the patio to the spot where she sat with her feet propped on a table. She braced for another round.

"Stopped by your room earlier." He looked out over the darkened pool. "What are you doing out here, hiding?"

"No."

"You get any dinner?"

"No."

He stared down at her. He'd ditched the suit jacket and tie and rolled up his sleeves. The light from the motel put shadows on his face, and his jaw was dark with stubble. He looked like a man who'd had a long day and probably spent way too much of it on a phone arguing with people.

Andrea pulled her feet off the table and pushed a chair toward him with her toe. He accepted the invitation.

"Sorry I blew up earlier." As the words came out, they surprised even her. She rarely apologized to anyone. In her male-dominated workplace, it was a sign of weakness. But she was feeling weak today. Her nerves were frayed. She thought back to that blue baby swing and felt heartsick.

"Sorry for keeping you in the dark about the timeline," he said.

He wasn't really sorry, but she appreciated the effort. And anyway, she'd been keeping him in the dark about a few things, too, such as her trip to the Delphi Center. And her hostile encounter back at Lost Creek Ranch. But if he knew everything she'd been up to, he'd probably force her to butt out, especially after seeing that bullet.

"I contacted my brother tonight."

His gaze narrowed. "You called him?"

"E-mailed him. I'm trying to get him to see me tomorrow." Her throat tightened as she spoke. "I still don't think he's involved, but maybe he knows something, saw something that can help you get a search warrant for the ranch or make an arrest . . . before anything else happens."

"If you let me talk to him, I can help him, Andrea."

"You can't promise that," she said quietly.

"I can try."

A silence settled over them, and she gazed out at the murky water. She was right, and he knew it. He couldn't promise her anything. As he'd said in the car, if her brother had committed a crime, he was going to be held accountable. Andrea closed her eyes and tried to make the knot in her stomach go away.

Jon's chair scraped over the pavement as he leaned back and looked up at the desert sky. "It's not so bad out here."

"Yeah." If you didn't mind the chill, which he obviously didn't. He'd grown up in cold weather. She hadn't. In only her thin blazer, she'd been shivering for the last half hour, but she hadn't wanted to camp out in her room, where she'd known he'd come looking for her.

He was right. She was hiding. She wasn't exactly sure what she was hiding from, but it had something to do with the way her pulse sped up whenever he argued with her. And the way he looked at her, as if he could see straight through every word she said.

He turned to look at her now. "What'd you think of the senator?"

She scoffed. "I think he's a prick. I know there's no 'correct' response to death, but isn't there a moratorium on golf or something?"

"I wouldn't know. I don't play."

"You don't?"

He looked at her. "You sound surprised."

"You're a doctor's kid."

"My dad doesn't play, either." He smiled. "That's a stereotype, Andrea. Like saying you grew up on a farm, so you probably lost your virginity in a hayloft."

"I didn't."

"There you go."

He gazed up at the sky again, and she did, too.

"You're right, though," he said. "About Kirby. If I were him, I wouldn't let my wife out of my sight."

"Yeah, well, you're not him."

Jon's protective streak was deeply ingrained. The senator had seemed more worried about his reelection than about his family. Andrea didn't know why she was so shocked by that. She'd always hated politicians, but actually seeing their warped priorities up close was pretty disturbing.

A gust whipped up, and she wrapped her arms tightly around herself.

"His own son," Jon said, "and I bet he hasn't even called the hospital."

She glanced over and saw the contempt on his face. "Not everyone gives a shit about their kids, North."

He looked at her, and she turned away, sorry she'd said anything. "You're talking about your mom?"

"My dad."

"Where is he?"

"No idea."

He gave her a sharp look. It probably sounded odd to someone who had grown up in a stable family. Andrea felt self-conscious. And maybe a little defensive, as she had for most of her life.

"My mom cared about us," she said objectively. "But she was an alcoholic. An addict. You've seen it." Anyone in law enforcement had seen it a thousand times. "She and my dad always drank a lot, but he could handle it. When he left, she couldn't anymore. It was like she became someone else."

Andrea remembered so many afternoons coming home from

school to find her mom passed out on the couch and Gavin camped out in front of the television, eating Froot Loops and chips, whatever was in the house.

"My childhood wasn't all bad," she said, thinking of Dee and Bob's farm. Their method of helping their grandkids deal with grief had been to put them to work. Andrea remembered hanging wash on the clothesline and feeding chickens. Dee would send them out with coffee cans to fill with dewberries so she could make pies.

She thought of those hot afternoons picking berries alongside her brother until their fingers ached. She thought of his flushed cheeks and his solemn eyes, and her chest swelled with love for him. He'd been such a quiet kid—almost painfully shy—even though Dee and Bob had done everything they could to draw him out.

"Salt of the earth." She looked at Jon. "That's what people say about my grandparents. They're good people. And they don't have much, but they take care of it. Especially family."

"That sounds nice."

"It is."

"But you didn't want to stay on the farm?"

"Not really my thing." Andrea looked at the sky again, recalling a female police officer with a tight brown ponytail. She'd waded into their messy living room, and with only a glance at the empty bourbon bottle, it was as if she knew everything about them. She'd walked up to Andrea and put a firm hand on her shoulder.

It's up to you now. You need to be strong for your brother.

Some total stranger had given Andrea the words she'd lived by for years.

She looked at Jon in the dimness. They came from such different places in so many ways.

"How'd you get into this?" she asked him.

"What, law enforcement?"

"The Bureau."

For a moment, he didn't say anything. "My uncle was DEA. He used to take me fishing a couple times a year. I looked up to him." He paused. "He worked in the Murrah Building in Oklahoma City, back in ninety-five."

"You mean—"

"He died in the blast."

Andrea cringed. "How awful."

"It was."

She didn't know what to say, so she watched him, hoping he'd fill in the blanks.

"I followed the trial pretty close," he said. "What amazed me was McVeigh. His complete lack of remorse. Those children he killed, he called them 'collateral damage.'"

Andrea shook her head.

"Total lack of conscience," he said. "I think we're dealing with the same thing now."

Andrea watched his face, noted the steely look in his eyes. She could see this case was personal to him. She admired that about him. People were always telling cops not to let the job get personal, not to take the work home. But she didn't think that was possible. The best cops she knew put their hearts into it.

She studied his profile, and her own heart fluttered. She looked away.

"Maybe he views it as a war," she said. "A take-no-prisoners type of thing. Maybe he's sick. God knows I've seen enough head cases on the job."

"Same."

They sat in silence for a while, with Andrea shivering and

wrapping her arms around herself to fight off the chill. She felt cold to her bones. "Ever wish you'd stuck with the law firm?" she asked, trying to lighten things up. "You'd be making more money."

"I like what I do." He leaned forward and rested his elbows on his knees as he turned to look at her. "I'm good at it."

He stated it as a fact, and she believed him.

"What about you?" he asked. "You like your job?"

"If I still have it."

He frowned. "Is that really in doubt?"

"Didn't you read the news stories?"

"You're talking about that article that said you should have shot the pistol out of his hand, like it's the Wild West? You can't worry about crap like that, Andrea."

It had been an op-ed column, and she *wasn't* worried about it. It was absurd. But the supposedly factual news articles that implied the same thing bothered her.

She looked at Jon again. He seemed so strong and competent. She was tempted to open up to him, and she sensed that he really wanted to listen. She'd never been in a relationship like that. Not with a man, anyway.

He was watching her, waiting.

"I broke protocol," she said. "I should have summoned backup if I'd thought the subject was mentally disturbed or there was potential for violence."

"Instead, you followed your instincts."

Her instincts. The same instincts that had made her look twice at the kid in the trench coat, the same instincts that had made her confront him—those same instincts had made her hesitate. And hesitation was deadly.

She'd walked into that kitchen and been ambushed by his humanity. The kid holding that gun was someone's son, someone's brother, someone's ex-boyfriend. And she'd ended his life. *She'd* ended it. And even now, with bureaucratic forces lined up on opposite sides against her—she'd acted too late, she'd acted too soon, she shouldn't have acted alone—none of that mattered now, because it was done, right or wrong, and she couldn't undo it.

Looking back, the situation was clearer. From her perspective, anyway. No matter what any review board concluded, she knew that her biggest mistake was that she'd hesitated, she'd frozen up, and in doing so, she'd put innocent people at risk.

Despite all her training, all her experience, she'd hesitated in a crisis, and now she questioned whether she really had what it took to be a cop.

Jon rested his hand on her knee. She looked at him, faintly shocked by the warmth of the contact.

"You did the right thing," he said.

She looked into his eyes, and she wanted so much to believe him. And selfishly, she wanted the review board to see it that way so she could go back to work.

She missed her job. Desperately. And she had no idea what she was going to do with herself if she couldn't get it back.

His fingers slid over her arm and found her hand, making her loosen her grip on herself. He squeezed her fingers.

"You're freezing."

She didn't say anything. She watched him. She could feel her chest rising and falling as she looked at his eyes, his mouth. He was warm and strong, and she hated feeling needy, but that was how she felt right now.

He leaned in, and she stiffened.

"Come here," he whispered, pulling her close. She let him. She leaned against him, and his breath was warm against her temple.

He kissed her, and she pulled back reflexively.

He sighed. "You don't trust me, do you?"

"No."

It was a lie. She did trust him. She didn't know why, but she did.

She wished things could be simpler. She wished they could just be two people getting to know each other, using each other for warmth. Maybe if they'd met under different circumstances, she could cave into what she was feeling right now, instead of burying it deep inside herself.

His hand slid down her neck, and he rubbed his thumb along her jaw. His eyes were dark now, and the intensity in them made her pulse pound.

"We're the same, Andrea." He kissed her temple again, then tipped her chin up and found her mouth. "We're both alone."

His mouth settled on hers, and she gave in this time. He tasted warm and male, and she leaned into his heat as his arms wrapped around her, and he shifted her almost into his lap. He pulled her closer and kissed her. There was a hungry insistence about him that reminded her of the way he'd looked at her the night they first met. She'd known then that he'd be this way. She'd known he'd be powerful and commanding, and it excited her.

He tipped her head back and kissed the underside of her jaw, and she felt the rasp of his stubble against her skin, and her pulse was racing now. The air around her was cool, but warm ripples ran up and down her skin as his mouth moved over the sensitive side of her neck.

She slid her arms around him, and his mouth found hers again, and she felt his fingers gripping her hip as he kissed her and pulled her even closer.

A phone buzzed, and she jerked back. For a second, she didn't move. Then she groped around and found the phone wedged under her leg on the chair. She stood up and turned away, ignoring Jon's gaze.

"Andrea Finch."

"It's Ryan."

The words were slurred, and she had to think a moment.

"Ryan Copeland."

"Ryan, hi. What's up?"

"Is it true?"

She looked at Jon, who was watching her intently. "Is what true?"

"About Carmen."

She glanced around, making sure they were still alone out here. "Carmen Pena died in an explosion last night. Her son is in the hospital."

"Oh, God."

"The incident is still under investigation."

Silence.

"Ryan?"

"I think I killed her."

chapter eighteen

"WHAT DO YOU MEAN, you killed her?"

Jon stood up and stepped closer, his brow furrowed.

"I didn't mean it. I never thought . . ." Ryan's voice trailed off into a muffled sob.

"I need you to explain what you're talking about."

"I never meant for this to happen."

"Ryan—"

"I talked to that reporter. I wanted her to get fired and—"

"You're saying *you* were the source of the rumor?"

"Yes."

"Was it true?"

She heard a rattle on the other end of the phone, like ice cubes in a glass. She felt a pang of sympathy for him and hoped he was home, at least, and not at some bar.

"Ryan, was it true?"

"*Yes.*" His voice was filled with misery. "But I didn't know this would happen. I just wanted her to get fired."

She didn't say anything, wanting to let him talk.

"You think it's the same guy, don't you? That killed Julia. He's going after all of them."

"I'm afraid I can't discuss details of the investigation." God, now she sounded like Jon. She looked at him, and he was motioning to her to mute the phone.

"Tell him we'll send an agent over tomorrow to talk to him," Jon said. "Sometime in the morning."

"Ryan, an FBI agent will be visiting you tomorrow morning to get a statement, all right? Until then, don't discuss this with anyone else."

Silence.

"Ryan?"

"I'll be here," he said, and hung up.

Andrea looked down at the phone in her hand. She looked at Jon. "He feels responsible because he leaked the story about Carmen and the senator to the press."

Jon gazed down at her, and she looked away. In the parking lot, someone started up a diesel pickup and pulled out. She watched it fade down the highway. Jon eased closer and reached for her hand. She stepped back.

"I should get to bed."

He watched her. "You can't hide from this forever, Andrea."

This what? This case? This . . . thing they'd somehow started that didn't make any sense? Her pulse jumped as he reached out and feathered her hair away from her face. The gesture was soft. Tender. And the look in his eyes wasn't hungry now but determined and patient.

And that made her pulse race even more, because she knew he wasn't going to let it go. He wasn't going to let her off the hook until she dealt with this.

He stared down at her for a long moment. Then his hand dropped, and she stood stock-still as she watched him walk away.

◆

She fell into bed thinking about him. She slipped into a restless sleep and woke with her heart hammering and her cheeks wet and a breathless, panicked feeling like someone was sitting on her chest.

She sat up and checked for her gun on the nightstand. It was right where she'd left it. The clock showed 6:14. She glanced across the room, and in the predawn dimness, she could see that the latch was still secured.

She closed her eyes and let the dream return. She was standing in the crowded kitchen. It was hot and airless, and everyone was staring at her, their faces twisted with revulsion. She looked down at the gun in her hand and touched the muzzle. Still warm. She lifted her gaze to the body sprawled across the floor. She took a step forward, and her feet were like cinder blocks. She took another step. Blood spread out along the floor grout.

Andrea shuddered, trying to shake it off. She felt the impulse to call Jon or go knock on his door. She'd been spending more and more time with him. More talks. More cracks in her defenses. Last night by the pool, she'd caught herself searching his eyes for something, as if he could understand her somehow or maybe even fill the void.

Andrea rubbed her forehead. It was probably the stress, the anxiety of the last few weeks wearing her down. A man couldn't fix her problems. She needed to tackle them herself.

Her phone rattled on the nightstand, and she answered without checking the screen.

"Hey, it's Ben," the caller said, and it took a moment for her to conjure up an image of the cyber-detective with the goatee. "Sorry to call so early, but I've been working on that info you wanted."

"No, it's fine." She got out of bed and pulled on the jeans she'd tossed over a chair. They had a flight to catch in three hours and still had to return the rental car. "Tell me what you found."

"Well, first of all, you were right. The FBI *was* missing something."

Her nerves skittered.

"But in all fairness, it's not surprising, given the situation."

"What situation?"

"The comm setup. They're using a SNAP, and it's a nice one, too. Not one of those crap-in-a-box things you buy on eBay."

She shook her head to clear it. "They're using a what?"

"An SIPR/NIPR Access Point. A temporary satellite terminal that allows for encryption. Although whether they're actually encrypting anything, I don't know."

"Wait. Back up. You're talking about a sat phone?"

"A temporary satellite *terminal*. It's portable, comes in a few tough boxes. You can hook up a laptop to it and get satellite Internet."

"So . . . they've got a satellite dish?" How had the FBI missed something so obvious? It would have shown up on the surveillance photos.

"Yeah, but like I said, it's portable. Looks like they put it away when they're not using it, which is most of the time. I ran a broad-spectrum analysis of the area for almost thirty-six hours before I picked up on it."

"So they *do* have Internet access at the ranch? And it's encrypted?"

"Yes and maybe," Ben said. "Someone's definitely accessing the Net, but I don't know if they're encrypting communications. Didn't get that far. To intercept what they're doing, I'd have to do node-to-node back-stepping. Are you familiar with that?"

"No."

"Well, it's a major pain in the ass, and now that the weekend's over, I'm not sure I'm going to be able to take that on. Is your agency planning to hire us, do you know? Alex made this sound pretty informal."

"No—it is. Informal. And thanks for your time on it."

"Not a problem. I had to work the weekend anyway. But like I said, intercepting the communications would be a bigger deal, especially if they're encrypted. Even if they're not, I wouldn't be surprised if the person using this is hopping on an anonymizer site to cover his tracks. Whoever's running this is pretty obsessed with invisibility."

Gavin was probably running it, which meant he'd lied to her about what he was doing at the ranch. What else had he lied about?

Andrea felt numb. People lied to her all day long. Every time a suspect's lips moved—lie, lie, lie. But somehow she'd thought that with Gavin, she'd know. After twenty-two years, she'd thought she'd be able to tell.

"You have no way of knowing what sorts of communications are going back and forth?"

"Could be e-mails, Web surfing, whatever. But the log-in times raise some red flags."

Andrea slumped against the wall, getting more depressed with every word. "How's that?"

"Well, like I mentioned, this is a portable terminal. Picture a laser that beams up at the sky. It's got to be outside and works best in clear weather conditions. I only caught two log-ins, both short, both around two in the morning. So whoever's using it is only setting it up in the dark of the night and then putting it away, which means they could be paranoid about surveillance. Maybe they know the feds are watching them?"

"Maybe." Andrea closed her eyes. She was running out of innocent explanations for all this. She was running out of *any* explanation that didn't have Gavin involved in something truly horrific.

"The FBI techies need to step up their game," Ben said. "This is a complex setup, not to mention expensive. We're not talking about some guy covering his tracks because he's cheating on his wife. When I see shit like this? It's usually people involved in a child-porn ring, bank fraud, drug distribution. Without intercepting the actual transmissions, it's hard to know for sure, but do you want to know what my Spidey sense is telling me?"

"What?"

"Whatever they're up to out at that ranch, it isn't good."

◆

The inn's fitness center consisted of only a treadmill and a weight bench, but Jon made good use of both before swinging into the lobby in search of coffee.

"Those biscuits just came out of the oven."

He glanced up to see the front-desk clerk eyeing him.

"Thanks," he said, putting a lid on his coffee. He thought about getting one for Andrea but decided against it. After spending an hour getting rid of all his pent-up energy, the last thing he needed was to see her sleepy-eyed face against the backdrop of a rumpled bed.

He grabbed a biscuit from the tray and nodded at the clerk as he slipped out. Andrea's room was still dark. He neared his own door and heard the muffled sound of his cell. He hurried inside and grabbed it before it could go to voice mail.

"This is Pete McMurphy in Philadelphia. I got a message here?" Jon had never met the man, but judging from his voice, he had some years on the job.

"I hear you're working the university bombing," Jon said.

"The Julia Kirby case, yeah."

So it was the "Julia Kirby case" now. After yesterday's press conference, the media had latched onto the theory that an Al Qaeda cell had targeted the senator's daughter as a political statement. Senator Kirby was on the Foreign Relations Committee, so speculation was running rampant about how that might have motivated a terrorist attack.

"Thanks for getting back to me." Jon set his breakfast on the table and glanced at his watch. He had a plane to catch, but he needed this guy's information. Everything he'd heard so far out of Philadelphia had been secondhand. "I'm on a task force down here looking into some antigovernment groups that might have had a beef against Senator Kirby."

"I know." So the guy had checked up on him. Jon was impressed.

"I wanted to see if you had any loose ends you haven't followed up on. Stuff I might be able to check out on this end."

Silence as McMurphy digested the question. It was touchy, because Jon was essentially accusing the task force of sloppy work. He muttered something Jon couldn't hear. And then he said, "You know, when I saw your message, I almost didn't call."

"Why's that?"

"Because so far, this case has brought me nothing but shit."

"How do you mean?"

Another pause. Jon heard cellophane crackling and pictured the guy tapping out a fresh cigarette. "How long you got on the job?" McMurphy asked.

"Eight years."

"I got nineteen. And a half, but who's counting, right? And I'm probably gonna get canned over this thing, but I'll tell you what. Reese can go fuck himself."

Alan Reese was the associate director who'd given the press conference yesterday.

"And I'll tell you something else: this case is radioactive. Don't say I didn't warn you."

"What did you think of yesterday's arrests?" Jon asked, hoping to get specifics.

"The arrests were fine. Textbook. Judge signed off on every-thing. But it doesn't matter, 'cause our evidence stinks. Videos, cell phones. We even been through the hard drives already. Word is, it's thin. And some piece-of-shit civil-rights lawyer from Miami already signed these guys up. He's gonna have a field day, this thing goes to trial."

Jon heard him sucking in a drag.

"Another problem? I'm hearing rumblings out of the ME's office. Something screwy about the autopsy."

Jon scrounged up a pen and looked for something to write on. "The autopsy for Khalil Abbas? I thought we had positive ID."

"We do. DNA checks out."

There was a carryout menu on the table, and he started jotting notes as the agent talked.

"This is something else," McMurphy said. "Don't ask me what, because I got no idea, and from what I heard, the guy was blown to bits. But what's left of him—the ME's got an issue with something. He called in last night, said he had to do 'additional testing.'"

Jon gripped his pen. Physical evidence was in question now. People could dismiss competing theories all day long, but concrete evidence was harder to ignore.

"Listen, what can you tell me about that bomb?" Jon asked. "I heard it was ammonium nitrate and racing fuel, but do they have any leads on where it came from?"

"Don't know, but I can ask around. ATF's all over it, so you know how that goes."

He meant there was a turf war, which wasn't surprising. It was conventional wisdom that any action by the FBI in a bombing case caused an equal and immediate reaction from the ATF. Maybe Jon could find someone over there who would talk to him.

"Hey, there's one other thing," McMurphy said. "Long as we're tossing this around."

Jon waited.

"These three suspects, they're all with this mosque in Philadelphia. Couple days ago, we got a tip about a DOA who turned up about a block from the church. This is some homeless guy they found in an alley on trash day. Took the locals a while to ID him because he didn't have a wallet or anything. Had to run his prints through AFIS."

"This is near the mosque?"

"Yeah, only a block over. Apparently, that's his stomping grounds. They posted the guy in Philly. Autopsy report shows a time of death consistent with the time of the bombing, give or take twelve hours. Maybe a coincidence? I don't know."

"Cause of death?"

"There's the interesting part. Single shot to the forehead, downward trajectory, like maybe he was sitting in a doorway or something, and someone walked right up to him—*bam*. Could be he got hit by some thug who wanted his cash or his bottle. But how many street thugs you know who use hollow-point bullets?"

"That's a little unusual."

"No shit."

"So you're thinking what? This guy witnessed something go down at the mosque and got killed for it?"

"I don't know. But someone should be asking questions about it, don't you think? I'd say that's a loose end, but far as I know, no one's taken the time to look into it. I made a push yesterday, but the brass shut me down."

"Why?"

"No idea. But I'll let you know if I figure it out."

Jon got off the phone and stared down at his scribbled notes. They wouldn't make much sense to anyone else, but to him, they made one thing clear.

Despite all the spin out of Philadelphia, the task force didn't have its case together. Jon suspected they knew it, too, which was why they'd sent a team down to cover the senator. If they were confident they'd neutralized the threat against him, they wouldn't have bothered.

Jon needed to get back to Texas. He'd planned to take the nine thirty flight, but there was still time to make the eight fifteen. He crossed the patio to Andrea's room, where a housekeeping cart was parked beside the door.

"Andrea?"

He stuck his head in and startled the maid who was stripping the bed. Jon glanced at the bathroom, but the door was wide open.

"The woman staying here," he said. "Where is she?"

"Sorry?"

"The woman in this room. *La mujer*. Have you seen her?"

"*Sí*." She nodded. "She took the taxi."

chapter nineteen

SHAY KNELT IN THE creek bed. He glanced at the range flag, then settled the bipod on the mound of sandbags and considered his shot. Moderate wind posed a challenge, but that was good. There was never a perfect moment, and he trained to be prepared.

He rested his face against the cheek piece, made his muscles relax, and filled his lungs with air. Then he looked through the scope and made adjustments for wind and gravity.

Another breath. Another heartbeat. He pulled the trigger.

A plastic drum exploded two hundred yards away. Ross stepped into his peripheral vision, and Shay shifted his earmuffs.

"You're using the fifty?"

He glanced at Ross, then down at his weapon, a Steyr-Mannlicher HS .50. The Austrian-made rifle fired a .50 BMG cartridge that could penetrate armor and bulletproof glass. Human flesh was like butter.

"Better to be safe than sorry," Shay said.

Ross nodded. He was on board with this phase of the mission. Message Two had been delivered and now Ross was himself again—a soldier unafraid to kill in the line of duty.

Shay loaded another round, enjoying the smooth sound of the Austrian engineering at work. He lined up the shot. The second target was three hundred yards. He peered through the scope and got his head in the game. Took a deep breath.

Boom.

Another kill. He sat back and smiled as he hooked the earmuffs around his neck.

"So I went into town," Ross said.

"Anyone see you?"

"Just the spic."

"Whose phone did you use?"

"Deb's at the gas station."

Shay glanced at his watch. "And?"

"And I talked to my brother. We're all set on that end."

Shay stood up and shook out his stiff legs. He stretched his neck. He rested the gun on his shoulder, liking the weight of it. It was a world-class weapon, and he was glad to own it, especially since it was outlawed on the Left Coast.

Ross continued to stare at him. "So this is getting pretty intense. You really think it's going to go down?"

"Yes."

They climbed out of the creek and started trekking toward the house. He looked out over the land he now called home. In some ways, it was the same as his family's—craggy ridges, weathered fence posts, dusty roads. But the old place had gnarled oaks and rich pastures, while this land was covered with cacti and thirsty scrub trees.

He thought of his mother in the nursing home, sitting in her chair, gumming her food like a baby, staring at the landscape for hours and hours without really seeing it.

He looked at the empty creek bed. Lost Creek. When he'd come here, it could have been called Lost Hope. But he'd found something here. He'd formulated his plan here, the plan that would redeem his family and send a message to those who would take away his property, his livelihood, his rights.

Message Three was coming.

"How do you know they'll be there?"

He looked at Ross and slapped him on the shoulder. "Trust me, they'll be there. I guarantee it." Shay was confident, because he knew his enemy. And he knew his enemy, because he was disciplined. It all came back to training—an irony that wasn't lost on him as he neared the zero hour.

They crossed a field, and a faint noise droned above as they ducked into the barn.

Ross checked his watch. "On time again."

Shay smiled up at the cloudless sky. "Like clockwork."

❖

Torres pulled up to the oil derrick and surveyed the line of vehicles. Two ICE pickups and two rental cars. The Lincoln would belong to Maxwell, which left the Taurus for the agents down from Philly.

A gray pickup zoomed up the road, trailed by a cloud of dust. North pulled up beside him and climbed out.

"How was Phoenix?"

"Fine."

"Where's Andrea?"

"No idea." He slammed the door.

Hey, ho. Looked like North got the brush-off. Torres had been rooting for him, but apparently, he'd blown it.

"You met these guys yet?" North scowled at the vehicles.

"Nope. Santucci and Theilman. Word is, Santucci's smart, Theilman's an asshole."

They entered the trailer and found everyone squeezed around the plywood table littered with coffee cups. A ravaged doughnut box sat in the center, with a few globs of jelly stuck to the lid.

Maxwell made the introductions. Special Agent Theilman was pale, pudgy, and balding, and Torres couldn't imagine anyone less cut out for the Texas border region. Special Agent Santucci was thin, dark, and quiet. He didn't say a word, just nodded from the end of the table.

Torres grabbed a seat while North hit the coffeepot.

"I think we should just pick him up, bring him in for questioning," Theilman was telling Maxwell.

"He could take the Fifth and leave us with nothing," Maxwell said. "And then he knows we're on to him, so he goes home to destroy any evidence he has before we get a search warrant. We need more evidence than we have now before we confront him."

"All due respect," Theilman said, without any, "what *do* we have now? I been briefed twice since yesterday, and I gotta tell you, I'm not seeing it."

"North?" Maxwell looked at him. "You want to bring our Philadelphia colleagues in on the latest?"

All eyes swung to North. Continuing with tradition, their SAC was letting him take the lead on this, just in case it fell apart.

North sat down and glanced around the table. "First off, we have surveillance footage showing Shay Hardin's pickup truck parking at the El Paso Airport three days before the bombing."

"But we can't prove he was on a flight," Theilman stated. "Our team ran the footage from the airport and didn't see this guy. So what's your theory?"

"I think he traveled to the East Coast on a fake ID," North

said, "then rented a vehicle and drove to Philly. The night before the bombing, he approached Khalil Abbas as he was leaving the mosque after evening prayers. We have witnesses who saw Abbas leave the building, but no one actually saw him get into his minivan and drive away."

Theilman's eyebrows tipped up. "You think Hardin kidnapped him?"

"And then murdered him so his remains could be found at the crime scene."

Silence dropped like a brick. North glanced around, probably noting all the skeptical looks.

"Why him?" Santucci asked.

"His vehicle, for one thing. He owned a minivan, which Hardin could use to hold the bomb. But more important, he was known to be radical. Hardin knew he'd grab our attention the second we traced the van."

"How'd he know we'd trace it?"

"We did it in Oklahoma," Torres said. "The VIN on the truck axle led us directly to the truck-rental company."

"After he had Abbas and the van," North continued, "I think he—and possibly an accomplice—spent the night assembling the explosive."

"Where?" Theilman asked, as if North had a crystal ball in front of him.

"I don't know. A rented storage unit? A warehouse? Could have been a lot of places. In the morning he drove to campus, parked in front of the designated building, and walked away. We have a stoplight cam that caught the minivan coming through an intersection nearby, just before the bombing. We have the plate, but you can't see who's driving. Then a few minutes later, according to ATF, the detonation was triggered by a cell phone."

Theilman shifted in his metal chair, looking constipated. "Where'd he get the explosives?"

"I don't know."

"You guys nail down where these clerics supposedly got the explosives?" Torres asked.

Theilman shot him a look. "No. But this still seems like a stretch, no matter how you look at it. There's a lot of supposition."

"But it would explain a few things," North said.

"Such as?"

"The DOA near the mosque."

Theilman looked puzzled. "What DOA?"

"You're talking about the homeless guy. I heard about that." Santucci looked intrigued now. "He turned up a block away with a bullet in his skull. You're saying he witnessed something?"

"Maybe."

"What about this Carmen Pena we been hearing about?" Theilman asked. "How does she fit in?"

"Kirby's mistress," North said. "She died in an Austin house fire, which first looked like a gas leak. Investigators say there *was* a gas leak, but they also recovered fragments of a pipe bomb that was on a timer. The device wasn't large, but together with the gas leak, it was enough to cause a deadly explosion. Kirby may be the father of her child, who was injured."

Theilman shook his head, and Torres glanced at Maxwell. He looked skeptical, too, now. Obviously, the boss wasn't yet sold on the Carmen Pena angle.

More ass shifting by Theilman. "Why all the subterfuge? If he wanted to kill this woman, why not come right out and murder her, make a big statement?"

"That's the thing," North said. "He's not making a big statement. Not yet. This statement is personal, and it's for Kirby. He's telling him, 'I know who you are. I'm coming for you *and* your children.' What's more terrifying than that?"

The room went quiet. The only sound was the wind whipping against the flimsy trailer walls.

"I don't know." Theilman shook his head. "I buy some of it but not all of it. So Hardin's a weapons guy. Maybe he's smuggling guns to Mexico or something. That would explain all the secrecy at his ranch. But covert assassinations? There's no physical evidence that says he did that. Meanwhile, we've got Khalil Abbas's van and Khalil Abbas's DNA *at* the crime scene."

"Exactly my point." North glanced around. "This is Hardin's game. Lead us in one direction, and we look all the more incompetent when it turns out to be something else. He did the same thing when he murdered a federal judge six years ago and set it up like a suicide. Our investigation was a dead end, just like he planned. One of his core objectives is to embarrass the federal government, and he's doing a great job of it."

"Which brings us back to the point of this meeting," Maxwell said, finally stepping up to the plate. "How, exactly, are we going to get evidence for a search warrant?"

"Gavin Finch."

Everyone looked at North.

"He's our best chance."

◆

Fear churned in Andrea's stomach as she bumped along the dirt road. Gavin had agreed to meet her at the deserted ranch adjacent to Lost Creek, but the odds of him bailing out on her were high.

She drove over a rise and pulled up to the old wooden windmill. No Gavin. She got out of her Jeep and looked around but saw no sign of the little blue Ford. The late-afternoon sun made the scrub trees cast long shadows across the yellowed grass.

She checked her phone. No e-mail messages. She checked her call history in case she'd missed something, which she hadn't. She'd spent her entire day on pins and needles, dodging Jon's calls and trying to figure out what she was going to say to her brother.

A faint hum in the distance had her turning and squinting as a speck of blue appeared on the horizon. She put her hand on her Kimber until the car drew near enough for her to see who was at the wheel.

Gavin skidded to a stop beside her and climbed out.

"I thought you went home," he said, slamming the door.

She met his gaze, and a lump formed in her throat. He seemed completely oblivious to why she was here. Annoyed, even.

"I know about Philadelphia, Gavin."

No change in his face. Nothing at all. He glanced away, and Andrea's chest convulsed.

This is what heartbreak feels like. She stood frozen for a moment, watching him. And then she lunged.

"You son of a bitch!" She pounded him with her fists. "How could you do it? How *could* you?" She clobbered his shoulders, his neck, his bony arms. "What is *wrong* with you?"

"Stop!" He ducked behind his arms.

"You just hate everyone? Is that it? You couldn't just kill yourself and get it over with?" She clawed his arms away from his face so he couldn't hide. She landed blow after blow after blow. "You selfish shit! *Where is your soul?*"

"Stop, God damn it! I didn't *know!*"

He shoved her away with both hands, and she stumbled back, panting. Her heart galloped inside her chest as she stared at his guilty face. "Bullshit! How could you not know?"

He lifted a hand to the scratches on his neck, and his fingers came away bloody. "Damn, Andrea."

"How could you not know?"

He glared at her. "I didn't, all right?"

She stepped back, hands bunched into fists. She didn't believe him. She didn't believe a word out of his mouth. "You're a liar." Her voice trembled with rage, and she could see the fear in his eyes.

"I didn't know. I swear. I found out this weekend."

For an instant, she clung to the words. She wanted them to be true. But something was broken now, and she no longer trusted him.

"You have to believe me." He stepped closer. "I swear to God, Andie. I had no idea he'd do anything. I knew he hated Kirby, but I had no idea about it."

"Right."

"You have to believe me."

"Then what'd you come out here for?" She gestured angrily in the direction of Lost Creek. "You think I believe you're out here as a ranch hand? You think I'm that dense?"

"He hired me to set up his system."

Andrea stared at him. Finally, something that sounded plausible. Her shoulders tightened as she waited for the confession she'd been dreading.

"He needed e-mail, Internet access. He wanted something below the radar so the feds couldn't eavesdrop on what he was doing."

"How can you say you didn't know? What'd you think he needed all the secrecy for?"

"I knew about the secrecy, all right? But he told me it was about guns. Hardin has a business. He needs to communicate with his customers and doesn't want to tip off the police."

"He's selling guns." She didn't hide her skepticism.

"To collectors. It's a good business. He deals with people who want to exercise their rights without having the government invade their privacy—"

"Cut the constitutional horseshit, Gavin! You helped him set up a criminal enterprise! You expect me to believe you didn't know what else he was doing?"

"I didn't," he insisted. "I didn't find out till Saturday."

Andrea squeezed her eyes shut. She wanted to believe him. More than anything. But it defied common sense.

"Gavin—"

"Just listen, okay? I saw the headlines in town about Kirby's daughter, but I didn't make any connection until I found some papers at the house—maps of Philadelphia, the bus routes, stuff like that."

She stared at him, her head spinning. This entire plot had seemed like such a distant possibility until right this moment. "You have to come with me." She took his arm. "You have to talk to the FBI. Tell them everything you know."

"I can't."

"Are you kidding me?"

"I can't leave yet. I need more time."

"You have to talk to them *now*, before anything else happens!"

"I need to go back and get some things, stuff I can trade for immunity. He might have evidence lying around. And what if he's planning something else? Maybe I can find info about what it is or who all's involved."

"You can *tell* them what you know. But you have to come now so they can act on the information."

"I can't go yet, Andrea." He shook off her grip. "I need more stuff, and I can't leave Vicky."

The words stopped her cold. She stared at him. "Vicky Leeland?" She gaped at her brother as everything fell into place—the summer job, the ditched semester, his burning need to be out here in the middle of nowhere.

"Jesus Christ, Gavin," she said through clenched teeth. "For a genius, you're amazingly stupid, you know that?"

He watched her warily.

"Ross Leeland is a gun nut. He is a combat veteran with a history of domestic violence. And you're screwing around with his *wife* right under his nose? Have you lost your mind?"

He just looked at her.

"If he finds out, he'll kill you."

"Andrea, listen." He stepped closer. "Ross doesn't like me much. If I disappear without an explanation, he'll know something's up, and he'll take it out on Vicky because he knows we're friends."

She bent her head forward and rubbed the bridge of her nose where a headache was forming. This was so messed up. "Fine, go get her," she snapped. "I'll wait here."

"I can't get her this *minute*. We need time to come up with a story."

"Yeah, well, tough shit, Gavin. Time's up."

"Twenty-four hours. That's all I'm asking." He glanced over his shoulder in the direction of the ranch. "I'll find a way for us to leave without raising suspicion."

"We don't have twenty-four hours. You need to talk to the FBI *today*."

"I'm not leaving without her." He crossed his arms. "He'll hurt her, Andie."

She looked at him, torn.

But then she thought of Jon in the car last night. He was convinced another attack was imminent. April nineteenth was just four days away. What if Gavin brought them evidence they could use to track down the other parties involved?

Andrea muttered a curse. She looked out at the ever-lengthening shadows made by the setting sun. She knew what she *should* do. She looked at her brother.

He'll hurt her.

"Twelve hours," she said. "Meet me back here at six A.M., unarmed, and be prepared to answer some tough questions. Vicky, too. Does she know about this?"

"She doesn't even know about the guns."

Andrea highly doubted it, but she'd let the FBI be the judge.

"Come alone," Gavin said. "Hardin's paranoid. He notices any cops sniffing around here, he'll know something's up."

She stared at him, wondering whether Hardin actually did know he was under FBI surveillance.

He knew about *her*—that was for certain. The bullet in her motel room had conveyed that message. And he'd gone to a hell of a lot of trouble to cover his tracks.

"I can't promise that," she said. "But know this, Gavin: you have one chance here. *One.* If you stand me up, you're screwed. You'll be in a world of hurt, and I won't be able to do a thing to help you."

"Fine." He held her gaze, and she saw something in his face. Distrust? The irony formed a bitter lump in her throat.

"Six A.M.," she repeated.

He climbed into his car, and she watched him disappear over the ridge.

She drove back toward the highway with the sinking feeling that she'd made a terrible mistake.

chapter twenty

JON SAT UP, INSTANTLY alert. Loco was barking. He looked across his darkened bedroom as a shadow moved—

He grabbed his gun just as the light switched on.

"Rise and shine."

"Holy shit, Andrea." He lowered the weapon. "What the hell? How'd you get in here?"

"Back door was unlocked." She propped her shoulder against the wall beside his bedroom door, and he looked her up and down, heart pounding. She wore jeans and a leather jacket over one of those thin T-shirts.

"I'm on my way to pick up Gavin," she said. "Figured you'd want to come."

He glanced at the clock: 5:12. He got out of bed and walked across the room to glare down at her, hands on hips.

All yesterday, she'd evaded his calls. He'd even gone by her motel looking for her. He'd started to think she'd gone back to Austin.

"You have a lot of nerve, you know that?"

"You want to come or not?"

He towered over her, trying to rein in his temper, when what he really wanted to do was throw her down on his bed. From the look in her eyes, she knew it, too.

Her gaze slid down his body, and she lifted an eyebrow.

"What?"

"Nothing." She shrugged.

He stared down at her. She had a pistol on her hip and all-terrain boots on her feet. Her cheeks were flushed, and he wondered if it was cold outside or if he'd actually managed to embarrass her with his morning hard-on.

He grabbed his T-shirt and tactical pants off the floor and watched her as he zipped up.

"When are we meeting him?"

"Soon."

He sank down on the bed and pulled on his boots. Then he strapped on his holster and grabbed his Sig from the nightstand, along with an extra clip.

"Chop chop." She glanced at her watch. "We're burning daylight."

Jon glanced at the window. The sun wasn't even up yet. He walked past her into the bathroom, and when he came out, she was standing by the door impatiently.

He locked his house as Loco went crazy next door, hurling himself against the fence. He followed Andrea across the patch of dirt to her Cherokee, and the cold morning air slapped him awake and made him realize what a crappy plan this was. Which was the whole point of it. She'd shown up like this to catch him off guard.

He eyed her over the roof of the Jeep. He didn't like being jerked around.

"What?" she asked innocently.

He slid inside without comment, and the aroma of fresh coffee hit him. Two tall cups were nestled in the console. "Where'd you get coffee this early?" Nothing in Maverick was open yet.

"Made it in my room."

He looked at her, but she didn't elaborate. She'd changed motels to avoid him, which ticked him off even more.

"We're meeting him at Las Brisas Ranch."

"Why?" Jon took a scalding gulp as she turned west onto the highway.

"In case he needs to come on foot."

"What's with the stealth? Can't he just leave when he wants?"

"I don't know."

He took out his phone, and she put her hand over his. "No calls."

He looked at her.

"We do this my way. Low-key. I don't want a big SWAT team showing up all locked and loaded."

Jon watched her for a moment. She was putting him in a terrible position here, and she knew it. He should call it in, but then he ran the risk of his supervisor putting everything on hold until they could get people in place. Which increased the likelihood of an armed standoff or, worse, a shootout.

"Please?"

He put his phone away and gazed out the window as they sped down the deserted highway.

"FYI, there's an attorney meeting us at eight o'clock. He's out of El Paso."

Jon shot her a look.

"Did you think I was just going to hand over my brother without getting him some legal advice? I don't want you guys throwing him to the wolves when the case unravels and you need someone to hang this on."

"You think I'd do that?"

"*You* aren't calling all the shots. I work for a bureaucracy, too, remember? I know how this goes."

The sign appeared, and she swung a left onto the narrow road. The pavement was old and pitted, and she only drove a few hundred feet before she slowed to a crawl and cut the headlights. Jon didn't say anything. It was still dark out, the only light coming from a faint purple glow on the eastern horizon.

She looked tense as she focused her attention on the narrow road, driving by feel.

"You've been out here before."

She didn't answer. The road had her complete attention. He looked ahead, at the thin strip of asphalt barely visible in the pre-dawn gloom. He felt a slight dip, a curve. She slowed even more and glanced around.

"What are we searching for?" he asked.

"A gate. It should be on the left."

He peered around her.

"There." She pointed.

"It's not locked?"

"Just some baling wire looped over the fence post. You'll see it."

He got out and pulled open the gate. He'd expected it to squeak, but it glided silently on its hinges. As the Jeep rolled through, Jon propped the gate open with a rock to ensure an easy exit if they needed to leave quickly. He slid back in. "Quiet gate."

"I oiled it."

"When?"

"First time I came out here."

She veered left, following the road.

"Guy who owns this land is about a thousand years old," she continued. "He lives in Fort Stockton. Used to raise cattle, but now he's down to about a dozen head, and he leases the mineral rights to an oil and gas company."

"They ever notice you snooping around out here?"

"I doubt it. They use the north access road, so I haven't seen them."

The pavement gave way to gravel. They made a slight dip. As they came over the rise, the sky was lightening, and he could make out the dark shadow of a windmill.

Andrea scanned the area. She maneuvered into the darkest niche of the landscape and eased to a stop.

"Now what?"

She checked her watch. "Now we wait."

◆

Worry gnawed at her as the minutes crawled by. Where was he? Had he run into trouble getting away, or was he blowing her off? With every passing second, Jon was getting closer to calling this in, which took control out of *her* hands and transferred it to people with guns.

"What time did you tell him?"

"Six thirty," she lied.

He checked his watch. "We'll wait till seven."

Andrea turned the key and buzzed down the window so she could listen. The front seat filled with cold air and the smell of creosote. She turned off the car again and reached for her coffee. Moment by moment, the sky was brightening, going from indigo to purple to lavender.

"When did you see him?"

She glanced at Jon in the passenger seat with his elbow resting on the open window. "Yesterday evening."

"What does he know?"

"He said he didn't know anything until Saturday, when he found a map of Philadelphia and put two and two together." She felt the tension elevate at this news.

"You believe that?"

She looked away. She didn't know what she believed. And it didn't matter anyway.

She stared at the top of the windmill as the sun began to paint it with light. The minutes ticked by. The muscles in her shoulders tightened. Sweat pooled beneath her arms, despite the chill. She checked her phone. No texts, no e-mails.

She glanced at Jon beside her as the sunlight slanted through the windows. She'd dragged him out of bed, and he looked tired, but there was something else in his face, and she couldn't decipher it. He was a difficult man to read. What did he think of her brother right now? Of her?

She shouldn't care, but she did. His opinion mattered, more than she wanted it to.

Gavin couldn't have *knowingly* helped commit these crimes. And yet the tiniest part of her doubted him now, and she was ashamed. All those years when they were each other's only ally, when it was them against the world—did that mean nothing anymore?

Come on, Gavin.

Jon glanced at his watch. She looked out the window, scanning the horizon, and she could feel his gaze on her as he took out his phone and made a call.

"Hey, it's me. You talk to Whitfield yet?"

She waited nervously as he exchanged a few more words and then clicked off.

"Pretty quiet last night, according to Torres," he said.

"Someone was here all night?"

"We had a CBP truck parked up the highway, hidden from view. Pair of agents is keeping an eye on the house at night."

"And during the day?"

"Too conspicuous. We rely on drones and drive-bys."

Andrea peered out the window, craning her neck to see anything coming from the direction of Lost Creek.

"Last night was dead," he said. "No vehicles in or out."

She checked her phone again. She'd been so sure he'd come. How could he tell her the things he'd told her and then think he could duck out of this?

Jon's phone buzzed. His face revealed nothing as he listened to the caller and gave a few brief answers.

He muted the phone and looked at her.

"First-pass photos just came in from the drones."

She held her breath.

"Gavin's car is gone."

"Gone?" She blinked at him.

"Either that, or someone moved it into the barn in the middle of the night."

"But when could he have left? I thought you said it was quiet."

He didn't respond, and she could see the tension in his face. This was partly her fault. If she'd given him the heads-up sooner, he could have doubled up on surveillance. He probably would have spent the night out here himself.

"What about the brown Dodge?" she asked.

"What about it?"

"Is it there?"

He relayed the question. A few more clipped words, and he hung up. "Dodge is at the house," he told her.

Andrea gripped her phone in her hand as she looked out the window at the ever-brightening landscape.

"What does Vicky Leeland's car have to do with this?"

"I think they might be together."

She glanced away, but she could feel his anger growing beside her, filling the space between them. "How long have you known about this?"

"Less than a day," she said.

"God damn it."

"What?"

"I don't believe you."

She drew back, stung. "Believe what you want. It's the truth."

He stared at her hard, as if by sheer force of will he could make her reveal something. It was a look that probably worked on a lot of people, but it wouldn't work on her.

"He's obviously not coming." His stared grimly out the window. "He either left last night or slipped out this morning."

Backtracking to the highway was faster with the benefit of daylight, and soon they were speeding toward Maverick. Jon called Torres and gave him a rundown of the situation before getting a more detailed report on the overnight surveillance from Whitfield.

Andrea focused on the road, trying to ignore the sour ball of dread filling her stomach as she listened to the conversation. She'd given Gavin a chance, and he'd blown it.

She'd been so naive. So confident she could do something, *fix* something. But she couldn't save Gavin from himself any more than she'd been able save Dillon in that restaurant kitchen. She was powerless.

And it was out of her hands now. Jon's entire team was pulled into the search for Gavin, and they knew he had information. Any illusion of her brother being uninvolved had vanished, and now a team of armed federal agents was looking for him.

Andrea made a loop through town, slowing as she passed the various motels, in case he and Vicky had decided to get a room. Yes, it would be a stupid move considering the size of this town and the chances of someone spotting them together. But Gavin's actions of late hadn't demonstrated much prudence.

She did a second pass down Main Street as Jon wrapped up another call with Torres.

"They think he left around five this morning," Jon said.

"How do they know?"

"They don't. It's just a hunch. Whitfield spotted a car on the highway headed toward Maverick, but it didn't come from Lost Creek."

"Maybe he cut through the neighbor's ranch to the west, then doubled back."

She studied Jon's profile—the firm line of his mouth, the determined set of his chin as he combed the horizon, searching for her brother. He looked at her. "Where do you think he'd go?"

"I don't know."

"He's your brother, Andrea. Think."

"Maybe he went to Fort Stockton."

"We've got a BOLO out for him. Where else? Where would he go around here?"

She tamped down her anxiety and thought about Gavin's routines—what little she knew about them anymore. "My guess is food. He'd go to a Dairy Queen or maybe a truck stop looking for breakfast. Something big and cheap."

She pulled a U-turn and headed back toward the highway,

where most of the restaurants were. She looped through the Dairy Queen parking lot, slowing to peer into the windows at the customers. She parked at a diner and got out to check the premises, including the restrooms, while Jon talked to the servers. No sign of him.

Andrea's chest tightened as they slid back inside the car. She shifted in her seat to face him. With his ICE T-shirt and his leg holster and the intent look in his eyes, he seemed intimidating. He *was* intimidating, and she hated what she had to do.

"I need to tell you something."

His gaze narrowed. He propped his forearm on the door and waited.

There was no going back. She was betraying her family. Her *brother*. Someone she was supposed to look out for, always.

But those victims in Philadelphia had families, too. So did Carmen Pena.

"You were right about Lost Creek," she told him. "They do have communications there. They're using satellite Internet hook-ups." She swallowed. "Gavin set it up for them. Hardin hired him for technical support."

Jon stared at her, and shame warmed her cheeks. "Why didn't you tell me this?"

"I found out yesterday. He told me he wasn't involved in any-thing else, and I believed him, but—" She looked out the window at the dusty highway.

"If he wasn't involved, why would he run?" Jon finished for her.

"You need to set up a satellite surveillance," she said. "You need to intercept whatever they're doing, see if you can pick up something you can use to get Hardin in custody."

"I know."

"How did—"

"It's already under way," he said. "Our surveillance team caught evidence of a satellite signal early Sunday morning. They're working on an intercept now."

Something flickered in his eyes, something like pity.

"Thanks for telling me," he said.

Thanks for giving us your brother. Thanks for handing him over so we can put him away for the rest of his life.

Jon took another call, and it sounded like Torres. She watched closely as his expression changed. "When?"

She held her breath.

"Where?" He glanced at her. "Okay, tell Whitfield. I'm on my way." He hung up. "CBP thinks they saw him earlier this morning headed southbound on three-eighty-five."

Southbound? Her heart sank. God, was he driving down to Mexico?

"This agent was northbound, but he noticed a small blue sedan suddenly veering west from the highway, going off-road. Here, get out."

"Why?"

"I'll drive. Torres gave me directions." He got out and walked around the front. She scooted over the console, just in case he had any ideas about taking off without her.

"You said CBP?" she asked, trying to visualize the scenario as Jon jumped behind the wheel and adjusted the seat.

"He couldn't pursue because he had two men in custody already, but he called it in." Jon thrust the Jeep into gear and swung back onto the highway. "Looks like no one followed up."

"So you're saying—"

"A blue car, possibly a Focus, went into the desert an hour ago. Torres is out there now trying to pick up the trail."

chapter twenty-one

HE FLOORED IT SOUTH, making good time as he cut through the swath of desert between Fort Stockton and Big Bend National Park, just north of Mexico. Signs marked the distance to the park, but Andrea knew that wasn't Gavin's final destination.

She spied a pair of white SUVs pulled over on the side of the highway. A roadrunner raced across the pavement as Jon pulled onto the shoulder and rolled to a stop.

Torres was standing beside his ICE truck, talking to a man in a border-patrol uniform.

"Is he real CBP or undercover?" Andrea asked.

"Real CBP."

They climbed out, and Torres looked up from the map spread out over the hood.

"We just got here," Torres said. "A small blue car was spotted leaving the roadway near this location about ninety minutes ago. Agent thinks it could have been a Focus."

Everyone turned to scan the sprawling landscape to their

west—just rocky plains dotted with scrub brush, as far as the eye could see. The opposite side of the highway looked the same.

"This private land?" Andrea asked, noting the lack of fencing.

"State-owned nature reserve," the CBP agent piped up. "About twenty thousand acres."

Jon tromped over to peer down at the map. "Let's not waste time. We'll divide into three groups. You take this wedge. Torres, you take this one. Andrea and I will search this piece. It's fairly flat through here?" Jon looked at the border agent.

"More or less. Couple dried-up creek beds, that's about it. Our chopper's tied up right now, but I've got another truck on the way."

"We'll make do with vehicles for now." Jon looked at Andrea. "Anything distinctive you can tell us about the car?"

She tried to shift into cop mode. Tried not to think about how they were embarking on a search for her brother, the fugitive.

"A Ford Focus," she recited. "Cobalt blue, gray interior, missing hubcaps."

"Everyone got that?" Jon looked around. "All right, let's saddle up."

Andrea slid inside her Jeep, content to let Jon do the driving. She felt numb. Cold inside.

She pulled out her phone as Jon fired up the engine and rolled forward, dipping down off the highway and onto the desert floor. No missed calls. No e-mails. No plausible explanation for why he'd failed to keep his promise.

"You need to help me look, Andrea."

She glanced up at him. His gaze was trained on the rugged landscape in front of them.

"He probably cut west to get away from the highway, then turned south. That means this section."

She stared out the window, suddenly getting his meaning. He'd divided up the sections so that *they* would have the greatest likelihood of finding Gavin, not some hotshot who couldn't wait to whip out his gun.

He drove silently as she scanned the bone-dry landscape dotted with boulders and cacti and skeletal-looking plants. She searched all of it without seeing her brother's car—without seeing anything, really, but desolation.

Jon's handheld radio crackled, and he picked it up. "Yeah?"

Andrea couldn't make out the garbled words, but Jon seemed to catch them.

"Roger that. We're on our way."

"What is it?"

Jon swung into a turn, throwing a spray of rocks up behind them. "Our CBP friend spotted the car." He looked at her. "It's empty."

◆

He floored the gas, and they bumped and lurched over the rocky earth as Andrea's mind reeled. He cut a straight line north, pushing the speedometer to fifty.

"There." She pointed at the two white vehicles near a clump of mesquite bushes. A patch of blue flashed in the mid-morning sun. She saw the glimmer of a windshield peeking out from beneath the foliage.

Jon jammed to a stop. Andrea jumped out and rushed up to the car. The driver's-side door stood open.

"We're running the plates now," Torres said.

"It's his."

Everyone looked at her.

"You sure?" Jon asked.

She ignored his question as she ducked under the branches to peer inside. It was Gavin's, no doubt about it. Two oversize fast-food cups were stuffed in the cup holders. Wrappers littered the floor. In the backseat was a wadded T-shirt.

She stood up and whirled around. "No sign of him?"

Torres traded looks with Jon. They weren't telling her something. She turned back to examine the car again, looking for what she'd missed.

Blood.

On the steering wheel, two dark smears. Andrea's heart lurched.

She glanced up at Torres, then darted a look at the CBP guy who was inside his vehicle on the radio, presumably running the plate. "Is this how it was, with the door open? He found it this way?"

"That's right."

Her pulse spiked. Maybe they had it all wrong. Maybe Gavin wasn't speeding *toward* Mexico but *away* from something else. Maybe someone was pursuing him.

And now his car was abandoned in the desert, with the door hanging open. She glanced at the blood on the steering wheel and looked at Jon, who was crouched beside the back tires, searching for something on the ground. Spent cartridges? Blood trails?

"No shells," Torres said. "We already checked."

Andrea knelt down to see for herself. She leaned into the front seat, careful not to touch anything as she searched for further signs of violence. Her chest tightened as all the possibilities flooded her brain.

"Footprints?" She looked at Jon, who knelt nearby, examining the ground.

"Too rocky." He glanced east toward the highway. "Same for tire marks. We can backtrack, see if there's a patch of sand between here and the road, maybe get something."

"I've got another unit on the way," the CBP agent said, climbing out of his truck.

Jon stood up and looked at him. "We're going to need at least two more. And a helicopter, ASAP."

"You think your suspect's still out here?"

Suspect.

Andrea looked at Jon, who was watching her.

"If he is," he said, "we'll find him."

◆

The sun inched high in the sky as they trudged over the arid land. Jon cut a path through the thorny brush, pushing forward while trying to dodge the worst of it. He could hear Andrea behind him, quietly keeping up with his long strides. The few times he'd suggested a break, she'd simply ignored him and kept going.

"How much have we covered?" she asked tersely.

"About five square miles."

They'd divided up the search area, and once again, Jon had chosen the highest-probability section for him and Andrea, figuring they had a better chance of picking him up without resistance. Now Jon regretted the strategy. They'd been out here more than three hours, and the odds of finding Gavin were rapidly fading.

Jon pictured the car again, with the blood-smeared steering wheel and the door hanging open. When he'd first seen it, he'd immediately imagined the driver being chased down, dragged from the car, and shot, then either left for dead or hauled away.

Andrea had probably imagined that, too, which was why she'd had that bleak look on her face when they set out on the search.

Sweat trickled down Jon's back as he picked his way over the uneven ground, trying to find firm footing so they wouldn't turn an ankle. He listened to Andrea's footfalls behind him and wished she would say something to break the silence. She was strong and resilient, and somehow he knew that she was too proud to talk to him about what was really hurting her right now.

The sound of her phone made him stop and turn.

"Hello?"

Hope filled her voice, but then her face fell.

"Oh, hi." She looked at him and gave a slight shake of her head. "No, I'm actually . . . pretty tied up at the moment. I can't really talk." She went still. Her gaze dropped to the ground, and she turned away. "Okay, thanks for the info . . . Yeah, I know . . . Say again? You're breaking up."

Jon glanced around, surprised she was even getting a connection out here. Cell-phone coverage was spotty throughout the area. If they got much farther away from the highway corridor, it would probably disappear completely.

She stood with her back to him, shoulders tense, and he could hear the tinny sound of someone on the other end yelling at her. He studied the back of her neck, pink with sunburn, as she talked on the phone.

"Nathan . . ." Her tone was defensive. "I don't expect you to tell them anything."

Jon eased closer.

"Yeah, well, I never asked you to. I can take care of myself."

A moment later, she huffed out a breath and stuffed the phone into her pocket as she turned around.

"Who was that?"

"Friend from work." She brushed past him and plunged ahead through the thicket of mesquite. Jon followed.

"He sounded upset."

"I'm supposed to be in today. I have a hearing at four."

Jon halted. She kept going. "*The* hearing? That's today?"

"I'll reschedule."

"You could lose your job."

"I'll handle it."

He checked his watch. She had four hours, which was still doable if she caught a flight out of Midland. "Andrea, we can cover this here. If you go back now, you could still make it—"

"Drop it!" She whirled around. "I'm not going!"

She strode ahead, and he watched her for a moment, a bundle of nerves and determination plowing through the bushes. She was intent on seeing this through, no matter what the outcome.

He caught up to her and cut ahead, taking the lead. He'd had a lot more practice tromping around the desert than she had. He picked his way over debris and around rock piles, shifting his gaze from the rocky ground to the distant horizon, trying to keep them on track while scouring the area in front of them. The desert was littered with all sorts of clues, both human and non-human, and Jon mentally cataloged everything. They passed deer and jackrabbit droppings, cigarette butts, food wrappers, empty water bottles discarded by people on the move. They passed spiny canes of ocotillo and spiky agave bushes and bony animal carcasses picked clean by scavengers. Jon trudged past all of it, keeping his mental map fixed firmly in his head.

And with every step deeper into the parched wilderness, he became more and more pissed off.

Andrea's boots clomped over the ground behind him. He heard her heavy breathing as she strained to keep up. She was intensely worried and intensely focused, and he knew she wouldn't stop until she had tracked down her selfish, no-good brother, no matter how much it cost her.

Her worry was justified. However this played out, the kid was in deep shit, and despite her determination, Andrea wasn't going to be able to dig him out.

Jon's gut tightened as he thought of Jennifer McVeigh, who'd been put on the witness stand at her brother's trial. The woman had idolized her older sibling. It was her obvious reluctance to testify that had made her such a compelling witness.

Jon pictured Andrea in the witness chair, with twelve jurors riveted by her words.

Gavin Finch hadn't masterminded anything. Jon knew that. But he *had* provided technical support, as Jon had suspected since the day he learned the identity of Lost Creek Ranch's newest arrival. It was going to be difficult, if not impossible, for Gavin to make anyone believe he'd set up Shay Hardin's communications and yet knew nothing about his schemes. Jon didn't believe it, and he wasn't even sure Andrea did. He doubted a jury would, either.

And a trial by jury was the *good* scenario.

Jon's gaze scanned the desert floor as he focused on a more likely one: Gavin Finch slumped under a mesquite bush, gut-shot and bleeding. Or dragged from his car, murdered, and tossed into a trunk to be disposed of somewhere no one would ever find him.

Was Hardin capable of executing a man who'd once been his friend? Absolutely. Andrea knew it, too. Since the moment she'd burst into the trailer with the news about Carmen Pena and her child, Jon had seen the shift in her. She'd suddenly realized they were dealing with a sociopath.

A faint buzzing noise made Jon stop in his tracks and squint at the sky. A chopper appeared like a gnat on the horizon and hovered over the site of the abandoned car.

"Who's that?" Andrea looked at him.

"Reinforcements."

◆

Andrea trekked over the rocky terrain. She skimmed her gaze over the bushes and boulders and cacti. The very *sameness* of it all was unnerving, and she'd stopped a few times to ask Jon to confirm that they weren't going in circles. But he assured her that they were moving in a steady crisscross pattern over their designated search area.

The now-familiar thrumming overhead made her shoulders tense. It was the ninth pass. She'd been counting. If a helicopter didn't spot him, what were the odds Gavin was actually out here? She'd been holding out hope because she couldn't stand the alternative. But with every passing hour, that hope diminished, and the stark realization of what had likely happened began to take its place.

"You'd be surprised how much a chopper misses."

She glanced up at Jon, whose broad shoulders she'd been following for miles now. She'd memorized his gait, his posture, the heels of his boots. He'd set a ruthless pace out here, and she liked him better for it.

"People get low," he said, "especially when they're injured. He could be under a bush or huddled up against a rock. Chopper could do a dozen flyovers, never catch a glimpse of him."

Andrea's response came out as a grunt. She'd hardly slept last night, and she'd skipped breakfast. Her legs felt like noodles. Despite all her jogging, her knees weren't used to so much up-

and-down, and her boots were giving her blisters. She studied the surrounding trees but saw nothing except the same monotonous pattern of rock piles and cacti and thorny bushes she'd been seeing for hours now.

"Water break."

Jon stopped, but she simply went around him.

"Andrea."

The sharp tone of his voice made her turn around. She was too tired to argue, so she trudged back. He set his pack on a rock and pulled out a fresh bottle. By some unspoken agreement, he was carrying all the heavy gear—the water, the walkie-talkie, the first-aid kit. She had only her phone and a granola bar stuffed in her pocket, alongside the black-tipped bullet she'd been carrying like a talisman. For days, it had bolstered her motivation.

"Here," he said.

She accepted the water and tipped her head back for a gulp.

"You need sunblock."

"I'm good." She lowered the bottle from her lips and squinted up at the sky.

"No, you're not. But I don't have any anyway, so you're outta luck."

She looked him over, noting his sun-browned skin and muscular forearms. His T-shirt clung to his skin, but he wasn't breathing heavily, which told her he did a lot more than pump iron to keep in shape.

Andrea stretched her muscles. Everything ached, and she wanted to collapse into a heap on the ground. Or better, collapse against Jon and just let it all spill out—her worries, her fears, her darkest "what ifs." She had the impulse to pour it all out to him, as if he could be her confidant, her friend in this situation—which, of course, he couldn't.

Frustration burned inside her. How had she ended up here? How had Gavin brought her to this? She couldn't stop thinking about the freckled little boy who used to call out to her when he had night terrors and how she would sit up with him and scratch his back and tell him everything was going to be all right. Andrea looked around at the boundless desert. Sweat trickled down her neck, and a lump of fear rose in her throat.

She handed back the water bottle, but at his disapproving look, she took another swig.

"We're losing a pint an hour out here."

"I'm not even sweating, really." Which wasn't true, but she didn't want to ease off the pace.

"Don't be fooled by the temperature." He dug into his pack and came up with some packets of table salt. Andrea had used them before when she was training for a marathon. He handed one to her, and she downed the contents as he opened one for himself.

"I got dehydrated once in twenty-degree weather," he said. "Nearly passed out, too."

"Was this when you worked the *Canadian* border?" she asked, alluding to the lie he'd told her the night they met.

"This was in Chicago. I was sledding with Jay and Missy."

"Missy's your sister?"

He smiled. "Our golden retriever. We were out all day, no water, surrounded by snow, but Jay and I were too stupid to eat any. We came home wrecked."

She took another gulp and passed the bottle back. Then she looked around. He was trying to distract her, and it was working. But they had more ground to cover.

Jon shouldered his pack, saving her from nagging. She pulled out her phone to check her messages again.

"Anything?"

She shook her head "I don't have a signal anymore, so—" A flash of white caught her eye. She squinted at it and stepped forward.

"What?"

"There! Through the trees!"

She dodged past him. Was it a T-shirt? A *person*? She scrambled over a pile of rocks and sprinted to a clump of mesquite trees. She dropped to her knees beside the white cloth and yanked the branches away . . .

"A jacket." She stared down at it, crestfallen. It was thick and puffy and streaked with dirt. It looked like a woman's size, and she pictured someone shedding it here as she moved furtively through the desert, desperate to blend in and remain unseen.

Andrea gripped the jacket in her hands.

She stood up, suddenly furious. She flung the jacket away. Then she picked up a rock and flung it, too.

"God *damn* him!" She picked up a bigger rock and hurled it into a clump of trees. "Where the hell is he?" Her voice sounded shrill, and she turned to Jon. "I'm sick to death of this!"

His look was wary as he walked closer. "You're tired."

"I'm not tired, I'm pissed! Why did he get into this mess? What is he *doing* in this godforsaken place?" She picked up another rock and hummed it, and it made a satisfying *thunk* as it ricocheted off a boulder. She reached for another one.

"*Andrea.*"

Her gaze snapped up. He was watching her with complete intensity.

"Do not move."

"What . . ." Her voice trailed off as something shifted in her peripheral vision. A faint noise filled her ears, soft at first, like a tambourine, growing steadily louder as her most primal instincts identified the sound.

Rattlesnake.

It was coiled on a rock, mere inches from her foot. It lifted its head slowly as if sniffing the air.

Andrea's gut clenched. The sound of that rattle filled her head, her universe. She reached for her gun.

"*Don't.*"

Jon eased forward, Sig in hand.

The rattle intensified. It saturated the air, making every molecule vibrate with warning. She felt the tremor in her body, starting with the soles of her feet and working its way up through her knees, her thighs, her chest. She shifted her weight to step away, and the noise grew louder.

"Andrea, please don't move," Jon said tightly.

She made a small, high-pitched noise as he slowly eased forward, aiming his gun.

He got within ten feet of her without taking his eyes off the snake.

"Are you going to shoot it?" she croaked.

"Not unless—"

The head lifted high above the giant coil of snake flesh. The rattling intensified, drowning out all other sound.

Andrea's knees quivered.

"Please tell me you're a decent shot."

He didn't answer, but his arm was rock-steady as he pointed the gun, seemingly right at her kneecaps.

She closed her eyes. She held her breath.

She heard a deafening *bang*.

chapter twenty-two

JON STOOD BESIDE THE SUV, listening to Torres's half of a conversation with their boss. At last, he hung up.

"Maxwell is back with reinforcements," Torres informed him. "They're going to set up in the trailer near the oil derrick."

"How many?" Jon asked. Budgets were tight everywhere, and you could tell how much priority an investigation had by how many agents were staffed to it.

"Maxwell plus two."

Jon shook his head. He looked at Andrea seated on the bumper of her dusty Cherokee, wiping rattlesnake guts off her jeans with a paper towel. His ears were still ringing from the gunshot, which meant hers were, too.

She glanced up and caught him staring at her.

"They've doubled up on the senator, though," Torres said. "He's now got two more at his house interviewing him, along with a surveillance team on him and his wife. Still the private bodyguards, which is either good or bad."

"Good," Jon said. "I met them in Arizona. They're supposed to be the best."

Torres nodded. "Well, something's up in Philly, because at least some of the momentum's shifting away from there."

"But not to us," he said bitterly. A couple of additional agents was nothing relative to the size of the case before them. Which told Jon that many people believed they still didn't *have* a case.

"Maxwell wants an all-hands meeting in thirty minutes," Torres said, "to give everyone a rundown."

"And this?" Jon jerked his head at the border agents clustered nearby.

"He wants CBP to take it from here." Torres paused. "What about Andrea?"

"What about her?"

"She seems pretty shaken."

"She is. And she's dehydrated. She needs to get back to town, get indoors. I'll take her when we wrap up here."

"Take me where?"

He glanced up to see her striding over, looking primed for a fight. "They're suspending the search for now," he said.

"Who is?"

"My SAC. He wants a team meeting."

Andrea glanced over her shoulder at the line of cars, where several CBP agents seemed to have gotten the word and were now packing up to leave. She glanced at the sky, where the chopper had disappeared. They'd been over this entire area, and it was obvious to everyone but Andrea that the chances of finding Gavin out here—injured or otherwise—were rapidly fading.

"The unit with the search dog's gonna stay on," Torres said, probably reading her expression. "If there's anything here to find, he'll find it."

Andrea looked at them, her face taut with worry. Despite the sunburn on her cheeks and nose, her skin looked wan. Jon wanted to get her out of here.

"I need you to drop me at my house so I can pick up my truck," he told her.

"Get someone else to take you. I'm staying here."

"Andrea—"

"*I'm staying.*"

Torres sent him a look. "Think I'll go talk to Whitfield, give him the update."

Jon felt his temper rising as Andrea glanced over her shoulder at the canine team. The German shepherd stood in the shade of the SUV, lapping up water from a plastic bowl. Andrea had to be at least as tired and thirsty as that dog.

"You've been at this five hours, Andrea. You need a break."

"I'm fine."

"CBP can handle it. They've got a search dog."

"And they've got me," she said, daring him to challenge her. The words *back off* were not in her vocabulary, and she was offended he'd even suggested it.

"Andrea." He struggled for patience. "You look sick. You haven't eaten today, and my guess is you didn't sleep much last night." He paused. "Am I right?"

"I had a granola bar." She looked out at the desert, avoiding eye contact.

"Andrea, we've got alerts out for him. We'll find him. All you're doing out here is working yourself into a panic. I'll call you as soon as we know anything."

Anger sparked in her eyes as she turned to face him. "Let me ask you this: if your sister was lost out here, injured and thirsty, would you sit back and let someone else find her?"

He didn't answer.

"That's what I thought." She pulled the shades off the top of her head and shoved them on. "Go to your meeting, North. I'm not leaving."

✦

"Let's start at the top," Maxwell said. "We've got an alert out for Gavin Finch at border checkpoints in El Paso, Presidio, Boquillas, and Del Rio."

"And with TSA agents at all the nearby airports," Jon added.

"Anything else turn up? Whitfield?"

The agent glanced up, startled. "Uh, nothing here."

Whitfield looked beat. Everyone did. It was after nine P.M., and they were suffering through the second team meeting of a grueling day. Everyone was ready to call it a night, particularly the new recruits from Philadelphia. Theilman and Santucci were still on East Coast time.

"Well, at this point, I think he's officially disappeared on us," Maxwell said, king of the obvious. "If he's running, that tells me he's probably hiding something. If he's not running, that tells me he's probably dead. North?"

"Sir."

"Your team's latest report says no one at that ranch has an active cell phone that we're aware of. Have you developed anything else? How's he communicating with his sister?"

"Occasional e-mails," Jon said. "Using the satellite Internet connection, the people on the ranch could be going online to check e-mail, Skype, send messages, whatever."

"And?"

"And our surveillance team's been running a scan ever since

we found out about the SNAP system," Jon said. "But so far, no intercepts."

The door swung open, and Torres tromped into the room, bringing a gust of wind with him. Like Jon, he was still in tactical pants and heavy boots. A thin layer of dust covered him from head to toe.

"Any news?" Maxwell asked.

He grabbed a seat beside Jon. "Just finished another search with the canine team and Andrea Finch. Nothing."

Expressions soured around the table at the mention of her name.

"This is the cop from Dallas?" Theilman asked.

"Austin," Jon said.

"I hear she's up on disciplinary charges. You really think she's reliable?"

"Charges?" Maxwell looked at him. Clearly, this was the first he'd heard of it.

"Detective Finch is on administrative leave following a shooting incident. It's under review now, but she's expected to be greenlighted to go back to work soon." If she hadn't been fired for missing her hearing today.

"Yeah, well, I don't trust her," Theilman said. "Maybe she's holding out on us. How do we know she didn't help her brother flee the country?"

"I was with her when she went to pick him up," Jon said. "He was a no-show."

"You been with her twenty-four seven? Maybe the meet was a ploy. Hell, maybe *she* drove his car into the desert and left it there so we'd be chasing our tails while he makes a run for the border."

"Let's keep our eye on the ball," Maxwell said. "Our primary objective is Hardin. When's the last time we saw him?"

"No visual on him today," Whitfield reported. "But his truck hasn't moved in the last thirty-six hours, so the assumption is he's still there."

"Who *do* we have a visual on from today?"

"Mark Driscoll and his wife left the property at eleven thirty-five A.M. to go into town. They stopped at the grocery store, then McDonald's, then went straight back home."

"You find out what they bought?"

Whitfield sighed and flipped open the notebook in front of him. "Cat food, milk, tampons, and a six-pack of Cokes." He turned the page. "Also a McRib sandwich and two large fries."

"I think we need to beef up surveillance around the property," Torres said. "We've only got eyes on two gates, and we might miss something."

"It's already happening," Jon said.

"Since when?" Maxwell asked.

"Since this morning, when we learned from Detective Finch that some people have been using roads on the adjacent ranches to come and go."

"We have to be careful," Maxwell said. "The last thing we need is for them to know they're under surveillance. Then we'll run the risk of a standoff, like the Ruby Ridge debacle."

"Why don't we just surround the place?" Whitfield put in. "Then at least we'd have the son of a bitch pinned down. Who cares if he knows about it?"

"A standoff means possible casualties, both law enforcement and civilian." Maxwell glanced at the faces around the table. "We're trying to minimize confrontation and avoid a showdown. And that comes from on high. We don't want another Waco."

"Why don't we just pick up Hardin and interview him?" Santucci asked in a rare display of speech.

"We've been over this," Maxwell said. "That tips our hand. I can't stress this enough: we need *physical* evidence against Hardin and his conspirators. The Justice Department is under huge pressure to bring this case to trial, and it's turning into a clusterfuck." He turned to Jon with a dark look. "What do we have on the car?"

"Prints just came back, and no hits in AFIS. But that's not surprising, because Gavin Finch has never been arrested."

"We're sure?" Theilman asked.

"He's got a clean record," Jon said. "Never even had a speeding ticket." Now he sounded like Andrea, but he needed to put it out there. "Some of the prints on the passenger side are smaller, possibly a woman's. My guess is Vicky Leeland."

"Why?" Maxwell's gaze narrowed.

"According to Detective Finch, her brother might have been having an affair with her."

"Where is she?" Maxwell's gaze shot to Whitfield.

"No visual on her today. And her car isn't there—or at least, it wasn't when we did the last flyover. No one's seen it reenter the property."

"It's possible she's with Gavin Finch," Jon pointed out. "Our alerts include her, too."

"What else do we know about the car?"

"Also recovered: a pair of pink flip-flops, women's size six. And a whole lot of trash. Plus the blood, obviously. Lab's working on that now, but it will take a few days, at least."

"Well, that's not much." Maxwell sighed. "I was hoping they might have found a bag of hundred-dollar bills we could tie back to one of these bank robberies. Guess that would be too easy."

"They did find some money," Torres said. "Evidence team recovered fifty-eight bucks from the glove compartment."

Jon exchanged a grim look with Torres. Most people wouldn't leave cash behind. If they had a choice.

Jon had a very bad feeling about this whole situation. He stared at the window as he thought about Andrea, combing the desert until she was ready to pass out. She'd been expecting to find a corpse. He'd seen the bleak certainty in her eyes.

Jon raked his hand through his hair. He truly hated this case.

"North, you've got a rapport with the sister," Maxwell stated. "You think she'll tell you if her brother reaches out to her?"

Rapport. That was one way of putting it.

"I don't know."

The hard truth was that even after everything they'd been through, Jon still didn't believe she trusted him.

"Keep tabs on her," Maxwell said. "She's our best connection to the brother. On the off chance he's still alive, he might know something that could break this thing open."

✦

The stoplight blinked yellow as Jon drove through town, scanning all the parking lots. No brown Dodge. No white Jeep. It was after midnight, and Maverick was shut down almost completely, with the exception of a single gas station, where a spotlight beamed down on a self-serve pump.

On the phone an hour ago, Andrea had said she was going to bed, and she'd sounded tired enough to be convincing. But he'd driven by her motel, and the Jeep wasn't there. He'd driven by all the local motels and had spotted no sign of her. Where the hell was she? He wouldn't put it past her to be traipsing around the desert by flashlight, still searching. It would be a desperate thing to do, but the last time he'd seen her, that was precisely the emotion engraved on her face: desperation. And fear, with maybe some anger thrown in to make the other two bearable. Jon didn't mind the anger—he welcomed it, in fact. It was better than seeing her scared.

Jon pulled out his phone and called, but it went to voice mail, and he skipped leaving another message. He made another pass through town and then headed out to his house.

He needed to stay away from her. He was too close, too involved, too biased now to be objective about his job. She had him actually *worried* about what happened to her brother. Not just about how to bring him in but how to help him avoid a fate of his own damn making. It was screwed up, and the solution was to put some distance between himself and Andrea—which seemed to be happening on its own now, anyway. *Keep tabs on her.* Right. He couldn't even get her to return a call.

Jon turned onto his street. A pair of headlights blinked into his rearview mirror. A punch of relief hit him, but it was quickly replaced by frustration.

He whipped into his driveway as the Jeep rolled to a stop in front of his house.

Jon climbed out. "Would it kill you to return a phone call?"

She didn't say anything, but her look was belligerent as she approached his truck. "What's the news?"

"Nothing." He slammed the door and turned to scowl at the Rottweiler going bonkers on the other side of the fence. When he turned back to Andrea, she was watching him, searching his face for answers.

And suddenly he felt like shit, because he didn't have any.

She crossed her arms over her chest, but it wasn't her typical defiant stance. She looked like she was hugging herself. She glanced away from him, and he'd never seen her seem so small.

"You look worse than you did earlier," he said. "Where've you been?"

"Out."

Not quite the comeback he'd wanted. The worried look on her face pulled at him. The logical part of his mind shouted a warning, but he ignored it.

"Come on." He took her hand. He must have caught her in a moment of extreme vulnerability, because she followed without the slightest resistance.

He unlocked his door and stepped into the cold, dark house that had been empty for eighteen hours. He flipped on a light and pulled her into the kitchen, where he opened the cabinet beside the sink.

"What's that for?" She eyed the bottle of Patrón warily.

"Comfort food." He took down two juice glasses and poured them each a generous shot—or three. He held hers out and stared her down until she took it.

"I hate tequila."

"You need it."

She lifted the glass reluctantly and examined its contents.

"No worms, I promise."

She surprised him by tossing it back. She plunked the glass on the counter and doubled over, coughing.

"God, that's *awful.*"

He downed his shot, savoring the fire as it slid down his throat. He rested his cup beside hers, and she stared down at the twin glasses, both with barely a sip left.

"Better?" he asked.

"No."

She drained the rest stoically, and he followed suit. When their glasses were side by side again, he looked at her and felt the booze kicking in.

The room fell silent. Even Loco had quieted. The air was charged with tension as he held her gaze and reached up to touch her cheek. He stroked his hand down and let it rest on her shoulder. He could see the pulse thrumming at the side of her neck as she eyed him mistrustfully.

Something twisted inside him. All this time together, and she still didn't know. She didn't have a clue how he felt about her.

He leaned his head down and kissed her.

chapter twenty-three

THE SLOW BURN SPREAD through her body as she lifted her arms up around his neck and their hips connected.

He kissed her forcefully, and her heart pounded. This was a bad idea. Her emotions were up. Her defenses were down. Which was exactly why she wanted his strong arms around her and his weight pressing against her body. His kiss was determined, insistent, as if he was done with excuses, and he knew she was done, too.

She combed her hands through his hair, and her fingertips tingled. *It's the tequila.*

But that wasn't all. The real intoxication was coming from the decision she'd made when she let him pull her into his house.

The burn spread, and she gave herself over to it. His hands closed around her waist, and he lifted her onto the counter, pushing her knees apart. His palms slid over her thighs, and when she leaned into him it was like an electric current passed between them. She wrapped her legs around him and drew him against her and kissed him, dimly aware of him tugging at her T-shirt, pulling it from her jeans. He kissed her with a hot, fierce urgency as his fingers slid over her ribs. His thumbs brushed her nipples, and he made a low groan in his chest as she pulled him closer with the heels of her boots.

"You feel good." His breath was hot against her ear, and she tipped her head back as he trailed kisses down her throat. His hands slid around, looking for the clasp of her bra.

She nudged him away, hopped off the counter, and picked up his hand. "Take me to bed."

His gaze heated, and he pulled her the short distance across the house. The only light was a wedge of yellow from the hallway as he leaned her back on the bed and stripped off her boots, then her T-shirt. He kissed her face, her neck, her collarbone. He slid the straps down her shoulders and moved to her breast, hovering until she looked at him, and then the hot pull of his mouth was a jolt that had her arching off the bed. She gripped his shoulders.

"God, I've wanted to do this for so long." He slid his mouth down her body. "You have no idea."

She managed to tug his shirt up while he kissed her, and she got her hands on all those firm muscles. He sat back and yanked the T-shirt over his head, and she was speechless at the sight of him in the dim light, all bronze skin and defined abs. He didn't seem to notice her gaping, though, because he was too busy un-buttoning her jeans and kissing her and stroking his hands over her arms, her breasts, her thighs. He eased her zipper down, and she lifted her hips as he peeled off the jeans, leaving only her white cotton bikinis.

He went still. "What happened?"

"What?" She sat up on her elbows and saw the alarm in his eyes. He reached over and switched on the lamp, and she blinked at the sudden brightness.

"Hey!"

"What the hell, Andrea?" He surveyed her bruises, which had faded to green and brown.

"I had a little run-in when I first got to town."

"A *run-in*?"

"I bumped into someone at the ranch one night. He didn't like me trespassing."

The muscle in his jaw jumped. His gaze skimmed over her body, and she shifted slightly, so he wouldn't see the still-dark bruise on her back. "Is anything broken?"

"I'm fine." She shimmied down the bed and hooked her finger into the waist of his pants. "Really, it's nothing. Turn off the light."

When he didn't move, she reached over and did it herself. Then she shifted to her knees in the darkness and ran her hands over his skin. He remained tense, unmoving.

"I'm fine," she whispered, leaning into him. She kissed her way up his neck and lingered at the spot just under his ear that smelled so warm and masculine it was making her dizzy. She wanted to distract him again. Tonight was about distraction. She took his hand and settled it at her waist, then slowly brought it up to her breast as her teeth sank into his earlobe. She inched closer and stroked her hands over his wide shoulders, his sculpted arms. *This* was what she craved most—the contrast.

She loved the scent of him, the feel of him. She loved his arms wrapped around her. He brought his mouth down to hers, and she could taste his desire again as he eased her back against the mattress.

She lost herself in his kisses, in the warmth of his hands gliding over her, the feel of his stubble rasping over her skin. She loved his strength. She loved the hard contours of his shoulders as he propped himself on his forearms, trying to keep his weight from crushing her as their bodies moved together and the heat built.

She closed her eyes and gave into it, letting the need spread through her entire body like hot wax. She stopped thinking and let herself feel and touch and be tasted. Finally, he stepped off the bed and stripped off the rest of their clothes, and she heard the soft tear of a condom wrapper. Her heart pounded wildly. The mattress shifted and made a loud squeak.

He eased her legs apart, and she clamped down on her resistance as he pushed inside and every nerve jumped. For an endless moment, she didn't move, didn't breathe. He rested his weight on his arms and gazed down at her, and she could feel the tension in his body.

"I'm okay. It's good," she whispered, shifting her hips.

She pulled him close, and then they were moving, finding their rhythm, and the bed was squeaking and squeaking as she felt her body coiling tighter and tighter. He kissed her fiercely, possessively, as they moved together, and she slid her hands down the valley of his back, over his corded muscles. The cool, controlled part of him was gone, replaced by pure need and intensity, and the power of him took her breath away. She wrapped her arms tighter, desperate to pull him closer as he set a ruthless pace that she strove to match. It was like before, like the hiking, with him pushing and pushing and making her keep up with him, and she loved that he refused to go easy on her. The heat gathered inside her body, and she could feel it coming, feel it bearing down on her as she dug her heels into him and felt the first tremor as she clenched around him.

"Oh, God . . . *yes.*"

A powerful thrust pushed her over the edge, and she tipped

her head back and came apart. A groan tore from his chest as he drove into her one last time.

She lay there, lax, just listening to his breathing and the sound of her own heart thrumming. He hovered over her, breathing hard but still not crushing her.

Her head fell to the side, against the cool bedspread, and they let the moment settle.

"You all right?"

She opened her eyes and smiled. He searched her face for another second before pulling away and climbing off the bed. He disappeared into the bathroom across the hall.

A chill drifted over her skin. She felt instantly, agonizingly alone, and she closed her eyes, shocked by the sting of tears. She never cried after sex. Her emotions felt exposed tonight. Her body, her nerve endings, everything tonight felt naked and vulnerable.

The bathroom door whisked shut. The mattress shifted and squeaked.

"Nice bed." She turned to look at him as he stretched out beside her in the dimness.

"Yeah, sorry. I usually only use it for sleeping."

"Usually?"

"Most nights, anyway."

He'd said it to needle her, which she took as a good sign.

They were still on top of the covers, and the room was cold, but he radiated heat. She scooted against him and was pleased to feel the sweat on his skin and know she wasn't the only one feeling the exertion. She rested her head on his biceps as she trailed her hand down his body.

She gave him a look. "Already?"

He kissed her forehead. "We can take a breather."

She smiled and closed her eyes. He was keeping it light. To-night was about distraction, and they both understood that.

She felt his fingers in her hair, combing it away from her face. Then he stroked his hand down her arm, and the touch was so gentle it put an ache in her chest.

Maybe there was more here.

But she didn't want to think that. She refused to let herself. Almost as soon as the thought formed, she forced it away. She needed to let tonight be what it was, not think beyond it.

His arm settled over her waist, warm and heavy, and suddenly she was so, so tired she couldn't form a single thought. She nestled against him and let the steady rhythm of his breathing soothe her to sleep.

◆

She lay in Jon's bed, watching the windows lighten. She hadn't slept well, and she resigned herself to starting yet another day feeling sapped of energy. Her gaze drifted to the man beside her, sleeping on his back with her thigh cradled snugly against his stomach. In the dimness, she watched the steady rise and fall of his chest. She looked at his muscled arms, his pecs, the shadow along his jaw where another day's worth of beard was coming in. It was his face that amazed her. Despite the hard lines, there was something soft about him in sleep, something that wrapped around her heart and squeezed.

He looked relaxed. It wasn't his typical state, and she felt lucky to catch a glimpse of him in their own private moment, locked away from everything else. What would it be like to see this private side of him every day? To really be *with* him and let her guard down? To learn each other?

The fantasy ended when she spied her phone on the night-stand. Still no word. She'd awakened twice during the night to check it, and twice Jon had pulled her back to bed and made her forget the soul-crushing worry.

Distraction. He was good at it. And despite the raw, physical way he did it, there was an aspect of friendship to it, too. She'd come over here last night looking for an escape, and he'd ful-filled her wish. It should have been enough, but now that they were cocooned together in the warmth of his sheets, she wanted more from him. The way he'd touched her and looked at her had kindled sparks of longing, which was so unlike her that she felt scared. She wanted . . . if she was honest with herself, she wanted him to want more of her. She wanted him to want her back, again and again.

It was a reckless thing to want. And it was impossible anyway, but that didn't keep her from letting the thought fill her mind as she skimmed her gaze over his face, his shoulders, the masculine trail of hair that started at his navel.

"You gonna look or touch?" He opened an eye lazily.

"You're awake." She slapped his arm.

A smile spread over his face. "How can I sleep with you lust-ing over me like that?"

"Ha." She turned to swing her legs out of bed, but he caught her around the waist and pulled her on top of him. It was one of their better positions.

"It's okay." His voice was still gravelly from sleep. "Lust all you want."

She squirmed into a sitting position and looked down at him, flattered when his gaze drifted to her breasts. She was far from voluptuous, but that hadn't stopped him from lavishing attention on her all night.

She reached out and traced a finger over his bristly chin. She felt flooded with wonder at the pure attraction burning in his eyes. He slid his palms up and pulled her down to kiss him. It started playful but quickly turned serious as she shifted on top of him. She couldn't seem to get enough of his taste, his kiss, the feel of his hands gliding over her body.

At the sound of her phone, she went rigid. For a moment, they were still, staring at each other. Then she climbed off him and grabbed the phone from the nightstand.

She checked the number and muttered a curse.

"Who is it?" He sat up on his elbows.

"Nathan from work."

"Don't you need to answer it?"

She sighed. "I already know what he's going to say."

"It could be about your job."

"It is." The phone chirped as he left another voice mail. She glanced up, and Jon was watching her, gaze narrowed.

"How do you know?"

"Because he left a message yesterday."

"And?"

"And the committee decided to let me go."

He leaned forward. "They fired you?"

She flinched at the word. "It's done."

"What do you mean, done?"

"It's over." She tossed the phone onto the nightstand and grabbed her shirt off the floor. "They set up hoops for me to jump through. I didn't jump. I missed three shrink appointments and a hearing. So they let me go."

"Aren't you going to fight for it? Can't you tell them you had a family emergency or something? Can't you call in a favor?"

"I don't need a *favor*." She whirled on him, infuriated by the suggestion. "I've been there six years. They know me. They have my case in front of them." She snapped her jeans up off the floor. "They either want me back or they don't, and they obviously don't."

He got up and pulled on the pants he'd shed just a few short hours ago. "Unbelievable," he said as he zipped up.

"*What?*"

"That's the dumbest thing I've ever heard." He glared at her. "Get some *cojones*, Andrea. You love that job. Go back there and fight for yourself."

"I'm not going to grovel."

"No one's asking you to grovel. They're asking you to show up."

"You don't understand."

"What don't I understand? You think if you throw your career away, it'll bring back that kid? He's gone, Andrea."

She stared at him, shocked.

"There's no going back. And even if you could, you wouldn't change it, because deep down, you know you did the right thing."

She shook her head. "You know what? Just butt out."

"What, and watch you make a really stupid mistake?"

"It's over! And it's none of your business, anyway."

His face hardened at that. She'd insulted him. Fine. He'd insulted her, too. She held her clothes against her body and tried to muster some dignity.

"I need to use your shower."

He looked incredulous. "You have to ask? Jesus."

She stalked into the bathroom and slammed the door.

✦

Jon stared after her, fuming. Six years on the job, and she'd thrown it all away. He wanted to throttle her. He wanted to throttle her brother even more.

The shower went on as he looked at the door. *His* shower. He could be in there with her right now, touching her. But instead, he was out here, pissed off.

He turned away from the door. God damn it, she drove him crazy. But she challenged him, too, and that was part of what excited him. He couldn't predict her. Last night in the dark, she'd mesmerized him, but this morning, she'd just as easily slammed the door in his face.

A phone beeped, and he looked at the nightstand. Both of their phones were there, but hers was the one glowing. He walked over to it.

Not a voice mail this time but a text.

Sorry 4 yesterday. New plan. Meet me @ DQ by 8 & come alone.

Jon glanced at the bathroom door. He picked up the phone.

chapter twenty-four

TORRES SWUNG INTO THE alley behind Walmart and pulled up next to North's pickup.

"Where's Maxwell?" Torres asked, climbing out.

"On his way, but I doubt he'll get here in time." North unlocked the toolbox mounted behind the truck cab and pulled out a Kevlar vest identical to the one he was wearing.

Torres peeled off his dun-colored jacket and tossed it into his truck. "Thought this was the sheriff's collar," he said, strapping on the vest.

"That's the plan."

Meaning if the sheriff's guys screwed up, North wanted to be ready to jump in.

"So how's this going down?" Torres got behind the wheel as North slid into the passenger seat.

"Quick and quiet. We need them out of there before anyone notices."

"What's our position?"

"Eastbound frontage road," North said, "which is their most

likely approach. Another deputy's stationed on the westbound side in case they come from that direction."

"And Andrea?"

"What about her?"

"She's not coming?"

"No."

Torres sensed there was a story there, but he didn't ask. He pulled out of the alley and crossed the near-empty parking lot to the access road that paralleled the interstate. The Dairy Queen was about a hundred yards up at an overpass, a prime location just across from a truck stop.

Torres spotted the sheriff's deputy parked in the grass, watching the exit ramp. He pulled in behind the Walmart sign, where the ICE truck was less noticeable but he and North would have a clear view of everything between the ramp and the restaurant.

Torres glanced across the truck. North was tense, and he figured it had to do with Andrea. Quick and quiet wasn't always doable. Some people didn't take kindly to a routine traffic stop, and everyone was operating under the assumption that Gavin Finch could be armed.

Torres took a deep breath to get himself in the zone. He checked his weapon. His pulse sped up, the way it always did before a takedown.

"Here we go." North reached for the radio as a brown sedan came into view on the feeder road. "We've got a brown Dodge on the eastbound frontage road."

"Roger that," the sheriff's deputy drawled. "I'm lighting 'em up."

The Dodge zipped past the lurking sheriff's unit, which immediately pulled off the grass and onto the road, lights whirling.

Both cars passed Torres before the Dodge driver even tapped the brakes.

"Finch is at the wheel, red baseball cap," North said into the radio. "No passenger."

Where was Vicky Leeland?

The Dodge abruptly slowed and pulled over not far from where Torres had parked. When the Dodge's one taillight went dark, the deputy killed the siren.

North's stress was contagious, and Torres's nerves started jumping as the sheriff's deputy hefted himself out of the cruiser. His hand rested on the holster at his hip as he approached the car. Finch buzzed down his window, and they exchanged a few words, with the deputy motioning at the busted taillight. Then he motioned for Finch to get out.

Torres waited, heart thumping. North eased his door open a few inches and watched intently. If this bust was going to go sideways, it would happen now.

But the kid climbed out and casually handed over an ID. He was as tall as the deputy but probably only half as heavy with his skinny build.

"Come on, come on," North muttered.

"He going to frisk him?"

"That's the plan."

There was some back-and-forth, probably about Vicky Leeland's expired inspection and registration. A visible sigh from Finch, and then he turned around and placed his palms on the roof of the car as the deputy checked him for weapons and came up with nothing. They exchanged a few more words, with Finch shaking his head. The deputy reached for his handcuffs.

Finch bolted.

"Fuck!" North was out of the car in a flash, with Torres right behind him. The deputy jerked his gun from the holster and shouted, and Torres and North rocketed past him before he even got his ass moving.

Finch booked it across the parking lot, with Torres and North hot on his heels. The kid was fast. He darted across a street, dodging cars. He missed being creamed by a Mack truck and then hurdled a ditch like a gazelle.

Sirens went up behind them. The deputy had given up the foot chase.

"The truck stop!" Torres yelled as Finch veered toward the interstate.

Torres set his sights on the sprawling complex, where dozens of rigs coming and going would give Finch a place to hide, maybe even a ride out of town. He and North waited for a break in traffic before hauling across the street.

"Go around front, I'll go in back!" North shouted as they hit the grass.

Torres leaped over the ditch and ignored the zing of pain in his ankle as he sprinted around the front of the building. North pursued around the back, to the row of pumps where eighteen-wheelers were fueling up. Torres ran past the diner and around the corner. He paused for a second and spotted a blur of movement between two rigs, quickly followed by another.

Torres took off for the farthest truck, hoping to head them off. As he ran, he realized he had his Sig in his hand, but he couldn't remember pulling it from the holster. Half of the rigs coming through here were gas tankers, making this a bad place for a firefight.

Sirens screamed behind him, and he glanced over his shoulder to see a pair of sheriff's cruisers flying across the lot.

Torres dodged between two rigs, determined to reach Finch before they did. He spotted the red ball cap just as North made a running leap and tackled the kid to the ground. In seconds, he had his hands behind his back and cuffed.

"You got any weapons?" North hauled him to his feet.

Finch scowled and muttered a no, but Torres was already searching him, well aware that North's sole objective right now was to get the guy under control before the cavalry arrived. The pat-down netted a wallet, six quarters, and a black plastic thumb drive but no weapons.

A stampede of footsteps and half a dozen deputies rounded the eighteen-wheeler, guns drawn.

"Pecos County sheriff! You're under arrest!"

◆

Jon entered the interview room and tossed an envelope down on the table.

Gavin Finch watched him sullenly, arms crossed over his chest. "This is bullshit."

Jon sat down and eyed him across the table. "You think so?"

"You didn't have to do this. I was planning to come in."

"Vicky says hi, by the way."

He sat up straighter. "Where is she?"

"Close by."

After finding a room key in the cup holder of the Dodge, a pair of agents had dropped in on Vicky at the Econo Lodge in Fort Stockton. She'd come in willingly and agreed to be interviewed, but they hadn't started yet. They wanted to see what Gavin revealed first and then see if she could corroborate.

"Where'd you get the fat lip?"

He lifted a hand to his mouth. "Tripped this morning, walking to my car."

Which might explain the blood in his car. It sounded as if he'd slipped out in the dark.

Jon watched him, letting him squirm.

Gavin cast an anxious look at the door, then darted his gaze up to the corner of the room, where a camera was mounted near the ceiling. He glanced down to the envelope again. "What's that?" he asked.

"I bet you can guess."

He eyed the shape of it. He seemed annoyed, and Jon fought the urge to reach across the table and pop him. "It's a thumb drive," Gavin said.

"Yeah, we got that far."

Gavin reached for the envelope and pulled out a small plastic evidence bag containing a compact storage device. "No, I mean literally. It's a thumb drive, as in you need a thumb to open it. It's biometric, only accessible with a designated thumb print."

"Yours?"

"Shay's. I can't open it, if that's what you're thinking."

Jon leaned back in his chair and watched him.

"Seriously, even if I wanted to. One of your techs could probably do it, but it'll take some time."

"What's on it?"

"How should I know? I told you, it's Shay's."

Jon stared at him, not liking the hint of smugness in his voice. "You're not helping yourself here, Gavin."

"What?" He was defensive now. "I really don't know, but it's something important. I know that. Shay keeps it in his room, in the back of a drawer. I went back there and got it so I could bring it to you guys."

"So you were on your way to do the right thing when you decided to turn south and head for the border, is that right?"

"You don't understand." He leaned forward. "I had to wait for Vicky. She slipped out after I did and came to pick me up at a designated spot. My car's a piece of crap. I didn't even have a full tank of gas, so—"

"Why didn't you meet your sister?"

"We were going to. Vicky and I were. But she got cold feet and . . . she was freaking out about Ross and Shay and everyone, and I took her to a motel to talk her down from the ledge and convince her we needed to come in."

"Was this before or after you had sex with her?"

His cheeks flushed, and he slapped the table. "I'm telling you what I know! I'm offering you evidence, and you haven't offered me shit!" He scowled and looked away.

Jon waited.

Gavin's gaze drifted up to the camera again and then back to Jon. "Where is she?"

Jon looked blank. "Who, Andrea?"

"Vicky."

"Don't worry about Vicky. She's doing fine for herself."

"Where is she?"

"Why?" He paused. "You afraid she's going to rat you out?"

"There's nothing to rat out."

Jon arched his eyebrows. "Driving without insurance? Expired registration?"

"That's bullshit."

"Possession of a weapon of mass destruction?"

"*What?*" It came out as a squeak, reminding Jon just how young he was.

"Our dog doesn't like your car, Gavin."

His brow furrowed. "There's nothing in there."

Jon shook his head. "The dogs don't lie. Our evidence techs are going over it right now with a fine-tooth comb. If they find even a trace of explosives residue—"

"There's nothing! There's never been anything in there."

"Yeah? And Shay never borrowed it?"

The kid went still. The only sound was the faint hum of traffic two floors below, in downtown Fort Stockton. His eyes looked worried now but not nearly worried enough. He still didn't grasp the gravity of his situation.

Jon leaned in close. "Your sister lost her job for you, you piece of shit. She keeps telling me how smart you are. But I'm not seeing it."

Jon held his gaze, and the moment stretched out.

"What's on that drive, Gavin?"

"I'm telling you, I don't know."

Jon leaned back and sighed.

Gavin's attention darted to the camera. Clearly, he knew he was being recorded. And he'd waived his right to an attorney. Andrea would be going ballistic watching this.

But she wasn't watching. Jon didn't know where she was or even if she'd figured out what he'd done. His gut tightened with dread, but he couldn't think about her right now. He'd deal with the fallout later, after he got this done.

He kept his gaze locked on her brother, *trying* to sweat him down.

Maybe it was good that he hadn't asked for a lawyer. In Jon's experience, there were two kinds of perps who failed to lawyer up: the ones who thought they were smarter than everyone else and the ones who thought they were innocent *and* smarter than everyone else.

Which type was Gavin Finch? He didn't know yet.

The kid leaned forward, clearly getting frustrated. "I'm telling you, I don't know what's on the drive. But I think it's important."

Jon watched him. It was a bold move, keeping up the denials. If he was involved in Hardin's plot, how could he be sure the thumb drive wouldn't implicate him in some way?

On the other hand, Gavin's former boss had called him a computer maestro. Maybe he'd created the drive and loaded it with evidence that would implicate Hardin but exonerate himself.

Jon glanced at the camera. He could almost feel the impatience bleeding through the wall as Maxwell and the team watched from the next room. The pressure was on. If Jon didn't get something soon, they were going to have to fly the thumb drive to Quantico so their people there could work on it, and time was running short.

They needed something *now* for a warrant, so they could bring Hardin in. They wanted every last one of his conspirators, too, which was why digital evidence of his plans was so important.

Which brought them back to the thumb drive.

Jon leaned in again and pinned him with a look. Nothing.

"What's it gonna be, Gavin?"

His blue eyes simmered. He lifted his chin defiantly, and the resemblance to Andrea was so strong, Jon figured any second now the kid was going to tell him to go to hell. "Vicky had nothing to do with anything," he said instead.

"Okay." Jon waited.

"I'm not lying about the drive. I don't know what's on it. I don't know about what Shay did or anything he's planning."

"What did he do, Gavin? What's he planning? I need something I can use now, *today*, and you need a get-out-of-jail-free card."

"I told you." His gaze shot to the ceiling. "I don't *know* about all that. He didn't tell me."

Jon stood up and grabbed the envelope.

"Wait! Where are you going?"

"It's Vicky's turn. You're wasting my time."

"But I'm telling the truth. He didn't tell me about Philadelphia or Kirby or any of that. I don't know about that, I swear. I just know about the guns."

Jon pulled out the chair and sat down again. "Fine." He nodded. "Tell me what you know."

◆

Torres stepped into the conference room, and he could tell by the defeated looks around the table that the news wasn't good.

"Get anything?" he asked North.

"No."

"Nothing at all?"

"I ran the entire list by ATF. Sixteen pistols, two revolvers, eight long guns. Plus a shit ton of ammo. It's a big cache of weapons, but everything's legal."

Torres glanced across the room to where Theilman was on the phone. "What about the sales?"

"Finch claims he wasn't there," North said. "He remembers e-mails back and forth and a few of the buyers' first names coming up in conversation, but that's not going to cut it. Maxwell decided to kick him loose so we can keep an eye on him, see if he reaches out to anyone."

Torres looked at Theilman again. He looked at North. Four

months they'd been busting their asses out here trying to build a case. Four long months, and it was finally coming to a head.

Torres sank into a chair, and North's gaze narrowed.

"You have something. What is it?"

Torres smiled.

chapter twenty-five

TORRES DRAGGED JON'S LAPTOP across the table. "Check your e-mail."

Jon logged in and found the message. No subject line, just an attachment from Torres, and based on the size, it was a monster. He clicked it open and waited for the file to load. When had Torres had time to run down something new? They'd been together most of the day.

"Whitfield came up with this," he said, reading Jon's mind. "Take a look."

Grainy black-and-white footage appeared, showing a busy checkout counter with four cashiers. Jon recognized the beer display near the door of the store. "The truck stop."

"Yep." Torres scooted his chair in and pointed to the screen. "Check out the customers."

Shay Hardin shuffled to the front of the line, a case of beer in one hand and a few bags of chips in the other.

"Whitfield noticed how he stops in there from time to time, even though it's busier and farther away than the little grocery store on Main Street. So this morning, he got curious."

"Followed him into the store?" Jon asked, watching Hardin approach the register.

"Nope. Waited outside. Okay, check this out." Torres paused the video as Hardin accepted a handful of change. "Seventy-two dollars, ninety-one cents change."

Jon's pulse picked up as he looked at the screen. "He paid with a hundred."

"Bingo." Torres grinned. "He pitched his receipt in the trash when he left, then Whitfield fished it out and followed up with the cashier. The bill traces back to a stack from the Del Rio bank hit."

"Does Maxwell know?"

"You bet your ass. He's working on our warrant right now."

Torres stood up and closed the computer. Jon stood, too, and there was a faint ringing in his ears as the new reality sank in. After all this time, they had him.

Torres slapped him on the shoulder. "You believe this? We finally nailed him. Forty-eight hours to spare, too."

Whitfield stuck his head in the room.

"Hey, I was just telling North about your C-note," Torres said. "Nice trash dig."

"Thanks. North, thought you'd want to know Maxwell's cutting Finch loose."

"I know."

"His sister's here to pick him up."

✦

Jon spotted her pushing through the doors of the sheriff's complex. She glanced over her shoulder, and their gazes met as she stepped outside.

"Andrea."

But she was already out the door. He caught up and saw her brother ahead of her in the parking lot. She hurried down the steps.

"*Andrea.*" He caught her arm, and she whirled around.

"Do not. Touch me." Her look was arctic.

"I understand you're angry."

Her brows shot up. "Angry? Is that what you think this is? You deliberately *deceived* me."

"Andrea—"

"Just—stop." She squeezed her eyes shut and held up her hand. "I can't do this. I can't even look at you right now." She turned and rushed down the steps.

He followed. "I did what I had to."

"Right," she tossed over her shoulder. "Because you're morally superior. I forgot, you're the only cop with any integrity."

"He's your brother, Andrea. I couldn't be sure what you'd do."

That halted her. She spun around. "He is my brother. Yes. And I have dedicated my *life* to protecting the public." Her voice was quiet, but there was a tremor of fury in it. "You think I wouldn't do anything under the sun to prevent more people from getting hurt? Do you even know who I am?"

Jon said nothing. The wounded look in her eyes blew a hole in his confidence that he was going to be able to fix this.

She stepped closer. "I'm a *cop*, Jon. I'm nobody's wife. I'm nobody's mother. I'm nobody's daughter. I'm a cop." She clutched her fist to her chest. "That's who I am." She shook her head and started down the stairs again.

"Would you please wait a second?"

"No."

He took her arm and she jerked back like she'd been singed.

"Do not *touch* me. Do not talk to me, ever again. I have nothing to say to you."

He dropped his hand, and she fled down the steps.

✦

Andrea's hands shook as she fumbled with her keys. The rage was like an earthquake rattling inside her. She felt as if she was breaking apart, and it wasn't just the rage but the hurt, the insult, the betrayal.

"I take it you know that guy?"

She looked at Gavin in her passenger seat. She couldn't bring herself to answer him, so she shoved the keys into the ignition. "Where to?" She shot backward out of the space. Where to, indeed? She had no idea.

She glanced at Gavin. He didn't seem to know, either.

She took a deep breath and steered out of the parking lot. "Well?" She looked at him.

"I don't know."

Of course he didn't. Andrea watched the Pecos County Sheriff's Office recede in her rearview mirror. If only people could recede like that. And stupid mistakes.

She thought of the expression on Jon's face, and the anger welled up again. How had she allowed this to happen? She'd awakened this morning trusting him, their intimacy wrapped around her like a blanket.

Don't think about it.

She took a deep breath and tried to focus on logistics.

"I can't drive you all the way to Lubbock today," she said. "I can take you to the bus station. Or I can take you to the airport, but you'll have to buy your own ticket." As of yesterday, she was officially unemployed.

Just the thought made her go cold, and she gripped the wheel, thinking of her new reality. Every landmark in her life seemed to have crumbled. She felt completely adrift.

"Well?" She looked at Gavin as he wiped his sleeve over his face. Holy hell, was he crying? "Gavin?"

He turned away.

"What is it?" she demanded. "What's wrong?"

A shaky exhale. "She's gone."

It took her a second to get it. "You mean Vicky?"

"She went to her parents' place in Midland." He swiped his nose with the back of his hand. "Said she needs to 'figure out her life,' whatever that means."

"Gavin . . ." Good Lord, she didn't need this right now. She tried to scrounge up some sympathy for him, but she had none. Zilch. She looked at him. "What did you expect?"

He looked offended. "I thought we'd be together. I thought she'd leave him as soon as she got the chance."

"Gavin, her life is a mess right now. I mean, come on. She's in an abusive marriage, she's being investigated by the FBI. She probably *does* need some time to figure things out, and anyway, you've got your own problems to worry about."

He turned away. "You don't understand."

She clutched the wheel, struggling for patience. She understood completely. Her brother was in lust with this woman, and now he was entertaining the absurd idea that they had a future together. How could he be so naive?

The irony smacked into her right away. Who was worse, her

or her brother? At least Gavin had the excuse of being young. For all she knew, this was his first rodeo.

Andrea trained her gaze on the road, trying—and failing—to avoid thoughts of Jon. But it was impossible. The memories were too fresh. She thought of his hands on her body, his mouth sliding over her breast. She remembered the heat of his gaze, his touch.

She remembered the icy shock of standing in his bedroom, alone, and realizing what he'd done.

Don't think about it. Don't, don't, don't.

She slid a glance at Gavin again, and suddenly, she *did* feel for him.

"I can't go to Lubbock," he said, wiping his nose on his sleeve.

"Why not?"

"I got evicted." He sighed. "That's what the money was for—that I wanted to borrow. I lost my job at the restaurant and got behind on my rent."

Andrea wasn't sure she believed him, but she didn't want to fight about it. "Where's your stuff?"

He looked at her, and his cheeks were splotched from crying. Finches were not pretty criers.

"Your clothes? Your things?" she prompted.

"I don't have much. My clothes are at the ranch, but I can't go back there. I don't want to anyway, now that Vicky's gone."

"You could stay with me for a few days." The words seemed to come out on their own. "While you figure out your next step. You can sleep on my couch."

He sighed and slumped against the door.

"You're welcome."

"Thanks." He looked at her. "I mean it. And for picking me up, too."

"It's fine."

It really wasn't, but what else could she say? For better or for worse, he was family.

He leaned his head against the window and stared out at the dry, empty scrubland.

What was going through his mind right now? She wondered if he had any clue about the scope of Hardin's cruelty. The FBI had had Gavin in custody for five long hours, and she desperately hoped he'd managed to help them and provide something useful. He claimed he'd been cooperative, but she didn't know if she believed a word he said anymore. They'd released him without charges, at least, which she took as a good sign.

Andrea's head throbbed, and she focused on the road. She'd memorized this drive now, and it didn't get better with practice. Flat, flat, and more flat. Rest stops and highway signs. She had five monotonous hours ahead, and she was exhausted, both physically and emotionally. Her muscles ached. Her eyes burned like acid. Her feet were still blistered from yesterday, and she couldn't remember the last time she'd eaten a meal that didn't come with ketchup and a toy.

She sighed and rolled her shoulders, trying to perk herself up. At least this time, she had someone to keep her company and share the driving. She glanced over at Gavin.

He was fast asleep.

◆

By the time the judge signed off on the paperwork, it was nine P.M. In what Maxwell called another "lucky break," Shay Hardin and Ross Leeland were pulling into the Broken Spoke when the warrants came through. The SAC liked this development, because now the takedown could occur away from the ranch, where the situation was less likely to result in a heavily armed confrontation.

Jon liked the part about arresting Hardin away from his arsenal, but he didn't like the "luck" part. Two lucky events in one day was too many. Something was going to go wrong tonight—he could practically feel it as he strapped on his flak jacket.

The plan was twofold. Part one involved taking advantage of Hardin's and Leeland's absence to execute the search warrant at the ranch. An FBI tactical unit out of El Paso, including two explosives experts, had shown up to assist. While Jon and the others had been busy moving into the staging area and gearing up, the demo guys had slipped through the fence and swept the ranch's perimeter for land mines.

They'd found nothing, but it was a good precaution. No one knew yet what sort of measures Hardin had in place to protect his homestead.

As for Hardin himself, he and Leeland would be picked up after they left the bar—most likely, in the parking lot. Maxwell had assigned himself to do the honors, along with Santucci and Whitfield, with a second, smaller SWAT team on hand in case things got dicey.

Jon and Torres were assigned to the ranch because they knew the place better than anyone else. They had Theilman in tow, though, which was putting a damper on their normally stealthy approach as they neared the west fence.

Jon stopped and lifted his binoculars. He scanned the area, looking for any surprises, especially cars that didn't belong. But he saw only the Driscolls' red pickup parked beside the fire pit near the house.

"Confirming a red Dodge truck," Jon said into his radio. "No other vehicles."

"Copy that, Bravo," the SWAT lieutenant's voice said.

The other teams chimed in to confirm. The Driscolls were home. No one could see past the window coverings, but odds were they were either in the living room or in the bedroom. According to the detailed layout of the home provided by Gavin Finch, the couple's bedroom was at the far back of the house.

Jon surveyed the area and spotted the low oak tree that he and Torres had decided would make a good entry point. He made a beeline for it, and the others fell in behind him.

Theilman halted suddenly. "What's that?"

"Where?" Jon looked over his shoulder.

"Over there. Under that tree."

Jon squinted at the shape. "It's a cow."

"It's huge." He gripped his rifle. "Think he'll charge us?"

Jon looked at Torres.

"If he does, aim for his balls." Torres dropped into a crouch and pulled out wire cutters, and Jon held his weapon for him as he went to work on the game fence. He removed a square of mesh and slipped through. Jon followed. Theilman crawled through last and snagged his flak jacket.

"Shit!"

Torres took the agent's rifle off his hands while Jon yanked the jacket free.

Theilman rubbed the back of his neck as he stood up.

"You okay?" Jon asked.

"Fine."

Torres darted Jon a look as he returned the gun, and Jon knew what he was thinking. This guy was loud and nervous, and his pasty skin practically glowed in the dark. Not someone you wanted covering your ass.

A last radio check-in before the final approach. Then Jon

led the way, crouching low and using the scrub brush for cover as they crossed the field between the ranch's western boundary and the barn. They neared the dilapidated structure, and Jon surveyed the ground, looking for trip wires or pressure plates.

Despite five windows, the west-facing side of the house was completely dark. All the shades were drawn, as usual, and not so much as a glimmer of light seeped through. According to Andrea's brother, Hardin insisted on keeping the windows covered—even the kitchen ones—at all times to protect his privacy.

"What are these guys, vampires?" Theilman was looking at the windows. They were within fifty feet of the house now, but he obviously didn't know when to shut the fuck up.

Torres checked his watch and held up two fingers. Two minutes.

Jon took a deep breath. He relaxed his shoulders. He adjusted the MP5 in his hands and focused his gaze on the back door. He'd been involved in dozens of raids, but this one was different. His heart thudded against his sternum. This was it. Months and months of work, all leading up to this moment.

Jon stared into the darkness, and his thoughts went to Andrea. He pictured her on the steps of that sheriff's office, and his chest tightened. He'd made so many sacrifices for his job that it had become second nature. But today was the first time he'd done something he wasn't proud of. He'd done something cold and calculating, and now he felt a surge of panic because he didn't know how he was going to make it right with her. Or if he'd ever get the chance.

Ninety seconds.

Jon forced himself to get his head in the game. He trained his gaze on the house as black shadows shifted and the assault team stacked at the back door.

His pulse pounded. Wind rustled through the trees behind him.

Thirty seconds.

A slight movement near the door. Jon held his breath.

"Bang and clear," came the command.

Boom.

The door buster echoed over the prairie, quickly followed by the loud concussion of a flash-bang.

Black-clad agents poured in. Shouting came over the radio.

"Bedroom one clear!"

"Bedroom two clear!"

Jon kept his gaze fixed on the back door. More shouting over the radio.

"You got 'em?"

"Bathroom one clear! Where are they?"

"What the hell?" Torres muttered beside him.

A blur of white darted from the house. Olivia Driscoll's blond hair streamed behind her as she raced for the barn. Jon was after her in a heartbeat. Torres made the tackle, and Jon covered them with his gun as he wrestled her arms behind her and zip-tied her wrists.

"Where is your husband?" Jon demanded.

Two SWAT guys rushed over. Olivia cursed and kicked as Torres rolled her onto her side.

"Where is he?" Torres repeated.

Her chest heaved as she stared up at them, wide-eyed. "They're not here! No one's here!"

Jon crouched beside her and got right in her face. Leaves clung to her hair, and she looked shocked and terrified.

"Where is your husband, ma'am? You need to tell us where he is."

"I don't know! He went with Shay and Ross!"

"Whose vehicle?"

She glanced at the house.

"Whose vehicle?"

"Shay's! They're in the truck. I'm the only one here!" She looked at the house again and burst into tears. "What is this? What's going on?"

Jon looked at Torres. She could easily be lying.

He glanced at the house and heard cabinets banging open as agents moved room to room, searching. The pickup's doors stood open now. Agents were in the barn, rooting through equipment.

"We got her covered," Torres said.

Jon jogged to the back door, where he found the SWAT lieutenant looking unhappy as his men turned the house inside out searching for a potentially armed man.

"That's Olivia Driscoll?"

Jon gave a crisp nod. "She says her husband's with Hardin."

"I thought it was just two of them."

"So did I." Jon pulled out his phone and called Whitfield. Torres walked over. Meanwhile, the search continued as men streamed through the structure like army ants.

Whitfield answered right away.

"Driscoll's missing," Jon told him. "His wife says he's with Hardin."

Silence.

"Hardin's still inside the bar," Whitfield reported.

"She says he was with Hardin and Leeland when they left the house, all in one vehicle."

Curses on the other end. "Lemme call Santucci. See if he'll go in there and get eyes on them."

"He's not already in?"

"He wanted to stay in his vehicle, stake out the parking lot. I didn't go in because I'm in ICE gear, didn't want to make everyone jumpy."

Jon gritted his teeth.

"I'll send him in, call you back."

Jon hung up and looked at Torres. "Unbelievable. They don't have eyes inside the bar. I thought Santucci was the smart one."

"Is he with them or not?" the lieutenant wanted to know.

A commotion in the shadows as Olivia Driscoll was brought over, hands behind her back, a commando on each elbow.

"This is bullcrap!" The tears were gone now, but her cheeks and nose were splotchy as she sank onto the porch steps. "I'll sue you!" she snapped at Jon. "I'll sue all of you! You can't just bust in here!"

"Ma'am." Jon crouched beside her, out of kicking range. "Can you confirm your husband's whereabouts?"

"He's with Shay! I told you! What is wrong with you people?"

Jon's phone rang. Whitfield.

"We got a problem."

A queasy feeling slithered into Jon's stomach. "What?"

"No one's here," Whitfield said.

"What do you mean, no one?"

"None of 'em. Hardin, Leeland, Driscoll. Santucci went in and looked. Then I went. Then Maxwell."

"How is that possible? You're telling me—"

"I'm telling you none of them are in there. Everybody's gone."

chapter twenty-six

WHILE JON AND HIS team hopped a helo ride to San Antonio, the FBI's assistant director of counterterrorism was landing at Lackland Air Force Base, signaling a major shift in the case. By nine thirty A.M., everyone was crowded around a table in one of the base's conference rooms.

A real table this time, no plywood.

"Hey, we're movin' on up." Torres slapped Jon on the back, crooning the *Jeffersons* theme song as he sank into a faux-leather chair.

Jon grabbed a seat and settled his gaze on his SAC, who was deep in conversation with Alan Reese at the end of the table. At some point in the last twenty-four hours—Jon wasn't sure when—the investigation in Texas had gone from low priority to high. Not only was the counterterrorism chief in town, but he'd brought an entire team with him.

Jon had expected to be knee-deep in agents by this point, but he only saw a dozen. And he realized what this was: the briefing before the briefing. Reese was rounding up his intel before he addressed his troops—by which time, Jon and Torres and everybody else would be long gone, and there would be no mistaking whose show this was. Jon didn't give a damn about the politics at this point. His sole objective was to see Hardin dead or in custody by the end of the day.

"First, some news."

Everyone quieted at the CT chief's voice.

"I've talked to the medical examiner in Philadelphia. The skull fragments recovered from the bomb site—Khalil Abbas's skull fragments—showed evidence of lead wipe." He glanced around the table to see if everyone understood the significance of this development.

"Someone shot him in the head?" Theilman asked.

"According to the ME, yes. We sent an evidence response team to the mosque to do some more searching, and they recovered a shell casing from a gutter in the alley behind the building. It's from an SS195 hollow-point bullet."

"Same type of bullet used in the killing of that homeless guy a block from the mosque," Santucci said.

Reese nodded. "Our lab ran the analysis, and they believe there's a 'very high likelihood' that the two rounds were fired by the same weapon. So now it looks like Khalil Abbas was murdered, which basically eliminates him as our prime suspect." His gaze zeroed in on Jon. "Shay Hardin has been bumped to the top of the list."

Silence settled over the table. Jon tried to get his head around the fact that the theory he'd been pushing for so many months had finally gained traction within the Bureau.

"Second piece of news—which most of you already know—we have reason to believe Shay Hardin and Ross Leeland are in

San Antonio," Reese said. "They may be driving a white Plymouth four-door."

This information was based on conjecture, but Jon believed it was solid. He'd personally interviewed a gas-station clerk in Fort Stockton who'd sold Leeland a map of San Antonio while Hardin was buying gas.

"I hate to torpedo this supposed 'lead,'" Theilman said, "but all we really know is that Leeland bought a map last night. So what? I mean, who uses actual maps anymore? People want to go somewhere, they look it up on their phone."

"Hardin doesn't use a phone," Torres said, clearly irritated. He didn't like the agent from Philly. "Neither does Leeland."

"It's part of our profile of the suspect," Maxwell told Reese. "He's extremely paranoid about government surveillance."

"I don't blame him," Reese said.

"He goes to great lengths to avoid anything traceable," Maxwell continued, "like cell phones, e-mails, even landlines. It's not surprising to me that he'd use a paper map instead of downloading one."

"So the question is, what's in San Antonio?" Reese looked around the table.

"Not Kirby," Jon said. "I checked with his scheduler a minute ago. She says the senator was supposed to address a group of business-school students at UT Austin this morning, but his security team convinced him to bag it. He's canceled all public appearances through the weekend."

"Okay, what are some other potential targets in San Antonio? Maxwell? This is your home turf."

"We've got several colleges, plus the Alamo, the River Walk. In terms of government targets, there's the FBI building, the IRS office . . . this base, obviously."

Jon shook his head, frustrated. None of this was "obvious" at all.

"You don't agree?" Reese looked at him. Clearly, someone had told him that Jon was the resident expert on Shay Hardin.

"No, I don't. Hardin's pattern is to target people, not places," Jon said. "The judge, the senator's daughter, the senator's mistress and child. I don't believe his objective is a place, no matter how high-profile."

"Do you think he's planning a suicide attack?" Reese asked. "Does he want to be a martyr for his cause?"

Jon was no profiler, but he gave his best answer based on investigating the man for months. "I don't think he's a martyr. And I don't think the 'cause' is really the cause of this. Hardin's a sociopath. He kills without remorse. His antigovernment ideology just gives him a rationale. So do I think he's suicidal? No. I think he's got a plan, and it includes getting away after his next attack, with or without his co-conspirators. Everyone in Hardin's world is expendable."

"What, you can read his mind now?" Theilman quipped.

"Okay, let's table that for a moment," Reese said. "What about those co-conspirators? What do we know about Mark Driscoll? And how did we lose track of him in the first place?"

All eyes swung to Whitfield.

"It's my fault," he said, not dodging the blame. "I was tailing the pickup. I didn't see Driscoll in it, and I didn't see him slip out. Which tells me Hardin knew he had a tail."

"We know he didn't get out at the bar," Santucci said. "I saw two men go in, and two men only: Shay Hardin and Ross Leeland."

"In hindsight," Whitfield said, "looks like Driscoll probably slipped out when they went through the McDonald's drive-thru before heading over to the Broken Spoke. That's the bar where they disappeared from view."

"It's as if they knew a raid was imminent," Maxwell said insightfully.

Whitfield nodded. "Probably tipped off when Gavin and Vicky left the ranch with some cooked-up story. I'd say they saw us coming."

"I'd say they've seen us coming for months," Jon said. "The SNAP system proves it. He's been paranoid about government surveillance since he first set up operations at Lost Creek."

"So he could be anywhere by now, assuming he has transportation," Reese said. "And I think that's a safe assumption. Based on the bank robberies, it looks like he has the ability to swap vehicles whenever he wants."

Jon glanced out the window as a Humvee zoomed across the tarmac. The base was jumping this morning, everyone going about his business, no idea that just a few feet away, an FBI team was scrambling to track down the most wanted man in America.

"So, it's back to our original question. What—or who—is in San Antonio?" Reese nodded at the agent to his right. The man gave a few taps on his keyboard, and a slide flashed up on the projection screen across the room. Jon turned in his chair and saw a giant image of what appeared to be a floor plan.

"We accessed the digital storage device provided to us by"—Reese glanced at his notes—"Gavin Finch. This is what was on it."

"That's all?" Torres asked.

"That's all," Reese confirmed. "Only this file. It looks to me like a floor plan. Anyone know where this is?"

Jon could tell by the tone that it wasn't a rhetorical question.

The assistant director of counterterrorism, with all the resources at his disposal, didn't have a clue what this image was. The sole file on Hardin's flash drive—a drive protected with biometric security—remained an enigma.

"Looks like a house, probably a big one." Torres leaned forward and squinted at the screen. "Maybe it's Kirby's?"

"It's not," Reese said. "And it's a pretty rudimentary floor plan—just showing a basic layout—but it appears to be on a fairly large lot, assuming this is drawn to scale."

Jon looked at the image. He wouldn't assume anything. The picture consisted of some computer-generated lines and rectangles, something any ten-year-old could have slapped together on a computer. The map appeared to show streets surrounding the lot, but they weren't labeled.

"What's that cross up in the corner?" Torres asked. "Is that a church? Or maybe a compass rose?"

"We don't know," Reese said. "We don't really know anything about this image, except that it was on Hardin's storage device and it might be a building in San Antonio."

"Are we sure it's Hardin's device?" Jon asked.

"His prints were on it."

Every face at the table looked disappointed. They'd been hoping the drive would provide a treasure trove of information.

"Again, it's back to figuring out where he is and what he's targeting," Reese said. "What's his connection to San Antonio? Does he have any friends here? Relatives? Army buddies? Maybe a former commanding officer he hates for some reason?"

"I'll find out," Jon said, thinking of Gavin. He was with Andrea right now. Maybe he knew something, although Jon had no idea whether Andrea would let him anywhere near her brother—at least, not without a lawyer present. He checked his watch. He didn't have time to fight about it—he'd just have to convince her.

"Another disturbing piece of news," Reese said. "We have new information about the driver of the white Tahoe that was spotted trying to meet with Hardin in the middle of the night last week."

Jon looked at Torres.

"Brian Floyd. I checked him out," Torres said. "He works at a quarry about twenty miles west of Stockton. They don't have any explosives missing, if that's what you're thinking."

"It is," Reese said. "We checked out his background, and it turns out he previously worked at a quarry near Las Cruces, New Mexico. They recently had a theft at one of their facilities. Manager there thinks it was an inside job, someone who knew the layout of their storage lockers. Whoever did it drilled out a few padlocks and made off with more than two hundred blasting caps and fifty spools of ignition cord."

Jon leaned forward on his elbows. "When?"

"March twenty-second."

"That's the week before Philadelphia." Jon looked at Torres. "Maybe that's why we never found him on a flight out of El Paso. Maybe he didn't fly out of that airport—he drove."

"In a rented vehicle," Torres suggested. "He could have picked up the goods in New Mexico and then motored cross-country to carry out the attack."

"Would he have had time?" Maxwell asked.

"Yeah, especially if he had someone to help him with the driving." Jon looked at Reese. "Two hundred blasting caps?"

"ATF says that's more than he needed for Philly, same for the ignition cord. So now we have reason to believe he's got another bomb in the works. Which again brings us back to what he's targeting in San Antonio. What's his connection to the city?"

"What about the bank robberies?" Torres asked. "Probably not a coincidence that three of four of them happened here in town."

Reese looked at Maxwell. "What's the status on that?"

"I've got an agent working on it—"

"*One* agent? Where is he?"

"She's . . . in the office, I assume." Maxwell's face reddened. "I can call her for an update."

"I'll call her," Torres said. "We touched base on this yesterday. She was running down the getaway vehicles. Maybe she's got something new."

"Find out," Reese said.

"I'll check with Gavin Finch," Jon said. "See what he knows."

"And we need to talk to Leeland's wife again," Maxwell said. "She's at her parents' in Midland."

"Don't waste time on details," Reese ordered. "Our object is to find these suspects and bring them in. And in the meantime, we need to figure out what or who their next target is." His gaze moved around the table and stopped at Jon. "If your theory holds and he's planning something for the OKBOMB anniversary, then the clock is ticking."

He pushed back from the table and stood up. "Let's go, people. We have less than twenty-four hours."

◆

Elizabeth pulled into a parking space and took out her file. Ten to the fourth. Ten thousand possible phone numbers. The computer database had eliminated more than half right away because they were not in use. But she'd been left with 4,400 numbers to check out, and she'd run down every single one of them. She'd whittled the list to a few dozen entries that merited further investigation, including her current prospect, an Adam R. Jones of A.C.C. Enterprises, listed at this address. Jones's record was clean, but the business name sounded suspiciously vague, so she'd decided to check it out.

Elizabeth got out of her car and read the sign atop the building: ALAMO CITY CHOPPERS.

A.C.C. Enterprises.

Well, goody for her. Maybe if the agent gig didn't work out, she could get a job with the Bureau's cryptanalysis unit.

Elizabeth sighed and glanced around. The entire front row of parking was reserved for motorcycles. She glanced beyond them at the glass windows of the showroom, which faced the street.

Elizabeth stepped into the building and peeled off her sunglasses. Her gaze landed on a low-slung bike with gleaming fenders and a fat back tire. She glanced at a few customers and felt immediately self-conscious in her tailored gray suit. But everyone seemed too busy to notice her. It looked as though half of San Antonio had decided to spend this sunny morning checking out custom bikes.

She stayed on the periphery, browsing until she could catch a free salesperson. A man in coveralls whisked past her, and Elizabeth followed him with her eyes as he walked out a back door and into what looked like a workshop. She meandered over to the window and looked out at the long line of service bays facing the parking lot. A car at the end of the row caught her eye: a late-model Ford Fiesta, sapphire-blue.

Elizabeth's pulse picked up. What were the odds? She stepped closer to the window and studied the car.

It had a dent on the back door, driver's side, just like the car from the November bank robbery.

She glanced around. She needed to get closer to confirm, but it might be the vehicle.

She started for the door but then thought better of it. A blonde in a business suit waltzing past the garage would attract attention. She needed to go around.

She made her way casually across the showroom and spent a few moments lingering in the apparel section. Then she pushed through a side door and stepped out.

A narrow strip of pavement ran along the property line beside a chain-link fence. She moved swiftly now, because she didn't belong out here. She dipped her hand into her pocket to silence her phone.

The repair shop was a corrugated-metal building with six service bays. The garage doors facing the parking lot were raised, but all the back doors were lowered, and she skirted behind them now to make her way around the building. A radio DJ's voice penetrated the metal doors. She heard tools clanging and men bantering back and forth. She paused at the corner of the building and cautiously poked her head around. Her phone vibrated, and she jumped back.

She took a deep breath to steady her nerves, then peered around the corner again. The blue car sat just yards away, and she had a clear view of the license plate, which had been obscured by mud in the bank's surveillance footage. She pulled a notepad from her pocket and jotted down the digits. She started back to her car, then paused. Switching her phone to camera mode, she crept back and peered around the corner. A quick glance at the garage to make sure the coast was clear—

She froze, riveted by the sight.

chapter twenty-seven

ANDREA HAD THOUGHT ELEVEN hours of sleep would restore her to her normal self, but evidently not. She couldn't seem to shake this low-grade anxiety that had taken hold of her. All morning, she'd felt short-tempered and edgy. The television's drone grated on her every nerve as she stared at her computer screen.

"You mind turning that down?"

The blanket-covered lump on her sofa didn't move.

She stalked across the room and switched off the TV. "Enough."

Gavin frowned at her.

"You need to get up."

"Why?"

"You can't just lie there. You have to do something. Get back in school. Get a job. I never said you could surf my couch forever."

Gavin glanced at his watch. "I've been here twelve hours, Andrea. And I don't have anywhere to be today."

"Exactly! That's a problem. You need to get up and do something."

He sat up and kicked off the blanket. "Like what?"

"Like . . . anything. Act like an adult for once, and take some responsibility."

He combed a hand through his hair, and it stuck out in all directions.

"Are you planning to go back to school?" she demanded.

"I don't know."

"Are you planning to get a job?"

"I don't know." He looked up at her. "I was thinking I could maybe go stay with Dee and Bob awhile."

She crossed her arms.

"You think they'll have me?"

"Possibly." They wouldn't turn him away in a million years. "They'll put you to work, though."

"I know." He fiddled with the TV remote. "I was thinking that'd be good right now. Keep me busy while I figure out, you know, what I'm going to do and everything."

She just looked at him. He wasn't exactly on fire with motivation, but at least he'd thought about it.

He stood up. "Mind if I grab a shower?"

"Fine."

He disappeared into her bedroom, and she stared after him. She wasn't cut out for this. She didn't like this nagging, bitchy side of herself. Thank God she wasn't a mother. Her kids would run away from home as soon as they learned to walk.

Andrea returned to her computer and opened an e-mail from Nathan. He'd continued to work Carmen Pena's murder case even after the feds put it on the back burner to focus on other angles. Now he was reaching out for help, wondering whether she'd come across the name of Todd Greene, who looked good for a match with the partial print recovered from the pipe bomb.

Andrea hadn't heard the name, but that hadn't stopped her from checking it out. The feds had their hands full, and she didn't necessarily believe they knew their ass from first base, anyway. So she'd decided to try to drum up some leads.

The name Todd Greene was exceedingly common. None in Maverick, but she'd found a guy by that name living in Fort Stockton. A few phone calls to the local police had netted some interesting facts. One, Greene had sobered up since the drunk-driving arrest that landed him in jail ten years ago and put his prints in the system. And two, Greene now worked at a Fort Stockton hardware store.

Andrea typed up an e-mail to the cop who was helping her and attached Shay Hardin's picture, the one with his eagle tattoo showing. She wanted to see whether Greene had ever seen him in the store before, maybe purchasing some pipe or bolts or ball bearings, for instance.

If the lead panned out, she'd send it to Nathan, who would be annoyed by her meddling but would follow up anyway because he didn't like Carmen Pena being overlooked.

A sharp rap at the door. Andrea got up to look and was surprised to see Jon on her doorstep in a suit and tie. He gazed directly at the peephole, as if he could see her standing on the other side.

She took a deep breath and opened the door.

"I'm here to see Gavin." He stepped inside without an invitation.

"How'd you know he was here?"

"As a condition of dropping the charges, he agreed to keep us apprised of his whereabouts. He left me a message last night when he arrived here." He paused. "He's cooperating with us, Andrea."

She pursed her lips. Gavin was cooperating with the authorities. It was, quite possibly, the smartest thing he'd done in months.

"He's in the shower," she said over her shoulder as she strode into the bedroom and pounded on the bathroom door. "FBI's here to talk to you."

She rejoined Jon in her kitchen, where he stood beside the coffeepot. The scene was unsettlingly familiar, but this time, they had the added complication of a failed romance between them.

She crossed her arms. "What is it you want with Gavin?"

He looked her over, and she could see the stress on his face. Despite the suit and the shave, he looked ragged and anxious. She almost felt sorry for him. "The raid went sideways on us," he said. "Hardin slipped through our fingers, along with Leeland and Driscoll. We think Hardin's in San Antonio and we're hoping Gavin might have some ideas." He tucked his hands into his pockets and watched her. "We also recovered an image from Hardin's thumb drive. We thought possibly he could identify it."

She lifted her eyebrows expectantly.

He pulled up a digital picture on his phone and stepped over to show her.

"It's a floor plan," she said, ignoring the familiar scent of him. "Recognize it?"

"Is it Kirby's?"

"No."

"I have no idea." She looked up, and something warm glinted in his eyes.

He tucked the phone away and reached up to touch her face. "You look tired," he said.

"Thanks."

He rubbed his thumb along her jawline, and her nerves skittered in response. "How are your bruises?"

"Fine."

She remembered his hands gliding over her hips. She remembered his mouth and found herself staring at it.

He tipped her chin up and kissed her. It was gentle at first, but then his hand slid down and pulled her against him. Hope surged through her, hot and fleeting, before she squashed it down.

She jerked back. "Don't." She stepped away from him, and his eyes were simmering now.

"Why not?"

"Just—don't." She looked away, and she could feel his gaze on her.

"I'm sorry about yesterday."

"Fine." She stepped around him and flipped shut her computer.

"Andrea?"

"I said it's fine."

"I was doing my job."

Anger flared inside her. "I don't fault you for doing your job, North. It's the way you did it that pisses me off."

"I said I'm sorry."

"Fine, it's done anyway."

"What do you mean, done?"

She rolled her eyes.

"Look at me." He closed the gap between them and towered over her. She cast an impatient glance at the bedroom. Where was Gavin?

"Don't pull that crap. *Look* at me."

She met his gaze.

"I made a mistake. Let's move on."

"I don't want to 'move on' with you. I just want to forget it."

"Well, I don't."

"Well, I do! It's done, so drop it."

He glared down at her. But then his hostility faded, and a look of surprise came over his face. "Oh, my God. I get it now." He stepped back.

"Get what?"

"This is just like your job. You're scared, and so you're running away."

"Whatever."

"You're scared of losing something good, so you throw it away with both hands. Before you have a chance to get rejected."

She felt as if he'd smacked her with a two-by-four. She turned away, and he caught her arm.

"I'm right, aren't I? I can see it."

"Oh, please. Spare me the psychobabble. This is not about my job. This is about *you* disrespecting me and doubting my integrity." She could tell he didn't believe her, and she felt a hot spurt of frustration. "This is about you being a prick!" She shook off his grip. "You left me *naked* in your house while you deliberately deceived me—"

A loud cough had her whirling around.

Gavin stood in the living room watching them, his shoulder propped against the wall. He looked at Jon.

"You needed to talk to me?"

She glanced at Jon, but he wasn't even looking at Gavin. His attention was still fixed solely on her.

Andrea crossed the kitchen and grabbed her computer bag. She stuffed the laptop into it and snatched up her car keys.

"I'm going to the coffee shop," she said, and stormed out.

◆

Jon watched her leave. For the second time in two days, she slammed the door on him.

"She has a temper."

He looked at her brother. "I know."

The kid sauntered into the kitchen and pulled open the fridge. He took out some orange juice and guzzled it straight from the bottle.

"We cracked the thumb drive."

"Okay."

Jon showed him the picture on his phone. "You recognize this?"

"Looks like a house."

"I know."

He frowned down at the image. "I don't recognize it." He looked up. "I heard you tell Andie the raid was a bust."

Which meant he'd heard a lot of other things, too.

"I'm not sure why Shay would go to San Antonio. He doesn't know people there, that I'm aware of."

"Are you sure?" Jon asked. "Can you think of any connection at all? Maybe an Army buddy?"

He shook his head. "I'll think about it, though. Call you if I come up with anything."

Jon glanced at his watch, frustrated. So far, his trip to Austin had been a waste.

He started to leave but turned when he reached the door. "One more thing. Does Shay have a car at the Broken Spoke?"

"What do you mean?"

"Does he keep a vehicle there? Or maybe he has a friend who does?"

"No."

Jon opened the door.

"Mark has a bike at the Pony, though."

Jon turned around. "The what?"

"The Painted Pony. That bar behind McDonald's? That's where Mark keeps his motorcycle."

"Why?"

"Got me. Maybe he doesn't want it getting beat up out at the ranch. It's a nice bike. He bought it off his friend who owns a shop somewhere."

◆

Elizabeth's hands trembled as she gripped her phone. She'd missed a call from Torres, and she quickly pressed redial. Her heart pounded in her chest as she waited through the rings.

Slowly, she lifted her head up to the grimy window and peered inside the garage. Workers streamed back and forth, coming and going as if it was a normal day. Maybe she was jumping to conclusions, but—

"Torres here. Leave a message." The beep seemed to take forever.

"It's Elizabeth." She ducked down and glanced around her, making sure she was still alone behind the building. "Listen, I'm at this garage." She glanced at her notepad and rattled off the address. "I think I may have found the getaway car from last week's robbery. But that's not all."

She poked her head up to peek through the window again to confirm it. Then she dropped down and glanced around. Her pulse was racing now, and she felt sweat pooling under her arms.

"This could be crazy, but . . . you know when we went to

dinner, and you said how the bomb in Philadelphia was made of fertilizer and racing fuel?" Her pulse thundered as she said the words aloud. "Well, I'm here at this bike place, and they've got four big blue drums lining the wall, all labeled 'Racing Fuel.' There're some other drums, too, but they're not labeled."

A high-pitched beeping cut her off. She peeked through a window again as a large white truck backed into one of the service bays. The driver hopped out and heaved open the truck's cargo door.

Fear flooded her as she looked around. Where had everyone gone suddenly? The garage was empty now, except for the truck driver and one other person. The two men muscled one of the drums away from the wall and rolled it up a ramp.

Her grip tightened on the phone. This was happening. She'd woken up this morning determined to slog through her list, the ever-diligent agent helping out with the case. She hadn't actually believed in the conspiracy until this moment. Now the scope of it hit her like an anvil. And although she had the power to do something, the very real prospect of failure overwhelmed her.

"A white cargo truck just arrived." Her voice shook. "They're loading the drums inside and—"

Something hard touched the back of her neck, and she gave a startled hiccup.

A hand reached around and slid the phone from her fingers. She recognized the tattoo instantly. Randy from the body shop. Her throat went dry.

"Turn around. Slowly."

She turned around. Slowly. He had a pistol pointed at her face.

chapter twenty-eight

ANDREA MANEUVERED THROUGH TRAFFIC aggressively, although she didn't even know where she was going. She just knew she had to get away from Jon, and her brother, and everything else in her life that was pushing her to the edge. She glided past familiar sidewalks and storefronts, past the hustle and bustle of people going about their routines, and she felt a sharp pang of jealousy. They had jobs, commitments, places to be. She had none of that anymore. In the space of a few short weeks, her entire life had undergone a tectonic shift, and she'd lost her footing.

Tears of frustration burned her eyes as she sailed through another intersection. *You're scared, and so you're running away.* Was he right? Was she running?

She'd never thought of herself as a coward. She'd always thought of herself as a scrapper, a fighter, but maybe that was a lie, just one more fiction she'd created to get herself through. Maybe it was no coincidence that her career had suffered the same fate as all of her dead-end relationships. She'd been so afraid to fail that at the first sign of trouble she gave up without a fight.

Or maybe she was simply speeding up the inevitable. Maybe people were meant to hurt each other. Trust was an illusion, and connections were as fleeting as the flush of sex.

Her phone chimed from the cup holder, and the screen said US GOV.

Jon. Her heart skittered. Her first instinct was to dodge him, but that would only prove his point.

She spotted an empty parking space up ahead and whipped into it. She took a deep breath as she picked up the phone.

"Hi."

Silence.

"Hello?"

"Detective Finch?" It was a male voice but definitely not Jon's.

She cleared her throat. "This is Andrea Finch."

"Hello, I'm with the FBI, and I'm calling about your request."

"My request?"

"Your threatening-letter assessment? You may recall you submitted a sample and—"

"The letter! Yes, of course I recall. Sorry . . . it's been one of those cases."

"I understand," he said, although, really, he had no idea. "I've got the results back, but you didn't list an e-mail address here, so did you want to go over this on the phone or—"

"That's fine," she said, dragging a notepad from her purse. She should probably direct this call to Jon, but it wouldn't kill her to jot down the info—although it seemed less urgent now that they had their warrant in hand.

"Well, as you probably know, the threatening-letter database is used primarily by the Secret Service, so the majority of our files contain letters received at the White House."

"Okay."

"We ran the sample you submitted and found no links to any threats against POTUS."

"POTUS, President of the United States?"

"Yes, and that's past or present, by the way. We run submissions through the entire database."

Andrea watched the cars race by on Congress Avenue as she waited for him to get to the point.

"We did find a link with something in your neck of the woods—a letter received in Austin. The letter isn't signed, but several passages from it duplicate almost verbatim the letter you submitted, which would indicate a strong probability that we're dealing with the same unidentified author . . ." His voice trailed off as Andrea's pulse quickened. "This is dated . . . let's see . . . April nineteenth, two years ago. That's the date on the letter itself, mind you. As for the postmark—"

"You said April *nineteenth*?"

"That's right."

"And exactly who in Austin received this letter?"

"Yes, I was just getting to that. It's addressed to the governor."

✦

Jon bullied his way onto the entrance ramp of the interstate that would take him back to San Antonio.

"He had nothing on the floor plan?" Maxwell asked over the phone.

"Nothing at all," Jon confirmed. "Just the motorcycle lead."

"Sounds like you wasted your trip."

Jon didn't bother to disagree. He'd netted practically no new evidence, and he'd managed to piss Andrea off again, too.

And now time was ticking down.

"I can't see it," Maxwell said, still hung up on Mark Driscoll. "They're not exactly going to deliver a truck bomb on a motorcycle. And there'd be no way to conceal a rifle, so that's out."

"The bike might still be part of the plan somehow. Maybe Hardin intends to use it as a means of escape after he parks a truck bomb. Or plants an IED somewhere."

"The question is where," Maxwell said, pointing out the obvious again. "I need you to get back here ASAP to help us figure that out."

Jon ended the call with a renewed sense of frustration. Time was running out, and he'd never felt so far away from solving the case. The three primary suspects were in the wind, and he no longer even felt certain he understood the target. The only thing he did know for sure was that an attack was imminent.

Jon swerved around a slow-moving rig and thought through the new intel since yesterday. He had the gnawing certainty that he'd overlooked something, some key bit of information that would explain how everything fit together.

The job depends on the tools.

His uncle's saying came back to him as he sped toward San Antonio. So what tools was Hardin using this time? A fertilizer bomb? TNT stolen from some quarry somewhere?

A thought hit him. He pulled off the freeway and swung into a gas station, then jammed to a stop and grabbed the hefty file folder from the backseat.

"Come on, come on, come on," he muttered, thumbing through papers.

And then he had it, in his hand, a list of the items seized from Lost Creek Ranch. Jon scrolled through the e-mails on his phone, looking for the exchange with the ATF agent who'd checked the list provided by Gavin Finch. Yesterday Jon's focus had been finding something on the list that could be grounds for a search warrant. Now he was hunting for something else entirely.

Jon skimmed the list on his phone.

He compared it to the list in his hand.

"Son of a bitch," he muttered. He threw the car into gear and sped out of the lot and back onto the frontage road. He reached for his phone just as a call came in.

"I can't talk right now," he told Andrea, jumping back onto the freeway. "Something just came up."

"The Governor's Mansion."

"What?"

"He's targeting the Governor's Mansion. That's the floor plan, I'd bet my life on it."

"Where did you—"

"I just heard back about Hardin's letter," she said. "Remember the one we submitted to the threatening-letter database?"

"We *think* it's Hardin's. We don't know for sure he wrote it."

"Just listen, would you? There's another letter that is word-for-word the same in places as the letter sent to Senator Kirby. This letter's addressed to the governor and dated April nineteenth."

Jon's gut clenched as he glanced in the rearview mirror and saw the Capitol dome that dominated the city skyline.

"I'm on my way over there now," she said. "I called Austin PD to give them a heads-up but haven't heard back from my lieutenant yet."

"DPS is in charge of the governor's security detail." He cut across two lanes of traffic.

"I know, but this needs to come from you. You're the fed. I'm not even on the job anymore. Damn it, where are you?"

"I'm headed toward the Capitol now."

"The mansion's right across the street."

"I know. Andrea, there's a fifty-cal rifle missing from the weapons we collected during the raid."

She didn't respond. Horns blared over the phone, and he pictured her cutting through traffic.

"So you're saying—"

"I think he's planning a sniper attack."

◆

Torres and Whitfield didn't get much of a welcome when they rolled into the Two Oaks trailer park. Kids stopped and stared. Men scowled from their lawn chairs. Even the pets seemed pissed off, and a chorus of barks went up from every direction.

"Hey, good thing we're in suits," Whitfield quipped as they bumped over the gravel road in the "unmarked" FBI vehicle.

Torres squinted at the numbers on the wooden posts in each yard. Their target residence was at the far end of the drive, a dingy white double-wide with a weathered wooden stoop.

"Here we go." Torres glanced around as he got out. The rusted frame of a motorbike lay on its side on the overgrown lawn. He was glancing around for a dog as a bark went up from inside the trailer.

Torres looked at Whitfield. "Cover me."

He walked up the steps and gave a few sharp raps. The barking reached a fever pitch, and Torres put his hand on his holster as the door cracked open. A woman's face appeared in the two-inch gap. Caucasian, thirtyish, frizzy hair.

"Ma'am, I'm Special Agent James Torres with the FBI." He held up his ID. "I need you to step out, please, and leave the dog inside."

Her blue eyes narrowed.

"Now."

The door thumped shut. He heard shuffling on the other side, some yelling. Then the woman squeezed out, eyeing Whitfield suspiciously as she pulled the door closed behind her.

"What is it?" she asked.

"Sorry to bother you, ma'am. We're looking for a Randall Leeland listed at this address."

She folded her arms over her chest, which was barely contained by a faded black top. The look on her face told Torres they'd found their man.

"Is he here?"

She sighed heavily, and he got a whiff of alcohol as she opened the door and poked her head inside. "Randy! Get your butt out here!"

She looked Torres up and down as footsteps thudded. A freckle-faced kid appeared. Couldn't have been more than twelve, and he should have been in school. A dog poked its nose out and gave a low growl.

Torres dug a notepad from his pocket.

"Uh, we're looking for a Randall Leeland, date of birth twelve ten eighty-three. He any relation to either of you?"

"Go back inside," she snapped at the boy, then turned to Torres. "He's my ex-husband."

"Is he related to a Ross Leeland that you know of?"

"That's his brother."

"Have you seen Ross recently?"

"Haven't laid eyes on him in years." She looked at Whitfield again. "What's this about?"

"You know where we can find your ex-husband, Randall Leeland?"

"Beats me."

"Any idea where he works?" Whitfield asked.

She darted a look at him, and Torres could tell she was impatient to get the cops off her property.

"Try Hill Country Automotive, up on the north side." She opened the door, and the barking started up again. "And if you see the son of a bitch, tell him he owes me three months' back child support."

She slipped inside and slammed the door.

"Hill Country Auto. I've seen that somewhere." Torres pulled out his phone as they got back into the car. He'd missed a call from Elizabeth.

"I remember now. One of her reports."

"Whose reports?"

"LeBlanc's." Torres slid behind the wheel and pressed play on the message. He shoved his key into the ignition. As Elizabeth talked, his hands froze.

Her voice stopped abruptly. Torres looked down at the phone, and his blood turned to ice.

"Oh, no."

"What is it?"

He slammed the car into gear and rocketed back, spraying up gravel.

"What? What is it?"

Torres stomped on the gas. "That was LeBlanc."

chapter twenty-nine

ANDREA REACHED THE GOVERNOR'S Mansion and spotted the unmarked FBI vehicle taking a sharp corner. She pulled into a loading zone and jumped out, frantically scrolling through her phone as she jogged up the sidewalk to meet Jon.

"What now?" he demanded, reading the look on her face.

"I just got off the phone with Kirsten, the senator's scheduler. North, it's worse than we thought. Kirby's on his way over here."

"*Here?* He said he canceled all his public appearances."

"He did, but this is private." She glanced over her shoulder at the white plantation-style building behind them. "Some luncheon for bigwig contributors hosted by the governor."

Jon glanced around, clearly alarmed. They were near the mansion's side entrance, where people who looked like waiters and caterers streamed in and out with boxes and carts of food.

"Did you tell Kirsten to cancel?" Jon asked, whipping out his phone.

"It's her day off. She's not even in Austin right now. Damn it, where is that number?"

"Who?"

"Teddy, the assistant." She looked at Jon. "Who are you calling?"

"Maxwell." His face looked grim as he surveyed the area. "Voice mail." He left an urgent message for his boss to call him back and then set off at a jog toward the mansion's front entrance.

Andrea hurried to keep up with him as she searched her phone for the number. "You think it's happening now, not tomorrow?" she asked.

"Yes." He didn't even hesitate. "This way, he gets Kirby and the governor. Twice the publicity."

An unmarked police car turned onto the street, and Jon flagged it down.

"This is us," he told her as two agents piled out of the vehicle.

"Jon North, San Antonio," he said, flashing his creds. "We have reason to believe a sniper might be somewhere in the area."

Everyone's gaze tipped upward. This was a nightmare scenario. The governor's estate was surrounded on three sides by office buildings and parking garages, providing literally hundreds of possible hides for a skilled gunman.

"We need to get high, get a vantage point." Jon pointed to an office building and nodded at the older-looking agent, who was thin and balding. "Get inside that gray parking garage. And you"—he made eye contact with the young, stocky one—"see if you can access the rooftop on that office building. You'll have a bird's-eye view of everything going on. You guys have radios?"

"In the car." The younger agent hustled back to retrieve them.

"There's a better vantage point two blocks south," Andrea said. "It's a five-story parking garage with visibility on all four sides. It's over on Lavaca Street."

Jon glared at her, and she could tell he didn't want her involved in this. She didn't wait to hear his reasons.

"Too bad, North, I'm in. We need all the eyes we can get."

"Sorry. You are . . . ?" The bald guy was frowning at her.

"She's Austin PD," Jon snapped, and his phone buzzed in his hand. He made eye contact with the agent. "Follow her lead. She knows the neighborhood."

◆

Dread settled over Jon as he watched Andrea and the agents rush away. He didn't like her here, but he didn't have a choice.

He answered his phone.

"We have a problem," Maxwell said. "I just got off the phone with Torres."

Jon jogged toward the guardhouse, pulling the ID folio from his jacket pocket.

"We think we've got a truck bomb on our hands," Maxwell said.

The words stopped Jon cold. And then he was moving again as his mind raced. "Where'd this come from?"

"Torres got a message from Elizabeth LeBlanc," Maxwell said. "She was at a warehouse following up on the bank robberies when she witnessed a white cargo truck being loaded with metal drums and—"

"Where?" Jon cut in.

"San Antonio. North side of town."

"What time?"

"Message came in ninety minutes ago, but he just listened to it. We sent a team of agents over. No Elizabeth, no truck, nothing. So now we've got a missing agent and a missing vehicle, possibly loaded with explosives. And we have no idea of the target—"

"The Governor's Mansion," Jon said. "At least, that's what I think. I think that's the floor plan we found on the flash drive."

"How—"

"Kirby's on his way over here. I can't explain it all now, but you need to get hold of his security team and have them keep him *away* from the area. I'm on my way in right now to talk to the governor's people."

"You're at the mansion?"

"That's right."

"Where's the governor?"

"I'm about to find out. Give Kirby's people the heads-up. I'll call back in five."

The trooper in the guardhouse was on his feet now, looking suspicious as Jon jogged over to him, holding up his ID.

"Who's in charge of the governor's security detail?" Jon asked.

"Uh . . ." The trooper glanced at Jon's identification. "That'd be my lieutenant."

"I need him on the phone. Now."

✦

It was an urban battlefield, and Shay felt good in it. He peered over the concrete wall and planned the shot. Carefully. Methodically. He took a deep breath and let his heart rate slow.

Gazing through the scope, it came back to him—his first kill. He remembered the instant of panic, then the bone-deep thrill. There had been others, and soon it wasn't a thrill but a duty. He did it out of necessity, with clinical detachment, same as now.

His country had trained him well.

The phone vibrated beside him and he glanced at the text.

Just turned north.

Shay settled in to wait. He'd been disciplined and patient. Now it was time for his payoff.

Time for Message Three.

The tree of liberty must be watered with the blood of tyrants.

◆

The location was a sniper's heaven. Andrea gazed up at the concrete canyon surrounding her and saw a dizzying array of potential hides: multilevel parking garages, apartments, office buildings that surely had vacant suites. The parking garages were the worst. Their concrete half-walls offered concealment and even the possibility that someone could get a shot off without leaving a vehicle.

She picked the highest garage on the block and took the stairs two at a time. She poked her head out at each level, scanning the rows of cars for anything suspicious, but saw nothing. When she reached the roof, she rushed to a corner and gazed out at the sweeping view of downtown.

From her vantage point, she had a clear view of all the buildings surrounding the estate and most of the mansion itself, except for the far southern corner, which was partially blocked by a church. She recalled the cross symbol on the corner of the computer drawing on Hardin's thumb drive.

This is it.

The thought crystallized in her mind as she scanned the area. She couldn't explain why, but she had a sudden certainty that everything, all the pain and exhaustion and disappointment, had been building toward this moment. Her shoulders tensed. The air hummed as she looked around. She could practically see Hardin crouched behind a wall somewhere, peering through his rifle scope and waiting for his target to arrive. What thoughts would be going through his mind as he waited to end someone's life? What had he been thinking as he waited for Carmen Pena? And Julia Kirby?

A chill swept over her. She glanced around to confirm that she was alone on the roof as she dialed Jon's number.

"Okay, I'm on top of the garage just east of the bank," she told him. "That's west of the mansion."

"New development," he said sharply. "We have intel about a truck bomb. Can't confirm the target, but we think the mansion's a good bet. How's your vantage point up there?"

"I can see everything." *A truck bomb?* She pictured the carnage in Philadelphia, and her stomach twisted into a knot.

"You see any white cargo trucks?"

"How big?"

"No idea. All I know is it's white."

Panic gripped her as she gazed out over the labyrinth of streets and alleyways. "God, North, I see . . . dozens. Practically every truck on the road is white."

"Focus on the parked ones. The ones closest to the mansion."

"You guys have to evacuate!"

"We're working on it."

"Work faster! There're people everywhere! Pedestrians, bikers—"

"Andrea, *stop*! Focus. Don't think about everyone else right now. I need you to take a careful look around and tell me what you see."

She swallowed her fear and tried to block out all the cars and innocent bystanders. She took a deep breath. "Okay, I see two white vans parked behind the mansion."

"Those are caterers. We're checking them now."

"I see a white cargo truck, fairly big, looks like two blocks north of the mansion. There's a pushcart next to it, so maybe he's unloading." Her gaze skimmed across the sloping green lawn in front of the Capitol Building, where people were strolling and picnicking. "I see a brown delivery truck just east of the Capitol. About half a block south of him is another white truck with a logo on the side, but I can't read it from here." She took a deep breath, scanning the streets. "A white cargo van just pulled off Congress, heading west now toward the mansion . . ." Her pulse picked up. "But it isn't slowing. Now it's turning north onto Lavaca."

"What else?"

Exhaust drifted up from the streets below, along with the traffic noise. *Too many cars, too many people. Why aren't there sirens yet?*

"Andrea?"

"I see a white cargo truck . . . No, maybe it's gray. It's two blocks east of me, which means four from the mansion—" She halted as a black SUV swung into view, dark-tinted windows, bristling with antennae. It was followed closely by a black Lincoln sedan.

"I see a black Chevy Tahoe, looks like maybe a motorcade. North, is it Kirby?"

"Shit!"

"Didn't someone call him?"

"Where is it? Tell me exactly."

"It's moving east on Eleventh Street, heading straight toward the mansion. Is it Kirby or the governor?"

She glanced around frantically, looking for a police car, a trooper, something.

Over the phone, she heard Jon shouting orders at someone.

Andrea tuned out the noise. She tuned out the traffic and the exhaust fumes and the din of road construction as she scoured every building, every rooftop, looking for the telltale jut of a rifle barrel. She tried to penetrate the shadows of the parking garages, looking for the dark silhouette of a gunman.

"Andrea, are there any cargo trucks parked near the route of the approaching motorcade?"

She snapped her gaze to the SUV. "No."

A flash of light caught her eye. A slight glint just above the wall of a parking garage—

"*Gun!* I see a scope!" She dropped into a crouch and peered over the wall. "Ninth and Lavaca! *Wait.* No, *Tenth* and Lavaca! Gray parking garage! Fourth floor!"

She had her pistol clutched in her hand but couldn't even remember pulling it. She aimed it uselessly over the wall, but the gunman was much too far away.

The pair of black vehicles glided past her, nearing the mansion.

"North, he's out of my range!" She heard commotion on the other end of the phone but still no sirens, no warnings.

She darted a look at the sniper hide. The shot was wide open. She couldn't disrupt his aim.

But she could disrupt his target.

She leaned over the wall and took aim at the SUV, realizing she was about to bring the wrath of every state trooper and bodyguard within miles down upon her head.

No hesitation. She lined up her sights.

Pop.

She hit the bumper, and the SUV lurched to a stop as a sharp *crack* reverberated and the driver's-side window exploded.

"He took a shot! They're hit!" Her gaze jerked to the garage, where she saw a blur of movement behind the wall. She sprinted for the stairwell, clutching her phone to her ear.

Tires squealed and sirens howled up from the streets below as she raced down the stairs.

"Shooter fleeing! Tenth and Lavaca! I'm in pursuit!"

chapter thirty

JON SPRINTED FOR THE parking garage, gun in hand. Tires shrieked. A gray pickup blasted through the wooden arm, sending splinters flying as it careened onto the street. Horns blared. Jon ran into the road, halted, and fired three shots in rapid succession.

The back window burst. The truck jumped the curb and crashed into a fire hydrant. Jon bolted toward it as the passenger door popped open, and a blur of white leaped out.

"He's getting away!" Andrea was beside him now, and they both raced after the gunman. White T-shirt, blue jeans, baseball cap—Hardin. He was moving fast, no rifle or handgun that Jon could see.

Jon dodged around the pickup and sidestepped the geyser spewing from the fire hydrant. He ran hard, clutching his weapon, but didn't dare pause for a shot until he closed the gap. He was gaining, gaining, gaining, with Andrea at his side. Footsteps slapped behind him as the other two agents strained to keep up. One of them was on his phone calling for backup. Andrea peeled off suddenly and darted down an alley.

Jon surged ahead, intent on his prey. He needed transportation. Maybe he'd carjack someone at a stoplight.

Hardin reached an intersection, paused to look around. Jon lifted his weapon, but then he disappeared around the corner, out of sight. Jon plowed through a pair of joggers and raced around the building. More people on this block, sidewalk cafés, a valet sign.

He instantly spotted Hardin's objective: a young woman tipping a valet attendant and sliding into a car. Hardin sprinted toward her as someone lunged from the alley. Andrea.

She was on him like a panther, and they slammed to the ground in a tangle of arms and legs. Jon crashed onto Hardin's back and pushed Andrea aside as he jammed his pistol into the man's neck.

"Check for weapons!" Andrea yelled, pawing at his shirt, his pants.

Jon wrestled Hardin's hands behind his back as the other two agents appeared, guns drawn. Gasps and yelps went up from the shocked onlookers as Jon jerked Hardin's wrists back and slapped on the cuffs.

"No weapons." Andrea stood up.

Jon was busy searching for a cell phone, a garage-door opener, anything that might be used to detonate a bomb. He came up empty. The stocky agent helped haul Hardin to his feet, and they pulled him away from the restaurant patrons and into the mouth of an alley.

Jon heaved Hardin against the wall and planted his forearm against his neck. "Where's the truck?"

◆

"Where is it?"

Still no answer.

Andrea watched them facing off against the side of the build-ing. Jon held his Sig loosely at his side, but he looked ready to kneecap the man if he didn't answer the question.

"Jon."

Hardin slid down the wall. He plunked one booted foot over another and glowered up at them defiantly. His lip was bleeding, probably from when Andrea had tackled him.

She pulled Jon away and lowered her voice. "The senator?"

"Injured but alive. Motorcade's en route to the hospital. But I don't think that's all Hardin had planned." A bead of sweat slid down Jon's temple as he glanced around angrily. "I mean, look at this place."

She didn't have to look, because she could hear. Sirens echoed all around them as emergency vehicles converged on the nearby Governor's Mansion. Every trooper in the city and probably half the Austin PD were responding to the attack. These were Andrea's coworkers, people she *knew*. If he'd wanted to target law enforce-ment, he couldn't have planned it better.

She looked at Hardin, sitting tight-lipped on the ground, a man who obviously knew his Fifth Amendment rights and wasn't talking.

His eyes were a startling shade of blue, she discovered. She'd only seen them up close through a camera lens. They were the kind of eyes women swooned over in bars. How could eyes like that hide so much evil?

Andrea stepped over. She dropped into a crouch beside him and tried to look relaxed, despite the adrenaline rushing through her body.

"Taken down by a girl, Shay. What will people think?" She

dug into the pocket of her jeans and pulled out the bullet she'd been carrying. She held it out in her palm. "Think you left something in my room."

A predatory gleam came into his eyes. "I watched you in the shower."

"Yeah? See anything you like?"

"I should have put a bullet between your tits when I had the chance."

She leaned closer, taunting him, daring him to brag. Sweat beaded on his upper lip. Despite the cool defiance, she could smell the fear coming off his skin.

There was more going on here. This wasn't over.

"Where's the truck, Shay?"

He stared at her.

"Do yourself a favor, and tell us where it is."

White-hot hatred simmered in his eyes. She saw the burning need to boast, to prove that although he was on the ground and handcuffed, he was still smarter than everyone.

Come on, Shay. Give in to the urge.

Tires skidded behind her, breaking the spell. She glanced over her shoulder to see an FBI sedan and a trio of DPS cars pulling up.

She looked at Hardin again. He made a wet hawking sound and spit on her shoes.

✦

The governor's estate was mayhem. Patrol cars, DPS units, and even a few sheriff's cruisers were parked haphazardly along the perimeter. Several red ladder trucks blocked the side streets, and troopers were hustling around with barricades, evacuating civilians and forming a perimeter around the perceived danger zone.

"Tell me if you see an armored vehicle," Jon ordered. "Our bomb unit should be here by now."

They reached a manned barricade. He waved his ID at a DPS officer as they jogged to the northeast corner of the governor's estate.

Andrea scanned the area for a possible truck bomb. She stopped short as she saw a group of schoolkids being hustled from the Capitol.

"Holy Christ," she murmured. They'd probably been on a field trip, and now they were in the epicenter of a terrorist attack. She spied their buses . . . one, two, three in a line, probably more than a hundred kids. Her heart squeezed as she glanced around, desperately looking for a white cargo truck.

"See anything?" Jon demanded.

"Two white vans behind the mansion."

"Caterers. We checked them."

She darted her gaze around, searching for all the white vans she'd listed off earlier.

"There!" She grabbed his arm. "The alley! That wasn't there before."

Jon unholstered his weapon, and Andrea did the same as they jogged toward the truck, picking up speed as they cataloged the same suspicious details: parked in the alley, no taillights, no driver visible nearby.

"Jon, this is it. Has to be." Her nerves jumped as they reached the truck.

Staying low, Jon ducked around to the driver's side and crept up to the window. Andrea did the same on the passenger's side, staring at the side mirror as she approached the door. She peered into the cab. Empty. She touched the hood. Still warm.

On the other side of the truck, Jon swore loudly.

"What?" She rushed around.

"My phone's not getting a signal."

A sharp whistle, and she glanced up to see a German shepherd charging toward them, towing a man in SWAT gear behind him.

"FBI Bomb Squad!" the man shouted. "Step away from that vehicle!"

Jon held up his ID. "We think this is it."

The German shepherd gave two sharp barks and planted itself at the back tire, brown eyes intent, ears pointed skyward. The dog stared with laserlike focus, as if nothing else in the universe existed except this dirty white truck.

The handler said a few words into the radio clipped to his shoulder.

"This your case?" he asked Jon, dropping down to look at the undercarriage.

"That's right."

"I understand this perp likes cell-phone detonators."

"He also likes timers," Andrea said, thinking of Carmen Pena.

"We're jamming all cell-phone signals within a ten-block radius."

"But what if it's on a timer?" Andrea asked. "Can you jam that, too?"

The grim look on the man's face told her the answer was no. Andrea glanced around, heart pounding. Troopers with bullhorns were hustling people from the Capitol lawn. Kids were still boarding buses.

"Andrea, you need to leave. Now."

She looked at Jon. "Are you freaking kidding me?"

"*Both* of you need to evacuate," the bomb technician said firmly. "Our team is on the way—"

"Shh!" Andrea held her hand up. "You hear that?"

A chorus of sirens whined around them. Beneath it all came a dull *thump*.

"Listen!" She walked around the truck and leaned her head against the side.

Thud.

Andrea looked at Jon. "God, is there . . . a *person* in there?"

His jaw dropped. "Holy shit. Elizabeth."

"Who?"

"Our missing agent."

She clutched her hand to her throat, horrified. "You think she's *in* there?"

"You people *must* evacuate," the bomb tech said, but both Andrea and Jon ignored him as they rushed to check the cargo door. It was secured with a heavy padlock.

Jon took off for the nearest fire truck.

"Ma'am, I insist that you move back—"

"Quiet!" She pressed her ear to the truck again and heard a series of sounds now—*thump, thump, thump*—like someone trying to signal. "Someone's definitely in there."

Jon rushed back with a long red ax.

"Sir! Step *back* from the vehicle. You *must* evacuate."

"We've got an agent in there."

He lifted the ax above his head, and the bomb tech caught his arm.

"Wait! We need to check if it's wired."

He pulled a cordless drill from the pocket of his cargo pants as two more black-clad bomb techs hustled over. They dropped bags onto the sidewalk and communicated in clipped phrases as they swiftly unpacked gear.

"Andrea," Jon said.

"Forget it."

"At least get behind that barricade."

His eyes pleaded with her, but she ignored him as the technician drilled a hole in the truck's side. Someone passed him a fiber-optic camera, which he threaded through the hole like a snake.

Jon's face was taut with tension as he gripped the ax and waited.

A bomb tech bent over a small computer screen, reading the grainy camera image. "No trip wires. We're good."

"Everyone back." Jon heaved the ax over his head. He swung it down. Chunks of metal flew. The bomb techs shoved up the door to reveal a cluster of white drums arranged like bowling pins.

Jon hitched himself onto the truck bed as Andrea peered inside. She smelled gasoline and something else she couldn't identify. Squinting into the darkness, she spied a pair of women's shoes peeking out from behind a drum.

"Here!" She hefted herself onto the platform. The woman was bound with cord and had a strip of duct tape over her mouth.

"We need a medic!" Jon yelled.

"Don't move those drums!" The bomb tech rushed over to help Jon pull her out, and Andrea jumped down as they lowered her to the ground.

"Is she conscious?" the tech demanded. "Ask her what she knows about this det device."

Andrea crouched next to her. She had bruises on her face, and one of her eyes was swollen shut, like a hundred battered women Andrea had seen over the years. She nudged Jon aside, hoping she'd respond better to a female voice.

"Elizabeth, are you with us? I'm sorry, but this is going to hurt, okay? Just for a sec, though."

Andrea peeled back the corner of the tape and gave it a sharp yank. The woman yelped with pain, which Andrea took as a good sign.

"Elizabeth, did you see the detonation device?" Andrea asked. "Was it a cell phone? A timer?"

She looked too dazed to answer. Or maybe she didn't know. Jon had a pocket knife out and was working on the cord at her wrists. The look on his face was calm determination as he cut loose the bindings.

Time seemed to slow down, and Andrea became hyperaware of everything—the howl of sirens, the sharp smell of gasoline, the warm weight of the woman slumped against her. The world was suddenly sharper, brighter, louder, and a surreal mix of joy and terror flooded her all at once. *Jon.* She should have told him. Why hadn't she told him?

His gaze locked on hers, and her heart seized up. If this was it, she wanted him to be the last thing she saw.

A loud whoop from inside the truck.

A bomb tech stepped to the door and gave a thumbs-up.

"We're all clear!"

chapter thirty-one

IN A MATTER OF HOURS, the FBI's Austin location went from being a sleepy satellite office to the headquarters of one of the largest manhunts in Bureau history. Agents in suits and SWAT gear lined the hallways, checking phones and jonesing for the orders that would send them in pursuit of the missing suspects. Shay Hardin was in custody, but his co-conspirators were still at large.

Meanwhile, Senator Kirby was in the hospital being treated for shrapnel wounds, the governor was all over the news, and reporters were giving breathless updates from the site of what had almost been a mass disaster.

Andrea squeezed through the throng of agents. Most were twice her size. All were armed to the teeth. After spending the past six hours being debriefed and cross-examined by men with big guns and even bigger egos, she felt whipped—a clear case of testosterone overload. She needed to get home.

She pushed through the building's side door and halted on the steps.

Media vans lined the street, their antennae reaching high into the night sky. Riot police manned barricades between the reporters and the parking lot. News crews crowded the sidewalk, setting up klieg lights and jostling for camera angles.

"Damn, this place is a zoo."

At the voice, she glanced over her shoulder to see Torres pushing through the door. He stopped beside her and slapped her back.

"Good work earlier," he said.

"Thanks."

A surge of warmth flooded through her. When was the last time she'd heard anything like praise from a fellow cop?

Jon emerged from the building, phone pressed to his ear. He scanned the crowd and frowned when he spotted her. He ended the call and tucked his phone away.

"Thought you'd be home by now," he said. No praise there. He was still angry that she hadn't followed orders and evacuated.

"Hey, I'm in the car," Torres told him. "Later, Andrea."

Jon gazed down at her. "You don't look good."

"Really? Because I feel good. Nothing like six hours in a metal chair being interrogated by MIBs."

He glanced past her at the growing crowd of reporters. "Looks like someone chummed the waters."

"Who?"

"Someone in the governor's office." His jaw tightened. "They heard we're moving the prisoner, so now they're lining up for a front-row seat."

"Do they even realize who he is?"

"You mean Philly? Yeah, I think they put it together."

He stepped closer and stared down at her. A few hours ago, she'd looked into those eyes and thought his face would be the last thing she ever saw. Now she looked at him and felt vulnerable, so vulnerable her chest ached. She wanted to fall into him and cling to him, but she'd done that already. She'd let her guard down and trusted him, and he'd betrayed her without blinking an eye. She couldn't let it happen again.

His phone buzzed. He pulled it out and checked the number, and she knew what he was going to say before he opened his mouth. "I have to go."

"I know."

"We have a briefing," he said. "It's important."

"I know."

"Listen, I'll call you later."

"No need. I'm fine."

He looked impatient. "You're not fine. *We're* not fine. But I can't leave right now." His phone buzzed again, and he glanced down and cursed.

"Better get that."

"Andrea—"

She turned and left.

❖

Elizabeth sat in her car, watching the door. Her stomach refused to settle. The entire drive in, she'd felt nauseated, and at one point she'd even pulled over and thought she'd get sick. But the moment had passed, and she was back on her way again.

She glanced in the mirror and felt a fresh flood of apprehension. Makeup concealed the bruises mostly, but nothing besides time could fix her swollen eyelid and the line of sutures marching across her forehead like ants. According to the intern who'd stitched her up, it would be at least three weeks before she looked like herself again. She didn't have three weeks. She had a job to do. And as afraid as she'd been of coming in this morning, she was even more terrified of staying home for days and days and losing the heart to come back at all.

Today was a workday like any other. She was going to treat it that way so she could get through it, one hour at a time.

She pushed open the door and gathered her purse. She walked briskly across the parking garage and filed in with all the other agents carrying computer bags and travel cups. She felt people's startled looks as they noticed her face and her sling and realized who she was. She kept her chin up as she stepped onto the elevator and rode to her floor.

The doors parted, and she headed across the bullpen, resisting the urge to duck into the bathroom and get sick. A hush fell over the room. Phone chatter quieted. She'd almost reached her desk when she decided to veer for the coffeepot. People were going to stare no matter what, so she might as well give them a chance to have a good look and get it over with.

She filled a Styrofoam cup with coffee she didn't want.

"Elizabeth?"

Jon North. She hadn't expected to see him first. She felt a sudden gush of emotions and had to look down.

"Hi. What's up?" She clumsily tore open a creamer and dumped the contents into her cup.

"I assumed you'd be out for a while."

"No reason." She sipped her coffee. "Just a few stitches, really, so the doctor cleared me to work."

She felt people's gazes on them. She knew what they were thinking, too, especially the ones who'd had their start in police work. She looked like a woman whose husband/boyfriend/pimp had beaten the shit out of her, like one of those women who called 911 in a moment of panic and then, when the cops showed up, turned around and begged them not to arrest the guy. She'd always thought those women were stupid and cowardly, but she understood them now in a way she hadn't before yesterday, when she'd been at the mercy of a man's fists for the first time. Now she knew they weren't cowardly—they simply had more faith in pain and retribution than they did in the system.

Jon was looking at her now, and she saw the worry etched on his face. He'd just helped apprehend one of the worst home-grown terrorists in American history. She'd expected him to look triumphant this morning. Maybe even smug. Instead, he looked stressed. Ragged. Even the suit and tie didn't help. Maybe he'd been up all night, too.

"Listen, Jon." She cleared her throat. "I need to thank you. For yesterday."

"Forget it."

"No, I mean it."

He gave a sharp nod, and she knew he understood. "I don't know if you heard or not," he said. "Ross and Randy Leeland were arrested early this morning at a border checkpoint in Del Rio."

Randy Leeland was in custody. She felt dizzy. She leaned against the counter and let the news sink in.

"They've lawyered up already, but we're not too concerned about that. Both of them had bomb residue on their clothes at the time of their arrest. Apparently, they were in charge of the truck bomb this time—possibly with Driscoll's help—while Hardin carried out the attack against Kirby."

"So what was their game plan?" she asked.

"We're not sure yet. Looks to me like they didn't think they'd get caught. When everything fell apart, they decided to make a run for the border."

"And Mark Driscoll?"

"Still missing, but I don't think that will last long. His face is all over the news."

The mention of news triggered memories of yesterday's chaos—the crowds, the helicopters, the TV cameras.

"The team's about to meet," Jon said, "but maybe you want to sit this one out?"

She glanced at the conference room, where all of her colleagues had gathered. Maxwell was eyeing her with concern. Torres glanced over, and the instant shock on his face underscored just how awful she must look.

It was going to be a long day. But she was glad she'd come. Randy Leeland was in custody. Hearing that one kernel of information firsthand made it worth the effort to be here.

"Elizabeth?"

She looked at North. "I'm coming. I'll be right there."

"You sure? No one's going to think less of you if you need some time."

"I don't. I'm fine," she told him. She almost meant it.

✦

It was a dead, motionless sleep, and Andrea awoke feeling slightly drunk. Her muscles ached. Her mouth felt sandy. Her head seemed swollen and heavy.

And someone was in her kitchen.

She dragged herself out of bed and pulled on the jeans lying on the floor before shuffling out to investigate. She'd expected to see Gavin foraging through her pantry for Pop-Tarts, but instead, she found him at the sink, rinsing a mug.

Bits of information pelted her all at once: the scent of coffee, the laptop sitting open on the counter, the basket of laundry on the floor beside her stacked washer-dryer.

Gavin's damp hair.

When had he showered? She'd been so comatose she hadn't even heard him.

When she finally made it home last night, she'd been on the verge of collapse. But then she'd mustered the energy to sit up with Gavin into the wee hours, flipping news channels and filling him in on what had happened. Finally, she'd had to shut it off. Shay Hardin had dominated her thoughts for far too long. Andrea wanted her life back.

She eyed the basket again. "You did laundry."

"Yep." He shut off the water. "That load's clean, just has to be folded."

She leaned against the counter and stared across the kitchen at him. He was showered and scrubbed, and something was definitely up.

"I'm heading out," he said. "Hope you don't mind I used your computer to look up bus schedules."

"How'd you get my password?"

He rolled his eyes at her as he put the milk back in the fridge.

So he was taking the bus. Okay, then. That would save her the drive. "Do Dee and Bob know you're coming?"

"I'm not going to Pearl Springs," he said. "I'm going to Midland."

"What's in—" She stopped short, realizing.

"Vicky's going through a tough time. Her whole world's imploded. I need to be with her."

Andrea looked at her brother, finally awake enough to really *see*. His shirt was neatly tucked in. He'd shaved. And the despairing look in his eyes had been replaced with hope.

Andrea cringed inwardly. He was going to travel three hundred miles to visit a woman whose life was fraught with problems and complications, all because of the absurd idea that he was in love with her. This plan had disaster written all over it.

And it finally hit her, in a sudden burst of clarity.

This isn't my problem.

Gavin was an adult. She wasn't his parent and never had been, no matter how many times she'd tried to fill that role. With every fiber of her being, she believed he needed to finish school and get a job, but instead, he was determined to go to Midland. It was a disaster for sure, but it was *his* disaster. She'd bailed him out for the last time.

Gavin picked up the sticky note beside her computer and tucked it into his back pocket.

"So I need to get going," he said. "The twenty-two comes at eight fifty."

He was taking a bus to the bus depot. He didn't need a ride from her.

And he was watching her now, clearly expecting something—probably a lecture.

Andrea cleared her throat. "Have a safe trip."

He gave her a funny look. And then he walked over and put his arms around her. She leaned her head against his bony chest and heard the thump of his heartbeat and felt a tug of fear. She didn't know when she'd see him next. Or where. Their lives were diverging and had been for a long time.

He planted a kiss on top of her head, and she walked him to the door. He didn't have any luggage, only himself and the promise of Vicky.

"Thanks for letting me crash here." He stepped out the door and turned to look at her. "And for everything else, too."

"You really love her, don't you?"

He smiled sheepishly. "Yeah. I do."

She watched him walk down the steps and forced herself to close the door. She went back into her silent apartment and stood beside her window, looking at the street streaming with morning traffic, and she felt the familiar anxiety percolating.

She had no job. No schedule. She didn't even have a brother to pester. Really, she didn't have anyone in her life who truly needed her. For a brief instant, she might have had Jon, but that had been an illusion, as fleeting as a cactus flower after a desert rain.

What she'd had that *was* lasting, her career, was over now. Done. And it was her own fault. She'd given in to her fears and let it slip away without a fight, and there was no way to get it back. Frustration and regret burned inside her chest.

Andrea turned and eyed her phone on the kitchen counter. Possibilities whirled through her mind, and every last one of them made her intensely uncomfortable. But even worse than her discomfort was the stinging memory of Jon's words: *You're scared, and so you're running away.*

She'd ignored his phone messages last night. Much like she'd ignored Nathan after the shooting.

Jon was right. And the absolute certainty that he was right was what pulled her toward the phone. Scrolling through her call list, she found the number, then closed her eyes and took a deep breath. Her heart thudded crazily. What was she doing? This wasn't her. This was the act of someone desperate. It wasn't something she'd ever dreamed she'd do in a million years.

The call connected, and she waited through the gatekeeper.

Her pulse pounded. What would she say? What if he refused to talk to her or blew her off?

He picked up. At the sound of his voice, she found her *cojones*.

"Hello, Senator Kirby. This is Andrea Finch."

chapter thirty-two

ANDREA RAN AT DUSK. The air was damp and warm, and she could taste the first hints of summer as she curved south from the lake and set a course for home. Traffic hummed around her. The evening mist became a sprinkle and then a soft drizzle that soaked through her T-shirt as her feet pounded the pavement. The rain cooled her skin, and she imagined it rinsing away all of the ugliness and pointless yearning, all of the regrets that had covered her like a layer of road dust for the past three weeks.

She neared her building and turned on a last burst of speed. She ran hard, sucking air until her lungs burned and her muscles throbbed. She reached her sidewalk and pulled up short as she saw the solitary man standing in the halo of a streetlight, gazing out over the parking lot.

A sharp pain pierced her heart. Never in her life had she seen anyone look so alone. She felt the overwhelming urge to reach out and touch him.

She approached, and he glanced her way.

"Hey," she said.

"Where's your Jeep?"

"In the shop. I drove my tires bald." She stopped beside him and tried to get her breathing back to normal.

Three weeks since she'd seen him. Twenty-one days. Plenty of time for one or both of them to get past the stubbornness.

Nerves fluttered in her stomach as he stared down at her. His suit jacket was wet with rain, and he'd loosened the tie around his neck. His eyes were bloodshot, and there was a glint in them that reminded her of how he'd looked at the height of the case. He seemed edgy and sleep-deprived, and she felt a twinge of satisfaction that she wasn't the only one.

"You look like hell," she said.

He sighed heavily and glanced out at the cars again. "It's been a rough week."

He turned back to look at her, and she waited. Was he here for work or personal reasons?

"We arrested Mark Driscoll today."

"I heard." She ignored the ripple of disappointment.

"Just north of Seattle. He was trying to slip across the border. Our lab technicians think he's a match for the UNSUB in the bank-surveillance tapes, so looks like he was Hardin's front man. The charges against him are stacking up."

"You came here to tell me that?"

"No." He gazed down at her. "Will you have dinner with me?"

Her heart gave a kick. She searched his face for clues, but this was one of those times she couldn't read his expression. "I need to shower first."

"Don't." He touched her arm, and she felt it to the tips of her toes. "It doesn't matter. We'll go to the Pig."

"At least let me put on a dry shirt."

He stayed at the base of the stairs while she dashed up to her apartment. She stripped off her sodden clothes and took a super-quick shower. She threw on a tank top and jeans, refusing to analyze what she was doing as she stuffed some money into her pocket and headed out the door. She joined him on the sidewalk, and they walked toward the food trailers.

Friday-night traffic buzzed around them, and the rain-slicked streets were a kaleidoscope of colors. An awkward silence settled between them.

"There's something I need to get off my chest."

She looked at him.

"That day at the Capitol." He stopped and gazed down at her, and the look in his eyes put her on the defensive. He tucked his hands into his pockets. "After we found the truck."

"Yeah?"

"All around us, everyone was evacuating, and I kept looking at you, and I wanted to drag you to the other side of a barricade." He paused. "And it was making me crazy because I knew you wouldn't go."

"You wouldn't go, either."

"Yeah, but it hit me all of a sudden, like a lightning bolt." He rubbed the back of his neck. "I had this realization, standing beside that truck bomb. I can't make you do a goddamn thing."

She stared up at him. "That was the lightning bolt?"

"Yes." He sighed heavily. "When I left you at my house that morning, I was driving away, and I was thinking about the arrest and what I had to do, but part of me was thinking about you. I knew you'd be mad. I even knew you'd be hurt, but still, I kept driving because I told myself I could fix it later. I'd say I was sorry, you'd forgive me, and that would be it."

Frustration swelled inside her, and she felt the sting of betrayal all over again. "So that's what you had to get off your chest?"

"No." His eyes looked impatient now. "The idea of not touching you again, not talking to you anymore—" He picked up her hand. "I don't want to do that. I don't want to walk away from you."

Her throat closed. Tears burned her eyes, and she laughed. "God, North. I never thought you were a romantic."

"I'm not." He lifted her hand and gently kissed her palm. "I just know what I want."

The determination in his eyes was her undoing. Her heart squeezed, and she looked out at the traffic as she tried to swallow the lump in her throat. "I took your advice," she said. "I called in a favor and got a new hearing last week. I got my job back."

He gazed down at her, and she could see that this wasn't news. He'd been checking up on her. "I'm not surprised. You helped thwart the assassination of a senator. And anyway, you're a good cop." He squeezed her hand. "I knew they'd take you back."

"Well, *I* didn't."

They started walking down the street toward the food court. Emotions swirled inside her.

"I've thought a lot about what you said. About how I was running away." She cleared her throat. "I realized it's kind of a habit of mine." She cut a glance at him. "I've never had anyone fight me on it before."

He stopped walking. She read the look in his eyes, and her heart beat faster. He pulled her into the shadows beside a tree and dragged her against him, and she felt the heady rush of all the things she'd been craving for a long, long time. She hadn't realized she needed someone. Someone she could push. Someone who wasn't afraid to push back.

She slid her arms around his neck and pulled him closer. He smelled good, he felt good, and the wool of his suit rasped against her bare arms. He slid his hands under her shirt, and his fingers were warm.

"I missed you."

The three little words brought a burst of joy. All her life, no man had ever said them to her. There were other words, too, but these were a start.

She pulled him down to kiss her.

Acknowledgments

I'd like to say thanks to the many people who contributed to this book by sharing their expertise, including Luke Causey, Jeffrey Simon, Jessica Dawson, Erik Vasys, Tom Adair, and Kathy Bennett. Any mistakes are all mine.

I am grateful to the hardworking team at Simon & Schuster, including Abby Zidle, Michele Martin, Jean Anne Rose, Jae Song, Marla Daniels, and the many dedicated sales reps. Thanks, especially, to Louise Burke for her unwavering support over the years. Also, thanks to Kevan Lyon for her friendship and professional guidance.

And a heartfelt thank-you to my readers, who make it all possible.